"So the contents of that box are for me?"

Luke asked, looking back up at his neighbor.

"Right." A small laugh tumbled off Brenna's pink lips. "Homemade doughnuts. They're sort of a welcome-to-the-neighborhood present."

"I moved in five months ago," he pointed out.

"Well, I've been busy, and it was a cold winter. The snow kept me away. You too, apparently, because I haven't seen much of you."

She seemed to wait for him to offer an explanation, which he didn't have. He'd been busy at the fire station where he worked, and when he came home, he preferred to avoid doing the neighborly thing.

"Do you do this for all the new neighbors?" he asked.

"It was a tradition of my mom's when I was growing up. We don't get many new neighbors around here though, because no one ever leaves the creek."

"Well, that's nice. Thank you."

She shrugged a shoulder. "Cooking and baking are what I do for a living. So if you're lucky, you might get more treats from me in the future." Her eyes widened as if she'd just made a pass at him. *Did she?*

Luke took a backward step, increasing the distance between them. She was beautiful, no denying that. And there was no ring on her finger or evidence of a guy coming around. If she lived anywhere other than right next door, he might even consider asking her out. But she didn't.

PRAISE FOR ANNIE RAINS AND HER SWEETWATER SPRINGS SERIES

Snowfall on Cedar Trail

"Rains makes a delightful return to tiny Sweetwater Springs, NC, in this sweet Christmas-themed contemporary. Rains highlights the happily ever afters of past books, making even new readers feel like residents catching up with the town gossip and giving romance fans plenty of sappy happiness."
—*Publishers Weekly*

"Over the past year I've become a huge Annie Rains fangirl with her Sweetwater Springs series. I'm (not so) patiently waiting for Netflix or Hallmark to just pick up this entire series and make all my dreams come true." —CandiceZablan.com

"*Snowfall on Cedar Trail* was a wonderfully complex holiday romance that dealt with many tough issues while keeping the story both light and swoony. What a sweet Christmastime read it was!" —TheGenreMinx.com

Springtime at Hope Cottage

"This delicious rom-com has plenty of heart and is ideal comfort reading." —*Publishers Weekly*

"Annie Rains puts her heart in every word!"
—Brenda Novak, *New York Times* bestselling author

"Such a sweet romance!" —TheGenreMinx.com

ALSO BY ANNIE RAINS

STARTING OVER AT BLUEBERRY CREEK

ANNIE RAINS

FOREVER

NEW YORK BOSTON

Copyright © 2020 by Annie Rains
Excerpt from *Skillet Love* © 2019 by Anne Byrn
Cover design and illustration by Elizabeth Turner Stokes
Cover copyright © 2020 by Hachette Book Group, Inc.
Bonus novella *Sealed with a Kiss* © 2020 by Melinda Wooten

Forever
Hachette Book Group
1290 Avenue of the Americas, New York, NY 10104
read-forever.com
twitter.com/readforeverpub

First Edition: February 2020

Forever is an imprint of Grand Central Publishing. The Forever name and logo are trademarks of Hachette Book Group, Inc.

The publisher is not responsible for websites (or their content) that are not owned by the publisher.

The Hachette Speakers Bureau provides a wide range of authors for speaking events. To find out more, go to www.hachettespeakersbureau.com or call (866) 376-6591.

ISBN: 978-1-5387-0086-0 (mass market), 978-1-5387-0084-6 (ebook)

Printed in the United States of America

OPM

10 9 8 7 6 5 4 3 2 1

For Dana.
My sister and my friend.

Acknowledgments

Words can't begin to express the gratitude in my heart for everyone who has helped me in this author journey. I have the most amazing friends and family in the world (in my humble opinion). Thank you to my husband and children for supporting me in so many ways. Thank you, Sonny, for bouncing around ideas with me. Thank you to my children for your patience and enthusiasm, including taking my books to Show and Tell. Thank you as well to Annette and my parents who support me in too many ways to count.

I also believe I have the most amazing publisher, editor, and agent in the world. (Yes, I'm biased.) A million thanks to my talented editor, Alex Logan. Four books and two novellas published and I'm still pinching myself over the fact that I get to work with you (and Jodi, Estelle, Monisha, Elizabeth, and Mari...The Forever team is truly wonderful). The same is true for my agent, Sarah Younger. I am so fortunate to have you in my corner!

I would also like to thank Chuck Younger who generously offered his time and expertise to answer my firefighter questions. I really appreciate it. Any mistakes in the text are my own.

Thanks and love also go out to the ladies who keep me going every day. This writing gig wouldn't be nearly as much fun without Rachel Lacey, Tif Marcelo, and April Hunt. We cheer each other on in our writing and our lives. You've become more than authors who I respect and admire. You're also my friends, and I love you ladies so much.

Since this book explores sibling relationships, in addition to romantic love, I would be remiss not to acknowledge my own sister here. So thank you to my lovely sister, Dana. I am so blessed to have grown up with you and so thankful that our relationship was never as complicated as Brenna and Eve's in this book!

Lastly, but certainly not least, a HUGE THANK-YOU goes out to my readers. I am humbled that you take the time to read my stories and even more so when you connect with me online and tell me your thoughts or share pieces of your lives with me. A lot of my readers have also become my friends, and I'm so honored and thankful for your support in the many forms you give it.

CHAPTER ONE

The aroma of sugar, spice, and butter filled Brenna McConnell's kitchen. Her mouth watered as she stirred the contents in her saucepan, breathing it in. A taste test was allowed but nothing more. This food wasn't for her.

A timer went off on her stove, signaling that the homemade doughnuts were done. She slipped a mitt onto her right hand and pulled open the oven door to retrieve them. They were golden brown and glorious—all except the one that had gotten a little too burned around the edges.

Her stomach twisted with hunger and then growled a little. *Yeah, yeah.* That imperfect doughnut could be hers. But only the one.

She set the tray down on the stove top and stirred the saucepan again before lifting it up and drizzling its contents onto the doughnuts. Her neighbor, Luke Marini, had been slow to warm up to her, but that would hopefully change with this friendly gesture. She usually brought housewarming treats to her new neighbors on Blueberry

Creek but she'd been too busy during the winter months to officially welcome him to the community like she normally would.

She'd met Luke at his mailbox a couple of times, and he'd smiled when she'd introduced herself, but that was all they'd shared. He hadn't hung around to make small talk. In fact, he'd kept his answers to her questions clipped, replying "yes" and "no" when at all possible. She'd tried to convince herself it was because of the biting cold outside. Or maybe he'd just needed to use the bathroom or excuse himself for some other unknown reason.

She assembled one of the pastry boxes she kept stocked in her pantry and loaded the doughnuts. After closing it, she tied a red-checked ribbon around the handle that reminded her of picnics and sunshine-filled spring mornings. "I'll just walk right over and knock on his door to welcome him to the neighborhood," she said out loud to herself, which was something she did a lot. It had started when her younger sister Eve had moved out last year. Brenna had grown tired of the silence and had started talking to herself. But now that Eve had moved back in, Brenna was still doing it.

Brenna grabbed the box of doughnuts, giving the runt doughnut one last longing glance before heading to her front door. Then her gaze caught on the stack of college applications that Eve hadn't touched since moving back home. Brenna had strategically placed it on the counter so that her sister could see it whenever she walked into the room. Either Eve hadn't noticed or she was actively ignoring it. No doubt it was the latter.

Eve didn't have big college dreams like Brenna always had. Dreams that had taken a nosedive with the twists and turns of life. No, Eve's dreams were very different in nature. Eve had recently graduated from the fire academy and was determined to follow in their late father's footsteps as a Sweetwater Springs firefighter.

With a heavy sigh, Brenna stepped outside into the warmth of the spring sun and headed across the lawn toward Luke Marini's home.

He lived in a quaint yellow house with a blue metal roof. She'd always admired the home, even when it'd belonged to the old couple who'd lived there since she was a baby. They'd put the house up for sale last year and were now living with their daughter in South Carolina as far as Brenna knew. Brenna had come here many times as neighbors, and the couple's home had always been open and inviting.

She climbed the front porch steps and rang the doorbell. After waiting at least thirty seconds, she turned to check the driveway where Luke's old-fashioned red Ford truck was parked. Unless he'd gone for a walk, he had to be home. She rang the doorbell again. "Hello?" she called. "Hello? It's Brenna McConnell from next door!"

"Around here," a deep voice finally called back.

Brenna spun toward the sound, seeing a midsize Jack Russell terrier dart from the opposite side of the house. She headed down the steps with her box of goodies, the sweet aroma wafting under her nose. The dog met her on the lawn, running circles around her at first and then propping the pads of his feet just above her knee. "Oh, hi," she said, realizing she'd never seen Luke's dog up close before. It was...well...

She narrowed her eyes, her smile slipping as she looked at the little dog with matted brown and white fur in some places and large patches of no fur, just pink scarred skin, in others. She sucked in a breath and nearly dropped her doughnuts, especially when Luke stepped up wearing a T-shirt that fit him like a second skin. She met his dark-brown eyes, the color of maple syrup. His hair, nearly a perfect match to his eye color, poked out from beneath his ball cap, curling at the tips.

"This is Max," he told her. "I rescued him from a warehouse fire in Whispering Pines last year."

Whispering Pines was a nearby town, and if she remembered correctly, it was where Luke had moved from.

"I'm trying to turn Max into the firehouse dog but I'm not sure it's going to work out. He's good for morale around the station but he's still a little skittish around smoke and fire."

She studied the little dog as her mind connected the dots between the warehouse fire that Luke had saved him from and the condition of his fur. Emotion swelled in her throat, and tears threatened behind her eyes. She swallowed and clutched the welcome gift in her hands. "I, um, didn't realize you were working outside this morning."

"I'm patching up the fence behind the house," he said. "There were a few loose boards when I bought this place that I hadn't gotten around to fixing until now. Max likes to run out there, and I don't want any wildlife to get in the fence and have a run-in with him." Luke looked down at his dog. "Although he's one tough canine. I think he'd probably win."

Brenna smiled at the way Luke's voice and expression softened when he talked about his pet. "Well, I just came by to tell you that if you ever need anything—eggs or milk or someone to take Max out when you're not here— don't hesitate to ask. That's what neighbors are for." She reached down to pet Max, who immediately began to lap his tongue over her fingers. "I probably smell and taste like sugar," she said, laughing as he licked her. Then she looked up at Luke and felt every drop of blood she had in her body rush into her cheeks. "Because I've been baking. For you."

* * *

Luke's next-door neighbor was hard to miss, even when he was trying his hardest. She had rich black hair that seemed to soak up the sunlight as she shifted back and forth on her feet. She smelled like something sweet, maybe cinnamon and butter. No wonder Max was running circles around her, jumping on her and panting with his tongue half out.

Luke hadn't missed the way she'd physically responded to Max's burn injuries either. She'd taken a subtle step backward, and her hands had shaken just a little. The light he'd seen behind her smiling eyes had also dimmed momentarily. Some might not have noticed but he was sensitive to that detail because the burn scars on his back had elicited the same response from people. He and Max hadn't been injured in the same fire, but they were bonded; both of them had survived against all odds.

Luke's experience had been during childhood, and he'd had time to distance himself from it and face a fire fearlessly. Max hadn't, and Luke wasn't sure his little dog would ever get over his fear of flames.

"So the contents of that box are for me?" Luke asked, looking back up at his neighbor.

"Right." A small laugh tumbled off her pink lips that contrasted with her olive-toned skin, dotted with pale freckles that only added to her beauty. "Homemade doughnuts. They're sort of a welcome-to-the-neighborhood present."

"I moved in five months ago," he pointed out.

"Well, I've been busy, and it was a cold winter. The

snow kept me away. You too, apparently, because I haven't seen much of you."

She seemed to wait for him to offer an explanation, which he didn't have. He'd been busy at the fire station where he worked, and when he came home, he preferred to avoid doing the neighborly thing. He'd learned his lesson on that front in Whispering Pines when he'd found himself dating his neighbor. That had turned out to be a huge mistake. One he wouldn't make again.

"Now that winter is over and spring is upon us," Brenna went on, "I thought I'd make the trek across our yards and give you an official welcome." She shrugged underneath her floral apron and then held the box out to him.

His fingers brushed against hers as he took it, and the touch buzzed around his body like one of those honey bees that had come after him earlier while he'd been patching the fence. Just like with the bees, he ignored the sensation. "That's nice. Do you do this for all the new neighbors?"

"It was a tradition of my mom's when I was growing up. We don't get many new neighbors around here though, because no one ever leaves the creek." She giggled softly, the sound just as sweet as the smell of the treats wafting under his nose. "That sounds like a horror movie setup, doesn't it? You move to the creek and never get away," she said in a playful voice.

He held up the box. "Well, thank you for these."

"It's no big deal. Cooking and baking are what I do for a living."

Luke knew she owned and operated A Taste of Heaven Catering.

"So if you're lucky, you might get more treats from me in the future." Her eyes widened as if she'd just made a pass at him. *Did she?*

Luke took a backward step, increasing the distance between them. She was beautiful, no denying that. And there was no ring on her finger or evidence of a guy coming around. If she lived anywhere else, he might even consider asking her out. But she didn't.

"Well, I better get cleaned up before I need to head to the station."

"Oh... right." Her cheerful demeanor faded a touch. "I don't want to bother you. I just wanted to say that if you ever need a favor, I'm right next door. My phone number is in the box, and yes, I give it to all the neighbors. Just in case."

"I'm sure I won't be calling you," he said, not intending to come off as rude. Judging by her expression though, that's exactly how he'd sounded.

Her mouth formed a little circle of shock. "I see. Well, enjoy those doughnuts, Mr. Marini." She'd called him Luke before. Then, without another word, she turned and headed back to her house.

He watched her walk away for a long moment, her hair and the strings of her apron dancing in the breeze. "Come on, Max," he finally said. They went inside, and he slid the box of doughnuts on the counter in front of him. A little red oval in the bottom corner claimed that they were "made with love." Just like Brenna, they appeared to be sugar, spice, and everything nice. And he was snails and shells and puppy dog tails.

Luke sat on a stool and pulled a doughnut out of the box.

Max whined softly. He knew better than to beg but he'd already gotten a little taste off Brenna's skin.

"Just one," Luke said before offering it. Max snapped it up, his tail wagging excitedly. Then Luke pulled a second doughnut out of the box and took a bite, his eyes closing momentarily because it was one of the tastiest treats he'd had in a while. Being nice to his neighbor could have its advantages.

But it could also put him at a very big disadvantage. And right now his focus was on building a long-lasting career here in Sweetwater Springs. Not a short-lived romance that could ruin everything.

* * *

Brenna was having a stare-down with the runt doughnut on her cookie sheet. She was just being friendly to her new neighbor, and he'd kind of treated her like a nuisance. He certainly hadn't been inviting.

Brenna grabbed the doughnut and bit into it, her feelings dissolving along with the sugar on her tongue. She inhaled the pastry in three bites and then immediately regretted it. And she blamed Luke Marini entirely.

She paced the kitchen for a moment, scanning the room and trying to decide what to do next. Her sister was handling things at A Taste of Heaven today. Brenna had been training Eve on everything needed to run the catering business since Eve was a teenager, but as soon as Eve could drive, she'd been more interested in volunteering at the fire station than cooking meals. Thankfully, there were no vacancies to fill at the Sweetwater Springs Fire Department right now, though, and with any luck, it would stay that way until Brenna could convince Eve to go to college.

Brenna gazed at the stack of college applications, just as tempting as that runt doughnut she'd devoured a moment earlier. She had only needed one more year to finish her own degree in childhood education when her parents died. Then she'd dropped out and moved back to Blueberry Creek to care for Eve, who'd been eleven at the time. Brenna had stepped into a guardian role and had taken over her mom's catering business, working alongside their aunt Thelma. She'd put everything on hold for the last seven years, telling herself all the while that she'd start living her own life again once Eve was eighteen.

Even though Eve had turned eighteen this past fall, she still needed Brenna, whether she knew it or not. Sometimes Eve made poor decisions, and when it was her turn to watch the catering business, like today, she slacked off on her responsibilities.

Brenna nibbled on her lower lip. "Eve is fine," she said out loud. "It'll just make her mad if I show up."

And it was time for Brenna to let go and focus on her own life.

Brenna tapped her fingers on the counter, trying to talk herself out of going downtown to check on her little sister. Unable to resist, she grabbed her keys and headed out the front door. She glanced over at the little yellow house next door and suppressed another impulse—this one to walk back over and snatch back her welcome-to-the-neighborhood gift.

$\mathcal{C}$ HAPTER TWO

$\mathcal{B}$ renna reversed out of her driveway and drove toward A Taste of Heaven, just around the corner from the downtown strip of quaint little stores on Silver Lake.

After a short drive, she pulled into the parking lot and sat in her car for a moment. Maybe she should take a walk downtown. Perhaps she could do a little shopping. It'd been a while since she'd had a day off. She could even go to Perfectly Pampered and get a haircut or a pedicure.

Instead, she pushed open the door of her navy blue Honda CR-V and headed toward the back entrance of A Taste of Heaven. As she stepped through the door, the dense air immediately made her cough and the smoke detector started to shriek.

Brenna blinked past the sudden sting in her eyes, and her heart catapulted into her throat. "Eve?...Eve!" Heart racing, she hurried toward the kitchen and located the smoke's culprit. One of the three convection ovens along the wall had charcoal-colored puffs coming out of the back vents.

Brenna yanked open the oven door, allowing more smoke to bloom toward her face, which only elicited more coughing. Then she snatched a mitt from the counter and pulled a tray of burned biscuits out, stashing them on the stove top. "Shh-shh," she said, using the mitt to fan the air in front of the smoke detector. "Please stop."

"What are you doing here?"

Brenna whirled to face Eve, pulling the mitt down to her side as if she'd been caught with her hand in the proverbial cookie jar. She hadn't done anything wrong by coming here though. And it was a good thing she'd shown up when she had. "I'm keeping the business from burning down," she shouted to be heard over the alarm. "Where's Aunt Thelma?"

Eve shoved her hands on her hips. "Aunt Thelma called and said she was running late this morning."

"Where's Nate?" Brenna asked then.

Nate Trapp was a new hire. He could follow a recipe well enough, and he had a mind for business, which was a plus. He also helped with deliveries and setup.

"He went to deliver the spread to the men's breakfast at Sweetwater Chapel."

Right. Aunt Thelma usually handled that, but since she was out, Nate would have taken on the task.

"Don't worry. Nate and I cooked the eggs, grits, and bacon. But we forgot the biscuits." Eve gestured at the oven. Her long red hair was pulled up in a messy bun at her nape. She'd gotten the full lot of their father's Irish features, unlike Brenna who'd only gotten the sprinkle of pale freckles on her nose. Brenna had gotten her black hair and brown eyes from their mom, making her and Eve look as different as their personalities.

"Great," Brenna huffed. "The men's group love their

biscuits and now they'll be disappointed. And thanks to all this commotion, Mrs. Roberts is probably calling the fire department from next door as we speak."

Eve rolled her eyes as the smoke detector finally stopped. "Yeah well, Mrs. Roberts is slightly neurotic. A lot like you." She cocked her head to one side and narrowed her pale-green eyes at Brenna.

Brenna stiffened. "Do you think this is funny?"

"The fact that my sister doesn't trust me with the job she begged me to do? No. It's a little insulting, actually."

"You fill our shop with smoke, and now you're giving *me* the guilt trip?" Brenna shook her head but the guilt trip had worked. Her insides twisted uncomfortably because she should have let Eve run the shop without interfering. She knew that, just like she knew she needed to apologize and leave right now before this argument gained momentum.

"It's not our shop. I don't want it. It's yours." Eve pulled her apron off and flung it on the butcher-block-style counter behind her.

Too late.

"Looks like you're no longer taking the day off so I will. Bye, sis." Eve headed toward the back entrance where Brenna had entered only a few minutes earlier.

"Wait!" Brenna called. "I'm not working today!"

"Should've thought of that before you drove here to mother me," Eve called behind her. "I mean smother me." She slammed the back door behind her.

Brenna sighed as she reached for the apron that Eve had discarded and pulled it over her head, preparing to make a new batch of biscuits. Even though the apron was light, it felt like a shackle weighing her down.

* * *

Luke glanced over at Brenna's house as he cranked the truck's engine and reversed out of his driveway. Guilt pinched under the Sweetwater Springs Fire Department logo on the chest of his T-shirt about the way he'd treated her. He didn't deserve the doughnuts she'd brought him, which was why he was bringing the rest to the station.

The crew would appreciate it. They were all young and endlessly hungry, a lot like a bunch of high school boys. When Luke had interviewed for the assistant fire chief position six months ago, he'd been intimidated to step into an authoritative role as the new guy. A few of the guys had given him a hard time at first, and one still did most days.

He drove a short distance and then parked behind the firehouse.

"You're thirty seconds late," Chief Brewer called from his office as Luke walked in with Max matching every step.

Luke lifted the box of treats. "I come bearing food."

"Forgiven." The chief stood and followed Luke and Max to the small kitchen behind the garage, where Luke laid the box on the table. The chief looked at it for a long moment. "Made with love." His gaze jumped back to Luke. "By Brenna McConnell, I presume."

"A welcome-to-the-neighborhood gift," Luke explained.

"You moved here five months ago," Chief Brewer pointed out, just like Luke had to Brenna herself.

"I know. I guess neither of us made an attempt to get to know one another." Or actually Brenna had on multiple occasions but Luke had dodged those efforts.

"I worked with her father, you know," Chief Brewer said, leaning against the counter along the wall.

Luke had already gathered that bit of information and

had seen the pictures of Aidan McConnell on what Chief Brewer called his wall of fame, a space dedicated to honoring all the firefighters who'd come and gone at the Sweetwater Springs Fire Department.

"I was the first one on the scene of her parents' accident too," Chief Brewer added.

Luke hadn't learned that tidbit yet. "What happened to her parents?"

He only had to see Chief Brewer's expression to know that whatever happened had ended badly.

"Accident on Forest Grove. Her mom was driving and had to pull over because of a migraine. She called Aidan, who was working that day. It wasn't a fire department call, just a family emergency, so he was the only one who went. When Aidan arrived, he told his daughter to climb into the cab of his truck. Then he tended to his wife." Chief Brewer paused before finishing the story. "An oncoming vehicle hit Jane's car a moment later. It didn't even slow down."

A sick feeling blanketed the bottom of Luke's stomach. "They both died?"

"Yep. Fortunately, Eve was safe in Aidan's truck. Not unscathed though. She saw everything. As you can imagine, there was a degree of lashing out after that."

"That's awful. Where was Brenna?" Luke asked.

Chief Brewer grabbed a doughnut from the box on the table. "She was grown and living on her own by then. After the accident, she came back to Sweetwater Springs to care for Eve." He bit into the doughnut and shook his head as he chewed and swallowed. "Those girls are like family to me. I was good friends with their dad. He'd want me to grill you if you're thinking about dating his oldest daughter."

"Don't worry about me, sir. I'm not interested in anything romantic."

Chief Brewer clapped a hand on his back. "I'm not sure how their father would feel about his baby girl volunteering with us either. I'm sure that possibility never even crossed his mind. But I must say, Eve is determined and a big help on the scenes."

The more Luke thought and talked about the McConnell women, the more he regretted being so abrupt with Brenna earlier. She was only being friendly but he was so guarded when it came to beautiful neighbors now.

Maybe he'd go apologize after his shift. He didn't need to roll out his welcome mat to everyone who lived on the creek, but if he planned on staying in Sweetwater Springs, he guessed it was smart to be in the good graces of the people who lived directly beside him.

"It's my shift," Luke said, returning his attention to his boss. "What are you still doing here?"

Chief Brewer shrugged. "My wife is upset with me. I can't seem to do anything right these days. Sometimes the station is my home away from home." He chuckled softly. "Anyway, I don't want to step on your toes."

Luke shifted restlessly, eager to get started on the list of things to do today. "You should take up a hobby that'll get you out of the house."

"Maybe so. I've never been one of those guys who can spend their day at the golf course. Not sure what other hobbies I'd pick up. Maybe fishing." He looked at Luke. "Anyway, don't take any flak from Ryan today, all right?"

Ryan Johnson was a young firefighter with an attitude. He didn't want to do his chores around the firehouse but he was a skilled firefighter. When the adrenaline hit his veins, he became a different version of himself.

"You should have a sit-down with him. Being a firefighter is more than working the scenes. It's also about what happens behind the scenes."

Chief Brewer chuckled. "Oh, I've talked to him more times than I care to count. Believe it or not, his attitude has improved since he first started working here. Can't expect someone to change overnight. He didn't have the best upbringing, you know."

Luke knew that Ryan's dad was in jail. If you considered that, the young firefighter's poor attitude was a minor complication. He kept an honest job and stayed out of trouble. Luke certainly understood the heavy weight of carrying your past on your shoulders. "I'll keep an eye on him today."

Chief Brewer bent and patted Max's head for a long moment, his tone of voice growing soft. "You're the best firehouse dog we've ever had. The bravest one too."

"He's the only dog the station has ever had, right?" Luke asked.

"Doesn't make that statement any less true." Chief Brewer straightened. "Well, I guess it's time for me to go home and make nice with my wife. Maybe I'll stop by A Taste of Heaven and see if I can get something of Brenna's that's made with love."

"Not a bad strategy," Luke said.

"Take notes. One of these days you'll be in my shoes."

Not anytime soon, and not with Brenna McConnell. Although Luke did intend to make a point of being friendlier to his beautiful neighbor the next time he saw her.

* * *

Exhausted, Brenna unlocked her front door and stepped inside later that night. As she walked down the hall, she found Eve exercising in the front room. She was watching someone on TV pound drumsticks on the ground and then in the air. Brenna thought she remembered the aerobic activity being called Pound. She remembered because it reminded her of pound cake, which she only baked on Thursdays for Mrs. Hoveland's bunco group.

As Brenna walked into the kitchen, she breathed in the aroma of a myriad of spices coming from the Crock-Pot meal she'd set up when she'd woken early this morning.

Eve stopped drumming the air and walked around to prop her elbows on the kitchen counter and stare at Brenna.

"How was your day?" Brenna asked.

"Boring."

Brenna decided not to mention that it wouldn't have been if she'd stayed and worked the kitchen. Instead she pulled down two plates for dinner. "Well, my day was fine too. Thanks for asking."

"I didn't ask," Eve said dryly.

"It's called sarcasm. You know it well." Brenna scooped the chicken and vegetables onto the clay plates her mom had cherished once upon a time. She'd purchased them from a local pottery artist in the valley, and she'd loved serving meals on them back when they'd been a complete family with a mom, dad, and two kids.

Those memories seemed so far away and that family seemed so different from the small duo that existed now.

When Eve didn't respond, Brenna continued talking. "We catered the men's breakfast at the chapel, as you know. I made some more biscuits, and Nate ran them over once he got back. Then we did an impromptu hospital event at lunch. We also had a few potential clients walk in and inquire about booking their upcoming events with us. It was a good day."

Brenna swallowed as another memory of her mother during the evenings growing up played in her mind. Every night, her dad would ask their mom how her day was, and she'd answer the same way every time. Those same words rose in Brenna's throat and tumbled over her lips, bitter-sweet as she reminisced. "Everyone was happier when they left than when they walked in."

Eve huffed. "I'm happier when I leave a room with you too."

Brenna froze. Her large wooden spoon dripped hot chicken gravy to the plate below, making a mess, but she didn't care. Her blood pressure was no doubt spiking because she was seeing starbursts in her field of vision. With an aggravated growl, she tossed down the spoon with a clunk against the plate.

Eve straightened. "Sorry," she said but her tone didn't sound at all sincere.

"Do you know how hard I've worked since Mom and Dad died? I quit college, gave up the life I was planning, and moved back here for you. I've cleaned house and cooked dinner and helped you through middle and high school. I lost my fiancé in order to be your guardian."

Eve didn't even bat an eyelash. "I didn't ask you to do any of that."

Brenna's mouth dropped open. "You're my sister. You didn't have to ask. But I would think you'd have a little appreciation. I'm tired of your ungrateful, uncaring attitude toward me . . . I'm sick and tired."

"Well, I'm tired of how overbearing and controlling you are. You're always trying to run my life. Get your own life!" Eve shot back.

"What?" Brenna asked.

"You used to be my fun, older sister. Now you're

just…" Eve shook her head. "You're no fun to be around at all." She looked pleased with herself for saying something she knew would hurt Brenna.

It did hurt. Brenna looked around the kitchen, suddenly desperate for some kind of release. Something that would make her feel better. Her gaze landed on the basket of fruit on the counter in front of her.

Apples are too hard…ditto with the oranges.

Finally, she lifted a banana from the basket and peeled it with shaky fingers.

"What are you doing?" Eve asked in a mocking tone.

"Being a sister," Brenna said, her voice trembling. She knew the thoughts running through her head were wrong. Eve was an adult now, that was true, but barely. And Eve was just in pain and taking it out on Brenna, just like she'd done for the last seven years. It was natural. Expected even.

But Brenna was in pain too. She still missed her family. And most of all, she missed her sister who was standing right in front of her.

Brenna broke a piece off the banana, pulled her arm back, and launched the piece across the room.

"Hey!" Eve squealed, barely dodging the flying fruit.

Brenna broke another piece of banana off and repeated her action. This was completely irrational—she knew it—and it felt incredible.

Eve ducked. "Have you lost your mind? Are you *crazy*?" Eve took several retreating steps, which was probably wise because Brenna had another half of a banana left, and she planned to use it. In fact, there was a full bunch in the basket.

She should do this more often. It felt amazing.

"Stop it, Brenna!" Eve demanded.

Brenna froze, her arm in the air, a piece of banana

primed. "Will you sit at the table and eat dinner with me tonight?"

Eve's lips pinched. "After you threw banana at me? No way. I'm calling Aunt Thelma and telling her that you've gone off the deep end."

Brenna dropped her arm down by her side. "We don't need to bother Aunt Thelma with our problems."

"I don't have a problem. You do." Eve grabbed her bag and marched toward the front door. "Enjoy eating your dinner alone," she said as she slammed the front screen door behind her.

Brenna stared after her sister for a long moment, her eyes burning and the banana still in her hand. It was squishing out of the peel now because she'd squeezed the life out of it. The same way everything seemed to be squeezing the life out of her, and had been for a long time.

A knock on her screen door made her jump. She blinked past her tears and saw Luke Marini. Without being invited, he opened the door that Eve had just slammed and stepped inside. "Everything okay?" he asked.

No. Nothing was okay. "Yes," she lied instead. "Everything is fine."

CHAPTER THREE

"I overheard the commotion while I was walking Max," Luke said, standing outside Brenna's open door. He'd intended to come over here anyway to apologize about this morning. He had the perfect excuse because a misplaced piece of her mail had landed in his box this afternoon.

Brenna's gaze bounced from Max at his feet and back up to him. "Sorry. Sister wars. They happen frequently over here at the McConnell household."

"Anything I can do?" he asked.

She looked away, hiding her face behind her hair for a moment. "No. Our fights always blow over eventually."

"I had two brothers growing up. We had our fair share of fights too."

Brenna looked at him now. "The difference is that you referred to your fights in the past. Eve and I haven't outgrown ours." She shook her head, looking flustered and beautiful. She was so attractive that it made him uncomfortable. He realized now that was unfair. He was perfectly capable of keeping his head on straight with Brenna without giving her the cold shoulder. And he didn't know if she'd be interested in him anyway.

"Would Max like some water?" she asked, gesturing for them to step inside. "I have homemade dog biscuits too, if he's hungry."

"I think Max would love that." Luke followed her into the kitchen, where she tossed the banana she was holding into the trash can and reached for a bowl in her cabinet. Luke watched as she brought it to the sink and filled it with water.

"Homemade dog biscuits, huh?" he asked as he sat on a barstool and Max curled at his feet.

Brenna set the bowl in front of Max and then headed to her refrigerator. "Believe it or not, we have a client who wants us to cater their animal rescue event. So we're cooking for the humans and the canines. I'm trying out a few dog treat recipes." She grabbed a large plastic Ziploc bag from her fridge shelf and lifted a medium-size biscuit out. "These are peanut butter flavored," she said, addressing Max as she crouched in front of him. "Let's see if you like them."

Max's tail started thumping erratically against the floor. Luke's heart was doing something similar against his ribs. "What do you mean you're trying them out? You don't have a dog."

"No, just a sister who pushes me to the edge." Brenna straightened, the motion bringing her much too close for Luke's comfort. His mouth went dry. At this distance, he could see the amber-colored flecks in her irises, a perfect match to the dusting of freckles along her cheeks. "Um, the biscuits can be eaten by people too," Brenna said. "I'm sampling them myself to see if they're any good."

Without thinking, Luke reached a hand toward her and grabbed a biscuit out of the bag she was holding, bringing it to his mouth.

"They're not that sweet," she warned, looking a little worried. "I didn't add sugar, because it's not good for dogs. But I personally still think they're tasty." She gestured to Max who was already halfway done with his. "See?"

"If they're anything like the doughnuts, I'm sure they're fantastic." Luke took a bite. The doughnuts were definitely better tasting, but these were edible. "Not bad."

"Really?" Brenna zipped the bag back up and stepped away to return it to the fridge. "I'm sorry about disturbing your walk just now."

"Teenagers are hard for everyone."

"How would you know?" she asked, turning to look at him.

"Well, my brother Nick started his family early. He has two teenagers of his own. I've talked Nick out of tossing bananas on many occasions."

Brenna brought her hands to her face, her cheeks turning a deep crimson color. "So you did see our food fight? I'm so sorry. That's never happened before. It was a momentary lapse of self-control. I usually don't react to her sarcasm and criticism."

"It happens to the best of us. I can't say it's ever happened to me, but…" Luke grinned. Then he pulled his gaze away from Brenna while he still could and zeroed in on the Crock-Pot behind her, just looking for a new conversation. "Whatever that is, it smells delicious."

Brenna glanced over her shoulder. "It's chicken and vegetables. You're welcome to have some. I have plenty since it's just me tonight."

"That's okay. Max and I need to finish our walk. He

waits patiently all day to sniff every patch of grass from here to the stop sign and back." Luke stood.

Brenna laughed, the sound as sweet as her doughnuts this morning. "How about I make you a container and stick it in the mailbox? You can grab it on your walk back."

"You've already gone out of your way for me today."

"It's no trouble. In fact, you'd be doing me a favor. I have more than enough and my freezer is already packed with leftovers."

"Okay, then. That sounds great." A warmness spread through his chest, a sure sign that it was time to go. His goal here was to be friendly, not romantic. He turned and headed to the front door.

"But there's a catch," Brenna called behind him.

Luke stopped walking and turned back to narrow his eyes at her. "What kind of catch?"

"Just don't tell the other neighbors that I was having a food fight with Eve. Gossip spreads like wildfire in a small town, you know."

He gave a humorless laugh. "Believe me, I know," he muttered, thinking of when he'd first arrived in Sweetwater Springs. Any detail he shared seemed to immediately become public information. "But it's only a fair food fight if your opponent has food to throw too. Just saying."

Brenna put a hand on her hip, and his gaze and mind unintentionally dropped there. "Next time," she said.

"You know where I live. Next time, give me a heads-up, and I'll come talk you down. You said yourself that you hate to waste food. Seems like a shame to ruin a good bunch of bananas."

"Touché. And thank you. I might take you up on that."

"That's what neighbors are for, right?" he asked, repeating her words from this morning.

He and Max stepped onto her front porch. "I, uh…" He shifted back and forth on his feet, readying the apology he'd been preparing all day, his throat suddenly thick. "I'm sorry if I came off as less than neighborly earlier."

She leaned against the door frame. "Apology accepted."

Luke let out a huge breath. Then he realized that he was still holding an envelope in his hand. "I almost forgot. Your mail landed in my box today."

"Oh." Brenna took the manila envelope. "Our new mail carrier keeps mixing up the neighbors' mail. This has happened a few times to me already."

Luke gestured at the envelope. "You're thinking about going to college?" he asked. "I couldn't help noticing the sender's address."

"Oh no, this isn't for me. It's for Eve." She looked away shyly.

Luke frowned. "But it's addressed to you."

"Yes, well, I sent off for the information for Eve," Brenna said, not meeting his gaze. "Just in case she became interested."

Luke scrunched his brow. "She just graduated from the fire academy. I thought she was waiting for a position to open up at SSFD."

Brenna nodded. "She is, but in the meantime, I'm trying to persuade her to go to school for something more practical for an eighteen-year-old woman. Something safer."

Luke decided against arguing. This wasn't any of his business and he'd just gotten back in Brenna's good graces. "I see."

"Anyway, the chicken and vegetables will be waiting for you on your way back," she promised, looking up at him with a smile that made him want to stay a little longer. Instead, he resisted the temptation and said good night.

* * *

There was a quickening in Brenna's heart as she watched Luke head down the street with Max jogging alongside him. Ignoring the sensation, she closed the door and headed into the kitchen and grabbed a plastic container from her cabinet to fill with dinner for Luke. Unable to help herself, she prepared a small baggie of dog biscuits for his little dog too. She loved feeding the people around her, even if she didn't exactly enjoy being a caterer.

Brenna placed the container and baggie in a larger paper bag that she folded down to be compact. Then she walked it down the driveway and slid it into her mailbox. She glanced down the road in both directions, catching a distant view of Luke, and once more her heart fluttered around like the butterflies that frequented her flower beds lately.

She believed in first impressions, and they were usually accurate. Being a businesswoman, she knew that they were so vital. A bad first impression could mean losing a potential client, who tells everyone they know not to use your services.

She'd first met Luke last winter, and he'd been brief with her, just like he had every other time she'd met him. Her first, second, and tenth impression of him was that, while gorgeous, he wasn't overly social. But this evening he'd walked over to check on her and had even offered to talk her down next time Eve made her lose her head. That was nice and unexpected.

Brenna turned and headed back up her driveway, her mind going to that envelope that Luke had carried over. She hadn't exactly told him the truth. Yes, she was encouraging Eve to go to college. But the letter was for Brenna. She'd always told herself that she'd finish her college degree one day. Eve was an adult, and Aunt Thelma had offered to handle the business if and when Brenna decided to complete her degree. It would only be a year, and Nate would help.

Brenna stepped inside the house and closed the front door behind her, staring at the envelope on her table. Thick was good and thin was bad, right? This one had a medium thickness, leaving her unsure of the answer inside.

She took a few deep breaths, gathering her courage. "If they say no, I'll apply somewhere else." Even though Western University was her first choice. That's where she'd gotten her first three years of credits. "And if they say yes—" Her cell phone rang in the middle of her pep talk to herself. Brenna pulled it out of her pocket, checking the caller ID before tapping the screen and holding it to her ear. "Aunt Thelma?"

"Hi, Brenna. I just wanted to let you know that Eve is here."

Brenna sighed. "Of course she is."

"She said you lost your mind and threw bananas at her?"

Brenna closed her eyes and leaned against the back of her front door. "Not exactly. I threw *pieces* of banana at her. Just one banana. But don't worry, Aunt Thelma. I haven't lost my mind, just my patience with Eve's ungratefulness and complaining...Everything is fine."

"I'm sure it is. Eve asked to stay here tonight, and I told her she could. I hope that's okay."

Brenna blew out a breath. "Yes, thank you, Aunt Thelma. I'm sorry for the inconvenience."

"Don't be silly. Family is never an inconvenience. I just wanted to let you know where she was so you wouldn't worry about her. I know you do. You're just like a mom in that way."

Aunt Thelma didn't mean anything by that remark, of course, but the words stuck under Brenna's skin. She was just like a mom and yet not at all the same. And she didn't want to be Eve's mom. She wanted to return to being just sisters but it was so hard going back. Maybe there was no going back.

"I also wanted to make sure you were okay," Aunt Thelma added.

"I'm fine. Thank you for asking. And for the call."

"Of course. I love you girls so much. Always have."

"I love you too," Brenna said, meaning it. She didn't know what she'd do without her mom's sister. Aunt Thelma hadn't stepped in to run A Taste of Heaven, and she hadn't taken guardianship of Eve after the accident, but Brenna couldn't fault her for that. She was getting older and taking over a business and the care of a teenager was a lot to ask. Even so, Thelma had always been there if Brenna needed something. She was only ever one phone call away. "I'll see you at A Taste of Heaven in the morning?"

"Yes, you will," her aunt said.

Brenna said good night and disconnected the call. Then she walked over to the kitchen table and plopped into the seat in front of the manila envelope, staring at it for an exaggerated moment. She'd never know until she opened it. "Just do it, Brenna."

Her fingers shook slightly as she lifted it and tore off the top. She pulled out the letter inside and sent up a silent prayer before reading.

Dear Ms. McConnell,

Congratulations! We are pleased to inform you that you have been accepted to Western University.

* * *

The sun wasn't even over the mountains yet, and Luke had already trimmed back the roses and taken care of the weeds that were popping up every time he turned around. A light came on next door, catching his eye. Brenna was awake. He imagined she was turning on her coffee maker and rubbing her eyes sleepily. Was she preparing breakfast right now or was she the kind that skipped the first meal of the day?

Luke rubbed a hand over his face. Where were these questions coming from? He didn't wonder about the details of the neighbor on the opposite side of him or the ones down the street. And he didn't need to wonder about Brenna McConnell either.

After an hour more of work, including washing his truck, Luke showered and dressed for his shift.

"Luke!" Chief Brewer said, meeting him in the station's kitchen once he'd arrived.

"You're here again?"

"Can't help myself," the chief said. "Looks like there were no calls yesterday."

"It was a quiet day," Luke agreed. "I stayed on Ryan's back to get the lawn maintenance done."

"I noticed when I drove up. Looks good."

"Yeah, well, I had Wally go back behind him and touch it up."

Chief Brewer shook his head in response.

"Tim is behind on his training. Again," Luke pointed out. "I checked and everyone else is all caught up."

"Sounds about right," Chief Brewer said. "I've been meaning to have a talk with him about that. I'll plan to handle that tomorrow when I'm on shift."

Someone knocked on the office door, interrupting the conversation.

Both men turned toward a tall, thin young woman with bright-red hair and pale freckled skin. She was Brenna's sister, who Luke had heard fighting with Brenna last night. He'd seen her at a few scenes working as a volunteer firefighter before too.

"Eve, what are you doing here?" Chief Brewer asked. He stepped over and gave the young woman a hug, obviously happy to see her. "We haven't had any calls this morning."

"I'm not here as a volunteer. I'm here because I want to be a real firefighter. I want a job," Eve clarified. "I've finished the academy. I'm trained and well qualified."

Chief Brewer held out his open palms. "As I've told you before, we don't have any openings just yet. Our workload justifies one, and I've sent a request to Mayor Everson, but he's the one who decides how many crew we're allotted." The chief scratched the tip of his chin. "But honestly, your sister doesn't even like you volunteering with us, Eve. She's given me an earful on that subject before."

Eve huffed. "Brenna needs to mind her own business and stop treating me like a child."

Chief Brewer slid his gaze over to meet Luke's as if looking for help. Luke intended to stay out of this conversation though.

Chief Brewer returned his attention to Eve. "You haven't come out to the last few calls with us. I thought maybe you saw too much. It's not an easy job, and I wouldn't blame anyone for having a change of heart."

"I didn't have a change of heart," Eve said with all the feistiness of young adults that Luke had ever known, himself included at that age. "I've been busy helping out at A

Taste of Heaven but I'm done with that now. My sister is a control freak in the kitchen."

Chief Brewer frowned. "I'm sorry but I just don't have any openings right now."

"So when you do, the job is mine?" Eve pressed.

Chief Brewer shared another look with Luke. They both knew that openings at the fire station were rare unless Mayor Everson approved another spot. Right now, there were only six guys on crew, including Chief Brewer and Luke's assistant chief position. They split the day shifts, and the other crew took turns rotating longer, overnight shifts.

"There are plenty of other fire stations outside of Sweetwater Springs," Luke pointed out. "Might mean moving but you'd be able to find firefighting work if you were willing to do that."

Eve shook her head. "I don't want a job anywhere else. This is where my dad worked. This is where I learned the ropes as a volunteer firefighter. I want to be at SSFD."

She was headstrong, and her passion shone through. Luke saw more than a little of himself in her. All his life, he'd wanted to be a firefighter, and once he had the training, he'd pretty much camped out at the door of the station in Whispering Pines. His chief there eventually had to give him a job because Luke wasn't giving up.

"I'll call you if a position opens," Chief Brewer reiterated. "That's all I can promise. But you could be waiting a long time, and there's a list of other firefighters who want to work here. Best to find another paying job in the meantime."

Eve sighed, her shoulders rounding forward in temporary defeat. "Well, I'm not working with Brenna, so don't even try to suggest that. It's bad enough that I have to live under the same roof with her."

"You don't," Luke pointed out.

Eve narrowed her eyes at him. "What?"

"You're an adult, right? You don't have to do anything you don't want to do. Right, Chief Brewer?"

Chief Brewer held up his hands. "Don't ask me. I'm staying out of this one." He headed out of the kitchen, chuckling softly.

Luke and Eve followed him down the hall toward the garage where the engines were kept. The smell of wax was thick in the air, and Luke spotted Ryan finally shining one of the engines. Luke had asked him to take care of that yesterday.

"It was nice seeing you, Eve." The chief glanced over his shoulder. "I missed you while you were away at the academy," he said. Then his legs slipped out from under him and he clawed at the air as he fell to the hard cement floor.

Luke didn't breathe. Eve screamed. And Ryan let out a few curse words as he tried to catch Chief Brewer or at least break his fall. In a quick second, Chief Brewer was sprawled on his back, face scrunched in a painful grimace, lying right beside a spilled bucket of wax and a few dirty rags.

"Chief, are you okay?" Luke ran over and squatted down beside him. "Don't move. Tell me where it hurts."

"Everywhere," Chief Brewer muttered and then groaned. "It hurts everywhere."

CHAPTER FOUR

Brenna sighed as she wiped down the stove top in the kitchen. She and Aunt Thelma had just cooked a large spaghetti dinner for a client's luncheon in town. Spaghetti wasn't necessarily fancy but the way she and Thelma made it was. The sauce was homemade with fresh tomatoes, minced vegetables, and meat. They had also prepared several trays of buttered bread and fresh tossed salad to serve as sides, along with a few jugs of sweet tea. Nate had taken the food for delivery while they cleaned.

"You okay today, sweetheart?" Aunt Thelma asked, looking over with concern as she wiped down the neighboring stove. "You've been unusually quiet this morning. Even if you aren't talking to me, you usually talk to yourself." Aunt Thelma broke into a wide smile that reminded Brenna of her mom. Brenna's mom and Thelma used to say that when they were young, they'd often been mistaken for twins. Both had dark hair that they wore up in a thick bun and equally dark eyes, set a little wider apart than most.

"I'm fine," Brenna said. "Just..." She shook her head as she finished wiping down the glass top. Then she stopped and turned to face her aunt, suddenly brimming with excitement. "I applied to Western University a couple months back."

Thelma straightened. "You did?"

Brenna nodded.

"You didn't say anything. Why not?" Thelma asked.

"Well, I guess I was worried that I wouldn't get in."

"Well, of course you'd get in. You've always been so smart." She narrowed her eyes. "You did get in, didn't you?"

Brenna nodded. "I did."

"Well, good for you, sweetheart! I know how much you want to be a teacher, and I know how great you'd be at it. Your mom would want this for you too. If she were here, she'd insist that you go finish that degree."

Brenna stepped toward her aunt and wrapped her arms around her in a big hug. "Thank you, Aunt Thelma. I'm so glad you understand." Brenna pulled away and looked at her.

"Of course I do. I'm thrilled for you, Brenna. Even though I'm a little sad for me. First, Eve took off to the academy for six months, and now you're going away for a year. When are you leaving?"

"I can start during the second summer session. If I accept, that is."

Thelma scrunched her brows. "Of course you're accepting. We'll have to hire more help." Aunt Thelma tilted her head. "Or... maybe it's time you sell this place."

"Sell A Taste of Heaven?" Brenna asked, shocked that her aunt would even suggest such a thing. They'd discussed it when Brenna and Eve had first inherited the place after the accident but their parents' deaths were still too raw back then, and Brenna had clung to anything that belonged to them. But now...

"If you get your degree, you're not coming back to work here. And I don't mind covering while you're away at college but I want to retire in the next year. It's time for me to chase my dreams too," Thelma said. "I've always wanted to travel and see the world."

Brenna knew Aunt Thelma loved reading about different destinations but she'd never considered that her aunt wanted to go visit those places in person. "You've put off your life to stay here with us, haven't you?"

"Just a little delay," Aunt Thelma said, holding up her fingers to measure an inch. "But family is never an inconvenience," she said, repeating what she'd told Brenna on the phone last night. "Eve doesn't want this business. We both know that. And you don't want it either—not really."

"Mom worked so hard to build this place," Brenna said.

"She did," Aunt Thelma agreed. "That was her dream, and she lived it while she was alive. It served its purpose for her. Now maybe it's time to sell this place to someone else who has a passion for catering. Just think about it."

"I will."

Thelma put her apron away and walked slowly to the door. "I'm off to go to my doctor's appointment now. It seems like when you get to be my age, you and your doctors become the best of friends." She laughed under her breath. "Why don't we have dinner sometime soon? We can celebrate your news and discuss plans for this place?"

"That sounds good." She watched her aunt wave and then head out the back entrance.

When Thelma was gone, Brenna released another heavy sigh as she looked around the kitchen. Her gaze stopped on the wooden rolling pin that her mom had hung above the main stove many years ago. It was the one that she and Brenna had used together when Brenna was growing up. They'd roll out a mound of dough with that pin, and her mom would sprinkle imaginary love all over. "Made with love," she'd claim, offering Brenna a wink. "Just like you."

Her mom had hung the rolling pin as a reminder that the secret ingredient to everything they cooked at A Taste of Heaven was love. Brenna tried to maintain that standard but it was getting harder to do when this kitchen was feeling more and more like a jail cell lately.

* * *

Two hours later, Nate's niece Hannah pushed through the door. Brenna had offered to tutor her at Christmastime when Nate had mentioned how upset she was over her grades this school year. Hannah was struggling and needed a little extra help.

"Hey, Hannah." Brenna pulled off her apron and pointed at Nate. "Let me know if you need anything. We'll be in the office."

Nate stepped over and gave his niece a hug. "You are more beautiful every time I see you," he said. "Go learn lots."

Hannah offered a sweet smile, revealing a mouth full of braces. "Thanks, Uncle Nate." Then she followed Brenna back to the office where they worked on algebra. For the first time all day, Brenna felt alive. She loved teaching, even if math was her least favorite subject. When she saw things click in Hannah's eyes, Brenna felt invigorated. They sat for an hour and finished Hannah's homework.

At the end of the tutoring session, Hannah pulled a piece of paper out of her backpack and slid it over.

Brenna's gaze jumped to the red ink on the top of the page, and her eyes burned with happy tears. "A one hundred? You got a perfect score on your math quiz?"

Hannah's head bobbed up and down excitedly. "Thanks to you, Miss Brenna."

"No, you earned this. You're the one putting in all the extra effort. You're a rock star, and I'm going to tell your uncle Nate that he has to take you out for ice cream before he drops you off at home today."

Hannah's eyes widened. "I wish you could come too."

"Next time. I need to close up this evening." Brenna stood from the desk. "Come on, quiz-acer. Let's tell your uncle the good news. He'll be so proud."

Not nearly as proud as Brenna. For the first time today, she was smiling. Teaching fulfilled her in a way that catering didn't. Keeping this business would only weigh her and Aunt Thelma down. Her aunt was right. It was time to put this place up for sale and move on.

Tonight, she would tell Eve about her plans for college and then discuss selling the business. Technically, A Taste of Heaven belonged to both of them. Eve would have to agree to sell but Brenna didn't foresee her sister objecting. She didn't foresee Eve objecting to Brenna leaving town either. In fact, she suspected Eve might throw her a going-away party.

* * *

"Chief's going to fire me, isn't he?" Ryan asked for the tenth time this afternoon. Every time he walked by Luke in the last several hours, he'd phrased the question differently.

"It was an accident," Luke said once again. "A stupid one. Who spills wax and doesn't clean it up immediately?"

"I was going to clean it up once I was done with the engine. One thing at a time. Isn't that what you tell us?"

Really? Ryan was trying to divert the blame on him? "Well, some things you stop for," Luke said. "If we'd gotten a fire call, you would've stopped, right?"

Ryan nodded. "Of course."

"Spilled wax is dangerous. Now Chief Brewer is in the hospital because he hurt his back," Luke told him.

"He's definitely going to fire me." Ryan's face was pale.

If Luke were chief, he wouldn't hesitate to do just that. Maybe he should just let Ryan fret over the outcome that he thought was inevitable. "Don't you have a task list to do?"

"I was going to do it later," Ryan told him.

"Guess again."

Instead of arguing, Ryan looked down at his feet, probably knowing that he was already on thin ice. Or slippery wax in this case. "I'll get started on it."

"Good." Luke's phone buzzed inside his pocket as he watched Ryan walk toward the picnic table outside. He pulled it out and read a text message from Chief Brewer.

I need to see you ASAP.

Luke's heart dropped into his belly. It hadn't been long since he'd left the hospital. Why would the chief be calling him back?

You okay? Luke waited nervously for the chief's response.

No. My wife is smothering me, and I'll be out of work for the immediate future. Leave Wally in charge and head over to the hospital.

On my way, Luke texted back.

"Wally!" Luke called, stepping out of his office.

Wally appeared from the kitchen. "What's up?"

"I'm going to check on Chief Brewer. You're in charge. Make sure Ryan stays on task."

Wally nodded. "Sure."

"If there's a call, I'll meet you at the scene."

"Roger that."

Luke grabbed his keys and then headed to his truck. A short drive later, he pulled into the hospital parking lot and went up to room 301, where Mrs. Brewer met him at the door.

"Oh, Luke, please talk some sense into my stubborn husband."

Luke walked into the room and looked between the couple. "What's going on?"

"He's refusing the pain medication the doctor prescribed. Why should he choose to be in pain?"

"I'm fine," Chief Brewer barked. "And it's my pain. I'll deal with it the way I want to."

Mrs. Brewer clucked her tongue. "See?"

"If you don't mind, dear, could you go get me some tea?" Chief Brewer asked, softening his voice. "I think that would ease my discomfort."

She looked at Luke and sighed. "He just wants to talk to you alone. I get it. I'll take my time before coming back with your tea," she told her husband.

When she was out of range, Chief Brewer looked at Luke. "She drove me crazy when we were dating but now she drives me crazy in a completely different way."

Luke sat down in the chair beside the chief's bed. "What's the verdict?"

"Strained back muscles. They did a bunch of tests to rule out anything serious. I still need to take it easy. No heavy lifting or heavy fire suits. He wants me to take a month off from work."

"A month?"

"I have a history of back injury so we're taking extra precautions." Chief Brewer shifted uncomfortably on the bed. "That's why I called you to come back here. You'll be acting chief while I'm out. As assistant chief, you're next in line." The chief held Luke's gaze. "You're a born leader. I knew it as soon as I interviewed you. It's one reason I made you my assistant. You came highly recommended from your previous chief, and quite frankly, I believe in you. The other guys will help out."

Luke's heart was racing as he processed what Chief Brewer was saying. The guys had given him a hard time when he'd first joined the SSFD. He figured it wasn't easy having a new guy come in and take a higher position. They were mostly cool now, even if Ryan still gave Luke attitude most days.

Chief Brewer gestured at his body. "My injury is a good reminder that mistakes can be costly. It's not just Tim I needed to have a talk with. I was going to review standards and expectations with the whole crew. I'm going to need you to do that for me now."

Luke hesitated as he looked down at his interwoven fingers and roped in his competing thoughts. He didn't think him harping on the guys about their work ethics and attitudes was going to be received as well as it would have been from Chief Brewer. "Yeah, I can do that."

"Good. Also, I got off the phone with Mayor Everson just before you arrived. My injury and impending absence has sped up the approval for another fireman at the SSFD."

"A new hire?" Luke asked, looking up. At least there was a bright spot to this conversation.

Chief Brewer pointed a finger at Luke. "Yep. That's your first job as acting fire chief. Hire someone for the department. I trust you to go through the applications on file and determine the right fit for our crew."

Luke leaned forward over his knees, overwhelmed by the sudden responsibility that had fallen on his shoulders. "Anything else?" he asked.

"Acting fire chief, a pep talk for the crew, and a new hire. That's all for today." Chief Brewer offered his hand for Luke to shake. "Good luck, son."

* * *

Brenna turned onto her road and drove along the creek toward her house. She'd texted Eve and asked her to meet her tonight for dinner. Eve hadn't responded to her texts yet. She was ignoring her. What else was new?

As Brenna drove into view of her home, she exhaled when she saw Eve's green Volkswagen Beetle in the driveway. Hopefully, Eve had cooled down since their fight last night and was ready to talk.

She parked and hurried up the steps. As she entered the front door, Eve came walking toward her. She stopped and heaved a sigh.

"Hi," Brenna said. "I was beginning to worry about you. You okay?"

"Never better," Eve said.

"Good. I'm glad to hear that. I didn't mean to step on your toes yesterday morning at work. I'm sorry. And I'm sorry about, um, the banana." Singular. Just one.

"I'm over that," Eve huffed. "And I don't want to cook big fancy meals for people who should learn to cook their own food anyway. I got a new job today."

Brenna forced a smile. "Well, I can't wait to hear all about it. We can talk over dinner. I prepared our meal at work today. It's still in the car. I just need to grab it and warm it on the stove."

Eve rolled her eyes and let out an exasperated groan. "I'm not staying to eat. I'm moving out. Right now."

"What?" Brenna noticed the suitcases against the wall now. "You can't move. This is our home. It's yours just as much as it is mine."

"No, this is my prison where you treat me like a child. Luke reminded me that I'm an adult, and I don't have to stay here if I don't want to."

"Luke? Our neighbor Luke?" Brenna asked.

"That's the one."

"When did you talk to him?" Because Luke never ventured over. Not until the noise from Brenna's fight with Eve had lured him to their front door. He'd been so nice. They'd come to an understanding. Or at least, she'd thought they had.

"Why does it matter when I spoke to him? Are you jealous?" Eve asked.

"No."

Eve smirked and reached for the handle of her rolling luggage. Then she lifted a carry-on bag over her opposite shoulder and took a few steps.

"Can we at least talk about this?" Brenna asked.

Eve kept walking.

"Eve, you're being irrational."

Eve whipped around to face her. "I don't want to go to college, and I don't want to live here anymore, okay? I want to be a firefighter at the SSFD, just like Dad."

Were they really going to go through this again? "There aren't any openings right now..." Brenna began, willing her voice to stay calm. She could always talk Eve down. There was no reason for either of them to argue.

Eve offered a satisfied smile. "Good news. The mayor approved a new position, and I got hired today."

Brenna blinked. "The Sweetwater Springs Fire Department is your new job?"

"Yep."

"Doing what? Like, a secretary?" *Please let it be a clerical job where it's safe.* Her father hadn't died while working but he'd had several close calls. Brenna barely had any family left, just Eve and Aunt Thelma. She couldn't lose them too.

"Are you for real?" Eve asked. "News flash, sis: Girls can be whatever they want. And what I want, what I've always wanted, is to be a Sweetwater Springs firefighter."

CHAPTER FIVE

Brenna gulped in the fresh air as she watched Eve back out of the driveway and speed away. She continued to stand there long after her sister's car had disappeared from sight.

"You okay?" a man's voice asked.

Brenna turned to see Luke approaching the porch from his yard. "No. I could scream right now."

Luke lifted one eyebrow. "Anything I can do to help?"

"I doubt it. Eve just moved out." Brenna tried and failed to keep her breathing and voice steady. She narrowed her eyes at the man in front of her, her heart kicking softly against her ribs. *Down, heart.* The only thing she was interested in where Luke Marini was concerned was giving him a piece of her mind. "She says you advised her to."

Luke's jaw dropped. Then he held up his hands. "No, it wasn't advice. I just reminded her that she was an adult, and if she wasn't happy with the way things were, she had choices."

Brenna leaned forward on the porch railing. "That sure sounds like advice to me."

"She didn't have to act on it. This is her decision, not mine."

"Maybe, but you're the assistant fire chief. She looks up to you. Of course she's going to act on what you say. And she apparently got hired on at the Sweetwater Springs Fire Department today."

"Yeah, I know," he said, flinching.

She narrowed her eyes. "Of course you do. I could just strangle the chief right now."

Luke put his hands in his pockets as he shifted back and forth on his feet. "Why are you so against her working at the fire department anyway?"

Brenna shook her head. "She's just a kid, Luke. She's not ready to charge toward dangerous situations. She's overeager and headstrong. She doesn't think before she acts."

"That's not the Eve that shows up as a volunteer for us. From what I've seen, she's passionate and eager to learn. She cares about people, and she keeps her head on straight at the scenes. That's important. When things get chaotic, a firefighter needs to be calm. I wasn't half as calm as her at that age."

Brenna fidgeted nervously, an undercurrent of anxiety still buzzing through her. "You became a firefighter at her age?"

"Soon as I was old enough, I was there. There was nothing else I ever wanted to do."

The same was true for Eve. "I just can't believe that Chief Brewer would hire her without talking to me first. We're friends. My dad worked with him."

Luke was looking increasingly uneasy, which she found curious. She guessed it was because she was talking about his boss.

"And what would you have said if he'd come to you first?" Luke asked.

Brenna shrugged. "The same thing I'm telling you. I would've told him that Eve isn't ready."

"She is ready," Luke reiterated. "You're the one who's not ready." He held up his hands once more. "Not saying there's anything wrong with that. But it's your problem, not Eve's."

Brenna's mouth fell open. "Excuse me?"

Luke continued to hold up his hands. "My mom wasn't ready when I became a firefighter either. You're not Eve's mom, I know that, but the way you're acting is kind of the way my mom did."

"What did she do?" Brenna asked.

Luke chuckled, lowering his hands. "She marched down to my fire chief and fussed him out in front of his whole crew."

Brenna straightened from the porch railing. "That's great advice, actually."

Luke looked startled. "I didn't offer any advice."

"I need to go have words with the chief," Brenna said. "Do you know where he is?"

Luke met her gaze. "Yeah... You're looking at him."

"You're not the chief."

"Acting chief. Chief Brewer had a fall earlier today. He's fine but he hurt his back. The doctor wants him to take it easy for the next month."

"I don't understand. You hired my sister?" Brenna asked. "It wasn't enough that you advised her to move out of the house she grew up in? You had to hire her to run into burning buildings too?"

Luke put his hands on his hips. "Wait a minute. If you want to be upset that someone didn't ask your permission, that person is Eve. But truthfully, you have no right to be upset with her either. You should be congratulating her. A firefighter getting their first job is one of the best days in their lives. It should be celebrated."

His frown and obvious disappointment in Brenna's behavior right now made her feel suddenly small.

"Honestly, I doubt it was my advice that drove Eve away," he added. "It was more likely her overbearing sister."

* * *

Luke took a step backward for his own protection because Brenna looked like she wanted to deck him right now. "Well, I better get home to take Max for his walk. Just wanted to make sure you were all right...Good night."

She didn't even respond. Instead, she made a low sound that sounded like a growl and went back inside, slamming her front door behind her. He guessed there'd be no more doughnuts in his future.

Turning, he walked across the lawn and entered his own house where Max stood waiting, leash in his mouth. "How'd you get a hold of that?" He'd placed it on the top of the washing machine, and Max was a small dog. A resourceful dog. "Never mind. I don't want to know. At least I can make someone happy tonight." He snapped the leash into place and went right back outside, stopping every couple of steps for Max to smell the air, the bushes, or the scent of a critter that had already come and gone.

As he waited, his mind played over his run-in with Brenna. He didn't understand where she was coming from. He understood her sister, Eve, more. Just like Eve at that age, Luke had been stubborn, and he'd done exactly what he wanted no matter what anyone else said. He'd wanted to be a firefighter with every fiber of his body. Still did. It was either in your blood or it wasn't.

Max tugged against his leash and then glanced back and barked at Luke, who apparently wasn't walking fast enough.

"I'm coming," he told his dog. They walked for about an hour before heading back in the direction of his house. Brenna's lights were all on in her home but he wasn't going to dare talk to her. In fact, he was going to stay as far away as possible from his pretty neighbor from now on. He should've stuck to that resolve in the first place.

* * *

The next day, Luke arrived at the station bright and early and sat at Chief Brewer's desk. It was his first full day as acting fire chief. Chief Brewer was putting his faith in him, and Luke wasn't going to let him down.

"Don't get too comfortable there," Ryan called as he walked through the door. "You'll be spit shining engines again once he's back."

"I know my place," Luke called back. "Do you know yours?"

"Right now it's the kitchen to see if there's any food. I didn't have time to grab breakfast."

Luke yawned. Last night's sleep hadn't been the best. He'd thought he would make up for it with a cup of coffee from the Sweetwater Café, but as he'd stood in front of the entrance, he'd seen Brenna inside. He'd promptly retreated to his truck and headed here.

He stood and walked to the kitchen as well, hoping to find coffee in the pot. No such luck.

"I'm here and ready to work," Eve said, entering the room behind him.

Ryan faced her. "Great. You can make our new fire chief here a pot of coffee. The stronger, the better."

Eve's mouth twisted into a scowl. She looked at Luke, her brow lifting subtly as if to say, *Are you going to let him talk to me that way?*

No, Luke wasn't. Things needed to change here at the station, starting with the level of respect that the crew were giving each other.

"Ryan, make a pot of coffee," Luke said, folding his arms over his chest.

Ryan whipped his head around to look at Luke. "You serious? I don't make coffee."

"And what makes you think that I do?" Eve shot back, her voice becoming shrill. Yeah, Luke could just see Eve and Brenna getting in a tangle. Both appeared to be strong women able to defend themselves. "I'm here to work just like you guys," she said.

"But you're a woman, not a guy," Ryan pointed out.

Luke couldn't believe the idiocy of his co-worker. "Do you talk to your mom like that?"

"No way. She'd poison my food," Ryan said.

Eve scowled harder and took a step toward him. "So would I."

"That's enough." Luke placed a hand up, holding it between them. "No homicidal threats at the station. Ryan, you need to apologize."

"What for?" Ryan asked. "She's the one who just threatened to poison me."

Luke raised a brow. "Apologize or go home without earning your pay today."

Ryan's jaw dropped. "You can't do that."

"I'm acting chief. I can, and I will. Chief Brewer wouldn't allow you to talk to another firefighter with that kind of disrespect, and neither will I."

Ryan looked between them, his defensive posture

seeming to soften. "It's not because she's a woman, okay? It's because she's bottom of the totem pole. We treat all the new crew that way. I was treated that way when I got here. She wants to be treated like the rest of us, and that's what I'm doing."

Ryan had treated Luke that way when he'd first arrived as well. Luke massaged his forehead. "Chief Brewer is expecting me to take care of things while he's away, and I need everyone's help to do that. If we're arguing, we're not at our best. Got it?"

Ryan shrugged. "Yeah, okay. I got it."

"Now apologize," Luke repeated, pinning the young firefighter with his gaze. "Or go home."

Ryan glanced over at Eve, hesitating so long that Luke thought he might choose to go home without pay. "Sorry," Ryan finally muttered.

Luke supposed that was as good as he'd get today. He'd have to work on Ryan's attitude and take baby steps to improve upon it. "Good. I can make my own pot of coffee." Luke looked at Ryan. "You have your jobs for the morning." He looked at Eve. "You're studying for your CDL, right?"

Her face lit up. "I know it's not required to drive the engines, but I want to have it."

"It looks great on a résumé. Find a place and keep studying. Later in the day, I'll teach you how to do maintenance on some of the equipment."

Her eyes widened. "That sounds awesome. I want to learn it all."

What Ryan Johnson had in attitude, Eve had in passion. "Pass the word. I'm having a meeting this afternoon at shift change," he told the two. "We have new rules to go over."

"You're one day in your new role, and you're already trying to change things?" Ryan asked.

"These rules come down from Chief Brewer. He's still our fire chief." Even though Luke was the one who'd stayed up last night outlining what needed to change around the station. He'd been observing the weaknesses of the department for a while. Chief Brewer's fall was an example of what could happen when things got sloppy. Yeah, it was an accident but it was also the result of a lax mentality. That was going to end on Luke's watch.

The phone rang from Chief Brewer's office.

"Meeting at shift change, no one leaves until we talk. It'll take fifteen minutes." Luke turned and headed to answer the call. He picked up the phone's receiver and held it to his ear. "Sweetwater Springs Fire Department."

"Yes, this is Donna Roberts from the seamstress shop downtown," the caller said. "I smell smoke coming from that catering place next door again."

Luke closed his eyes. Donna Roberts called at least once a week to complain about Brenna's business. Usually Chief Brewer rode out there and settled the older woman's nerves, assuring her that her shop wasn't about to burn down. Today, however, Luke guessed it was his job. Lucky him. "I'm sure it's nothing but I'll come check it out right now to make sure."

"Oh, thank you so much," Mrs. Roberts said. "Please hurry."

"Yes, ma'am. See you in a few minutes." He hung up the phone and turned toward a knock on his door.

"Was that a fire call?" Eve asked. "Can I go along?"

Luke started to tell her no. The seamstress shop was right next door to A Taste of Heaven, and Brenna was already upset with him. Bringing Eve along might look like he was rubbing Eve's new job in Brenna's face.

Then again, Eve was his new hire, and she deserved as

much on-the-job training as she could get. That was his duty as her acting chief, and he wasn't about to neglect it over a dispute with his neighbor.

He looked at Eve and gave a nod. "Sure. Let's go."

* * *

Brenna coughed. A smoky kitchen was her pet peeve. She never worked in a smoke-filled kitchen, mostly because she always had a clean oven and never burned the food. She was a professional, after all.

This morning, however, she'd burned the bottoms of her bread loaves. It was unlike her and she knew exactly what was to blame. Or more accurately, who. Luke Marini. Ever since he'd moved next door, she'd been distracted. After their run-in yesterday, her mind had warred against an unruly attraction to the man and her desire to walk next door and lay into him.

Brenna coughed again and turned toward the freezer to get another loaf of bread to bake. The smoke wasn't enough to cause the smoke detector to go off, but knowing Donna next door, she was already dialing up the fire department.

"Please don't call the station," Brenna said out loud. It was better when Nate was here; that way she didn't feel like she was talking to herself. But he was out delivering food this morning.

Brenna glanced out the window and sighed as a red truck marked with the SSFD logo parked against the curb. Yep, Donna had called to complain.

Brenna was hoping not to run into the town's acting fire chief again for at least another week. She wanted time to cool down. If he hadn't given Eve a job, Eve would still be helping here at A Taste of Heaven instead of putting her life in danger. She also wouldn't be able to afford to move out—although Eve was sleeping in Aunt Thelma's guest bedroom until her first paycheck.

Brenna sucked in a sharp breath as she watched Luke step out of the vehicle. The passenger door swung out over the curb, and then Eve stepped out too. Brenna watched the two head inside the shop next door and then grabbed her pan with the new roll of French bread and slid it into the oven. She set the timer and started pacing the kitchen. It was only a matter of minutes before the smell of smoke led Luke and Eve here, and in that short amount of time, Brenna needed to collect her emotions. She needed to play it cool, maybe even congratulate Eve on her new job like Luke had suggested. Even though Brenna was still mad at him.

The bell over her entrance jingled, and Brenna straightened. Then she turned to face Luke, who was strolling in her direction. Eve wasn't with him.

"You okay?" Luke asked. "We got a call—"

"As you know, Donna will call the station if she so much as thinks she smells the scent of smoke."

Luke glanced around. "I have to admit I could smell it a little over there too."

"I burned the French bread," Brenna told him. "No cause for alarm. My fire detector didn't even go off."

Luke looked at the detector on the ceiling now, stepping past her and toward the closest one. "It should have."

"I know Eve's with you. Where is she?" Brenna asked, ignoring his concern.

He glanced over his shoulder, an apologetic look in his eyes. "She didn't want to come in. She's outside."

"Why didn't she want to come in?" Brenna could hear her tone unintentionally rising.

"Maybe she doesn't want the guilt trip for following her dreams."

Brenna sucked in a deep breath. "I was going to congratulate her on the new job, if you must know."

Luke nodded as he grabbed a step stool and climbed up. He popped the lid off the detector on the ceiling. "Do you have new batteries? These are bad."

"Really?"

His expression was serious as he studied the inner workings of the device. "When was the last time you changed them?"

"I can't remember."

"Which means it's probably been a while."

"Isn't the detector supposed to make a little beep sound when the batteries are bad?" she asked, opening the closet where she kept a container full of batteries.

"Supposed to. Maybe yours is a dud. You need a functioning detector in the shop, especially if you're going to go around burning bread."

Brenna grabbed some AA batteries and headed toward him. "I rarely ever burn anything," she told him. "I'm a professional."

He smiled at her, and the little dimples in his cheeks did funny things to her stomach. "If that's true, then why does Donna call the station so often?"

Brenna's mouth fell open. Then she placed her hands on her hips and watched him slide the batteries into the detector and secure the lid back into place. "Nate has a habit of burning things. He's a little forgetful in the kitchen."

"Then why do you have him working here?" Luke asked.

Brenna shook her head. "He's still learning, and when he isn't burning the food, he's proving to be a talented cook... You ask a lot of questions, Chief Marini. You know that?"

He lowered his hands away from the ceiling and looked at her. "Fixed. Next time you burn the bread, the detector will make sure that the whole street knows about it."

"Thank you ... I think."

There was that smile of his again, carving dimples in his cheeks and chipping away at the wall around her heart. He climbed off the step stool and put it back before starting for the door.

"Wait."

Luke stopped and turned, one eyebrow lifting subtly.

"Tell Eve ... tell her ..." Brenna wrung her hands in front of her. She didn't know what she wanted to tell her sister. She just wished things were easier between them. "Tell her I said congratulations on the new job. I'm sure she'll do great."

"You mean that?" Luke asked.

"Halfway," Brenna said, shrugging one shoulder. "Okay, not really. I just want her to be safe. And happy too, of course."

"Me too," Luke said. Something sincere in his tone of voice struck her. "I'll look out for her, same as I would any of the firefighters on my crew."

Brenna nodded. It was a huge relief to know that there was someone else looking out for Eve's well-being. She couldn't be everywhere for Eve anymore but loosening the reins was so much more difficult than she'd expected it would be. "Thank you for saying that."

"They're not just words. I mean it." He offered another little smile. Then he headed out the door, leaving Brenna standing there with a fire of her own that needed putting out.

CHAPTER SIX

That evening, Luke caught Ryan on the way into the parking lot. "I told you we were having a meeting before shift change."

Ryan rolled his eyes. "Right. I forgot."

Luke didn't believe that for a second. Ryan probably knew most of the things that Luke wanted to go over pertained to him. Not all, of course. There were other things that needed to be addressed at the station. When he'd spoken to Chief Brewer earlier today, the chief had relayed some of the things he'd wanted to bring up with the crew. "Back inside. It won't take long."

Ryan sighed and headed back into the garage where the crew was already gathered. Luke felt like an impostor stepping in front of them. They'd been here longer, except for Eve, and they knew Chief Brewer and the inner workings of the SSFD better than he did. But the inner workings needed a tune-up, and that's what he'd been tasked to do.

"I've already spoken to all of you but I'll recap. Chief Brewer is going to be out for at least a month, and as the assistant chief, I'm in charge. I'm not going to lie. That's pretty intimidating. This is my first job as assistant chief, and now I'm running the station on my own. I need you all to help me out over the next month." Luke scanned the group. "Can you guys—"

Eve cleared her throat.

"Sorry," he said. "Can you all pitch in so that Chief Brewer can rest easy, knowing we're okay?"

"We're a team, and we have each other's backs. What do you need from us?" Tim asked.

Luke exhaled softly, relieved that not every firefighter on the crew was bucking his authority. "Well, we need to keep things neat and organized. Safety comes first, always, no exceptions." His gaze slid to Ryan before looking at the other guys. "And we have to respect one another."

"Why do you keep looking at me?" Ryan asked.

"Because you don't respect some of us," Eve hissed in his direction.

Ryan gave a small laugh, which seemed to make her madder. Her fair skin bloomed a dark shade of red that matched her hair.

Luke waved his index finger between them. "That kind of interaction can't happen. Like Tim said, we need to have each other's backs. No more bickering. New rules starting now. You get your jobs done every day, no excuses. You do them without complaining. You stay up-to-date on your training. If you don't, you don't go on the scenes. We'll call in more volunteers if we have to."

Tim narrowed his eyes. "You can't keep us from doing our job." Tim was a great firefighter but Luke had noticed that he was overdue for a couple of trainings. Trainings that Luke had reminded him of last month.

"Chief Brewer made me acting fire chief, and as such,

I decide if you go to the scenes or not. The trainings are important. We need to stay informed. We should condition our minds just as much as we do our bodies." He looked at Eve. "You're inexperienced. Not your fault, but you have a lot to learn." He looked at the guys. "That means we have to teach her. She needs to learn the right way to do things because it might be your back she's saving."

"Or yours," Ryan said, talking to Luke.

Luke didn't think Ryan was saying he wanted anything bad to happen to him. Ryan was just a young guy who couldn't control his mouth or his attitude. "We all have room to do better. Actually, better isn't good enough when lives are at stake. We need to do our best."

A long second passed between Luke and the crew. He wasn't sure if this pep talk was enough. Chief Brewer said he'd been planning on having a talk with the crew before he'd gotten hurt. What would he have said? How would he have said it to make sure it sunk in? Luke was new at this leadership thing and wasn't sure if he'd relayed his message effectively.

Wally stepped forward. "So, in short, you want us to do our job. Right? Because all the stuff you mentioned is what I signed on for. And I'll be the first to admit that I've gotten a little lazy lately."

Luke nodded. "We all have room for improvement. Even me."

"Is that all you wanted to discuss?" Ryan asked, making a point of looking at his watch. "Can I go home now? My shift was over five minutes ago."

Luke pinned him with a stare before looking at the others. Based on their response, he had a feeling he'd be revisiting this conversation with some or all the firefighters here before this month was over. "That's all. For now."

He wanted to go home too. There were a lot of chores to do around the house, and he wouldn't mind taking a walk along the creek with Max. And, as much as he hated to admit it, he also wouldn't mind another run-in with Brenna. She was beautiful and feisty, and even though he was a guy who shied away from drama, he didn't mind clashing with her. Some part of him was kind of enjoying it.

* * *

Brenna got into her car and drove home, glancing in the rearview mirror every few minutes to see that Luke was right behind her. He wasn't stalking her. He just happened to live right next door. She couldn't get away from him even if she wanted to.

She pulled into her driveway and stepped out.

"Fancy meeting you here," Luke called from the neighboring driveway.

She popped her trunk and grabbed a few bags of groceries she'd picked up after work. "I know Chief of Police Alex Baker, sir. Following me home is cause for a restraining order."

She heard Luke's laughter as she walked up her driveway with her bags and closed the door behind her. She didn't want to see Luke or hear him. She didn't want to think about him either because her thoughts weren't all bad. Some were good. And others were completely inappropriate.

As she started to put away her food items, her cell phone buzzed from the pocket that she'd stuffed it in. She pulled it out and glanced at the screen.

Where were you this morning?

It was a text from Halona Locklear, who owned the flower shop downtown. Brenna sometimes met Hal at the Sweetwater Café for coffee in the mornings before work.

Sorry. I overslept because I had a hard time sleeping last night.

Uh-oh. Eve stressing you out?

Always, Brenna replied.

What did she do now?

That list was too long to share over a text. I need to see your face for this one. Coffee tomorrow?

I know something's up when you tell me you want to see my face, LOL ... Yes, coffee in the a.m. Don't stand me up! ... I have something to ask you.

That piqued Brenna's curiosity. She finished unloading her bags and then started thumbing through her mail. "Are you serious?" she asked out loud. She stared at a piece of Luke's mail in her hand. Unfortunately, it looked important.

She growled as she stood in her kitchen and then headed back toward her front door. She walked across the yard, knocked on his door, and heard Max barking ferociously from the inside. She wasn't fooled; the little dog was sweet. When Luke didn't immediately come to the door, she knocked again. Max barked louder.

Finally, the door opened, and Luke stared back at her. He was wet...or his hair was. Drops of water clung to his cheeks, dripping down to his bare chest and shoulders where he'd draped a towel. Standing before her, bare chested and wearing only a pair of low-slung jeans, he looked like he belonged on the cover of a romance novel. She would definitely read that one.

Brenna dragged her gaze down and away. "Um, I'm here to, um..." *Why am I here again?* Her mind was suddenly blank.

He looked at the envelope in her hand. "Another case of misplaced mail?"

Brenna looked down at the envelope. "Oh. Yes." She couldn't seem to help the fact that she was staring at him in all his glory. Well, not *all* his glory, but her imagination was bidding to fill in the rest.

"I always step into the shower once I get home to get the dust off me."

She felt the furrow of her brow as she looked back up at him.

"That's what my dad always used to say when he got back from the factory where he worked. Now that he's retired, he collects his dust at the fishing pier."

"I see," she said, trying and failing not to find him so attractive.

A smoke detector started shrieking from behind him.

"Sorry. I left some turkey sausage in a pan on the stove." Without waiting for her response, he turned and headed down the hall.

Brenna stood there, watching him for a moment as shadows danced across his back. Then she gasped softly as she realized what she was looking at. His back was scarred on one side, the skin uneven and discolored. Her mouth went dry even as her eyes grew wet.

She was about to turn around and head home but realized she hadn't done what she'd come to do. The piece of mail was still in her hand. She supposed she could just put it in his mailbox. Why hadn't she thought of that to begin with?

She knew the reason. Some part of her wanted to see him. To talk to him. To flirt innocently. That part of her still wanted those things despite the sudden ache in her heart from seeing his scars.

She stepped over the threshold. "Luke?" she called as she followed him down the hall and into the kitchen.

He turned from the stove where he was standing and met her gaze. She watched a shadow of something flicker in his eyes. She guessed she hadn't fully hidden her reaction from seeing his back.

"I'm sorry," she felt the need to say. Although she wasn't sure what she was sorry for. She couldn't help her response. What had happened to him?

Luke didn't say anything. Instead, he turned off the stove and smoke detector, and then moved the smoking pan to the back burner. "I'll be right back." He walked briskly down the hall, leaving her standing in his kitchen, heart aching from the pain she'd felt radiating off him. Following him inside was a mistake but it was too late. Now all she could do was wait for him to return and do her best to pretend like what she'd seen was no big deal. Even though it was. Scars like his only came from a life-threatening experience.

Brenna remembered comforting Eve after their parents' accident. Eve had seen it happen. Eve had only been minutes removed from being in that car with their mom and dad. After that, Eve had rebelled. She had survivor's guilt. She'd gone through periods of anger and depression. And then she'd started acting dangerously, leaving Brenna up many a night worried about her. At least Eve had channeled that into something positive by becoming a firefighter.

Brenna swallowed past the growing lump in her throat. She'd never looked at Eve's transformation quite that way before. A sudden sense of pride came over her. Eve had come so far from the eleven-year-old girl that Brenna was guardian over.

Brenna's gaze trailed down the hall where Luke had disappeared. What had he been through? It was none of her business. She didn't need to know but she wanted to.

* * *

What was wrong with him? Luke usually made it a point to keep his shirt on so that he didn't make others feel uncomfortable, and judging by the look on Brenna's face, she felt more than a little bit of discomfort.

Luke had just turned the sausage when the doorbell had rung. When he'd gone to answer, he'd suspected that the person knocking was the UPS person delivering a package that he was expecting. Luke headed to the door without even thinking. He'd never expected to turn his back to anyone, much less his beautiful neighbor.

Thoughtless. And now Brenna was standing in his kitchen with a bunch of questions he didn't want to answer. That, or she'd run back to her own house to escape the horror of what she'd seen.

Luke lifted a hand to massage his temples. They were just scars. For the most part, he'd accepted them, but he didn't expect others to. He pulled on a T-shirt and headed back to the kitchen to find Brenna at his stove, trying to salvage his burned dinner.

"You could've just left the mail on my table."

She glanced over her shoulder. "I know. But your overcooked dinner wasn't something I could walk away from."

"A bit of a control freak, huh?" he teased, hoping to lighten the mood.

Brenna slid him a look as she used a butter knife to scrape off the burned sections. She must've gone through his drawers to find the utensils. He didn't mind. He'd just shown her the only thing he had to hide—his scars.

"You've been listening to Eve. That's what she calls me," Brenna said.

"You should loosen up a bit where she's concerned."

Brenna's lips pinched. "Easier said than done, I guess. After our parents died, a lot was put on my shoulders. My entire life seemed to be spiraling out of control. I was in college but I had to drop out and come back to care for Eve." She looked at him for a moment. "Well, I didn't have to, I guess, but the alternative would've put Eve with Aunt Thelma, whose health isn't the best, or with distant relatives who we've never even met."

"Sounds like you became a single mom in a way." Luke watched her scrape the sausage with increasing force while laying her story out there for him. He found that fascinating. He was the opposite. He didn't like to talk about himself or his past. Not that his childhood and life until now was all bad. He just didn't feel the need to share the details with strangers the way she seemed to do so readily. "That couldn't be easy."

"That's an understatement. I inherited A Taste of Heaven from my mom. I knew the business so I stepped into the role almost seamlessly." Brenna looked at him. "I'm sorry. You didn't ask, and I'm talking too much, aren't I?"

"It's okay. I like learning more about you."

She shrugged. "Well, that's pretty much me in a nutshell."

"I somehow doubt that's it. I think there's a lot more to you than meets the eye."

Her eyes widened just a touch, and he realized that he'd probably sounded like he was flirting. He wasn't trying to. He'd already drawn that line in the sand where she was concerned. Not only was she his neighbor, but she was also his employee's sister. Not happening.

"Anyway, this sausage won't be salvageable on its own. Hand me a knife and I'll slice it. I can make gumbo," she said.

"You want me to hand you a knife?" he asked, stepping up to the drawer that held his cutlery. "I'm not sure handing a woman who hates my guts a knife is a wise decision on my part."

She looked over at him. "I only halfway hate you."

"That's progress, I guess. And the other half?" he asked, which probably wasn't a wise decision either because he thought he knew the answer. The sexual tension between them could be cut with that butter knife she was wielding, even though she'd seen his back up close and personal. She'd seen it and hadn't run. Instead, there was an unmistakable heat in her gaze as she stared back at him.

She looked away. "The other half of me likes being with you way too much. Which is why it's probably best if I go home right now."

CHAPTER SEVEN

The next morning, Brenna walked into the Sweetwater Café and looked around for her best friend, Halona Locklear. Halona hadn't arrived yet so Brenna headed to the counter and greeted the café owner. "Hi, Emma!"

"Good morning," Emma said. "Your usual?" she asked, which didn't surprise Brenna one bit. Emma made it her mission to memorize her customer's favorite drinks. Sometimes she started making it as soon as Brenna walked in.

"That would be great, thanks." Brenna watched as Emma started pouring the dark brew into a to-go cup. She added the almond milk and lots of sugar for Brenna's sweet tooth. Then she placed it on the counter in front of Brenna. "I love you," Brenna said, grabbing her beverage.

Emma rung Brenna up. "Wow. If only my coffee-making skills invoked that declaration from the single men who walked in, maybe I wouldn't still be single."

Brenna offered her debit card. "Those men must be blind because you're a catch."

"I could say the same for you," Emma said as she swiped the card and handed it back to Brenna. "Enjoy."

"Thank you." Brenna took her drink and headed to the corner table where she and Halona usually sat. Her mind wandered back to last night as she sipped and waited for her friend.

After her heated moments with Luke in his kitchen, her sleep had been restless. Her mind had even taken the liberty of contemplating kissing him until she'd woken with a start. Then she'd gotten up to get a glass of water from the kitchen sink and had looked across the lawn to see that his house was lit up. He must have been having a hard time sleeping as well. Because of her?

"Hey," Halona said, plopping down in front of Brenna with her coffee.

"You already got your drink?" Brenna asked with amazement. "I didn't even see you walk in."

"I texted Emma this morning and told her I was coming. She had my drink prepared as soon as I stepped inside. You looked like you were too lost in thought to wave at me when I got here." Halona took a sip of her coffee. "Must be a juicy story to share this morning."

Brenna felt her body warm. "I don't know how juicy it is. Luke and I seem to argue as much as we flirt."

Halona grinned. "I call that foreplay."

Brenna narrowed her eyes. "Maybe for you and Alex. I have enough to worry about right now without complicating things with a crush on my neighbor. He's gorgeous, yes, but now he's Eve's boss."

"Wait—what? Eve got a job?" Halona asked.

That's right. Brenna hadn't mentioned that detail yet. "Yep, at the Sweetwater Springs Fire Department, just like she wanted."

"That's awesome."

Brenna nodded instead of being a Debbie Downer on her sister's good news. "So you see, there are too many reasons for me to stay far away from Luke."

Halona seemed to consider the information. "I hate to admit it but that actually makes sense."

Brenna reached for her cup of coffee. "I'm trying hard to make amends with my sister. I'm not thrilled about her working in such a dangerous job, but I am proud of her for following her dreams. I even got her a little congratulatory gift."

"That's mature of you," Halona said.

"It's not easy letting go, but if I hold on too tight, I'll lose her." Brenna swallowed. "And you know how Eve is. If I start dating Luke, she'll accuse me of only dating him to spy on her."

Halona grimaced. "That wouldn't be pretty."

"Probably not."

"Even so, you can't let your little sister stand in the way of your own happiness, Brenna. If you like Luke, you should go for it."

Brenna wouldn't be in town much longer so any relationship with him would be over before it started. The thought of that made her feel hollow inside. "New subject, please."

Halona placed her hands on the table in front of her. "Actually, I do have something I want to discuss."

Brenna tilted her head. "If I'm not mistaken, I think *you* have something juicy to tell."

Halona's grin spread even wider. "I'm getting married next year, and I need a favor."

"Of course. Do you want me to cater it? Because you know I'm already planning to do that." Even if she sold A

Taste of Heaven. She had a stove at home, albeit just one, and was perfectly capable of cooking.

"No. I mean, yes, I'd love for you to cater," Halona said, "but Nate will have to be the one running the show because I need you by my side. As my maid of honor."

Brenna's mouth fell open. "Are you serious? What about Josie? She's your sister-in-law."

"But you're my best friend. Are you trying to say no?" Halona frowned.

"Of course not. I'm saying yes. Definitely yes." A jolt of excitement shot through Brenna's chest, quickening her heart. She stood, walked around the table, and wrapped her arms around Halona. "Thank you for asking me."

When they pulled away from the hug, Halona pointed a finger. "It's not just a title. There's work involved in being the maid of honor."

Brenna sat back down. "It's not work if you love what you're doing. And I'm going to love every minute of making the happiest day of your life perfect. This is going to be so much fun."

Halona smiled. "Well, there's nothing for you to do just yet. I just wanted to make sure you were willing."

"Oh, I'm willing." Brenna lifted her cup of coffee in the air. "A toast?"

"To what?" Halona asked, lifting her cup of brew to hold in the air next to Brenna's.

"To happily ever afters," Brenna said.

"For both of us," Halona added, tapping her cup to Brenna's. Brenna wasn't so sure her HEA was coming. She'd been close once—so close—and it had all fallen apart at the first little bump in the path. She didn't want to go through that again. At least not now when her focus was on following her longtime dream of finishing her college degree.

Halona stood and collected her drink in one hand and her bag in the other. "Now I have to get to the flower shop."

Brenna stood as well. "And I have to get to A Taste of Heaven."

"Maybe I'll catch you again one morning this week."

"Hope so." Brenna waved as they left the café and turned in opposite directions.

When she walked into A Taste of Heaven a few minutes later, Aunt Thelma was in the kitchen. "Morning, sunshine," she called. Just like Brenna's mom, Thelma was happiest behind a stove. Brenna envied that.

"Good morning. Any new calls?"

Thelma looked up, seeming to go through a mental Rolodex. "Yes. Mrs. Anderson called to thank you for handling the event last week and the senior Mrs. Everson wants you to call her back. She wants to talk to you about her upcoming event that we're catering."

Brenna would hold off on making that call until her caffeine fully kicked in. The mayor's mother wasn't the easiest client to work with. They'd already scheduled the main menu. Now Mrs. Everson wanted to finalize the desserts and appetizers. "Is that it?"

Thelma gestured at the stove top. "I'm just prepping some vegetables for a stew."

Like her mom, Brenna's aunt made stew several times a week. People in Sweetwater Springs often stopped in to buy it for their dinners at night. Sometimes they called and ordered it ahead of time. It wasn't traditional catering but it was something Brenna's mom had started and Thelma carried on. And if no one purchased the stew, Brenna took it home for her and Eve. Or just herself, now that Eve didn't live at Blueberry Creek anymore.

Brenna helped Thelma prepare some vegetables and

then went to the office to push around some paperwork. The day flew by until the afternoon when Hannah came walking in, lugging her book bag on one shoulder.

"Hi, Hannah," Brenna said, perking up more than she had all day. "How was school?"

Hannah groaned. "Just when I figure out something in math, my teacher teaches something new, and I'm lost all over again."

Brenna tipped her head toward the kitchen. "I made cookies. How about we eat and figure it out together?"

Hannah's expression brightened. Most likely because of the treat, but Brenna's excitement stemmed from an opportunity to teach. She couldn't wait until that was what she did all day. Maybe once that was the case, she could focus on finding her own happily ever after.

* * *

The next day, the fire alarms at the station went off an hour into Luke's shift. This wasn't merely a call because Donna at the seamstress shop smelled a little smoke. No, this was an all-hands-on-deck kind of call with two engines deployed.

Luke suited up and hurried to check on Eve, who was also on shift this morning.

She looked at him with a wild excitement in her eyes. Something about her expression reminded him of Brenna, and for a moment, Luke's mind stuttered to a halt.

He'd hardly slept a wink after Brenna had left his house the other night and his brain had been returning to thoughts of her ever since. She was distracting him, even when she was nowhere around.

Luke watched Eve jog over to the engine and climbed

on behind her, reaching for the safety bars as the engine screamed out of the parking lot.

"What's going on?" Ryan asked, leaning into him to be heard over the sirens.

"Ronny Hill's barn is on fire," Luke told him.

"Just his barn?" Ryan asked.

Luke understood what he meant. A barn fire would mean that search and rescue would be unlikely. It would mean he and the crew could stand back and hose the flames at a safe distance. There was no risk to human life or of bodily harm. Those were the best calls.

"As far as I know," Luke answered. He looked straight ahead as he rode for several minutes. Then the engine slowed and turned onto Ronny Hill's road. Luke had met the middle-aged man before. He was nice, although quiet. He used to keep horses on his property but he had sold them several years back, from what Luke had heard. The barn would be empty.

Flames were already licking at the air above the barn's roofline as they approached the scene.

"Let's go!" Luke called to the crew. He turned to Ryan. "Keep an eye on Eve."

"Babysitting duty?" Ryan scoffed before walking ahead. Luke hoped the lack of staying to protest was him accepting the duty, because there was no time to argue.

The men and Eve unloaded and started deploying the hose toward the structure.

"Stand back!" Luke yelled at Ronny, who seemed dazed as he stood in front of his barn.

Luke headed over to the man and laid a hand on his shoulder. "You okay?"

Ronny gave a small nod. "There's a litter of kittens in that barn. I checked on them just last night."

"Kittens?" Luke asked, his mind leaping from one option to another. The barn was in a blaze. As much as the thought pained him, human life couldn't be risked for kittens.

"Where are they?" Eve asked Ronny, stepping up beside Luke.

Ronny's gaze slid to her. "Back corner on the right."

"How many?" she asked.

"Six. But the mama cat took one with her. So five." Ronny gestured to his back porch where a black-and-white cat was holding a small ball of fur in her mouth. The cat's eyes were wide and pinned to the engulfed structure.

Luke's heart plummeted. The back-right corner looked like the most dangerous section of the barn right now. The roof above was on fire and could cave at any moment. "Poor cat."

"She's a good one," Ronny said. "Keeps the mice away. I call her Millie." Ronny looked at the fire again.

The men had the hose out and were spraying but Luke was starting to doubt it would be enough to salvage the barn. Or save the kittens. And he couldn't go in after them. Not at their location.

Eve had been a volunteer firefighter before so she knew the ins and outs of what was happening right now. Because this was just a structure fire, the job was to stand back and minimize damage while they put out the blaze as quickly as possible.

Luke looked over at her. "Eve?" She wasn't next to him anymore. Wasn't with Wally or Tim, who were operating the hoses either.

"Eve?" Luke's gaze jumped to the barn, where the ceiling was caving under the weight of the water and the damage from the flames. Movement caught his eye, and a curse word tumbled off his lips as he realized Eve was heading around to the back of the barn. He didn't have to wonder why. She was going in for those kittens, and she didn't want anyone to stop her.

Luke took off running. If Eve didn't get caught by the flames, she could be trapped if the roof fell through. He'd promised Brenna to keep an eye on her, which was supposed to be the easy job. Turns out Brenna was somewhat right about her sister. Eve McConnell was a loose cannon and not as easy to contain as this simple structure fire.

Luke turned the corner of the barn and headed toward the back entrance, which was engulfed by a thick shroud of dark smoke. He charged inside, calling Eve's name while heading toward the back-right corner like Ronny had described.

"I can't carry them all!" Eve shouted to him, holding the kittens against her stomach. They were barely squirming in her arms, which wasn't a good sign.

Luke scooped three of the kittens from her hands. "Get out of here!" he ordered through his mask, gesturing in the direction from where they'd both come.

Eve passed him, two kittens in hand. Luke watched her clear the building, relief flooding his veins as she made it out. He stood there a second longer, listening to the crackle of the flames, the memory from his childhood surrounding him as thick as the smoke that hung like a heavy blanket around him. He remembered calling his brother Marco's name. Again and again, his voice competing with the sounds of the fire. Marco had never answered back.

Luke pushed those memories away and headed toward the barn door. The kittens in his hands needed fresh air and their mama. And he needed to clear this building fast before the roof caved.

* * *

Something was off this morning but Brenna couldn't quite put her finger on it. Her instincts were on overdrive. She felt restless.

The catering shop's phone rang, and Brenna wiped her hands on her apron and headed over.

"A Taste of Heaven Catering. How can I help you?"

"Yes, hi," a woman's voice said. "My name is Ava Diaz. Do you cater classroom birthday parties?"

Brenna straightened slightly. "Well, we are capable of catering any celebration at almost any location."

"My son is a second grader, and he wants to have an ice-cream party for his birthday. I could go buy some ice-cream cartons, I suppose, but I want it to be special for him. With lots of flavors and toppings."

Brenna frowned. She'd gotten a lot of strange requests over the years, and this one was going on that list. "Ice cream? My services usually involve cooking."

"I was thinking that A Taste of Heaven might be open to preparing sundaes and banana splits. Are you capable of doing that?"

"Well, we're definitely capable..." Brenna wasn't sure how to respond. She guessed there was no real reason to decline the business. It would be easy enough, and going to a second-grade classroom would be fun.

"I know it's short notice, but his birthday is this week, and if you say no, I don't know what I'll do."

The mother could buy the ice cream herself but Brenna's other clients could cook their own meals too. There was something special about having someone else do it for you. "We have room in our schedule and we can certainly prepare the ice cream party for your son."

"Oh, thank goodness." The mother gave Brenna the details over the phone, and Brenna put the new event in her calendar. When she hung up, she stared at the notes she'd jotted down for a second before being reminded of the uneasiness in her gut that she'd been feeling all morning.

The bell on the front door jingled, and Brenna headed toward the counter to attend to her visitor.

"Eve." Brenna froze at the sight of her sister, who was avoiding her last time she checked.

Eve could never hide the fact that she'd been crying. Her fair skin stayed ruddy for the rest of the day as did her red-rimmed eyes.

"What's wrong?" Brenna asked.

Eve groaned. "I don't know why I came here. You're just going to gloat." She turned to walk back out of the shop.

"That's not fair, Eve. You know I love you, and I would never be happy over something that caused you pain."

Eve faced her again and her eyes welled with tears.

"You're upset. Talk to me. Let me help."

Eve really did look awful. "Do you have any brownies?"

Brenna smiled. "I always keep some made in the freezer—you know that. I can pull them out and pop them in the oven to get warm. Come on. Sit down at the table back here. There's coffee in the pot, and I'll have brownies in ten minutes flat. Then you can tell me what's going on."

"That sounds good." Eve headed past Brenna toward the table she'd mentioned and then turned back for a moment. "Thanks, Bren. I know I've been kind of a bratty younger sister to you lately."

"What's new about that?" Brenna asked.

"I know I can be difficult. I get that from you." The smallest smile lifted Eve's lips but it didn't reach her eyes.

Brenna's emotions warred as she watched her sister continue toward the back room. Was it wrong of her to be happy that whatever had happened in Eve's life to upset her had brought her here? Brenna missed Eve and needed her as much as she wanted to be needed.

She preheated the oven and then grabbed the bag of frozen brownies from the freezer and laid them out on a cookie sheet. Ten minutes later, Brenna placed a plate of warm, gooey fudge brownies at the center of the back room table and sat down in front of her younger sister. "Ready to tell me what has you so upset?"

Eve met her eyes, and Brenna could tell that she'd shed more tears while Brenna had been preparing their little treat. "It's over. I messed up."

"What are you talking about? What's over?"

"I really wanted this for myself, you know? I was so excited about being part of the crew at the SSFD. They're like a bunch of brothers that I never had, and I kind of felt like I was home there." Tears spilled off Eve's bottom lashes, splashing onto her cheeks. "It's been so long since I felt like I had a home, and the station felt that way for me. It'll probably sound silly to you but I felt closer to Dad somehow being there." Her voice cracked right along with Brenna's heart.

Brenna reached across the table and laid a palm on Eve's hand. "I don't understand, Eve. Did something happen at the fire station?"

"You'll probably even throw a little celebration about the news," Eve muttered.

"What news?" Brenna pressed a little more forcefully.

Eve's face scrunched as more tears flooded her eyes. "I got fired today. Chief Marini doesn't want me there anymore."

"Luke?" Brenna's mouth popped open. "Why would he do such a thing?" Brenna asked, even though this was exactly what she'd wanted to happen when she'd first heard the news of Eve being hired. Little by little, she'd started to change her mind about that, however.

"I made a mistake and he won't give me another chance. I mean, everyone makes mistakes, right?"

Brenna nodded. "I make more than my fair share."

"Please don't suggest I come back to work here," Eve said. "I'd rather be a nanny or be a dog walker—anything except cooking and serving food."

"Actually, I'm thinking about putting A Taste of Heaven up for sale," Brenna confessed. "I was going to talk to you about that but there hasn't been a good time. I wanted to make sure you were okay with selling."

Eve blinked, making one loose tear slip down her cheek. "I know it was Mom's but I don't have sentimental feelings toward this place like you do. It's just a kitchen, and I hate to cook."

Brenna had learned that a long time ago.

"But what will you do?" Eve asked.

Brenna reached for a brownie, needing something in her hand to temper her nerves, both good and bad. "Actually, I'm going back to college to finish my degree."

"What?" Eve's mouth fell open. "Wow. All this time you've been pushing me to go to college, and now you're the one going. And the one thing I wanted more than anything I've already screwed up." Eve's face fell into her hands dramatically.

"No, you haven't." Brenna reached for Eve's hand, pulling it down and looking her sister in the eye. "Maybe Luke just needed to cool down. Let me talk to him."

Eve's brows dove toward her nose. "Why would he listen to you?"

Brenna shrugged. "I don't know. Maybe because I'm a neutral party."

"You're anything but neutral. You're my sister," Eve said.

"Which is why I want to help. Let me."

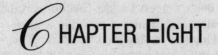

CHAPTER EIGHT

$\mathcal{L}$uke was still fuming from this morning's scene. Eve had acted recklessly. What was she thinking?

His whole body felt restless, and he needed to release the excess energy flowing through him. He was on shift so he couldn't go for a run. Talking to his brother Nick always helped, but that would have to wait until his shift was over.

He got up from his desk and headed toward the kitchen to see if there was something edible to take the edge off.

Ryan approached him as he passed through the garage. "Chief, can I talk to you for a minute?"

Luke had a good mind to tell the young firefighter no but he was a leader now. Leaders were supposed to be there to talk whenever their crew needed them, right? Luke exhaled and looked at Ryan. "Sure. What's up?"

Ryan looked around as if making sure that none of the other guys could hear him.

"Let's go in here." Luke turned and headed back into

his temporary office. "Something on your mind, Ryan?" he asked once they were inside.

Ryan shoved his hands into his pockets. "It's just... don't you think you were a little hard on Eve? Firing her for one mistake?"

Luke plopped down in the chair behind his desk and looked at Ryan. "Since when do you want her here? If I remember correctly, you were bullying her and acted like she didn't belong on this crew."

Ryan frowned. "She does belong. That was just me being stupid and jealous of how good she was for a rookie. And I'm not proud of the way I acted. I'm trying to do better."

Luke felt a surge of pride for the young firefighter, not that this change of attitude had much to do with him. "Eve acted foolishly, and she's lucky that no one got killed."

"I know that," Ryan said. "But I've done stupid things before, and Chief Brewer always gave me second chances. I think Chief Brewer would give Eve another chance too—that's all." Ryan held up his hands. "No disrespect to you." He put his hands on his hips. "I kind of feel like it's my fault. I was supposed to be watching out for her like you told me to. If you need to fire someone, fire me."

Luke wasn't sure he recognized Ryan right now. "I'm not letting you go today, Ryan. I'm pretty impressed with you at this moment. You worked this morning's scene like a pro, and you might've failed to watch Eve's back at the barn but you're watching it right now."

"Trying to, at least."

Luke massaged his forehead. "You failed to do a job I asked you to at the scene. Do you want to make it up to me?"

Ryan shrugged. "Yeah, of course. How?"

"By taking care of this litter of kittens." Luke gestured

to the corner. "The veterinarian, Dr. Lewis, stopped by. The mama cat is stressed out from the fire. She's not nursing her kittens right now."

Ryan frowned. "I hate to hear that."

"Me too. The kittens seem to be doing okay but Dr. Lewis wants to give the mama cat time to calm down. He plans to reintroduce them in about twenty-four hours or so. Until then they need to be bottle fed."

"They're Ronny's cats," Ryan said.

"Ronny Hill can't care for a litter of kittens. He's old, and frankly, he doesn't want to." Luke stared at Ryan across his desk, willing the younger firefighter to accept the responsibility. "Dr. Lewis left the milk and the syringe that you'll be feeding them with on the hour. You can do that here and take them home with you at night."

Ryan's eyes widened. "Sorry, sir, but I'm allergic to cats, and I have dogs at home. Big ones."

Luke's heart sank.

"But if you hired Eve back, I'm sure she'd do it." The corner of Ryan's mouth quirked.

"I just fired her," Luke said. "I'm not going to rehire her just because of a litter of kittens."

The sound of a woman clearing her throat got both of their attentions. "Why would you fire my sister?"

Luke closed his eyes. Under any other circumstances, he'd be happy to have Brenna barge into his office. It'd been a couple of days since she'd stood in his kitchen, looking at him with an unmistakable heat in her gaze. He'd thought about that moment ever since, letting his imagination fill in the possibilities of what might have happened if she hadn't hurried home.

Maybe they would've shared some more flirty banter. Maybe an opportunity would have arisen to kiss her. In reality, that would've been a mistake, but in his fantasies, it felt good.

"Luke?" she prodded, still standing behind him.

He turned to face her, and something kicked in his chest. Letting himself fantasize about her wasn't helping, because his instinct was to immediately reach for her and pull her into his arms. Judging by the look she was giving him though, that would only cause more problems.

Why did Brenna look so angry? He would have guessed firing Eve would make her so happy she could kiss him. Instead, she looked like she wanted to kill him.

* * *

Brenna looked between the two men in the office. "I just spent a half hour with my devastated sister, and I want an explanation." She put her hands on her hips to keep them from shaking.

"Are you serious right now?" Luke asked on a laugh. "The other day you were upset with me for hiring her. Now you're mad that I let her go?"

"You crushed her spirit. I've rarely seen her so upset. I guess I was in denial about how set she was on being a fireman. Or a firewoman...fire person?" Brenna's cheeks burned. She felt like such an idiot now that she was here. On the drive over, she'd rehearsed what she was going to say. "Eve made a mistake. Everyone makes mistakes, right? That doesn't mean she can't learn from it and do well at this job."

Luke was looking at her as if she were crazy. Brenna *felt* crazy right now.

"What happened?" Brenna asked.

Luke's jaw hung open for a moment. "I guess when she

was complaining to you, she didn't mention the fact that I saved her butt this morning. Or that I'm the reason she was even in your shop this morning versus a hospital bed or worse."

Brenna swallowed. "I, uh...no, she didn't tell me that."

"Did she tell you that she ran into a burning structure without backup and without telling anyone what she was doing?" Luke asked. "Did she tell you that I was prepared to have my crew follow her into danger to save a litter of kittens?"

Heat flooded Brenna's cheeks. "No. All she told me was she made a rookie mistake and you wouldn't give her a second chance. That you yelled at her and fired her without letting her explain."

"That's true," Luke said on a nod, "but I didn't need an explanation. I made the right call."

Crap. Brenna wondered if she should back herself out of the room slowly or continue forward with her plan not to leave without getting Eve's job back. "I came over here because I thought maybe you were too strict with Eve on my account. That maybe you fired her for me." Guilt curled in her stomach. "You knew I wanted her to go to college instead of being a firefighter. I thought maybe you would've been more lenient on her if not for me."

"Let me ease your mind: I wouldn't have." Luke folded his arms over his chest. "She was reckless, foolish, and impulsive."

"But she's also eager and determined. She's passionate about this job. She understands better than anyone here how important a firefighter's work is. She'll be amazing at it," Brenna said, unable to believe she was even fighting for Eve when, a week ago, her sister working here was the worst thing that could have happened. "Can you please hire her back? For me?"

Luke ran his hands over his face. "It's official. I will never understand women... You're asking a lot of me right now."

"I know," she said quietly.

"Sir," Ryan said, "I agree with Brenna. Eve deserves another chance."

Brenna glanced at Ryan, surprised that she had an ally here. Then she turned back to Luke. "I'll talk to Eve about her actions. I'll make sure she knows this is her last chance."

Luke looked between them and sighed. "Chief Brewer left me in command. I can't allow someone to put the crew in danger. If I give your sister another chance, that's it. If she pulls another stunt like she did this morning, she won't be coming back no matter how much you two plead. Clear?" he asked.

"Got it," Brenna said.

Ryan looked between them. "Me too. Thank you."

Luke offered Ryan a pointed look. "And next time I ask you to look after our new hire, follow through."

"I will, sir." Ryan gestured to the door. "I'll just go back outside and return to my to-do list."

"Good idea."

Ryan walked out, leaving Brenna and Luke alone.

Her heart kicked hard when he met her gaze. "Thank you," she said again. "I know I didn't want Eve working here, and you must think I've lost my mind, but I love my sister. I just want what's best for her. I want her to be safe and happy."

"She's not safe when she acts the way she did earlier today."

Brenna frowned. "She won't do that again. Today was a wake-up call for her. For me too, I guess." Her eyes had been opened to a lot of things lately. "Except, even though I want you to hire her back, can you promise me that you'll protect her? Don't let her do anything that she's not ready for."

"I already told you—that's how I would treat anyone at the station. Eve is no different."

Brenna looked down at her interlocked hands, wishing she could take a few retreating steps and get out of here now that she'd accomplished what she'd come to do. "Thank you."

Luke cleared his throat. "If I give Eve her job back, would that mean you owe me?"

Brenna looked up. "Owe you?"

"The way I see it. I do you a favor, and you do one for me."

She narrowed her eyes. "Did you have something in mind?"

He tilted his head. "Matter of fact, I'll be caring for a litter of kittens at my place over the next twenty-four hours while the mama cat recuperates. I could use a little help."

"You want me to help care for kittens?" she asked. That would involve seeing more of Luke, which part of her wouldn't mind. She could resist him but she had never been able to resist a kitten. "Fair enough. I'll come by your place tonight."

* * *

Luke wasn't sure how Max would react to the kittens but his dog took to the wiggling fur balls like they were his own. Max plopped down on the floor of the kitchen and allowed the kittens to snuggle against him for warmth.

"Good job, buddy," Luke told his dog as he walked by.

Max rolled his eyes upward, his tail thumping the floor at Luke's praise.

Between kitten feedings, Luke had showered and cleaned

up the house a little bit, knowing that Brenna would be here soon.

When the doorbell rang, he couldn't help the jolt of adrenaline he got as he went to answer the door. He pushed it away. He was not going to act on his attraction to Brenna tonight. And he wasn't going to kiss her, he reminded himself as he headed down the hall and opened the door. Even if he was tempted to.

"Hi." She shifted back and forth on her feet as she stood on his front stoop. Her gaze dropped below his neck. "You're wearing a shirt today."

He looked down as well. "You sound a little disappointed," he teased, before being hit with the memory that she'd seen him without his shirt on. She'd seen all of him, waist up at least, and she hadn't run for the hills. And she hadn't asked him questions about his scars either. Not yet at least.

"A little, maybe," she said, tilting her head to one side and letting her hair spill down her shoulder. "I, uh, came for the kittens. I know this is supposed to be some kind of trade-off for you giving Eve her job back, but honestly, this isn't a sacrifice. I laid my stuff down when I got home and practically ran over here. I can't resist a kitten."

Luke gestured for her to come inside. "Sounds like you and your sister are cut from the same cloth."

"Hardly," she said on a laugh as she followed him in. "Sometimes I wonder if one of us was switched at birth because we are nothing alike. We never have been. We've always butted heads."

"You're pretty protective of her," Luke pointed out.

She entered his kitchen and waited for him to look at her. "Well, yeah, she's my sister."

"I get it. I grew up with two brothers. They drove me

insane sometimes but let someone mess with one of us and the other two went after that person with a vengeance."

"I bet you guys created quite the trouble in your town. And quite the stir with the women." Brenna looked away shyly as if realizing what she'd just said. She cleared her throat. "I can't believe you're stuck with these kittens. I'm sure Eve would take care of them, you know. She's a sucker for an animal in need."

"That'd be like rewarding bad behavior," Luke told her. "She's lucky she got her job back. Thanks to you and Ryan."

"I was happy to see one of the crew sticking up for her so much," Brenna said.

Luke leaned against the counter. "Me too. Ryan gave Eve a little bit of a hard time but truthfully, he gave me a hard time when I first got hired too. His respect has to be earned, and Eve has already started doing that."

"You have too, apparently," Brenna noted.

Luke pulled in a deep breath. "I guess so."

The corners of Brenna's mouth quirked. "It's kind of funny that you're the one babysitting the litter."

"What's funny about it?" He folded his arms over his chest as he watched her.

"Well, you're this big, bad fireman, and those kittens are small and sweet."

"Opposites attract, right?" He heard the teasing tone of his voice. Why was he flirting? It was as if his mind and mouth just weren't communicating with one another these days.

"So, where are the little cuties?" she asked. As if understanding her clearly, one of the kittens cried out from the corner of the room where it was cozied up next to Max.

Brenna whirled in the direction of the noise, and her

hands went up to cover her mouth. "Oh my goodness. How sweet is that? Your dog loves them."

Luke followed her gaze. "Yeah. I'm surprised. I wondered if Max might try to eat one of them but it's as if he knows they're orphans and need to be taken care of right now."

Brenna glanced back. "Well, Eve tells me that the mama cat is still alive so, technically, they're not orphaned."

"You spoke to Eve?"

"I called her on the way home. She's meeting me for breakfast at the café tomorrow. I plan to stress to her how seriously she needs to take her second chance at this job. If you decide to give it to her, that is."

"I called her this afternoon too and asked her to meet me at the station in the morning." He hadn't told Eve he was giving her another chance at being an SSFD firefighter yet. He thought he'd let her sweat a little first. "So why the one-eighty? You didn't want your sister being a firefighter before."

Brenna narrowed her eyes. "Would I prefer that she go to college? Yeah. But while I don't necessarily want her running into danger, I want her to love what she does. My parents always said that the most important thing in life was that you were happy. It didn't matter if you had a huge house or a small one, a new car or a clunker. As long as you were happy, none of that mattered." She looked down at her hands for a moment.

"Well, it's mature of you to let Eve live her life the way she wants."

Brenna nodded and looked up. "The truth is I'm thinking about selling the business."

"Selling?" Luke asked. "Why would you do that?"

"Because I, um…Well, I got into college, actually. I

was close to finishing my degree when I had to come back here after my parents' car accident. Aunt Thelma wants to retire soon, and I've always wanted to be a teacher, so…" She shrugged. "There's no reason to hang on to A Taste of Heaven anymore."

"I see." Luke felt a pang of regret at this new information but he wasn't sure why. He was set on his intention not to get involved with Brenna. Her leaving should've been good news. "When are you leaving?"

"This summer."

"Congratulations are in order, I guess. That's great news."

"It is." She nodded. "It's something I've been wanting to do for a long time. My sister has inspired me. She doesn't let anything stop her from getting what she wants."

"Seems to me she gets that from you. From my vantage point, you're the same way. You even persuaded me to give Eve her job back. You're one hard woman to resist, Brenna McConnell."

Brenna smiled shyly, sweeping her hair back behind her ear. Something about that gesture, unsure and insecure, had Luke stepping closer.

"What are you doing?" she asked.

"I have no idea. I told myself that I wasn't going to kiss you tonight," he said, his voice dropping even lower.

"Oh?" He saw the muscles of her neck constrict as she swallowed. "That's good to know because I told myself the same thing on the way over here." Her gaze stayed on his, her pupils large. The tip of her tongue poked out to wet her lips. She was definitely giving him the green light for a kiss.

"So we agree. Neither of us is kissing the other," he said.

"I'm just here to feed the litter," she confirmed, her words coming out a little breathlessly.

"You want me for my kittens. I see how it is."

She leaned toward him, and he did the same until her hands went up to brace herself against his chest. "I want you for your body, actually."

He felt his every muscle tense. His body pulsed with desire for hers. He could totally kiss her right now and lose himself. "Give me one good reason why I shouldn't kiss you right now."

Her lips parted as she looked at him. "I'm leaving, for one. And my relationship with my sister is just getting back on track. Kissing her boss could derail it."

"That's two reasons." Both very good.

"What do you have?" Brenna asked.

He sighed. "You're my neighbor. If things go south, I'll be stuck with you next door. At least until you leave this summer." And if they didn't go south, she was leaving. Dating casually had never been his thing. He didn't fall easily, but when he did, he fell hard. Looking at Brenna, that was a real possibility.

Brenna laughed humorlessly. "That's a good reason too."

"Yep." His gaze flicked to her lips and then back to her brown eyes. Standing this close to her, he studied the different shades of brown in her irises. There was even a little bit of green poking through.

One of the kittens cried out again.

"All right," he said, gathering his willpower and taking a step backward while he still could. "Then we agree. We'll keep our hands and lips to ourselves."

CHAPTER NINE

$\mathcal{B}$renna cradled a whining kitten in her arms. She and Luke had almost kissed. Her body had thought that was a good idea, still did, but her head knew better. Kissing Luke would have opened doors that were better left closed.

Luke glanced back from the stove where he was heating a kettle of hot water. "Thanks for giving the kittens a little TLC."

"Anytime." She watched as Luke tipped the kettle over two mugs. She assumed one was for her, which was welcome. She wasn't ready to leave just yet despite her frayed feelings. After a moment of pouring and stirring, he walked toward her at the table and set a mug in front of her.

"Hot tea?" she asked, getting a whiff.

"It's too late for coffee." He set his own mug down and sat next to her at the table. "This is decaf."

She pulled the claws of the kitten's paws from her cotton shirt, one by one, and then set the wiggling fur ball back in the bunch still snuggled into Max's belly. Her gaze snagged on the dog's skin before turning back to Luke. "You said that Max was injured in a fire?"

Luke's jawline hardened. "Yeah. Seems like burning structures are the best way to find a pet."

Brenna reached for her mug of tea and lifted it to her mouth, feeling the steam on her skin. "I'll pass on getting a pet, then. You and my sister are braver than me."

"Or just fools."

"I'm sure Max and those kittens don't think that. To them, you're heroes. To the town, you're heroes. I admire you both."

Luke laughed a little, looking humble, which made him even more attractive in her book. Her ex-fiancé hadn't known anything about humility. In hindsight, he'd been selfish and self-serving. He hadn't understood why she would sacrifice anything for someone else, not even her own sister.

Brenna swallowed and wondered if she should ask Luke the next question that waited on the tip of her tongue. It was none of her business but she suddenly needed to know. "So, what exactly happened to your back?"

She noticed Luke's fingers wrap more tightly around his mug. He seemed to be thinking about how to answer her question or whether he was going to at all. Then he sucked in a breath, let it out, and his gaze flitted up to meet hers. "It's not something I talk about much. It happened a long time ago," he finally said.

She was suddenly embarrassed by her nosiness. "I'm sorry. I shouldn't have asked." There was pain in his expression when she looked at him. She'd put it there, and for that, she felt regret.

Luke's lips moved to speak but then one of the kittens cried out from the floor, where its brothers and sisters had pushed it out of reach of Max's warm body. Max nudged his nose at the others, making room. He gave an extra nudge at the little kitten as it squirmed toward him.

Brenna returned her attention to Luke. "I think that's the equivalent of a Max kiss."

A long silence passed between them, and Brenna knew it was all her fault. She swallowed, searching her mind for a new topic to shift the mood in a different direction. "So, I have a confession," she said.

Luke narrowed his brown eyes at her.

"While I'm excited about going back to college, I'm also a little nervous. It's been a while since I've taken classes."

"I'm guessing it's like riding a bike," he said. "Once you get started, you'll fall into the rhythm of it all."

"I hope so. I'm trying to reclaim my life. It's time."

"Now I'm the one admiring you."

She met his gaze, and her heart sped up. "Really?"

"Yeah. Running into burning buildings doesn't scare me, but running into a college building—now, that's intimidating."

Brenna tilted her head, a dreamy sigh tumbling off her lips. "I've always loved classes. I love sitting in them, and I've always imagined myself standing at the front of one." She shrugged a shoulder, feeling exposed and a little foolish. But she'd rather that than to make Luke feel any more uncomfortable by asking questions that were none of her business. "I'm thankful for the catering business but I think it's okay to be thankful for what you have and still want more."

They stared into each other's eyes for a long moment. She didn't just want more in her professional life. She had other desires as she sat here with Luke.

"I've already forgotten why I'm not supposed to be kissing you," he finally said.

She swallowed. "My reason seems to have slipped my mind too," she said quietly, as her breaths grew shallow and her heart thumped against her ribs.

"I'm concerned that if I don't get up right now, I might kiss you anyway."

"I have another confession. I'm concerned that you might not." She leaned in, eyes still locked on his.

Then Luke met her halfway and kissed her, a need exploding out of him that surprised her. She needed this kiss too.

His hand wrapped around her lower back, finding the place where her shirt had ridden up. She willed that hand to go higher but it stayed rooted. He was a gentleman, and that was as frustrating as it was hot.

"It appears I can't be with you without wanting to kiss you," Luke said when they broke free, both breathless.

"Appears that way."

"The last thing I want to do is lead you on, Brenna, and it sounds like neither of us are looking for a serious relationship right now."

"Definitely not. A relationship would only complicate things. My life is complicated enough," she agreed.

"So maybe, if we can't seem to keep our lips to ourselves when we're around each other, we should make a point of avoiding one another."

"Not so easy to do when we're neighbors," Brenna pointed out.

"Not when the shop owner next to you is always calling the station either."

Brenna laughed. "You could always send Eve. She knows the drill."

He nodded. "I guess I could. And if this is our new plan, I guess I'll take care of these kittens on my own. I can recruit the crew during the day."

Brenna glanced back at the sweet little fur balls wiggling closer to Max's belly. She didn't want to stay away from them. And she didn't want to stay away from Luke; she was enjoying his company entirely too much lately. But he was right. Keeping their distance from each other was for the best.

Brenna stuck out a hand for him to shake, unwittingly luring one last touch from him. His hand slid against hers, and her whole body seemed to buzz with awareness. "Okay, then," she said. "I can agree to that if you can."

* * *

Luke stared up at his ceiling. He was always restless right after a fire. It was hard to come down from the adrenaline high, and seeing flames always brought memories of his childhood fire to mind. He tossed from one side to the other, shut his eyes, and willed his mind to quiet to no avail. Finally, he sat up in bed and reached for his cell phone. His brother Nick was a night owl, and he'd told Luke a hundred times that he could call him anytime, day or night, if he needed to talk.

Luke pressed Dial and waited for the call to connect.

Nick answered almost immediately, a sign that he wasn't asleep. "Hello?"

"You awake?" Luke asked.

"Yes, but the chick beside me isn't."

Luke chuckled softly. "Do I know her?"

"Not the way I do," Nick teased. "Nah, man. I'm kidding. I'm alone. What's up?"

"Just wanted to say hi," Luke lied.

"At two a.m.? Not buying it. You okay?"

Luke sighed. "I went into a fire today. Or I guess it's yesterday now."

"Everyone okay?" Nick asked, his tone of voice turning serious.

"Yeah. It was just a barn fire but a rookie decided to go in. She didn't ask, just ran inside to save a litter of kittens."

"Kittens? So you got the rookie and the kittens out?"

"Yeah. Couldn't save the barn, unfortunately." Luke was sure Nick was thinking the same thing that he was. A barn could be rebuilt but human life couldn't. They both had firsthand experience with that.

Luke shook his head, even if Nick wasn't around to see it. After the fire that had devoured their childhood home, Luke had been terrified of even the smallest of flames. If someone so much as flicked a cigarette lighter, he'd jump several inches off the ground. Back then, he'd had nightmares nearly every night and had slept with the lights on. He'd never been one to let fear rule his life though. When he was afraid of something, instead of running the other way, he faced it head-on.

He'd started by learning how to make campfires in Scouts. He'd had his father teach him to work a grill as a teen. Then he'd joined the volunteer fire department as soon as he was old enough. Instead of hiding, he'd devoted his life to fighting fires and saving lives.

"Now I'm stuck taking care of the kittens for a day or two," Luke told Nick, making him roar with laughter.

"That's hilarious. I can't wait to spread that around Whispering Pines. My little brother caring for a helpless litter."

"Don't you dare," Luke warned.

"That's chick bait, man. You can use that to your advantage," Nick said.

Luke massaged his forehead, feeling slightly better just

talking to his brother. "Feel free to come here and help out and use the kitten angle for your own dating life. I'm not interested in dating right now."

"Maybe you should be. Don't let the work consume you, bro," Nick advised, knowing Luke all too well. "You might sleep better if you had other things to focus on outside of work."

Luke headed to the window to look out at Brenna's house. "What do you suggest?"

Nick chuckled. "If not a woman, maybe you should find a few friends and go have some drinks?"

That wasn't a terrible idea. Luke hadn't made a lot of close connections since he'd moved to Sweetwater Springs but a few came to mind. "I know a couple guys I could ask."

"Great," Nick said. "I wouldn't recommend calling them tonight. Most normal people are asleep at two a.m."

Luke laughed. "Right. You're not normal."

"And neither are you. How's everything else going?" Nick asked. "I haven't heard from you in a while."

"Busy. My fire chief got injured at work so I'm leading the station while he recuperates."

"Wow. Big job," Nick said.

"You're telling me." And some part of Luke still wondered if he was up for the challenge.

"How's it going so far?" Nick asked.

"Pretty smoothly, other than a reckless rookie." But even Ryan was falling into line.

"Well, busy or not, you need to make time to come home pretty soon. Mom misses you."

"Tell her I'll take a Sunday off and come by for lunch." Their mother loved to cook after Sunday-morning church services. She always made too much food to lure family and friends to her table.

"She'll be happy about that." Nick broke into a yawn. That was Luke's cue to disconnect.

"Thanks for answering the call," Luke said.

"Call me anytime. I'll send you a bill," Nick joked.

Luke swallowed past the sudden tightness in his throat. "Who needs a therapist when they have you as a brother? Maybe that's what you should be doing instead of playing in the snow all day." Nick was a ski instructor in Whispering Pines. Unlike Luke, he'd dealt with the tragedy of their past by having fun—the more, the better.

Nick chuckled. "I play, and they call it work. This is the life."

Luke was a little jealous.

They said their goodbyes, and Luke disconnected the call. He stared for a second longer out the window at Brenna's house, and then he got himself a glass of water and went back to bed.

Perhaps, later today, he'd consider taking Nick's advice and maybe grab a few drinks after work with a couple of guys he knew. He wouldn't be taking Nick's initial advice and finding a woman though. He'd already found one, and she was another reason he was losing sleep tonight.

* * *

Brenna was halfway through her coffee, seated in the back corner of the Sweetwater Café and waiting for Eve, who apparently wasn't going to show.

They'd said they would meet this morning, and Brenna had prepared her pep talk for her sister. It wasn't a lecture. Brenna just wanted to ensure that Eve understood that she needed to get her impulses under control if she wanted to be part of the fire department. She had to work with a team instead of plowing forward with her own plans. That was the only way she could do the job safely.

The door to the café opened, and Brenna turned eagerly, hoping it was her sister. Instead, it was Halona. Brenna had already texted her friend and told her she couldn't meet this morning.

Halona looked at the empty chair across from Brenna and beelined toward her. "She left already? Did you two get into another argument?"

"Try again," Brenna muttered over her coffee cup before taking a sip. "Eve didn't even show."

Halona frowned. "What was her excuse?"

"I don't know, seeing that she didn't even text or call to let me know that she wasn't coming."

"Ouch. I thought you two were making progress."

Brenna shrugged. "I'm trying on my end. But you never know with Eve."

Emma headed toward them with a cup of steaming coffee. "Here you go. Just like you like it." She handed Halona the drink. "I saw you walk in so I thought I'd beat you to the punch."

"One of the many reasons I love you," Halona said, taking the cup. She reached toward her purse.

Emma held up a hand. "Don't worry about it. I'll put it on your tab for next time."

"Perfect." Halona looked at the empty chair across from Brenna. "I'd love to keep you company but I have a lot of arrangements that need to be prepared at the flower shop this morning."

"Funeral?" Brenna asked.

"The family is calling it a 'celebration of life,'" Halona said. "The man was from Wild Blossom Bluffs. He was ninety-seven and lived a long, happy life from what I'm told."

"Well, don't worry about me. I'll wait here a few more minutes just in case Eve slept in and really isn't standing me up."

Halona frowned. "I'll text you later. Maybe we can meet up tomorrow. I need to hear about what's going on with you and Luke."

Brenna grew hot as memories of last night's kiss flooded her thoughts. She shifted restlessly.

"Whoa!" Halona pointed at her. "I don't know what happened, but whatever it was, it looks like it was steamy. Can't wait to hear all about it."

Brenna laughed. "I'll talk to you soon." She watched her friend leave the café, letting her gaze linger on the door. Eve wasn't coming. Of course she wasn't. That would be doing exactly what Brenna wanted her to do. She knew that things between them wouldn't change overnight, but she really missed her sister.

Brenna pulled out her phone and tapped a text to Eve.

Sorry I missed you at the café this morning. Maybe we can have a rain check soon?

She didn't want to nag Eve. More than anything, she wanted her relationship with Eve to return to the way it used to be. Once upon a time, Brenna would come home from college and take Eve out. Then Eve would spill all the details of what was going on in her life. She'd ask for advice and actually take it.

Brenna scooted back from the table and collected her coffee. She needed to get to work. It was a full day, which was good. That meant she didn't have to dwell on being stood up by Eve this morning or obsess over kissing Luke last night or how she was going to avoid him from now on.

Brenna waved at Emma and headed out of the café, taking her time as she strolled downtown toward A Taste of Heaven Catering. Nate was in the store waiting for her when she finally arrived.

"No coffee for me?" he asked with mock insult.

"Sorry. It's your husband's job to shower you with treats."

Nate rolled his eyes. "Chris? You need to talk to him. He's been working so hard these days that he's letting the romance wither on its vine."

"You're so poetic sometimes," Brenna said on a laugh. She set her purse under the counter and cupped both hands around her cup of coffee. "I'm not married, of course, but I imagine it's kind of like having a sister. You have to work at it, almost like a job. You two should go out more often."

"His new job is so demanding. I think he's stressed, and I wish he'd just quit…Hey, maybe going out would be fun though. Why don't we all go to the Tipsy Tavern tonight?"

A beat passed between them until Brenna realized that Nate was waiting for her to respond. "You're inviting me to be a third wheel on your date with your husband?"

Nate frowned as he iced some cookies for the classroom party today. In addition to ice cream and a wide variety of toppings, they were preparing cookies for the second grader's special day.

"It's not like I haven't suggested to Chris that we need to go out more. He promises he will but puts it off. I need an excuse."

"And your excuse is me?" Brenna asked. "I'm not sure Chris will buy that. Why would I need you and Chris to come out with me to the tavern tonight?"

"Because you're struggling with your sister. Eve has taken this job at the fire station, and I'm worried about you." Nate's expression transformed to one of concern.

Brenna laughed. "You are not worried about me."

"Chris is a softie for a damsel in distress," Nate continued. "And it's not a lie. Eve really is driving you crazy. And I am concerned, although not about you and Eve."

Brenna narrowed her eyes. "What are you concerned about, then?"

"Your dating life. You don't have one, and I think it's past time. Another reason we should go out tonight."

Brenna decided not to tell Nate about her collision of lips with Luke. She'd only gone over there in the first place because she'd agreed to help with the kittens. And per their agreement, she wouldn't be going over again.

"You're going to turn into an old maid, and I can't have that. Not on my watch," Nate said.

He leaned into Brenna. "I'm not taking no for an answer about tonight."

Brenna leaned into him as well. "No," she said.

"Great," Nate said with a wink. "Then it's a date."

CHAPTER TEN

Luke was surprised at how easily he'd fallen into command over the crew. Chief Brewer had seen leadership skills in him that he hadn't even realized he had. And Luke thought he was doing a pretty good job, or at least he wasn't terrible at it.

Eve knocked on his office door and then stepped inside, looking sheepish and worried.

Luke gestured to the chair across from his desk and she dutifully walked to it and sat down.

"Let's cut to the chase," Luke said. "You can have your job back." He pointed a finger across his desk. "But if you pull another stunt like you did yesterday, there won't be any more chances."

Eve nibbled on her lower lip. "I'm sorry about that. I just couldn't leave those kittens in that barn. They were helpless, and the mama cat was so upset."

"I understand why you did it but you can't act on your own. We're a crew. What if no one had seen you go in? What if you'd gotten hurt while you were in there?"

Eve looked down at her feet for a moment. "It won't happen again, sir."

"See that it doesn't."

"Thank you, Chief Marini. This job means everything to me. I've dreamed about working here forever."

"Is this job everything you expected?" he asked.

She hesitated. "Well, we've only had one real fire call. That's not what I expected."

"Don't forget the one where you came with me to check out the seamstress shop and A Taste of Heaven."

Eve rolled her eyes. "Seriously? I wouldn't peg that as a real call."

"I have to track our calls, and that one counts." Luke preferred the calls that turned out to be no big deal. That meant that people were safe.

"As a volunteer, I just went on the big calls. I guess I never saw too much of the slow side of things."

"Take advantage of the slow side," Luke advised. "It gives you time to train."

Eve stared at him a moment. He could almost see the wheels turning in her mind. "So, I know Brenna was the one who helped persuade you to give me my job back. Is she really okay with me working here?"

"Yeah. I think she's trying to be, at least," he said.

"It's just hard for me to believe that."

"She's your sister. She wants to see you happy."

Eve gave him another sheepish look. "I was supposed to meet her for coffee this morning."

"She told me," Luke said, not thinking.

Eve narrowed her green eyes. "When? We made the arrangement last night."

Luke swallowed. "She's my neighbor, Eve. I see her pretty much on a daily basis."

Eve's eyes narrowed even farther. "I used to be your neighbor, and I rarely ever saw you."

Good point.

"She came over to help with the kittens." He tipped his head at the sleeping litter in the corner. He'd fed them half an hour ago and would probably need to do so again in the next hour. Unless he could persuade someone else to do it.

"Oh," Eve said quietly.

"All right. Are you prepared to start back today?" Luke asked then. "Because we need you."

Eve smiled and nodded. "Yeah. Of course."

"Good. I'd like you to help Ryan do maintenance on the equipment this morning."

Eve blushed, which he found curious. "Got it. Anything else?"

"Nope."

"I'll just go grab my stuff from the car. Thank you again, Chief." She waved and headed off.

The phone rang, and Luke grabbed it quickly to keep it from disturbing the kittens, who, for as tiny as they were, could be loud and demanding when they were awake. "Acting Fire Chief Luke Marini."

"How's my station holding up?" Chief Brewer asked on the other end of the line.

"Great, sir. How are *you* holding up?"

Chief Brewer groaned. "My wife won't leave my side. I need an update on things to keep me sane...but not over the phone."

"I'll head right over."

"Thank you," Chief Brewer said. "I already owe you for taking care of the station in my absence. After this visit, I'll owe you double."

Luke laughed. They disconnected, and then he got up and headed out the door. "I'm heading over to check on Chief Brewer," he told Ryan, Eve, and Wally. "Wally, you're in charge here. Ryan, we're all a crew, and none of us is your mother. Eve..."

She looked up eagerly. "Yes, sir?"

"You have your orders."

She blushed and glanced at Ryan, which struck Luke again. What was that about?

"Also, I need you to feed the kittens in my office," he said. Hopefully tomorrow, Dr. Lewis would give the okay to reunite them with their mother at Ronny Hill's place and his responsibility for them would end.

Eve's eyes lit up at the new order. "I can handle that."

* * *

"You want me to serve the second graders?" Nate asked, putting his hands on his hips. "Are you insane?"

"Nate, please. It's just an ice-cream party. I'll interact with the kids. All you have to do is help me set up and make the banana splits."

"Why can't Thelma help you?" he complained.

"Because she enjoys cooking but not serving. You know that." And Brenna respected that. She was just thankful to still have her aunt helping out A Taste of Heaven after all these years.

"It's not that I don't like kids. I love my niece," Nate said, pushing his glasses up on his nose. "But little kids are just a lot more demanding. And they change their minds constantly."

Brenna placed a hand on his shoulder. "You'll survive. We'll even have fun—I promise. They can't be as bad as

Mrs. Everson, who is coming back this week to finalize the menu for the upcoming event, by the way."

Nate held up his hand. "I'll help cater the classroom party but I'm not sticking around for Mayor Everson's mother. That's my condition."

"Truly, I'd rather you be here with me when she comes in. For moral support, if nothing else."

Nate started packaging up the cookies for the classroom party. "Mrs. Everson is tough, hard to please, and nothing like her son."

Brenna looked at Nate. "Do you think Brian knows how hard his mom is to deal with? Because if he did, why would he send her to do his errands?"

"To keep her out of his hair, I'm guessing. Poor Jessica. Mrs. Everson can't be an easy mother-in-law. I should have a cup of coffee with her one day," Nate said, putting the plastic containers of cookies in a large bag. "I have experience with difficult in-laws."

Brenna remembered Nate telling her that his in-laws hadn't accepted him and Chris being married at first. They were supportive now but his marriage had had a rocky beginning.

"Do you need help loading the delivery van with the ice cream?" Brenna asked.

Nate lifted the bag in his arms effortlessly. "I'll carry this and then come back for the rest."

"Great. I'll meet you over there," Brenna said. "I have errands to do afterward so I'll need my car." After the party, she was hoping to stop in at Mountain Breeze Realty and discuss putting A Taste of Heaven on the market. It was a big step but it felt like the right thing to do.

"As long as those errands don't keep you from coming

out with Chris and me tonight," Nate said. "You need me now, and I need you later at the Tipsy Tavern."

Brenna laughed. "Don't worry—I'll be there."

* * *

An hour later, a little jolt of excitement lit through Brenna as she stepped inside Allison Winters's second-grade classroom. Brenna loved the chaos and noise of the children. Always had. Even when she was an elementary student herself, she'd loved walking into a room full of desks and computers, construction paper and scissors, crayons and pencils.

Brenna looked around and spotted Allison immediately along with the birthday boy's mother. For a moment, Brenna found herself envying Allison. She got to hang out in this room with the students all day. She got to listen to the laughs and whispers and direct the children in their lessons. She got to read them books and have them write creative stories. Someday soon, this would be Brenna's life too.

Allison spotted Brenna and waved her over. The mother looked up and waved at Brenna as well. Just as the parent had requested, Brenna had brought every banana split topping imaginable. It was a good thing that it was the end of the school day because the children in this classroom were going to be on a sugar high like their parents had never seen before.

Brenna made her way across the room to where the teacher and mother were standing. "Hi, Allison," Brenna said before turning to the mother. "Hello, Mrs. Diaz."

"I must say this is exciting," Allison said. "The students have hardly been able to concentrate all day once they found out there was going to be an ice-cream party."

"Not just any ice-cream party," Mrs. Diaz pointed out.

"Definitely not. I have more flavors than Baskin-Robbins today." Brenna didn't really but it made the women laugh. Brenna gestured to the table against the wall. "I'm assuming this is where you want me to set up?"

"Yes, that would be great. Do you need any help?" Allison asked.

"No, Nate is coming," Brenna said. "He should be here in just a few minutes with some more of the supplies."

Allison went to give the students some busywork while they waited. Two minutes later, Nate walked into the room pulling a cart of ice cream behind him. He had a huge smile on his face as the children cheered him on like a rock star. Brenna guessed that he was to them, considering that he came bearing chocolate, vanilla, and strawberry ice cream.

Brenna noticed Halona's son, Theo, sitting in the back corner. For the last couple of years, he hadn't spoken a word. That had changed at Christmas, however. He was still shy but now he spoke to the people he was familiar with. Brenna stared at him for a second until he looked over. She offered him a thumbs-up, which he returned.

"I still don't understand this," Nate muttered as he stepped up beside Brenna and started unpacking the cart. "We didn't make this ice cream. This isn't catering."

Brenna rolled her eyes. "No, but we're making the sundaes and banana splits. And I'm not going to turn down business or an opportunity to spend the afternoon with children."

Nate leaned in to whisper in her ear. "Let's see if you're still dreamy eyed when this job is over. We have to do cleanup as well, and I predict these eight-year-olds are going to be messy eaters."

Brenna laughed as she shook her head. "I don't care

what kind of mess they make. I'm going to have a blast while we're here."

A half hour later, when the school dismissal bell rang, Nate was right. There was more food on the floor than Brenna thought got inside the second graders' mouths. She used a wet cloth to get up all the sticky ice cream and toppings off the floor so that the custodians didn't have to later.

"You must have the most fun job in the world," Allison said, walking back into the classroom after taking her students to the buses and car pool line.

Brenna looked up at her as she wiped some chocolate syrup off the floor underneath one of the student desks. "Are you kidding me?"

Allison shook her head. "Not at all. You get to feed people and make them happy."

"Trust me, my customers aren't always smiling," Brenna said, thinking of her scheduled appointment with Mrs. Everson. Brenna gestured at Allison. "But you get to teach these kids. They'll remember you for the rest of their lives. At least I still remember my second-grade teacher."

Allison cocked her head to one side and folded her arms over her chest. "Okay, pop quiz. What was your second-grade teacher's name?"

Brenna didn't even have to think before answering. "Mrs. Jacobs. She was near retirement age, always wore a long charcoal-gray cardigan, and she laughed so hard she usually doubled over. I adored her."

Allison leaned against the desk behind her as she listened to Brenna talk. "I have no idea who my second-grade teacher was. My dad was a marine, and we were always moving. I think I had two different teachers that year because we moved right after Christmas, and I didn't warm up to either one of them. After my dad retired, we moved here."

"So what made you decide to be a teacher?" Brenna asked. She just assumed the only reason anyone would take on the job would be because they were passionate about it.

Allison held up a hand. "Don't get me wrong. I love teaching. I just wouldn't say it's what I always wanted to do. But it's rewarding to know you're making a difference in these children's lives."

Brenna understood that. In college, she used to volunteer at a local elementary school and found the work satisfying. Tutoring Hannah and even babysitting Halona's son, Theo, were also satisfying. "Well, I think I'm all done here. Nate has already packed up all the ice cream and toppings to take back to A Taste of Heaven."

"Thank you so much for this afternoon. The kids had a great time. Hopefully, we'll see you here again soon."

Brenna laughed. "I'd be shocked if another parent had me cater their child's classroom birthday party."

"You never know," Allison said. "Perhaps we'll invite you for our end-of-year party in a couple months."

"I'd love that." Brenna gathered her stuff and waved at Allison before heading down the long hall toward the principal's office. She admired the students' artwork hanging on the walls as she walked. If not for her parents' accident, she would have finished college. She might even have been one of Allison Winters's colleagues here at Sweetwater Elementary School right now. Maybe she still would be one day soon.

* * *

Luke had a freshly topped-off glass of sweet tea in hand, and Mrs. Brewer wasn't letting it fall under the halfway point as she hovered between Luke and her husband.

"You see what I mean?" Chief Brewer asked when Mrs. Brewer stepped out of the room. "It's constant. And I'm laid up with a bad back so I can't get away."

"Can't you ask her to give you space?" Luke asked.

The chief lifted a thick brow. "Then she'll want to talk about why I want space. Then I'll never get her out of my hair." He sighed. "I love her. This is my doing, and I know it. For years, I've put too much time in the job. She's missed me. She's begged for me to take time off and go off with her for something fun. I always told her I would but you know how it is. There's always some kind of fire to put out. Pun intended there." He grinned at Luke.

"I understand, sir."

"No, you don't. You're single. You have no idea. Not yet, at least. But you will. How's the crew doing?" he asked, changing the subject.

Luke clasped his hands on his lap. "Ryan is giving me less lip. And Tim is all caught up with his trainings. Everyone is pitching in to help me while you're gone."

"That's good to hear. That's how it should be, like a family in its own right," he said. "You know, we used to have picnics back in the day. A couple times a year, our families would gather, and we'd all hang out. We were one big, extended family." Chief Brewer's eyes seemed to light up at the memory.

"Sounds nice. Why don't we do that anymore?" Luke asked.

Chief Brewer's expression fell, and the light in his eyes dimmed. "Brenna and Eve's father was part of the crew. After he died in the car accident, it didn't feel right to enjoy a happy occasion without him. We were all mourning just like the girls, I guess. Once you cancel one picnic, it's easier to cancel the next. Aidan McConnell was integral to those picnics. He was the grill master and DJ at the same time. A picnic wouldn't be the same without him."

Luke felt a wave of sadness for Brenna as he listened. Her father sounded amazing.

"When you mentioned the crew, you left Eve out," Chief Brewer said. "How is she working out at the station?"

Luke looked up. "I fired her."

The chief's jaw dropped. "You what?"

"Don't worry. I rehired her."

Chief Brewer seemed to relax. "I bet Brenna was thrilled when Eve got fired."

"You would think but she's one of the reasons I gave Eve another chance," Luke said, shaking his head. "I can't figure her out."

Chief Brewer's eyes narrowed. "Uh-oh. You like her, don't you?"

Luke's body tensed. "Sir?"

"Brenna. You have a thing for her?"

Luke swallowed. "I'm not sure what you mean by *thing*. We're neighbors." Neighbors who had agreed to avoid each other because they couldn't seem to keep their hands off one another otherwise.

Chief Brewer chuckled.

Then they heard Mrs. Brewer humming as she walked back down the hall in their direction. Luke stood. "Pretend like this is a vacation," he told Chief Brewer.

"One where I need pain meds?" the chief asked.

"You told me Mrs. Brewer has been lonely. This is a great time to hang out with her. I'll check back in a day or two," Luke promised, stepping away.

"Oh, Luke, you're leaving already?" Mrs. Brewer asked.

"Afraid so. I have a station to watch. I need to make sure it's running smoothly for when Chief Brewer returns."

Mrs. Brewer frowned. "He needs to take care of himself for that to happen. Did you tell him?" she asked.

Luke glanced back at his chief. "I did but it's worth repeating. Take care of yourself, Chief."

From what Luke could tell, Mrs. Brewer was a kind, thoughtful woman, and Chief Brewer was lucky to have someone who cared so much about him. She led Luke to the front door, insisted he come back soon, and then waved as he headed down the steps.

Luke got into his truck and drove back toward the station, feeling good about how things were going in his life. And he was taking his brother's advice tonight and going out for a few drinks with friends.

The closest thing Luke had to buddies here in town so far was Granger Fields, who owned a tree farm, and Jack Hershey, a local park ranger. Luke had found himself sitting with them at the Tipsy Tavern's bar a couple of months back when he'd first moved here, and they'd gotten along great. They'd exchanged numbers and had talked about doing it again but hadn't yet. Tonight, hopefully, they would.

CHAPTER ELEVEN

*B*renna felt sick to her stomach as she walked into Mountain Breeze Realty and sat down. Janelle Cruz had used Brenna's catering services before for a few business events but Brenna was here to solicit Janelle's services this time.

Was she really going to sell A Taste of Heaven?

Brenna glanced around the small, professionally decorated office as she waited, her emotions warring until Janelle walked in. She wore a bright-red pencil skirt and matching high heels. "Hi, Brenna! It's been a while," she said, walking around the desk and taking a seat. "How can I help you?"

Brenna sucked in a deep breath. Eve didn't want the business, and Brenna was going to college. This was the right thing to do, even if it was going to hurt letting go of her mother's legacy. "I want to sell A Taste of Heaven."

Janelle's smile dropped. "Well, I wasn't expecting you to say that. Really?"

Brenna nodded and then gave Janelle the short story of what was going on.

"Well, as fate would have it, I have a client who is looking to buy a kitchen to start up their own catering business right now. I'm not sure if A Taste of Heaven would meet their needs but I'll check. And if not, I'm sure there will be a lot of interest. The location is amazing."

Brenna nodded as she listened, that sick feeling in her stomach dissipating. It would be ideal if the buyer kept the business intact. The town needed a catering business, and A Taste of Heaven already had a full book of clients.

"I'll draw up some paperwork for you to sign in the next few days," Janelle finally said.

"Thank you." Brenna stood on wobbly legs and shook Janelle's hand.

"Congratulations on your college acceptance, by the way. That's a huge deal."

It was. And it came with huge sacrifices—the theme of Brenna's life. She was always sacrificing something.

* * *

After leaving Mountain Breeze Realty, Brenna had gone home to change before coming to the Tipsy Tavern with Nate and Chris. She'd had to be talked into coming along tonight but now she welcomed the thought of going out and having fun. Even if she was the designated driver and would only be enjoying one alcoholic beverage.

"Penny for your thoughts," the bartender asked as she sat in front of him.

Brenna turned from the dance floor, where Nate and Chris were having a blast, to look at him. "Just that I could really use this drink after the day I had."

"You own that catering place, right? Can't be too bad to work there," the bartender said while keeping his hands busy shining the glasses.

"Depends on the customers."

He gave a knowing look. "Yep. I understand that."

"But I'm behaving myself so I can drive my friends home tonight." She glanced at Chris and Nate again and giggled as Nate attempted to show Chris some moves.

"You must be a good friend."

She narrowed her eyes at the bartender. "And you're doing that bartender thing where you try to get me to talk about myself, unload my worries, and give you a bigger tip."

He laughed loudly. "I don't do it for the tips. I do it to pass the time."

Brenna took another sip of her beer, wishing she could just gulp it and grab another. Next time. "Maybe I should leave catering and take up barkeeping. I bet you know the scoop on just about everyone in here."

His amused expression told her that was probably true.

"Do you know stuff about me?" she asked. She didn't think there was anything interesting to know but one never knew what rumors floated around a small town.

"Your sister, Eve, has been in a few times."

"She's not old enough to drink," Brenna objected.

"And she doesn't. But that doesn't keep her from trying and then having a Coke on the rocks and unloading on me."

Brenna laughed. "Is she one of the customers we were just discussing? The kind that make or break a shift?"

He laughed but didn't agree. He didn't disagree either. Then his gaze snagged on the door behind her.

Brenna turned to watch three guys walk in. She knew

them all. She'd grown up here with Granger Fields and Jack Hershey. And recently she'd gotten to know Luke more than she probably should.

"Ah-ha," the bartender said behind her.

She turned back to look at him. "What?"

"Which one is it that you have your eye on? I'm fairly sure they're all single."

Brenna looked down into her beer. "What makes you think I have my eye on any of them?"

"I know the signs. I see it enough in here," he said. "Granger is a single dad of two small children. Not sure you want to take that on, being the busy woman that you are. Jack only dates casually. He's not the kind of guy that becomes your boyfriend. At least that's what I've heard from the women who've been in your seat sulking over him."

"And what about Luke?"

The bartender gave her a knowing smile. "Ah, well, he hasn't dated anyone since he's been in town. This is only the second time he's been in here. I watched a few women try to talk to him last time but he didn't seem too interested. If I had to guess, I'd say he's not on the market. Someone would have to work to win him over. Of course, that's just my speculation but I'm a good reader of people."

Brenna glanced over her shoulder to watch Luke, Granger, and Jack grab a table near the far wall. She'd do better to go after Granger or Jack than her neighbor, who also happened to be Eve's boss. But neither of the other two men were her type.

"So Luke, huh?" the bartender asked. "Well, who knows? Maybe you'll be the one to turn his head. Maybe you should go on over there and try."

Brenna shook her head quickly. "No. He's my neighbor, and I'm not looking for anything romantic. I'm just surprised to see him here." She looked at the bartender, who continued to polish glasses even though she was pretty sure he'd already done them all. "I'll just sit here and wait for Chris and Nate to wear themselves out. Then I'll take them home."

And she would go home too—alone.

"Uh-oh. Don't look now," the bartender said.

Brenna turned to look despite the warning, just in time to see two beautiful women walk over to the table where the guys were seated. One put her hand on Luke's shoulder, her eyes pinned on him.

A thread of jealousy and possessiveness ran through Brenna. She'd seen the woman around town before but didn't know her personally. Just because it was a small town didn't mean that everyone knew everyone.

"You sure you don't want a second drink?" the barkeep asked. "Don't worry about being the DD. I have an Uber on standby to drive our patrons home. I take care of my customers."

"Still after that big tip, huh?" Brenna teased. She didn't feel like smiling though. She felt like walking across the bar and pulling Luke away from the blond and onto the dance floor.

* * *

Luke didn't appreciate the woman standing next to him with her hand on his shoulder. If she saw the scars underneath his shirt, she'd probably get squeamish. She was pretty, the kind of woman who probably peeked through her fingers at the sight of bugs. Prying her hand off his shoulder would be awkward and maybe even embarrassing for her so he reached for his beer instead.

That's what tonight was about after all. Friends and drinks. The only thing he needed to do was relax and let go of this tension.

Granger smirked at him, appearing to read Luke's mind about the woman. Not that he was doing anything to help.

"Wanna dance, sweetheart?" the blond asked. Luke couldn't remember her name. He'd been too distracted by the chaos and noise to pay close attention when she'd introduced herself.

"I'm afraid I'm not much of a dancer. But I think Jack over there is." Luke gestured at his friend across the table.

Jack looked up at the woman. "I might head out there in a little bit. Right now, I'm just going to sit and watch. Sorry, Rachel."

Rachel. That's right.

"Well, I'll be out there if you want to come find me," she said. "Unless someone else finds me first." She removed her hand from Luke's shoulder and headed in the direction of the dance floor.

"If we were all just going to sit around and drink, we could've done that at Jack's place," Granger teased.

"Why not yours?" Luke asked.

"I have two little girls who would insist that we play board games with them instead." Granger lifted his beer to his mouth. "My parents are watching them tonight, hoping that my going out means I'll meet the next Mrs. Fields."

Luke didn't miss the word *next* but he decided it was best not to ask right now. They didn't know each other well but he hoped to change all that. In addition to tonight being about relaxation, Luke was looking forward to becoming closer friends with these two. "Maybe my place next time, then," he said.

"On the creek? Yeah, that would be nice," Jack agreed.

"So, Jack, any interest in Rachel?" Granger asked.

Jack looked at the dance floor where the blond had gone. "She's nice enough. But she's interested in every guy in here." He tipped his head at Luke. "Don't feel too special, buddy."

Luke chuckled. "Here I thought we were the most eligible bachelors in the room, and that's why she walked over."

"We're the most eligible bachelors at this table. How about that?" Granger said on a laugh.

Luke shook his head. "I'm fine just sitting here."

Granger frowned. "Just because we don't want to find our soul mates at the moment doesn't mean we can't look for a woman to spin around on the dance floor though." He reached for his empty bottle and set it on its side. Then he rubbed his hands together. "Let's play a game."

"Spin the bottle?" Jack grimaced. "I'm not kissing either of you two frogs."

Luke laughed, feeling his tension slip away. "What kind of game?"

Granger shot Jack a pointed look. "At least Luke is willing to hear me out. We each take a turn spinning. The first woman it lands on, the spinner has to send her a drink. If she takes the bait and comes over, the spinner has to ask her to dance."

Jack rubbed his chin thoughtfully. "What happens if she doesn't walk over?"

Granger shrugged. "Nothing. We just keep playing."

"Boring," Luke said. "If she doesn't walk over, the sender has to drink."

Jack held up his hands. "I don't do drinking games."

Luke had noticed that Jack didn't seem to do drinking either. He had a Coke on the rocks that he was sipping occasionally. "The last time I played a drinking game was when I was in the fire academy," Luke said. "I had to crawl into bed that night."

"Let's hope you hold your alcohol better now," Granger teased.

"Or that the woman you send a drink to finds you interesting enough to walk over," Jack added.

They chuckled a little. They weren't really going to play. They were just joking around and talking.

Then Granger leaned in, grabbed hold of the bottle, and gave it a spin. "I guess I'll start the game." The bottle spun at least a dozen times, finally slowing until it pointed at the table in front of theirs, where three older women were seated.

"Ohh." Jack grinned. "That's my old high school math teacher."

"She's probably married," Granger said hopefully.

"Nope. Single. Buy her a drink, bud," Jack said on a laugh. "This was your idea and your rules."

The teacher waved from the neighboring table when she got her drink but didn't walk over, so Granger had to order a shot.

"I might as well order half a dozen," he said, "because we might be striking out a lot tonight."

Jack took his turn next, even though he didn't have an alcoholic beverage in front of him. The bottle slowed on a table of guys. "No women. My turn is skipped."

"Was that a rule?" Luke asked. "Don't you spin again?"

"Nice try," Jack told him. "Your turn, buddy."

Luke sighed and spun the bottle. He got the English teacher's friend, who was also in her midfifties.

"My high school language arts teacher," Jack informed him.

She didn't walk over either.

Luke lifted a shot glass and looked between his two friends. "If this goes on, we're calling an Uber to take us all home. Agreed?"

"Unless you find a woman to give you a lift," Jack said. "Now, drink."

After three shots, Luke was ready for someone to walk over just so he didn't have to knock another back. Jack was already on the dance floor without having to even take one shot, and it was just Luke and Granger at the table.

Luke leaned forward and grasped the bottle between his thumb and pointer finger, and then he gave it a twist. The bottle spun and spun, around and around. Then it slowed and stopped, pointing to the bar.

Luke blinked through the buzz of alcohol as he focused on the back of the woman sitting where the bottle had pointed. She had long, dark hair and a slender frame.

"Send over a drink," Granger said.

Luke sighed before signaling the waitress who'd been weaving to and from their table, understanding that they were making frequent requests. "Over there this time," he said. *Please let this be the one.*

"Sure thing," the waitress said.

Luke watched the waitress deliver a drink to the woman. Then the waitress pointed in Luke's direction. This game was fun, albeit a little embarrassing. The woman at the bar turned, and Luke sucked in a breath.

Brenna waved, reached for her drink, and stood.

"Oh, she's walking over," Granger said. "Hey, that's Brenna McConnell. Looks like she might be interested in you, buddy."

Luke swallowed. He was interested too, and he'd had just enough alcohol tonight to forget why he wasn't supposed to be.

CHAPTER TWELVE

"Thanks for the drink," Brenna said, standing in front of Luke's table. She was surprised to find him here of all places. He didn't seem like the type to hang out in a crowded, noisy place. Then again, neither was she.

"You're welcome," Luke said, his gaze heavy on her.

"How are the kittens?"

Luke gave her one of those bone-melting smiles of his. "They went home this afternoon. I dropped them by Ronny Hill's place because the mama cat was released from Dr. Lewis's care."

"Aw, that's good news," Brenna said, even though she was frowning. "I have to admit I was kind of hoping to see them again."

"I'm sure Ronny wouldn't mind a visitor," Luke said.

Granger cleared his throat, reminding them they weren't alone. Luke had forgotten that detail for a moment.

"We're playing a game," Granger told Brenna. "Since you accepted the drink and walked over, Luke here now has to ask you to dance."

"Oh." Brenna narrowed her eyes at Luke. "So you only sent me the drink because you had to?"

Luke grimaced. "Guilty. And now, apparently, I have to ask you to dance."

Brenna cocked her head to one side. "Sorry, but my answer is no."

"Oh man!" Granger slapped a hand down on the table. "Rejected."

Luke chuckled.

Brenna pulled out the empty chair between them and sat down. "I don't dance but I do appreciate the drink. Unfortunately, I'm the DD for my friends tonight so I can't accept it." She slid it in front of Luke. "Afraid you'll have to drink it yourself. I'll stick to my Coke." She pulled her soda in front of her.

"You are striking out all over the place," Granger told Luke.

"So drinking games tonight, huh? Can I play?" Brenna asked.

"But you're not drinking alcohol," he pointed out. "There's no downside for you to drink."

"Not true. Too much sugar makes me crazy." The corner of her mouth quirked. "Let's play Truth or Lie."

"I don't know that one." Luke turned to Granger. "Do you?"

He nodded. "We say something about ourselves, and the others have to guess if it's the truth or a lie. If you get it wrong, you drink."

Luke looked at Brenna. "Is that how it goes?"

"Yep, I'll start. I love to dance in my kitchen while I'm cooking."

Luke laughed. "Lie. You said you don't dance."

She giggled softly. "I misspoke. I only dance in my

kitchen when no one is watching." She pointed at his shot glass. "Drink," she ordered.

He groaned before grabbing the ready shot and tipping his head back.

"Your turn. Tell me about your first love," she said.

"You get to pick the subject?" he asked. "Why didn't I get to ask you a question, then?"

Brenna grinned. "Because I'm making up the rules as I go."

Luke side-eyed Granger, who gave him a bewildered look. Then he refocused on Brenna. "The first girl I ever loved cheated on me with my best friend."

Brenna narrowed her eyes. "I say that's a lie. What foolish girl would do something like that?"

Luke tipped his head at her Coke. "Drink up. That's the truth."

"Aw, that's sad," she said, smile dropping.

Granger clapped a hand on Luke's back, right above where Brenna had seen his scars. "That is sad, buddy."

Luke didn't seem to feel any physical or emotional pain. "I got over it," he told them.

"Are you still friends?" Brenna asked Luke.

"Nope. They got married and didn't even invite me to the wedding."

Brenna's lips parted. "Really?"

"No. That's a lie," Luke said. "I was a groomsman. Take another drink of soda."

"Hey, you don't get to have two turns." She narrowed her eyes.

"If you can make the rules, so can I." He turned to Granger. "Your turn, bud. Tell us why you're still single."

Granger looked between Luke and Brenna. She knew some of Granger's story. The mother of his kids had walked away from their family right after his youngest child was born. "So I can date a new woman every night," he said on a laugh. Then he reached for his drink. "Yep, that was a lie, and you both know it."

* * *

Maybe it was the alcohol buzzing through Luke's veins, the sound of Brenna's laughter against the cacophonous tavern, or the soft lighting that made her look like she was glowing in the dark, but he couldn't take his eyes off her.

She grabbed her Coke and took a sip before leaning in to talk over the noisy background. Every time she leaned in, Luke got a whiff of some tropical scent she was wearing, a blend of coconut and mango.

"I got one," Granger said, reminding Luke that his friend was still at the table. "Truth or lie: You two have already kissed."

Luke glanced over. "Truth."

Granger looked between them. "But you decided it was a bad idea."

"Truth. You're on a roll," Luke said.

Granger pinched his chin between his thumb and forefinger thoughtfully. "So you two decided to just be friends."

"That's three for three," Brenna said. "Luke and I are just friends."

Granger chuckled and pointed at her Coke. "Now, that is definitely a lie."

Luke looked at Brenna for a long second, and then he turned back to Granger, lifted his drink, and took a long, hard sip.

"Luke Marini," someone said, stepping up to their table.

Luke looked up at the older woman that he'd sent a drink to earlier. "Yes?"

"I'm Loretta Lambert. I've heard about you. You're the acting fire chief while Chief Brewer is recovering. I wanted to come over here and thank you for the drink you sent me."

"You're welcome," he told her. "It was my pleasure."

"And to ask you if you wanted to dance," she said, surprising him.

Luke stuttered for a moment. "I, uh, well…"

"You have to agree, bud," Granger whispered as he leaned over for only Luke to hear. "That was the rule."

"Remind me to never play another drinking game," he whispered back. Then he looked up at the woman. "I'd love to." His gaze fell to Brenna as he pushed back from the table and stood. He didn't dance but he would to wrap his arms around her.

Mrs. Lambert led him to the dance floor and showed off some moves he'd never seen before. For a woman her age, she danced like a twenty-year-old on a sugar high. Luke did his best to move just enough to appease her, all the while planning his escape route for when the song ended. As the music lulled, Mrs. Lambert grabbed both his arms and pulled him to her.

"I never get to dance during the slow songs. This is a real treat for me," she said.

Luke didn't have the heart to pull away. The woman was sweet, and she seemed so happy.

Then someone tapped his shoulder, gaining his attention.

"I'm cutting in," Brenna said.

"Oh phooey." Mrs. Lambert reluctantly stepped away. "But I guess Luke might rather dance with you anyway." She smiled brightly. "Maybe I'll cut in on someone else."

"Thank you for the dance," Luke told Mrs. Lambert as she stepped away and Brenna took her place.

She tipped her head back to look up at him. "Looked like you were having fun to me."

"I was thinking of you the entire time," he said.

"Lie?"

"Completely true." Drinking made him admit things probably best left unsaid.

"And what were you thinking?" she asked, her body pressing against his.

"About this. Dancing close, holding you, smelling you."

She pulled back and gave a small laugh. "Smelling me?"

Luke nodded his head. "I think it's your shampoo." He leaned in closer and breathed her in.

"I daresay you're drunk, Luke Marini," she teased.

"That's probably true."

She beamed up at him as the song continued. "I told your friends I'd take you home. I offered to take them too but they're calling an Uber for themselves."

"It seems I'm racking up a lot of debts tonight."

Brenna tilted her head to one side. "I'm sure I can find a way to call it even."

The song ended, and she stepped away. Then a fast beat flooded the sound system once again.

"I need to find Chris and Nate. I'm their DD tonight," she told Luke.

"I'll wait for you at the table."

"Sounds good." She gave him a small smile before leaving him standing there, smitten and slightly intoxicated. Then he headed to his empty table. Granger and Jack were gone so he sat alone and watched the goings-on around him. His gaze moved around the room. He recognized some patrons and didn't others. He sobered up just a little when he looked at one couple seated at a table against the wall.

What were Eve and Ryan doing here together? Whatever it was, it looked like they'd overcome their differences and were enjoying each other's company. It also appeared that Eve wasn't drinking a soda like her sister. Ryan was twenty-one but Eve was underage.

"Chris and Nate want to stay longer. I already arranged for the bartender to call them a ride," Brenna said, stepping up to where Luke was seated.

He snatched his gaze away from Eve and Ryan, not wanting Brenna to notice them. "All right."

"I'm just going to use the bathroom, and then I'll be ready to leave."

"I'll wait right here for you."

"Don't let anyone drag you back to the dance floor," she teased before walking away and weaving through clusters of people. Once she was out of sight, Luke stood and headed toward Eve and Ryan.

Ryan nearly dropped the drink in his hand when he noticed Luke.

"We'll talk about this tomorrow," Luke said, willing himself sober enough to be taken seriously. "Tonight, you call a cab, an Uber, a friend, I don't care, and get both of yourselves home safely. To your own homes," he clarified, looking between them.

Eve's expression looked pained. "I've only had one, sir."

"One too many considering that you're eighteen," Luke told her.

"Please don't tell my sister," she pleaded.

He narrowed his eyes. "You just got your job back, and you're more worried about your sister knowing than your boss?"

She grimaced as the color of her cheeks grew darker. "No, I'm worried about that too."

"Good. You should be." Luke straightened and started to turn away, calling one last directive over his shoulder. "In my office. Tomorrow."

* * *

Brenna enjoyed the quiet of the ride home after spending the last couple of hours in a noisy tavern but Luke's silence left her unsettled. "That was fun," she said, looking over at him.

He gave a small nod. "I can't remember the last time I did something like that. It's good medicine."

"Drinking?" she asked, looking for clarification.

"No. That's never good medicine. Being with friends is what I meant."

She focused on the dark road as she drove. "I didn't realize you were close with Granger and Jack."

"I'm not. We met at the Tipsy Tavern a couple months back and clicked. My brother advised me to find some friends and hang out. He had a lot of advice but that was the best of it."

"Interesting. So what was your brother giving you advice for?" she asked.

Luke fell quiet again. "The alcohol puts me at risk for being too honest with you right now."

She glanced over. "That's not such a bad thing, is it?"

He didn't respond, and apparently, he wasn't going to. She suspected she knew the answer. He had a past like everyone else, and like everyone else, he was doing his best to deal with it in his own way.

She turned onto Blueberry Creek Road, followed it

down to her driveway, and pulled in. "Want me to walk you to your door?" she asked as she stepped out.

"Unless you want me to fall into the bushes."

"You're not that drunk," she teased.

"No, I'm not. But I'm probably drunk enough to kiss you at the door. So maybe you better not walk with me."

She swallowed, wishing her heart wasn't suddenly racing at the idea. "No, I think it's best that I do. Sleeping in the bushes doesn't sound comfortable." She pulled out her cell phone and turned on the flashlight app to light their path as they walked through his front yard and up his porch steps.

"This is backward," Luke pointed out. "The guy is supposed to walk the girl to the door."

"And the guy is supposed to kiss the girl," she said, stepping into him. "But since I'm making my own rules tonight…"

"And also doing your fair share of breaking them," he pointed out as one corner of his mouth quirked.

"That too." But she didn't care. They had both agreed to keep their distance but that wasn't easy to do in a small town or when living right next to each other. "Since I'm breaking the rules…" She went up on her tiptoes and pressed her lips to his, satisfied when his arms latched around her waist, securing her there. Not that she was planning on going anywhere else. Luke tasted like beer and scotch. He felt like a heavy blanket on a chilly spring night. And she wanted him like she'd never wanted any man before.

She pulled away and swallowed hard, her chest heaving softly under her blouse. "One good-night kiss never hurt anyone…Good night, Luke."

"Night."

She watched him reach into his pocket for his keys and come out empty-handed. He reached into his other pocket. "What's wrong?" she finally asked when he returned to the first pocket to check again.

He lifted a hand to his face. "I think I left my keys at the Tipsy Tavern."

"What about a spare?"

Luke shook his head. "I don't have one."

"You can't get inside your home?" she clarified.

"Well, I guess I could break in. Maybe pick the lock, but it's dark and my coordination is a little dulled at the moment. I'm not sure I could do it right now."

Brenna swallowed, ignoring the little voice in her head already protesting what she was about to suggest. She said it anyway. "Well, I guess we have no choice, then. You're coming home with me."

CHAPTER THIRTEEN

Brenna unlocked her front door and walked inside, feeling Luke's footsteps behind her. Max ran ahead of them. They'd gone to Luke's back fence, and Max had come out through the doggie door. She'd considered crawling through to unlock Luke's door for him but Max was a little dog and she didn't fancy getting stuck.

"You sure it's okay for Max to be here?" Luke asked.

"Of course. I don't have any dog food but I saved a few of the dog biscuits I gave him the other day. Just in case he came back for another visit."

Luke closed her front door behind him and locked it. "Thanks."

She swallowed, unsure of what to do with Luke now that he was in her house. "Are you hungry? I can whip something up."

"I'm starving but I'd hate to trouble you."

Relief flooded her. If he hadn't been hungry, she would have had to find something else to pass the time, and the only other thing she could think of right now was kissing him again. "I don't mind, and I'm starving too." She gestured for him to follow her back to her kitchen, where he sat on a barstool. "In college, after a night out with friends, I would come home to our apartment and make pancakes."

"Pancakes?" he asked, resting his elbows on her counter and watching her.

"Do you like pancakes?"

"Love them. That would be fantastic right now."

She opened her cabinet and started pulling down the ingredients. "I bet you were expecting something fancier from a caterer, huh?"

"I've realized that you're not at all what I expected, Brenna McConnell."

She considered asking him to elaborate but she didn't need an explanation. She'd been a little crazy where he was concerned. One of his first impressions of her was her throwing bananas at her sister.

Brenna turned and started preparing their midnight snack, working without any kind of recipe or measuring tools. "My mother and I used to cook together all the time when I was young. She loved cooking for others." Brenna grabbed a large spoon and stirred the flour, milk, and eggs into a bowl. She swiped at a lock of hair in her face, dusting flour on her cheek. "Oops." She glanced over at Luke, who grinned back at her.

"I like it," he said, his tone flirty.

She laughed softly and then brought the bowl to the stove, where a skillet was heating. She gestured for him to join her. "Wanna do the honors?"

"Me?" He got up and walked over, his body towering beside her and making her stomach tie itself into tiny knots.

"I've never invited a man to my stove before. You

should feel special." She handed him the large spoon in her hand.

"They won't come out pretty. I can promise you that."

"Sometimes they taste better when they're ugly."

He gave her a curious look as he scooped batter into the pan. "Are you subtly implying that I'm ugly?"

She laughed out loud. "We're talking about pancakes, not people. And no, you're definitely not ugly. I think you're fishing for compliments."

"True," he admitted. "And maybe for another kiss. It seems the more I try to convince myself to steer clear of you, the more I can't stop thinking about you."

She swallowed. "I'm having the same problem."

They stared at each other for a long moment until the pancake in the pan started smoking.

"But we should stick to eating ugly pancakes that taste delicious," Luke said. He pulled his gaze from her. "And I want to see if you really dance in your kitchen."

Brenna shook her head. "Only when I'm alone, remember?"

"We'll see about that." He grabbed a spatula and flipped the pancakes. "I have good persuasive skills."

She decided not to tell him that he could probably persuade her into a lot of things tonight.

* * *

Luke had sobered up midway through the largest stack of pancakes that had ever been set before him. They'd both poured half a bottle of syrup on their stacks and had joked until the hurt in their bellies was just as much from laughing as from eating too much. "Okay, let's see it," he said, sliding his gaze over to her as they sat at the kitchen counter.

She gave him a curious look. "See what?"

"I want to see you dance in the kitchen."

She ran her tongue over her lips, clearing off the syrup residue. "Only if you dance with me." Brenna tapped the screen on her cell phone, and some slow music started to flow through the speaker. Then she grabbed his hand and tugged him off the stool.

Luke let her pull him into the middle of the kitchen, and then she turned to face him, her face dangerously close to his. Without thinking, unable to resist touching her any longer, his hands looped around her waist and pulled her toward him, her hips swaying beneath his grasp.

Her brown eyes seemed to dance right along with her body, and he'd never seen anything sexier than this woman in front of him. "I'm guessing this isn't how you usually dance when you're alone."

She looked at him under her lashes. "Not exactly. But I kind of like this better."

He liked it too. Holding her close was an addictive feeling. One that he could bask in all night. And one that could lead to other things if they weren't careful. His gaze fell to her mouth, and the desire to kiss her was so strong. Would her lips taste syrupy sweet?

The corners of her mouth twitched as if she could hear his thoughts over the music. Then she went up on her tiptoes and brushed her mouth over his. He latched on to the kiss, deepening it, just as hungry for her as he'd been with the pancakes. "I love dancing in the kitchen with you," he whispered once they'd pulled away from each other.

She held his gaze, stirring all kinds of contradictory feelings inside him. Stay, leave. Touch, resist.

"Maybe we should amend this arrangement of ours," she said.

"I'm listening. What did you have in mind?" he asked.

"I'm only here until this summer but we can have a lot of fun until then. It doesn't have to be anything serious."

"We can just be two people enjoying each other's company," he agreed.

"Exactly. Something slightly more than friends."

Luke kind of liked the sound of that. A relationship of convenience with no strings attached. He'd always been the kind of guy who was all-in when it came to relationships. After losing so much in his childhood fire, he tended to hold on fervently to the people and things who came into his life. But if he knew there was no forever potential here, he could keep his heart in check. It was only a few months—just long enough to enjoy Brenna's company a little longer.

Luke dipped and kissed her again, allowing himself to fully enjoy the moment. "I like this new arrangement."

"Me too," she said, pulling away and looking directly into his eyes now with an undeniable hunger. He felt it too. Kissing and spending time together was one thing though; going further than that was another.

He kissed her one more time and then stepped back. "I'll, uh, sleep on the couch," he offered, collecting his willpower while he still had it. He didn't want Brenna to think that he was going to try to sleep with her tonight. And he didn't want her to suggest it, because he might not be able to resist.

"Right." She grabbed her cell phone to silence the music. "I'll get you some blankets. Be right back."

A moment later, she returned holding two blankets and a pillow. "Here you go. Want me to help you?"

"That's okay. You're probably tired," he said, needing distance if he expected to maintain his willpower. Otherwise, they might end up kissing the entire night.

"I am. At least Nate is opening the shop tomorrow. I can sleep in."

Luke was also supposed to have the day off but he'd told Ryan and Eve to meet him in his office first thing. He wasn't sure how he was going to handle that situation. "I won't bother you if I wake early," he promised. "I think we had enough pancakes for that to count as breakfast."

She took a retreating step, laughing softly under her breath. "I agree. Well, good night, Luke."

"Sweet dreams, Brenna." He watched her head down the hall, wondering at the flutter of feelings in his chest.

No feelings allowed.

He tucked one of the blankets into the couch cushions and then draped the other over his body as he lay down. Brenna was tucked away in her bed, where she belonged. And he belonged out here with Max, staring at the ceiling with that dance and those kisses on replay in his mind.

* * *

Brenna needed a glass of water. She'd woken at one a.m., an hour after retreating to her bedroom, and her mouth was dry. She cracked open her bedroom door and looked out, not wanting to disturb Luke.

As she tiptoed down the hall toward the kitchen, she peeked at Luke fast asleep on her couch with Max on the floor beside him. Her heart kicked softly. She continued toward the kitchen and poured herself a glass of water quietly, drank it, and then retreated to her bedroom.

Crap. She'd left her cell phone on the kitchen counter. What if Eve needed her? Brenna hesitated before lying down. Eve was an adult, and she never called at this hour anyway. But what if she did this once? Or what if Aunt

Thelma needed help for some reason? Unable to resist the need to have her phone, Brenna cracked her door back open and crept down the hall toward the kitchen.

She grabbed her phone off the counter and started to tiptoe back when she knocked her foot against the water bowl she'd set down for Max. It scraped loudly on her wood floor, the sound sending Luke lurching upright in the darkness.

"Luke, it's just me. Brenna."

She saw his shadowed figure look up at her, and without thinking, she headed toward him, turning on her cell phone's flashlight app and lighting up the space between them. "It's just Brenna," she said again. "Sorry to startle you." Although by the way he'd shot up, she wondered if he'd been having a nightmare. Maybe it was a good thing she'd woken him.

"It's fine," he reassured her, reaching out for her hand.

She looked down at her hand in his, the feel of his skin, tough and calloused against hers, arousing her senses in the dark. "Okay. Can I get you something?"

"No. Thanks."

He'd seemed upset when he'd woken. It didn't feel right to just leave him. "Want me to stay here with you? Or...you could stay with me. In my room."

In the dark, the interaction didn't quite feel real. It felt more like a dream, and in a dream, you could do anything without worrying about the consequences.

"Probably not a good idea," he said.

"But it's not the worst idea," she said softly. "Maybe I don't want to be alone tonight either." She waited for his response, wanting him to say yes. When he didn't, she tugged on his hand. "Come on."

He hesitated only for a moment, and then he stood and

followed her down the hall and into her room. Into her bed.

"I know we agreed to enjoy each other's company while you're here, but I don't expect to..." He paused. "I, uh, I'll keep my hands to myself," he said, climbing in beside her.

"You don't have to," she whispered. Then she took his hand and led it to her body, draping it over her waist. She felt him grow rigid beside her. She wiggled closer, her eyes locked on his in the dark, and then she pressed her mouth to his. She'd lost count how many times they'd kissed now, but each time, it only got better and left her wanting more.

"Are you sure?" he asked, his body pressed against her like a second skin. Even so, she didn't feel close enough.

She swallowed past the lump in her throat and all the second thoughts circulating in her mind. "No. You?"

"No," he whispered against her cheek. "Just say the word. I can stop if you want me to."

"I can't," she whispered back before kissing him again.

* * *

The next morning, Brenna stirred in bed, her eyes cracking open almost against her will. Yep, the sun was up, and daytime had found her again. Something moved beside her, and she nearly screamed before remembering that Luke was in bed with her. The other memories from last night flooded into her mind as well.

She sucked in a deep breath, trying not to panic. What had she done? He was her neighbor. He was Eve's boss... He was the guy she'd been crushing on for months now.

Luke stirred again and then settled into a quiet sleep. Careful not to wake him, she stood and shimmied down the hall toward the kitchen just like she'd done in the night.

She used the guest bathroom farthest from her bedroom and then started the coffee maker before pulling out her cell phone and texting Halona.

I can't come this morning. It's my day off.

It took a moment for the dots to start bouncing on the screen as Halona typed a return text.

A day off never stopped you before.

It's just, well, I have company.

At six o'clock in the morning??? Who?!

Brenna covered her face for a moment. I'll stop by the flower shop this afternoon. We can have coffee and chat there.

Don't stand me up! Halona texted. I need details!

A noise from the bedroom got Brenna's attention. Luke was awake.

She grabbed two mugs from the cabinet, setting one down for him to get when he was ready. Then she poured some hot brew into her mug and got the creamer from the fridge. When her coffee was ready, she sat down with it at the table and waited for Luke to walk into the kitchen. She listened to him stir around in her bathroom before his heavy footsteps walked down the hall.

Brenna held her breath, her hands trembling around her coffee mug. Why was she suddenly so nervous? So they'd had sex. It didn't mean anything; they'd already decided that when they'd discussed a no-strings-attached relationship until she left for college.

"Good morning," he said, stepping into the room. His dark hair was rumpled, and he looked equally adorable as he did hot.

"Good morning. I made coffee. There's a mug on the counter for you and cream if you want it."

"Coffee sounds delicious." He turned his back to her, revealing the scars she'd seen the day she went to his house to deliver a piece of mail. This time they didn't shock her. Instead, she found herself studying them. The skin was surprisingly smooth and shiny, almost rippled like a piece of artwork.

Luke turned and caught her staring. "It's okay. I don't mind."

Brenna swallowed and reached for her cup of coffee. "Do they hurt?"

He shook his head as he poured creamer into his coffee. "Not anymore. My skin gets tight sometimes but I stretch daily. It helps."

Brenna watched him turn and head toward her. He pulled out a chair at the table and sat down as if waking up together was completely normal. Maybe it was for him. Unless she counted Eve, Brenna hadn't had someone to wake up with since her fiancé seven years ago. This was foreign to her but it felt nice.

"The scars happened a long time ago, when I was seven. My family's home caught fire while my youngest brother and I were upstairs. There was so much smoke that I couldn't go down. I went to my window and saw my parents and my older brother Nick on the street, looking frantic. They didn't know where my brother and I were. When I pounded on the upstairs window, my mother screamed so loudly that I could hear her over the flames." Luke looked down at his mug, seeming to take a breath before continuing. "I thought I might die that day. I was trapped, and the flames were closing in."

Brenna reached for his forearm. "That's so awful. What...happened?"

He looked up, shaking his head softly as if loosening the memory in some far-off place. "It's kind of a blur. This huge firefighter barged through the smoke. I begged him to take my brother first but there was another fireman coming up behind him. He would get Marco." Luke paused again, taking another breath, this one longer and deeper. "The firefighter wrapped me in this fireproof blanket and picked me up like I weighed nothing. It happened so fast that the next thing I knew, I was outside, coughing on the lawn. I was loaded into an ambulance with an oxygen mask on my face and rushed to the hospital."

Luke hesitated. "I wanted to be a firefighter from that point on."

"Your burns?"

Pain pooled in Luke's expression. "I spent some time in a burn unit and had a few surgeries that my family couldn't afford, especially after we lost everything in the fire."

She wasn't even sure what to say right now. She held eye contact, seeing so much more to this man than the outer sexy shell. He was strong, protective, a hero. He'd just opened up to her, and she was grateful that he trusted her enough to do so.

Luke looked down into his coffee. "When I'm having a nightmare, it's hard to wake up in the dark. Like last night. The nightmares aren't as frequent as they used to be, but...sometimes something happens to trigger them."

"Like the barn fire with my sister?"

He looked up and gave a small nod. "That's when I have

the dreams. It's a helpless feeling, being all alone and not knowing which way is up or down."

She ran her hand from his forearm to cover his hand with hers. "I won't ask any more questions."

He took another sip of his coffee. "It's fine."

"Should we, um, talk about last night?"

"That's a question." Luke grinned. "And I can't this morning. I have something I need to take care of at the station."

Brenna's heart sank a notch.

"But we should talk tonight," he added.

Her heart floated on a bubble back into her chest, knocking around against her ribs. It wasn't supposed to matter whether he wanted to see her again. That was the beauty of a no-strings-attached relationship.

"My place or yours?" he asked.

"Yours."

CHAPTER FOURTEEN

*L*uke would rather that he was still in Brenna's bed this morning. Instead, he'd gotten a ride from Jack back to the bar to retrieve his keys and vehicle and had headed in to the station.

"What are you doing here?" Tim asked. "Thought I was on duty today."

When Luke had a day off, Wally was in charge. Next in line was Tim. There was a strict chain of command that the guys were actually following and respecting, at least a little bit, these days.

"I'm not staying," Luke said. "Just have something I need to take care of."

"Anything you need me to help with?" Tim asked.

"Yeah. You mind telling Ryan and Eve to come see me? I want to talk to them in my office."

"Sure." Tim started walking toward the back. He didn't buck authority like Ryan.

Luke headed to his office and sat down at the desk. He

didn't like conflict or having hard conversations like the one he was about to have. He hadn't forgotten that the last hard conversation he'd had with Eve ended up with him firing her.

Someone knocked on his door, and Luke looked up. Eve's face was pale, and her eyes were wide.

"Come in," he said, gesturing at the chair in front of him.

"I feel like I'm being called into the principal's office."

He narrowed his eyes. "I'm going to take a wild guess that that happened a lot."

She chewed on her lower lip, looking more like a teenager than an adult right now. He had to remind himself that she was still straddling that line. The transition between the two didn't just happen overnight. It was a slow fade. "I got called into Principal Smith's office more than once. Brenna wasn't happy about it."

Luke took this comment in, thinking about how Brenna had been put into a place of leadership without asking for it. And as a leader, she micromanaged. Yeah, she was a bit controlling, but her heart was in the right place. Brenna had a huge heart. It was one of her most attractive aspects, in his opinion. "She wants what's best for you."

"Are you going to tell Brenna about last night?" Eve asked.

"I don't typically tell my neighbors about the goings-on of the station. This is work. You're an employee, and if I have an issue, I take it directly to you."

Eve's mouth pinched tightly. "Thank you."

They both turned as Ryan knocked. He walked in without being told and plopped down in the chair next to Eve, folding his arms tightly over his chest.

"Eve is underage," Luke said, jumping right in. "I

don't need to ask how she got that drink in front of her, do I?"

Ryan sighed. "Come on, Luke. You know you drank before you were twenty-one. Everyone does."

Luke didn't comment. "It's illegal, and I won't have my firefighters breaking the law. We represent the SSFD whether we're on duty or not."

"It was just the one," Eve clarified. "And I asked him to buy it for me."

"More like begged," Ryan muttered under his breath, winning a scowl from Eve.

Luke looked at her. "I thought you didn't even like each other."

"You're the one who told us to try and get along," Ryan pointed out.

"I didn't say date one another." Luke looked between them.

"Well, you didn't say not to either," Ryan argued.

"Well, I am now. Dating at the workplace creates a messy situation. You two need to be able to have each other's backs while you're here. If you're having a lovers' quarrel, that puts your lives and everyone else's in jeopardy. It's not allowed."

"You're not even the real chief," Ryan said. "You can't tell me who I can date and who I can't."

"I can." Luke stared at Ryan until Ryan looked away.

"Chill out. We're not even dating anyway," he muttered. "It was just us going out for drinks."

"And it was just one drink," Eve repeated. "I didn't even finish it. I'm sorry. It won't happen again."

Luke looked at her. "See that it doesn't. I'm glad you two are getting along but keep it at the station."

Eve glanced over at Ryan, hurt flashing across her face.

Something told Luke that she had considered last night's outing a date, no matter what Ryan claimed. "That won't be a problem," she said.

"Good. Now I'm leaving." Luke reached for his keys to make his point. "It's my day off. Don't make me have to come back."

Eve and Ryan stood and walked out without another word.

Luke watched them for a moment. He thought he'd handled that relatively well. If Ryan and Eve truly liked each other though, they wouldn't be able to stay away from one another. That was a hard lesson he and Brenna had recently learned.

* * *

Brenna bypassed A Taste of Heaven as she walked downtown. Aunt Thelma and Nate had things under control today. She continued past the Sweetwater Café and stepped into the Little Shop of Flowers where Halona worked.

"You didn't stand me up," Halona said, a little surprise evident in her voice.

"Of course not." Brenna breathed in the scent of fresh flowers. "I wish I could smell flowers all day instead of spices and fried foods. After several years standing at a stove, those aren't yummy smells anymore."

Halona laughed. "It's a slow day here. Want some coffee? I have a pot brewing in the back."

"Sounds perfect." Brenna headed behind the counter and sat down at a small table, where she and Hal had sat many times. "Slow, huh?"

"Well, except for yet another visit from Mrs. Everson to discuss Mayor Everson's upcoming charity function."

Halona poured two mugs of coffee and sat across from Brenna.

"Oh, that's right. You're working that event too," Brenna said.

Halona cupped her hands around her mug. "I am. She wants flowers, and only the freshest and most beautiful in the land will do." Halona snorted. "Nothing is too good for her son's events."

"How did Mayor Everson fall so far from that apple tree?"

Halona laughed quietly. "It's the mother bear in her, I guess. I get it. Whenever Theo has something important going on at school, I'm right there making sure it goes smoothly. And you get that way with things involving Eve," Halona pointed out.

"I guess Mrs. Everson can't help it but I wish she'd lighten up just a little. Perfection is overrated," Brenna said.

"So?" Hal looked at her above the mug she was holding. "You had company early this morning, and I want the details."

Brenna shook her head. "There isn't much to tell."

"Liar." Halona set her mug down and pointed a finger. "When I was just dating Alex, you demanded all the details, and now it's my turn. Was it Luke?"

Brenna felt her cheeks flare.

"It was!" Halona bounced softly in her chair. "This is so exciting. Was it just a one-night thing or the start of something more?"

Brenna nibbled on her lower lip. "We haven't talked about it since it happened."

"What do you mean? What did he say this morning?"

Brenna thought about it. "Well, he woke up and said he had to go to work. Even though it's his day off."

Halona's smile dropped.

"Then he said we'd talk later. Tonight." Brenna could read what Halona was thinking, and maybe she was worried about the same thing. Was that a bad sign? Not that it mattered. They'd decided before they went to bed together that they were just having fun.

"Did he kiss you on the way out?" Halona asked.

Brenna nodded.

"A peck kiss or a lingering lover's kiss?"

Brenna thought about it. "A peck."

"Oh." Now Halona looked completely grim.

"What?" Brenna asked. "You think that means he regretted what happened?"

"I don't know. What do you think? Do you regret it?"

Brenna heaved a sigh. She wanted to regret it but she didn't. Last night had been amazing. The way Luke had touched her, as if he might break her. As if he might break if he didn't have her.

She looked at Halona. "No regrets."

Halona's lips parted. "Oh, wow."

"What?" Brenna asked.

"You're falling for him. I can see it on your face. That must've been some night."

Brenna looked away. "It was but he knows I'm leaving for college this summer. This is just casual between us. That's all it can be."

Halona thought for a moment. "I had no intention of falling for Alex last year. It just happened. I don't think you get a choice in the matter. Unless you lock yourself inside your house and avoid him from now on."

That was the original plan, and it hadn't lasted a day.

Brenna swallowed. "We only had the one night together."

"But you're feeling something. And that doesn't happen every day."

Brenna shook her head. "No, it doesn't." In fact, it had only ever happened to her once, and that hadn't worked out so well. That's why she needed to stick to the arrangement. Just fun, no feelings.

* * *

Luke wasn't quite sure what he was doing at Merry Mountain Farms but the only other alternative was going home. He and Brenna were seeing each other tonight, and he didn't want to see her before then. Not until he was ready to talk about last night.

"What are you doing here?" Granger asked, walking toward the farm's entrance.

"Seeing if you made it home safely last night," Luke lied.

"Aw, you care about me—that's sweet." Granger chuckled and waved him back. The farm got most of its business during the holidays when people came for trees but Luke knew that it was also an orchard, selling apples and peaches during the summer and fall months. "I didn't feel my best this morning—I'll say that. The girls still woke me up at six a.m., demanding that I cook breakfast and play with them. There's no rest for a single dad," Granger said.

"I guess not." Luke followed him around the perimeter of the farm, chatting about the weather and some nuisance birds that had been eating the fruit.

"I'm afraid I won't be making a habit of hanging out with you and Jack," Granger said, circling back to their initial topic. "Maybe once a month. We could form our own little group like the ladies in town have."

"I've heard about the Ladies' Day Out group," Luke said

"Oh, I'm sure. They're hard to miss." Granger stopped to check on a strawberry plant with wilted leaves. "Good thing we have an irrigation system. It's drier than usual around here this season."

"Dangerous time for forest fires," Luke added. "We've been lucky so far."

Granger righted himself and continued walking. "I'm guessing you're not here to discuss the weather though."

Luke laughed. "Not exactly. I have the day off, and I've been wanting to check this place out."

"Well, I'll give you the tour while you tell me what happened between you and Brenna last night after you left the Tipsy Tavern."

Luke nearly tripped over his feet.

Granger gave him a curious look and then chuckled to himself. "I see. You're lucky all around these days, huh?"

Luke hadn't come here to discuss Brenna either. In fact, he'd come for just the opposite. He wanted to stop thinking about her for a little bit but that seemed like a lost cause. "Did you know her parents?"

"Yep. Everyone did," Granger said. "They were involved with the community. They never missed an event and volunteered for most things. Salt-of-the-earth kind of people."

"Did Brenna have anyone to support her during that time?" Luke asked. He wasn't sure why he did but he couldn't stand the thought of her losing both parents and being there alone.

"Yeah." Granger nodded. "She had her fiancé with her."

"Fiancé?" This caught Luke's attention.

Granger glanced over. "Guess you two don't know each other as well as you thought."

"I had no idea she was divorced."

"She's not. She never made it down the aisle. The guy left her after her parents passed. Rumor is that he couldn't handle having to share Brenna with Eve. I can relate, I guess. A lot of women get scared off when they realize I have two little girls to care for."

"So she lost her parents and the man she was going to marry?" Luke asked.

"And became responsible for a spitfire teenager. I remember Eve in those days." Granger gave him a look that said the Eve Luke knew was much milder than the one she'd once been. "Brenna dropped everything and came home."

"That's a huge sacrifice." Luke already knew most of this story, but he hadn't known about Brenna's fiancé.

"You're interested in her. More than just a fling?" Granger asked.

"No. Neither of us are interested in anything long-term."

Luke and Granger passed the strawberry patches and headed along a fence toward what Luke guessed was the Christmas tree farm. He'd skipped putting up a tree this past holiday because he'd just moved to town but maybe he'd swing by this year and get one. He didn't even have to decorate it. He could just enjoy the pine scent that reminded him of home. Or maybe Brenna would be back from college and help him string the lights and hang the ornaments.

Luke's mind stuttered. One night and he was already thinking months ahead.

He cleared his throat and reached for a new subject. "Being acting fire chief is proving to be a little harder than I anticipated."

Granger glanced over. "Oh yeah? What's wrong?"

"I've had to be a little hard on the crew. Jobs weren't getting done. Attitudes were poor. There was a lack of respect for one another and the job. One of the reasons Chief Brewer hurt his back in the first place is because things weren't getting done the right way."

"I had no idea."

"Yeah, well, don't say anything."

"I wouldn't." Granger shook his head. "So you're in charge, and you're shaking things up. Big job for a newbie."

Luke blew out a breath. "A lonely job too. I've never been the boss before. People do things behind your back because you're the one that could get them in trouble."

Granger chuckled. "Yeah, I do things behind my dad's back all the time. He technically isn't my boss here on the farm but he's my dad so it feels that way." Granger stopped walking and looked out at the trees.

Luke mimicked his position. They were beautiful, full trees. Working in an environment like this every day would be nice. He hadn't grown up wanting to farm trees though. He'd grown up wanting to be the hero, coming to save the day the way someone had done for him and his family. Unfortunately, his hero hadn't been able to save everyone. Mistakes happened, and sometimes they proved fatal.

"Before I left the tavern last night, I saw Brenna's sister, Eve, with another firefighter," Luke said. "They were drinking."

Granger raised both brows. "Underage for her."

"Add illegal activities and dating in the workplace to the long list of things going on at the SSFD."

Granger offered a chuckle that started out small but gained momentum.

"Why are you laughing?" Luke worked hard to maintain his frown but it eventually turned into a smile as he watched his friend seem to find entertainment in his situation.

"I'll never feel sorry for myself again. Your life is upside-down at home and work. No wonder you showed up at my farm of all places on your day off."

Luke chuckled too. "I guess that is kind of funny."

"It is. Want some apple cider?" Granger asked after his laughter had died down. He started walking again. "My mom and aunt make it from the apples in the orchard. We don't sell it or anything. It's only for friends and family."

"That means I'm official?" Luke asked, following beside him.

Granger glanced over. "I'd say you need a good friend right about now."

Luke would have to agree.

"I have to warn you though," Granger cautioned. "If you walk inside my parents' house, you will instantly become Abigail and Willow's new best friend. And as such, you'll be obligated to play dolls at some point."

Luke's steps slowed. "Are you serious?"

Granger grimaced. "Afraid so. Second thoughts?"

He shook his head. He'd been looking for something to distract himself from thinking about Brenna today. This would work. "Sounds great to me. I can use all the friends I can get right now."

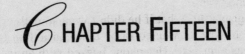

CHAPTER FIFTEEN

*B*renna just happened to be looking out the window thirty minutes ago when Luke had pulled into his driveway.

Okay, she'd been stalking the window, unable to help herself from looking out. They hadn't decided on a time to meet tonight. They'd just decided that they would talk at some point. She wasn't sure if that meant they would also eat or if they'd watched a movie on TV. Or if they'd have a repeat of last night.

All the butterflies fluttered in Brenna's stomach. "You've already decided, Brenna," she said out loud to herself. "No sex tonight, no matter what." She'd worn her worst bra-and-panties set just to make sure. Things were already moving way too fast between them, and she didn't want to get in over her head. She was leaving this summer so she needed things to slow way down.

Her cell phone buzzed on the coffee table behind her.

What time were you thinking about coming over?

Brenna's entire body lit up. Anytime. Should I bring something? Wine?

She grimaced. What if he didn't want something so intimate? Maybe he wanted to be quick in telling her last night was a mistake. Her phone buzzed with an incoming text.

No, I have wine and steaks to grill. You do like steaks, I hope.

Her foolish heart skipped as she typed her reply. Steaks and wine sound perfect. I'll be right over.

See you soon.

Brenna squealed a little in her empty house. Then she reconsidered her choice of underwear before forcing herself to stick with the plan. She grabbed her keys, closed the door behind her, and cut across her lawn toward Luke's.

"Around back!" he called as she made her way to the front porch. She detoured to the back where Max darted toward her with a single bark. He circled her once and then propped his paws on her thigh, panting with his tongue hanging out.

"Hey, there!" She rubbed Max's head, her hand moving to the area of missing fur where he'd been burned. It didn't seem to hurt him. When she looked up, Luke was watching her. The look in his eyes made her chest ache. She was in so much trouble with this neighbor of hers.

"Want to help?" he asked. "You're the cook after all."

Brenna straightened and climbed the steps of his deck. "I'm good in the kitchen but I'm awful at the grill." She stepped up beside him. "But I don't mind watching and taking notes."

He looked over, his brown eyes locked on her. The way he was looking at her revealed that he had no intention of telling her that last night was a mistake. The way he was looking at her was like a man who remembered what she looked like naked.

"Here's the trick," he said, turning back to the steaks on the grill. "You let them cook until they're done to your liking, and then you take them off."

Brenna watched him turn the steaks. "Oh, is that all there is to it?"

He glanced over. "Shh. Don't tell anyone my secret."

She pretended to zip her lips. "My lips are sealed."

His gaze clung to her mouth, making her breath freeze inside her. "I've been thinking about last night," he said in a low voice.

"Oh?" She swallowed.

He angled his body toward hers. "I was drinking. My judgment was clouded."

Her fluttering heart started to free-fall into her belly.

"Otherwise, I wouldn't have left my keys at the bar. I wouldn't have gotten locked out of my own house. And I wouldn't have spent the night in your bed."

"You weren't that drunk," she said, feeling her defenses rise.

"No, I wasn't drunk at all. I said I'd been drinking. Just enough to let my guard down around you."

"So you regret what happened?" she asked.

Luke just smiled.

Why was he smiling?

"You're putting words into my mouth. I wasn't drunk, and I don't regret anything."

She felt her brow furrow. "You don't?"

"In fact, I've been trying to convince myself to regret it all day but I can't. I enjoyed last night." He gave her a long look, his gaze steady and warm. "Maybe that's all there is to it," he said with a half shrug.

"What does that mean?"

"I have no idea. We said we'd keep things casual. I think that includes not overthinking things too much, including last night."

"Right." She was definitely overthinking things. Maybe last night didn't have to mean anything at all. If they truly were in a no-strings-attached arrangement, there was no reason to even talk about what happened.

Luke stabbed each steak and plopped them onto a plate. Then he picked up the plates and carried them to his table with a view of the creek. Brenna watched as he reached for a bottle of wine, poured them both a glass, and sat down. She did the same.

"Baked potatoes too?" Brenna asked, noticing a dish already at the center of the table. "I'm impressed with your skills, Chief Marini. Or should I say Chef Marini?"

"Which skills would that be?" His eyes seemed to dance as he looked at her.

Heat flooded from her toes up through her body. He was flirting with her and possibly, probably, thinking they were going to have sex again tonight. "I have something to tell you before I lose my nerve."

His eyes stopped dancing, and concern lined his brow. "Okay."

"I'm not staying over tonight. In fact, I think that I should probably stay out here on your deck while I'm here." She braced herself for him to protest, argue, or look at her differently. A no-strings-attached fling in her mind implied that things were strictly physical, and here she was, removing that from the table.

Luke reached for his glass of wine and took a sip. Then he tipped his head back and looked at the sky before returning his gaze to look at her. "Dinner under the stars with a beautiful and smart woman. Sounds like the perfect way to spend a night to me."

* * *

Luke was a hot-blooded male but he was a little relieved at Brenna's decision not to go inside with him. Last night had been incredible but slowing things down and getting to know one another better was a good idea. "Leave the plates. I'll get them later."

Brenna put the plate down. "Okay." She turned to look out on the creek. "Your view is better than mine," she noted. "I'm a little jealous."

Luke followed her gaze. "The view is what sold me on the house."

"Mm. I've always loved this house," Brenna said.

"But it's too big for one man. I wouldn't have bought it if not for this view. It's nice to come home from a bad day and just sit and absorb the beauty of something like this." He glanced over. "It's a piece of heaven on earth."

Brenna smiled. "A taste of heaven, you might say."

"Just like your catering business." He reached out to touch her, unable to resist. They'd agreed to stay outside but they hadn't said anything about keeping their hands to themselves. "How's the plan to sell going?"

"Well, I've met with a Realtor. That's the first step.

Next step is that she'll officially list it, and we'll see who bites." Brenna sighed and looked over at Luke. "The Realtor thinks it'll sell well, whatever that means."

Luke nodded. "That's good." The tension between them crackled, maybe a little too intensely considering they were slowing things down. "So what should we do tonight?"

"Definitely not another drinking game," she said on a laugh. She tipped her head back and looked up at the stars. "I'd suggest stargazing but I don't know anything about the stars."

"Me neither," he admitted. "Some Boy Scout I am."

"Eve and I used to go outside, lie down on a blanket, and watch the stars, waiting for one to shoot across the sky so we could make a wish." Her voice grew quiet as she remembered.

"How old were you?" he asked, glancing over.

"I was fifteen. Which would have made her five. There aren't a lot of things two kids so far apart in age can enjoy together but we both loved doing that."

"What did you wish for?" Luke slipped his hand from under hers and ran the tips of his fingers over her skin, loving the softness of her.

"A little bit of everything," Brenna said. "A fifteen-year-old girl wishes for the love of her life to come sweep her off her feet."

"That's a little early for that," Luke said.

Brenna shook her head. "Nuh-uh. We start dreaming of that from the moment we hear our first fairy tale. When Eve was a fifteen-year-old girl, however, she didn't stargaze and wish for love. All she wanted was a normal life with both parents." Brenna looked back up at the stars. "It just seems so unfair."

"I'll tell you another secret," Luke said. "There is no

normal life, and a lot of kids don't have both parents." He was sure she knew that but right now she seemed to need reminding. "You've given up a lot to make sure she got what she needed." He remembered what Granger had told him about her fiancé. "It's more than enough, Brenna."

"Thanks. Now I'm trying to figure out how to just be her sister again."

"You just told me you two used to stargaze and wish on falling stars together," Luke pointed out. "You seem to remember pretty well."

Brenna sighed. "I'm not sure I could just ask her to lie outside on a blanket with me anymore." A soft laugh tumbled off her lips. "She'd think I was insane. She already does."

"I know my brothers were always my best friends growing up," Luke said, turning to look back up at the sky. "I can still call Nick anytime, day or night, and he'll answer. I know I can tell him anything, and he'll always support me, no matter how stupid and crazy it is. That doesn't mean he always agrees with me. But brothers have your back, no matter what. I'm guessing it's the same for sisters."

"Hmm." From the corner of his eye, he saw Brenna tip her face upward again. "I wish Eve and I could return to being close like that."

"You can. You just got to keep trying and never give up, just like you would with anything you want. Like you're doing by going back to college."

"Some part of me feels selfish for leaving to finish my dream," she confided. "Like I should be here for her, even if I'm letting go. Or I should stay to keep my mom's catering business alive. And Aunt Thelma is getting older. How can I even think about leaving for a year? What if she needs me? She has no other family. Just me and Eve."

"Brenna"—Luke reached for her hand—"you know staying is not what Eve or your mom would want you to do. Or Thelma. Everyone wants you to be happy."

"Everyone?" she asked.

"Including me. But it doesn't matter what everyone wants. What matters is what you want. You have to go after this. No second-guessing. You can't let anything stop you, most of all yourself."

"You're pretty smart, Luke Marini. Not just a pretty face." She winked at him, and something about that gesture did things to him. "Thanks for the pep talk. I needed it." Then she leaned over and kissed the side of his cheek.

"Anytime," he said, turning his face to meet hers while she was still close. Then he brushed his mouth to hers. "Gotta take my own good advice and go after what I want right now."

She giggled softly, leaning into him. "You're easy to make happy."

The opposite was true though. He'd struggled to find true happiness in his adult life. There'd been flashes of it but it wasn't a dominant feeling in his day-to-day life. When he was with Brenna though, the feeling stuck around. Maybe that's why he couldn't seem to get enough of her these days.

* * *

When Luke arrived at the station two days later, the crew was already busy with their jobs. There was no bickering going on. Instead, Luke followed the sound of laughing toward the back bunks. "Something funny?" he asked.

Tim and Ryan straightened when they saw him.

Yeah, being the boss was kind of lonely. "I'm guessing I don't want to know," Luke said, turning away.

"No, that's not it, Chief. We're just looking at some firefighter blunders online. They're pretty funny," Ryan said.

Luke looked back. "Yeah?"

"But we've already taken care of a few things. It was just a quick look," Tim added.

Luke folded his arms over his chest as he turned to face them. "I think I saw those. Did you see the one where the rookie handled the water hose and it knocked him backward into that cactus garden?"

The guys laughed.

"That rookie must've been picking cactus spines from his body for weeks," Tim said.

"Chief Brewer's slip would've been a good one . . . if he hadn't gotten hurt." Ryan blew out a breath. "Yeah, that wasn't funny at all. I feel awful about the wax. Is he still doing okay?"

"He'll be fine," Luke said. "His wife is taking good care of him."

"That makes me feel worse," Ryan said but he was smiling now. "We all know that the chief doesn't like to be fussed over."

"Well, I'm guessing it's long overdue." Luke turned to head back to his office. He had a report that he needed to work on today showing their fire calls for the month. Luke was sure the numbers would be down, which was good for the town but not so much for the station. They needed the calls to justify the need for manpower and equipment.

"See you later, Chief Marini. Don't worry about us," Tim said. "The cell phone is being put away, and I'm about to work on the community fire safety training."

"And I'm going to help him," Ryan said.

Luke turned to look at them. "Sounds like teamwork to me." There was no report to put that on but Chief Brewer would be happy to hear about the positive changes here. It meant Luke had done a lot to clean up the fire station just like he'd been asked to do and that it was running like a well-oiled machine.

* * *

Brenna sat on the edge of her bed, giving herself a moment before succumbing to the morning rush. Then she got up, hit the shower, and plowed through the morning. Halona hadn't been able to meet for coffee at the café so Brenna had gotten her coffee to go and headed back to A Taste of Heaven to prepare for her follow-up meeting with Mrs. Everson. As promised, Nate was tucked away in the office, preferring to do the paper-pushing side of the business rather than deal with the upcoming customer.

Aunt Thelma wasn't working this morning either. She had another doctor's appointment and would be taking the afternoon off too. She'd insisted that it was just routine and there was no reason to worry. Thelma was just getting older. She wouldn't work at the catering business forever.

Brenna took a moment and tidied up. Then the bell rang at the front door, and Mrs. Everson breezed in with a large purse on her arm and a larger hat on top of her head.

"Brenna!" she exclaimed as if she were greeting a long-lost relative. "I'm so excited about this meeting. I could barely sleep a wink last night, debating all the options we might discuss."

Brenna, on the other hand, had spent a portion of the night dreading all the dessert and appetizer options that she and Mrs. Everson might discuss. They'd already had one meeting to finalize the main entrees. "Let's get started, shall we?"

An hour later, Brenna had a headache that made her forehead pound with every movement. Mrs. Everson had changed her mind about Mayor Everson's charity banquet menu at least five times. Then she'd rearranged the plans that Brenna had already put together.

"I was thinking we could offer key lime pie. It's a very popular choice right now."

"Oh no. That won't do. I want something more classic. I think cheesecake is best, don't you?" Mrs. Everson looked up at Brenna.

"If that's what you'd prefer." Brenna resisted rubbing her forehead or pinching the bridge of her nose. She also resisted calling Nate in on the conversation but she needed someone to keep Mrs. Everson in line.

"But what about the gluten-free people in the group? We should have an option for them, shouldn't we?"

"Of course. I can prepare a fruit salad," Brenna offered. "That would be safe for most food allergies and sensitivities."

Mrs. Everson's eyes lit up. "Yes, perfect!... Maybe we should offer a key lime pie after all. Those two options complement each other better, don't you think?"

Brenna shook her head, which only made pain splinter between her eyes. "We can offer all three options if you'd like."

"And maybe we need a fourth option with chocolate. People will be so disappointed if there isn't a choice with chocolate. Can we do that too?"

Heaven help me.

"You can't please everyone," Brenna said with fake cheer. Most of all Mrs. Everson.

Mrs. Everson continued to change her mind back and forth for another half hour before moving on to the next detail.

"Have you arranged for the servers yet?"

Brenna nodded. "I scheduled those after our first meeting." She had a list of people she contracted for events such as these. Most were friends in the community with regular day jobs, who just wanted a way to make extra money every now and then. Brenna had extended the invitation to Allison Winters at the school the other day since she seemed to think the job looked fun.

"And you'll be there to supervise them?" Mrs. Everson asked.

Brenna held her smile even though she'd had this conversation with the older woman a dozen times as well. "Nate or I will stay to make sure the food is okay."

Mrs. Everson grimaced. "Does it have to be Nate?" she asked, dropping her voice to a whisper.

Brenna lowered her brow. "Why not Nate?"

"Well, he's chatty with the guests."

"And that's a bad thing?" Brenna asked.

"Well..." Mrs. Everson's expression pinched. "My son's event is so important. I'd rather the guests be chatting among themselves. Not with the help."

"The help?" Brenna repeated. She'd been called a lot of things in her life but never "the help." It wasn't so much the words as it was the tone in which they were said. Good thing Brenna had learned to bite her tongue a long time ago.

"I only hire help that knows their place," Mrs. Everson went on. "I had a maid once who signed for a package at my door. That wasn't her place, and I let her know it. It's the same with talking to the guests at Brian's event. The help should serve quietly."

Brenna grabbed her pen. "I'll make a note of that and make sure I discuss it with all of my employees," she said. "If Nate helps with the event, I'll tell him that you'd rather he do so silently," Brenna said through her teeth.

Mrs. Everson gave a sheepish smile. "Oh, I hate to complain."

Yeah, right.

"I just want the best for my Brian. I'm so proud of him," Mrs. Everson said like she did every time.

Brenna agreed that Mayor Brian Everson was a good man. His mother should be proud, even if Brenna thought it had nothing to do with Mrs. Everson's parenting.

When the meeting with Mrs. Everson was over, Brenna leaned in the office's doorway and sighed as she watched Nate work. "I'm so glad you love doing that kind of stuff."

"One of the reasons we make such a good team," he said, winking at her. "I'm glad you enjoy working with problem customers."

"I never claimed to enjoy it. I tolerate it. Mrs. Everson was here in full force today. I have a headache."

Nate frowned. "Sorry."

"I owed you, I guess. How's Chris?" They hadn't had much time to discuss their outing the other night. That was mostly because Brenna wanted to avoid telling Nate how she'd ended up spending the night with Luke.

"Good. We should hang out again sometime," Nate suggested.

"If things are good, what do you need me for? I'm a third wheel."

Nate raised a finger. "Our lovable third wheel. We discussed maybe helping you find someone. We're both tired of seeing you single."

Brenna choked on a laugh. "Seriously? I'm your pet project now?"

Nate offered an apologetic expression. "Real pets are too needy. You're perfect for us."

Brenna decided to keep it to herself that she didn't need to be set up. There was something brewing between her and Luke, even if it was only short-term. "I do need your help with something though," she told Nate. She'd been looking for a good time to tell him her plans but there wasn't going to be the perfect moment. Soon there would be a sign in front of the catering business, and she didn't want Nate to be sideswiped. He deserved to know as soon as possible.

"What kind of help?" he asked.

"Well..." She plopped into the chair in front of the desk. "As you know, I've always wanted to be a teacher."

Nate nodded. "Right. And you do amazing with Hannah."

Brenna took a deep breath. "Thank you. The thing is I applied to return to college a few months ago, and I got in. I'm going back to Western University for the second summer session."

Nate blinked quietly across the desk. "Wow. I was not expecting that."

"Sorry to take you by surprise. There's more." Brenna wasn't sure how Nate was going to react. This business probably meant more to him than it did to her. She knew that he loved working at A Taste of Heaven even if he complained about some of the menial tasks. "I'm selling the business."

Nate's jaw dropped. "Selling? Seriously?"

"Yeah. It's time. It's not what I want or what Eve wants."

Nate looked crestfallen suddenly. She hated disappointing him but Luke was right the other night when he said that no one expected her to trade her happiness for theirs. Each person was responsible for their own joy.

"Are you okay?" she asked when he didn't say anything for a long moment.

"Yeah, yeah. Don't worry about me. I'm just a little shocked. And sad, of course. I'm also pretty proud of you. I was guessing you'd never let Eve out of your sight after you caught her drinking the other night."

Brenna pulled back slightly. "What are you talking about?"

"At the Tipsy Tavern. Didn't you see her there?" Nate asked.

Brenna shook her head. "No."

"I saw Luke talking to her and some guy. I thought you knew that our little Eve was drinking underage."

Brenna folded her arms in front of her now. "You saw Luke talking to Eve at the tavern? Are you sure? Maybe it was someone who just looked like her."

"Someone else with long, fiery-red hair like that?" Nate grimaced and held up a hand. "I don't want to be in the middle of this. No sister drama, and definitely no lovers' quarrels." He picked up his pen and pretended to start working on the order list in front of him.

"Are you sure she was drinking?" Brenna asked. "It could've been a soda, right?"

"There was a bottle in front of her. I assumed Luke told you," Nate said when she didn't move. "Otherwise, I would have."

She swallowed hard. "Because you're a good friend and you would never keep something so important from me."

Nate looked up. "You're a good friend. How long have you been keeping the fact that you're moving away and tossing me back into unemployment?" he asked.

Guilt curled in Brenna's belly. "I'm sorry, Nate."

He waved a hand. "I'm sure you had your reasons. Just like Luke probably had his reasons. I'm guessing he was trying to protect you."

"But it's my job to protect Eve."

"I did my fair share of drinking when I was eighteen," Nate pointed out.

"I waited to drink until I was twenty-one and able to buy them myself," Brenna said. "It's illegal. Eve could've gotten hurt. And who was the guy? Did he take her home?" she asked as questions filled her mind. Had the guy taken advantage of her intoxicated sister? And Luke knew and didn't stop it?

"You'll have to ask Eve yourself. Or maybe just let it go," Nate suggested.

Brenna got up and headed toward the door. "I'll be back to tutor Hannah before she gets off school," she called behind her.

"I probably don't need to ask but where are you going?" Nate called from the office.

"To talk to Eve." But first, she was going to lay into Luke.

$\mathcal{C}$HAPTER SIXTEEN

$\mathcal{I}$t was a slick, rainy morning so the SSFD had been busier than the norm. They'd already been on two accident calls. One had been a teenager who took a bend too fast. The driver had walked away without a scratch but her car had been totaled after hitting a tree.

The other accident had been a two-car collision. Both drivers had been taken away by paramedics but they were conscious and talking when Luke had seen them go.

The crew had worked as a team. No one had complained. No one had even needed Luke to tell them what to do. They'd worked smartly and efficiently.

"I want to see you in my office," Luke told Eve as they returned to the station garage and stepped off the engine.

She whirled around and narrowed her eyes at him. "What? Why? Did I do something wrong?"

"I don't know. Did you?" He suppressed a smile as he walked toward his office.

"Well, I need to use the bathroom first if that's okay with you," she called to him.

"Take your time. I'm in no hurry." Although the way this day was going, they might be on another call soon. He walked into his office and sat down behind his desk. Thankfully, he'd packed his lunch because he was starving and didn't fancy going out in this weather to get a bite to eat.

Although the idea of stopping in Brenna's shop sounded nice.

A knock on his closed office door got his attention. He'd told Eve to take her time but he guessed she was eager to know what he wanted to talk about. It wasn't anything bad. He just wanted to tell her what a good job she'd done today. Watching her, no one would've known she was a new firefighter. She was skilled, and he wanted her to know it.

"Come in," he called, pulling his brown-bag lunch to himself. Luke looked up as the door opened, thinking he'd find Eve in front of him.

Instead, Brenna walked in, her mouth pinched tightly.

"I would say this is a nice surprise but you don't look like you're here for a friendly visit," Luke said.

Brenna slammed the door behind her, confirming that suspicion. "I don't appreciate you keeping secrets from me."

Luke tried to think of what she was talking about but nothing came to mind. "What secrets are you referring to?"

"Eve. She was at the Tipsy Tavern the other night, drinking with some guy, and you knew about it. You even spoke to her when I wasn't looking."

"How do you know that?" Luke asked.

"Really? That's what you're worried about? It doesn't matter how I know. I know, and now I want an explanation."

Luke hoped the crew outside couldn't hear Brenna

yelling. "Eve works here. Ryan works here. I handled it as the acting fire chief."

"Ryan is the guy buying her drinks?" Brenna asked.

Maybe Luke shouldn't have revealed that tidbit for Ryan's safety. "I handled it as a work matter," Luke said again.

"She's my sister."

"She's my firefighter." Luke didn't let his gaze waver from Brenna's until tears began to form in her eyes. *No, please don't cry.*

She blew out an exasperated breath and then plopped down in the chair in front of his desk, looking defeated. "Was she drunk?"

"No," Luke said. "She'd only had the one drink, and I ordered them to call someone for a ride. I would never let her or Ryan drive home after drinking."

Brenna's expression softened. "Thank you. Of course you wouldn't. Maybe you made the right call not telling me. I would've flipped out and made a scene if I saw her drinking at the tavern, and that would've just pushed her away even more." Brenna covered her face with one hand. "I really do want to be her sister instead of an overbearing guardian."

Luke got up from his chair and walked around the desk to sit on its edge. "You care about her. No one can fault you for that."

She narrowed her eyes as she looked at him. "You still should've told me after we left the tavern. Or yesterday. I shouldn't have heard it from Nate."

"Nate, huh?" Luke tilted his head.

"He just assumed you would've told me." She stood, the motion bringing her standing only a few inches from him. "Next time, tell me yourself."

"Only if I can wait to get you in private and give you ample time to calm down."

She smiled softly. "Deal."

His gaze dropped to her mouth. He'd only ever kissed her in the privacy of their homes. He couldn't kiss her here but that didn't stop him from thinking about it. "You left work just to come yell at me?"

She leaned in closer. "It seemed like the right thing to do."

"You sure some part of you didn't just want to see me?" he asked. Because he didn't mind seeing her. She'd walked in upset but even so she'd managed to brighten this gray and stormy day.

A knock sounded on his door, and before either Luke or Brenna could respond, the door was pushed open.

"Eve," Brenna said, turning away from Luke. "I didn't know you were on shift today."

Eve looked between Brenna and Luke. "News flash—I don't have to tell you my schedule anymore. What are you doing here?"

Luke pinched the bridge of his nose. He hated secrets and lying and getting in the middle of drama. But the McConnell sisters didn't seem to give him much choice. "I wanted to talk to her," Luke said.

Brenna whipped her head around to look at him, a questioning look in her eye.

"You did? Why?" Eve's green eyes looked suspicious.

"Well, Chief Brewer said the station used to plan fun events a couple times a year. I'm planning a little get-together for the SSFD. A picnic to boost morale and get to know each other a little better."

Brenna's lips parted. "Oh, wow. I remember my dad bringing us along to the firehouse picnics. We got to know the crew Dad worked with and their families. They became like our families in a way."

"I remember too." Eve placed her hands on her hips. "But what does Brenna have to do with that? She's not a firefighter."

"No, but she's a caterer, and I was thinking about asking her to help us with the picnic." Luke met Brenna's eyes. He hadn't planned on asking Brenna. He was going to ask the volunteers to take care of food preparations. But this was better. This would allow Brenna to support the fire station, which now included her sister.

"Why didn't you just walk next door and ask her tonight?" Eve asked. "Why'd she have to come here?"

Eve had so many questions.

"I could've done that, I guess. But this is a work matter," he told her, just like he'd told Brenna a few minutes earlier. "And as a work matter, I think it's best for her to come here."

"I was in the area," Brenna added.

Eve looked skeptical. "You can say no if you want. I know you're busy this time of year, and the fire station is probably the last place you want to show your support. Now that I'm working here, that is."

"That's not fair. Dad worked at the SSFD. I love this place. And I'm getting used to the idea of you working here." Brenna slid her gaze to Luke and then back to Eve. "I would love to help out with the event. The fire station does so much for the community. It's the least I can do."

"Really?" Eve asked, her arms dropping down by her sides.

Brenna nodded. "I think it's a great idea. When are you thinking of having it?" she asked Luke.

"I'd love for Chief Brewer to be able to attend. Maybe that weekend before he returns. Is that too soon?"

Brenna nibbled on her lower lip. "No. I have an event to cater for Mayor Everson this weekend, but after that, I'm open for big events until early summer. I can do that."

"Thank you. I'm sure we can do a potluck, and each family can bring a dish or two to share. It's just the big stuff I'll need help with. Figuring out how to handle the drinks and maybe some of the main food items."

"That sounds simple enough," Brenna said.

Luke nodded. "It doesn't have to be fancy. This is about fun and family. Maybe we can discuss it more later."

"Yeah." Brenna nodded quickly. "Sounds good."

Eve cleared her throat. "Perfect. Anyway, you said you wanted to talk to me, Chief?"

"Right. I did."

Eve slid Brenna a pointed glance. "Unless you two have more to talk about?"

"Oh. No." Brenna pulled her purse up on her shoulder. "I need to get back to the shop and help Nate. Hannah will be getting off school soon, and I'm supposed to tutor her on some math." Brenna started to head out and then turned back. "Have a good rest of your shift," she told Eve.

"Do you mean that?" Eve asked.

"Of course I do." She glanced over at Luke, who gave her a subtle nod.

"We can discuss the picnic tonight maybe," he said.

"Yeah. I'd love that." Brenna waved and then closed his office door behind her.

Eve cocked her head as she faced him. "Please tell me you and my sister aren't dating."

"Why would you ask that?"

"She's nervous around you. Brenna is not a nervous

person. That means she likes you." Eve stared at him, seemingly waiting for him to answer.

"We aren't dating," he said. It only felt like they were. "I asked you in here to tell you that I thought you did a great job today, and it didn't go unnoticed."

Eve's face lit up. "Really? I thought you were going to ream me out for something I did wrong."

"From what I saw, you did everything right. Good job. I'll make sure Chief Brewer knows too. I'm stopping in to see him this afternoon."

"Thanks. Is that all?" Eve asked.

"That's it."

Eve didn't budge. Her expression suddenly turned sheepish. "Did you, um, tell my sister about the whole drinking thing?"

Luke swallowed. "*I* didn't tell her," he said honestly. "But you should. I wasn't the only one at the tavern who saw you. She'll hear about it one way or another... You can talk to her, you know. She was your age once too."

"Ten years ago. She's forgotten how it felt to be eighteen," Eve muttered. She said it as if twenty-eight was ancient.

"You'd be surprised," Luke said. "Try her."

Eve frowned at him. "I don't want to be difficult. I know she's doing her best."

Luke waited quietly, feeling that Eve was choosing her words carefully.

"It's just one moment she was my cool, big sister who came home from college on the weekends. The next she's a completely different person, and she's ordering me around, telling me what Mom and Dad would want if they were here." Eve stared at the wall behind Luke. "It felt like I didn't just lose my mom and dad. I lost my big sister too."

"You felt betrayed?" Luke asked. "By Brenna?"

Eve blinked and dropped her gaze back to him. "I felt abandoned by her, even though she dropped everything to take care of me. I know that sounds crazy but that's how it was."

"It kind of makes sense," Luke said, surprised that he understood.

"Anyway, I know she's trying, and I know I probably look like an immature brat on the outside."

Luke wobbled his head back and forth. "Maybe a little. But I learned a long time ago not to draw conclusions on things I know nothing about."

Eve smiled back at him. "Thanks."

"For what?" Luke asked.

"I don't know. Listening. Understanding. Hiring and firing me. And hiring me back." Her smile grew wider. "And for moderating between me and my sister. I know you asked her to help with the picnic for me."

Luke laughed lightly.

Then Eve pointed a finger. "I also know that you asked her to help because you wanted her there too. Deny it if you want but you have a little thing for Brenna. I don't think you two would be a good match though."

Luke pinched his brow. "Why not?"

Eve shrugged. "Well, because she's leaving, for one. But even if she were staying, it wouldn't work. She could never date a firefighter long-term. She worries too much, and when she worries, she's a complete mess. She'd drive you nuts."

Luke shook his head. He supposed this prediction should make him feel better but it didn't. And he didn't buy it anyway. If Brenna were staying, it'd work between them.

If she worried too much, he'd calm her down. And if she drove him nuts, he'd just kiss her until they were driving each other nuts in a completely different way.

Eve turned to leave but stopped and pointed at him again. "Don't tell Brenna all that stuff I just said about me and her, okay? I don't want her to feel bad."

"I won't tell. It's between you and her," he said. And he definitely wouldn't tell Brenna that Eve thought they were a bad match.

* * *

Brenna had expected the knock on her door this evening. She and Luke had unfinished business from this afternoon. She'd showered and changed clothes in anticipation of seeing him tonight, which was maybe overkill considering they didn't have any official plans.

She opened the door and gave him a once-over. "Hi."

"You're not cooking dinner, are you?"

She cocked her head to one side. "Not yet, but I was thinking about it. I'm starving, and I missed lunch today."

"How could you miss lunch? You're surrounded by food all day," Luke said.

"Food for other people. You'd be surprised how often I miss a meal." And if she acted on her impulse to pull Luke inside her home and shut the door behind him, she might never get a meal today.

"I missed lunch too. It was a busy day. Then this beautiful woman stormed into my station, and I couldn't focus on anything afterward."

She gave him a shy smile. "Sorry about that."

"I'm not." He stared at her for a moment. "I was thinking about going out for pizza but then I'd have to eat it all by myself." He rubbed the side of his face. "But you're probably a pizza snob, right?"

Brenna leaned into the door frame. She could invite him inside but it was a nice night and the threshold between them was keeping her needy hands in check. "There's one pizza place in town that no one can hold a candle to. Not even me."

"Yeah?"

"Joe's Pizzeria. Joe offers the full Italian pizzeria experience."

"I've been in Sweetwater Springs for five months. How is it possible that I haven't discovered this place yet?"

She shrugged. "Joe's Pizzeria doesn't deliver. I'm guessing the guys at the station only want a pizza that can be delivered."

"That's true," Luke agreed.

"Joe's is at the end of Red Oak Street."

"Yeah, I know where that is. It's all the way across town but I have a craving that needs to be curbed."

Brenna grinned. "That's what you get for asking a caterer her thoughts on pizza. I do make my own pizza but it's an ordeal that you probably don't want to hear about."

"Another time maybe. Or"—he pulled his keys out of his pocket—"you can tell me on the way to Red Oak Street."

Brenna tilted her head, making her hair fall against her cheek. "Are you asking me out, Chief Marini?" Except for a dance at the Tipsy Tavern, they'd kept their relationship here on Blueberry Creek.

"Well, I can't eat an entire pizza by myself."

"You don't have to. He sells it by the slice."

Luke frowned. "If you don't want to be seen with me in public, just say so," he said in a teasing tone.

Brenna loved the easy banter between them. "What will the folks of Sweetwater Springs think?"

Luke reached for her hand. "I don't know about the women but the men will think that I'm the luckiest guy in town."

Her heart melted just a little. "Aw. How could I ever say no to that?"

"You couldn't, I hope."

She smiled. "Such a charmer. Okay, then. Pizza at Joe's sounds good."

"If it isn't, I'll be bugging you to make one for us another time."

Us. That word struck her. They'd spent a lot of time together lately. So much that they were starting to feel like an *us*.

"Let me just grab my bag." She turned back inside and slipped on some shoes. *Slow down, Brenna.* This thing between them was short-lived, and she didn't want to leave town with a broken heart. She couldn't keep Luke even if she could already tell that leaving him was going to be much harder than she'd anticipated.

She grabbed her bag, locked up, and met Luke at his truck, where he opened the door for her.

"I bet your family makes great pizza," she said once he was seated behind the steering wheel.

Luke chuckled as he reversed out of the driveway and headed toward the other side of town. "My mom is the pizza snob. She'd be insulted to know that we were going to eat pizza anywhere but at her house tonight."

Brenna had heard Luke talk about his brothers but never anyone else in his family. She suddenly wanted to know everything about him.

"Mom's pizza is great but her lasagna can't be touched,"

he continued, his gaze sliding across the seat. "Watch out. Best in the area."

"I love lasagna."

"It's my dad's favorite so she makes it at least once a week for him. It's one of the things I miss most about living in my hometown."

"Sweetwater Springs isn't too far from Whispering Pines."

"Not really," Luke agreed.

"I get a lot of business from that area," Brenna noted.

"Yeah? Interesting. It looks like you're already busier than you can handle. I was half expecting you to turn the fire station picnic down when I popped the idea."

"I don't turn down friends," she said.

"Friends, huh?" He glanced over.

"Eyes on the road. I don't want to spend my first date with you in the ditch."

Luke faced forward, a large smile spreading through his cheeks. She studied his side profile and the shadows that danced across his face as he drove.

"I spent a date like that once," he said.

"Really? Did you get a second date?"

Luke shook his head. "Nope. Her dad wouldn't allow it, and I don't blame him."

Brenna laughed. "Well, I can tell you that my father would have loved you."

"You think?" Luke asked.

A thick lump formed in Brenna's throat unexpectedly. Luke was talking about his family so it was only natural that she'd bring up hers too, but she didn't expect the topic to come with such emotion. "He always told me that I couldn't date any of the firefighters on his crew."

"I'm confused. That means he wouldn't have liked the idea of me and you spending time together."

Brenna shrugged a shoulder. "I'm older now so I think he would've liked the idea. My dad was a firefighter through and through. Brave and focused on the well-being of everyone around him, no matter what. You remind me of him." Brenna looked over. "He would've loved you."

Luke nodded. "And what about your mom?"

Brenna laughed. "She sounds a lot like your mom. She would've cooked for you. And because you're a single man, living alone, she would've stocked your freezer with precooked meals."

"Wow." He reached for her hand. "Your parents sound great."

There was the emotion again. "Yeah. They were."

"I'm sorry I won't get to meet them," Luke said softly.

Brenna didn't even try to hide the fact that her eyes were tearing up. "Me too. I promise I'm not going to be a downer tonight though. I'm not sure where this is coming from."

Luke squeezed her hand. "You can be whatever you want tonight. I haven't met a side of Brenna McConnell that I don't like yet."

"You keep saying things like that to me and you might get lucky after dinner," she teased, trying to return the mood to flirty and playful.

Luke squeezed her hand. "I'm already the luckiest guy in Sweetwater Springs, remember?"

* * *

Luke couldn't take his eyes off Brenna.

She laughed at something he'd said. Then she reached

for a napkin to dab at some pizza sauce on the corner of her mouth. "Messy but delicious, right?"

Luke picked up his own slice. "Almost as good as my mom's. I'll be hitting this place up once a week now, and it's all your fault."

She laughed again, back to the lighthearted woman she seemed to be most often. He didn't mind the stormy side of her that got upset about her sister or emotional about her parents though. Or the silly side that danced in the kitchen.

"I'll have to stow away in your truck and come along every time you come to eat here," she said.

He reached for his soda and took a sip. "It's nice for other people to cook for you for a change, right?"

Brenna sipped from her Coke. "I rarely get out to restaurants, unless you count the Sweetwater Café."

He was glad he could take her here tonight. "Eve looked surprised that you agreed to support the SSFD."

Brenna pointed a finger across the table. "I think you planned that."

"Truthfully, it just happened." He lifted his slice of pizza and let it hover in front of his mouth as he spoke. "And the request was partly selfish on my part. I'm getting used to having you around."

She gave him a thoughtful look, and he wondered if she was thinking about the fact that she wouldn't be around for much longer. For some reason, the mood tonight kept wanting to swing to an emotional one.

She pinched off a piece of her pizza crust, clearing her throat slightly. "I bet your family misses having you around."

"Mom calls a couple times a week," he told her. "As long as she knows I'm eating well and have a roof over my head, she's happy. Dad usually wants to hear about what happened on the job when we talk."

Brenna smiled. "Not a lot happens in Sweetwater Springs, I'm afraid."

"I embellish the tales for his sake."

This made her laugh, which was his intention. "When I spoke to him the other day, I told him about the kitchen fire at the local catering business."

Brenna's brown eyes widened. "You didn't," she said with a small gasp.

"No, I didn't," he admitted. "But that's one I can build up for him. The blaze from that French bread nearly scorched the entire town."

Brenna giggled. They talked and laughed some more as they ate. Then they played tug-of-war for the last piece and finally decided to split it. She argued just for a moment when he picked up the bill too but this was a date, and dates didn't pay in his book.

The sun was down behind the mountains as they left the restaurant and drove back toward Blueberry Creek.

"Good thing you live right next door because I'm tired tonight," he said. It wasn't exactly true. He was just building up his excuse for dropping her off at her doorstep and not going in. He didn't intend to invite her inside his home either. She'd told him the other night that she wanted to take a step back and slow things down physically, and he assumed that was true tonight as well.

"Me too." She gave way to a yawn. "And I have to wake early tomorrow because I promised Halona I'd meet her at the Sweetwater Café."

"What will you two talk about?"

"Probably you," she said, winning a look from him. He tore his gaze from her and pinned it back to the road.

"So my ears will be itching tomorrow morning?" he asked.

"The saying is that your nose will be itching," she corrected.

"Maybe my town says it differently." He pulled his truck into her driveway.

"You could've just parked in your driveway. I can walk across our lawns."

"I can take you to your doorstep." He parked and pushed open his truck door. Then he walked around to open her door for her. They climbed the steps, and she pulled out her keys, fumbling awkwardly for the right one before turning it in the lock.

"Tonight was fun," she said, turning to look at him.

"Yeah."

She did that thing where she looked at him and appeared to be waiting for him to do or say something. "You're going to kiss me good night, right?" She rolled her lips together, wetting them in the process.

His gaze pulled down to notice their soft, rose-colored perfection. "Good night, Brenna," he said before dipping his head and lowering his lips to hers in a kiss that left him wanting more.

"Good night, Luke." Then she stepped inside, leaving him standing on her porch alone.

They were taking things slow but his racing heart had somehow missed the message.

$\mathcal{C}$HAPTER SEVENTEEN

$\mathcal{L}$uke was once again standing on Chief Brewer's porch. Since the chief had gone on medical leave two weeks ago, Luke had been trying to stop in at least a couple of times a week to update him on what was going on at the fire station.

"Come on in, Luke," Mrs. Brewer said, opening the front door for him. "He's in the living room having coffee. Would you like some?"

"No, thank you." Luke followed her down the hall toward the large room in the back where he usually found Chief Brewer lying down on the couch. Today he was sitting up in a leather recliner.

"Hey, Luke. I was hoping you'd stop in today."

Luke took a seat on the couch. "You're looking great, sir."

"Feeling great too," the chief said.

"Does that mean you'll be coming back early?" Luke asked, feeling a little hopeful and also a little disappointed at the idea. He'd only been acting chief for a short time but he was finally in the groove.

"Nah. The doc said one month, and I'm going to take it in full. A week ago, I might have jumped at the chance to get back to work but I'm starting to enjoy myself. I read a book for fun the other day. That hasn't happened in over a decade."

Luke noted the suspense novel on the chair beside Chief Brewer. "Good. You deserve the time off."

"Nancy deserves it too. We've watched a few movies together. And I've been able to get up and take a small hike through the woods every day for the last week. She comes along, and we talk. It's been good for us."

"They say things happen for a reason," Luke said.

"Maybe so. I've always been stubborn so perhaps it took a back injury to knock some sense into me."

"Well, don't worry about things at the SSFD. We're doing just fine." Luke told the chief about the motor vehicle accidents this week and how the crew had worked together. He left out finding Eve and Ryan drinking at the Tipsy Tavern. That issue was taken care of, as were most at the station for now. "And Brenna has agreed to help out with the semiannual picnic that we're reimplementing."

Chief Brewer's eyes lit up. "You're organizing a picnic?"

"You said the station used to have one a couple times a year. I think it's time we get back to that tradition. It'll be good for morale."

The chief chuckled. "And Brenna is catering? The department doesn't have that kind of money to put into something like that."

"She's doing it for free," Luke told him. "And it's not a full catering job. We're going to do a potluck and have everyone bring a favorite dish to share. Brenna and I are going to handle a few big dishes together. More her than me since I'm not that good in the kitchen," Luke added with a laugh.

"I see." Chief Brewer scratched his lower chin. "So how long have you two been seeing each other?"

Luke looked down at his hands for a moment. "It's not like that."

"So you're not dating?" Chief Brewer asked.

"We're spending time together but it's not serious."

"Uh-huh. Well, since her father's not around to give you a hard time, I guess that job lands on me."

Luke looked up and narrowed his eyes. "You don't want me to see Brenna?"

"I didn't say that. Are you going to treat her well?"

"We're barely dating," Luke said. "But I can promise that I would never hurt Brenna."

Chief Brewer gave him a stern look. "If you do, you'll be polishing the engines for the next year. How's that for giving you a hard time?"

"Sounds like cruel and unusual punishment to me," Luke joked.

"Good. Then we understand each other." The chief folded his arms in front of his broad chest. "So when is this picnic you two are planning?"

"The weekend before you come back. We're having it at Sweetwater Springs Park. I've already set it up. Families are invited too, of course. And the volunteer firefighters."

"Just like the old days. I love the idea," Chief Brewer said. "Good job, Luke."

Luke looked down at his hands again because it meant a lot knowing his chief thought he'd done well at the task he was given. "Thank you, sir."

"Any problems to discuss or have you put everything and everyone in their place?"

"No station is perfect but I've got things under control. Just enjoy the rest of your time off." Luke stood and shook Chief Brewer's hand. Then he said goodbye to Mrs. Brewer and drove back toward the station to finish out his shift.

Things were quiet when he arrived. He guessed Eve was completing some online trainings he'd asked her to do. Ryan was probably tinkering with something in the back.

Luke bypassed his office and went looking for them to update the crew on Chief Brewer's status. As he walked, he heard a giggle from the kitchen and walked in that direction, stopping in the doorway.

Eve was sitting on the kitchen table, and Ryan stood in front of her, his mouth only an inch from hers. Eve giggled again as Ryan whispered something that Luke couldn't hear.

Luke cleared his throat. "Ah-hem. Am I interrupting something?"

Ryan looked at him but took his time stepping backward. He was showing Luke more respect lately but he still had issues with authority.

Eve placed her hands against Ryan's chest to push him away faster. "This is not how it looks."

"It looks like you two were about to start making out at work," Luke said dryly.

"Then it is what it looks like," Ryan said with his usual sarcasm.

Eve swatted him.

Luke took a deep breath. He'd just gotten through telling Chief Brewer that the station was running smoothly.

That the crew's work ethic had improved and the overall environment was much more professional.

He looked between the two lovebirds and sighed. "Do whatever you're going to do," he finally told them. "I can't stop you. Just don't do it here, okay? When you're on duty, you're professional."

"So you're not going to yell at us?" Eve asked.

Luke frowned. "Have I ever yelled at any member of the crew?"

"No." She shook her head. "Not even when you fired me."

"Then I'm not going to start now." He turned to leave but then faced them again. "Next time I catch you doing that kind of stuff on the job though, you'll be polishing engines for the next year. Got it?" he asked, stealing Chief Brewer's line.

Eve nodded quickly. "Yes, sir."

Ryan seemed unfazed by the threat. "Got it."

Luke narrowed his eyes. "Good." As he walked away, he felt a little bit of pride. He'd handled that well. He was getting good at this leadership thing.

* * *

On Saturday night, Brenna scanned the large banquet-size room where Mayor Everson usually held his political and charitable events. She'd spent most of the week preparing for this event, and she'd been up since three this morning cooking. Nate and Aunt Thelma had come in around seven and had joined in the efforts.

"Relax. Tonight will go off without a hitch," Nate said. "Then you and I will high-five each other and go home."

"And hopefully Mrs. Everson won't drop by with complaints tomorrow." She knew that was probably a futile hope. Mrs. Everson always stopped in the next day with a list of minor things that could've been better. "Thanks for asking Chris to join us tonight. Aunt Thelma was exhausted after cooking all day."

"He was happy to help," Nate said.

Brenna had solicited help from Halona and Allison Winters as well. "I didn't dare ask Eve this time. She would've taken the request as me trying to get her to leave the fire station."

"And you've given up on that? For real?" Nate asked, suspicion heavy in his tone.

Brenna shrugged. "Yeah, I have. I'm working on following my own dreams now."

Nate nodded with approval. "I'm proud of you. I even admire you."

She poked her elbow into his ribs. "Stop it. You're making me blush."

They stared out at the room of people, all seated at small round tables with white lacy tablecloths, waiting for their dinner and Mayor Everson's speech. Tonight's event would help fund the Everson's Mentor Match program, which they'd started last year to connect outstanding members of the community to a child who might need a good role model.

"Don't look now," Nate said, leaning in close enough for Brenna to hear him.

She turned to look at what he was referring to.

"I said don't look," Nate grunted.

She slid her gaze to him. "Is it just me or does Mrs. Everson look unhappy?"

"Always," he muttered.

Brenna inspected Mrs. Everson's body language. Her arms were folded tightly at her chest, and the frown she was wearing was growing deeper by the second. "No, she's definitely more unhappy than usual right now. And here she comes." Brenna straightened and pretended to look like she was anxiously awaiting her next task.

"Brenna, there you are!" Mrs. Everson said. "I've been looking everywhere for you. For a moment, I thought you'd bailed on this very important event."

Brenna took a small breath, keeping her happy hostess face on. "I would never back out on the night of an event. We have the appetizers you picked out set up along the wall for those who can't wait for their meals." She gestured at the large variety of hors d'oeuvres for attendees to snack on. "And the plates of filet mignon and stuffed eggplant are about to be carried to the tables."

Mrs. Everson's brow furrowed. "I thought I asked for roast beef."

"No. You considered that option but changed your mind," Brenna reminded her, still maintaining a cheerful tone of voice.

Mrs. Everson shook her head. "I could have sworn I went with roast beef."

Brenna bit her tongue. "I can show you the paperwork that you signed and agreed to at our initial consultation if you'd like."

Mrs. Everson waved a hand. "Oh, that won't be necessary. I trust you, dear."

Could've fooled me.

"Is there anything else you need, Mrs. Everson?" Nate asked, interrupting their conversation. Usually he shied away when Mrs. Everson was around but Brenna appreciated him sticking by her side this time.

The mayor's mother turned her gaze to him. "Oh, I didn't see you there, Nathan."

Nate's jawline tensed. "I was standing here the entire time."

"Yes, I suppose you were." She smiled but it was obviously insincere and didn't reach her eyes. Mayor Everson's mother could be so difficult to deal with.

"Would you care for some punch while we wait?" Brenna asked, saving Nate right back before he said something he shouldn't.

Mrs. Everson's eyes widened. "Punch? Oh, that sounds delightful. I don't remember asking for that either."

"Well, you did, and it's over there. Feel free," Brenna said, her tone of voice losing its cheer.

"Yes, I think I will." Turning, Mrs. Everson headed to the table where Brenna's watermelon punch was set up. It had actual chunks of watermelon. She'd cut them up and marinated them last night before bed.

"I'm never working another job for Mrs. Everson again," Nate declared when she was out of earshot. "I guess that's one positive outcome of you selling the business."

Brenna formed a steeple with her hands in front of her chest. "Thank you for being here tonight. I couldn't do this without you."

He slid his gaze over. "You're welcome, and yes, you could. It just wouldn't be as much fun."

Brenna pulled out her phone and glanced at the time. "I guess it's time to start serving." She turned and headed toward the kitchen, feeling Nate follow behind her.

Half an hour later, after everyone had been served their meal, Mayor Everson took the stage with his wife, Jessica, and they spoke about the Mentor Match program, offering the crowd a few stories from the winter pilot efforts.

"Maybe I should be a mentor one day," Brenna whispered to Halona, who stood beside her in the back of the room now. She'd helped set up the floral arrangements in the room and then had stayed on to help with the catering. "After I get back from college."

Halona frowned. "I can't believe I'm going to have to go through a whole year without you. Who will I drink coffee with?"

"Your future husband, maybe?" Brenna suggested on a laugh. But the thought of being replaced as a coffee buddy stung.

Halona shook her head. "Alex drinks black coffee alone. And he prefers to be completely quiet while he drinks it."

Brenna giggled. "He sounds like a very serious coffee drinker."

"He is...Is that Mrs. Everson smiling?" Halona asked then. "Or are my eyes playing tricks on me?"

Brenna inspected her client closely, feeling her eyes widen in surprise. "She *is* smiling. That's so weird because she was already complaining when I spoke to her before the dinner was served. Then I sent her off to get some punch."

"She's gone back to that punch bowl several times. Must be good punch," Halona said before gasping softly. She covered her mouth with one hand. "Oh no."

Brenna glanced over. "What?"

"Janice Murphy is here tonight, right?"

Brenna nodded. "I think so. Why?"

"Janice Murphy," Halona said again. "Alex had to threaten jail time last summer because she spiked the beverage at an event, and it wasn't the first time either. For some reason, she likes to add her own not-so-secret ingredient at these social gatherings."

"You think she spiked the punch at Mayor Everson's charity event? She wouldn't do that, would she?" Brenna asked in growing horror.

Halona shrugged. "Mrs. Everson is tipsy for sure. I mean, look at her. She's dancing in place and there's not even any music playing."

Brenna watched Mrs. Everson shake her hips as her son delivered a speech. "No, no, no. This is a disaster." Brenna sprinted over to the mayor's mother. "Mrs. Everson?" she said, stepping up beside the older woman. "How are you doing? Everything okay?"

Mrs. Everson offered up a delightful smile, so much more sincere than the one she'd had for Nate earlier. "Oh yes, sweetheart. This is the best event you've ever done for us. Everything is wonderful. Just perfect."

Yep. Mrs. Everson was definitely drinking spiked punch. Hopefully, no one else had gotten a good taste of it yet or Brenna would have a lot of explaining to do.

* * *

Four hours later, after serving, cleaning, and packing up her supplies, Brenna breathed a sigh of relief as she pulled into her driveway and cut the engine. Mayor Everson's charity event had been a success, despite having to pour the punch down the drain and having Chief of Police Alex Baker threaten Janice Murphy with jail time again. Brenna also had to sober Mrs. Everson up without the mayor's mother even realizing that she was halfway intoxicated.

Thankfully, Nate and Chris were able to convince Mrs. Everson that she looked far too tired to drive, and they'd gotten her to agree to let a friend take her home. Overall, it was an eventful but successful night.

Brenna glanced next door. The lights were still on at Luke's, even though it was past midnight. She got out of her car and started to head inside her house but Luke's voice called out to her.

"You're home late," he said from his back deck.

She headed in his direction, petting Max's head when he ran up to greet her. "Tonight was Mayor Everson's Mentor Match charity event. I can't believe he didn't rope you into going."

Luke's chuckle carried on the night air, and she was drawn to it just like Janice Murphy was to her petty crimes. "He asked but I have my hands full with the station right now. Plus, I did it in the pilot round."

"I'm surprised he asked someone who was new in town," Brenna said as she approached.

"Chief Brewer volunteered me. He wanted someone from the SSFD to be involved but he didn't want to do it himself. He said he was too old to be chasing kids."

Brenna laughed as she climbed his deck steps. "Stargazing again?" she asked.

He pulled his gaze from the dark sky and looked at her. "Waiting for you, actually."

Warm tingles traveled up her body from her toes to her racing heart, which skipped like a rock across Blueberry Creek. "Why are you waiting for me?"

He gestured to the chair next to his. "Thought you might want a nightcap. Unless you're too tired."

"I'm exhausted," she said, plopping down in the chair beside him anyway. "But a nightcap sounds lovely."

He reached for a bottle on the deck table and poured them both a glass, pushing one toward her. "How was the event?"

"Good. There was a lot of interest in the program, a lot of donations, and Mayor Everson's mom got drunk and started dancing in the corner of the banquet room."

Luke nearly choked on a sip of his drink. He coughed as he set his glass down and lifted a subtle brow at her. "That sounds like an interesting story."

"Don't tell anyone. It's a secret. Mrs. Everson doesn't even know she was drunk so let's keep it between us."

"We're sharing secrets now?" he asked. "Things must be getting pretty serious."

Brenna knew he was just joking but some part of it felt true. Her feelings were plunging deeper every moment she spent with him. "I've done serious before," she said. "I'm not up for doing it again right now. Someday, maybe."

Luke reached for her hand, the touch as arousing as it was soothing. "Granger told me you were engaged at one point."

Brenna swallowed. "Gossip never dies in Sweetwater Springs."

"Your fiancé left because of Eve?"

Brenna laughed dryly. "Oh, that's the story you got. That's the one most people around here have heard but I don't think it was that simple." She tipped her face up to the night sky, imagining that one star was winking back at her. "The real version is that he left because he didn't love me enough to stay. When I moved back to Sweetwater Springs, he stayed behind for his job. We did the long-distance thing for a while but he became frustrated. He said I wasn't there for him and he needed more."

"The guy sounds like a jerk," Luke said.

Brenna slid her gaze over. "The funny thing is he wasn't. He was a nice guy. Smart, funny, good-looking. Mr. Perfect. He just wasn't my Mr. Perfect."

"Do you wish he'd stayed?" Luke asked.

"No," she said quickly. "I've asked myself that question enough times to know that answer. If he would've stayed,

I don't think we would've been happy. Looking back, we weren't really happy together in the first place. We were just comfortable, and I guess when Eve fell into my lap...well, he became less comfortable."

Brenna looked out into the darkness. It was a beautiful night. Not one to waste on past regrets. It was a night to focus on the here and now.

"So, no plans to run away and get married anytime soon?" Luke asked, his tone casual.

She took a sip from her glass. She'd wanted a glass of wine at the charity banquet but she didn't allow herself or her team to drink on the job. Now she savored the bittersweet taste of the wine on her tongue. "My plan for the time being is to finish college and get a job at a school somewhere. Hopefully back here." She glanced over at him, some part of her hoping he would still be here when she came home. She knew better than to think he'd wait for her but maybe another woman wouldn't come along and catch his interest.

Luke lifted his glass once more and took a healthy sip. "You don't need to know everything up front. All you need to know is what you want in the moment." He leaned toward her, pinning her with his gaze. "So what is it you want in this moment, Brenna?"

"You," she said simply.

His gaze narrowed. "You want me to do what? I don't want to misunderstand anything."

She reached for his glass and set it on the table. "I'm pretty sure you're not misunderstanding."

"I thought we were taking things slow."

"We were," she said. "Past tense. Unless, of course, you have objections." She watched his throat constrict as he swallowed.

"No objections here. You're the one setting the pace." He continued to watch her. "Are you sure?"

"I'm sure," she said, before kissing his mouth, her body revving from zero to sixty in half a heartbeat.

"Next question," he said. "My place or yours?"

CHAPTER EIGHTEEN

Luke clung to sleep until he felt the sensation of skin brushing over his. He opened his eyes and found Brenna lying on the opposite side of the bed watching him.

"This is a nice way to wake up," he whispered, the sound of his voice still raspy from sleep. He lifted an arm and ran his hand along her bare side, unable to resist touching her.

"I've been awake for an hour already. I didn't want to wake you."

"So you've just been staring at me?" he asked.

She shook her head shyly. "No, I've been mostly lying here thinking. And I texted Nate to make sure he was going to open the shop."

"All that while I was asleep?" He trailed his index finger over the curve of her hip. "What were you thinking about?"

"This." She snuggled in and brushed a kiss against his lips.

"Funny, I was thinking about the same thing. I wish I

could stay under these covers with you all day but I have to get to the station."

She pulled back and frowned. "But it's Sunday."

"I have to go check on some things but after that I was planning on driving to Whispering Pines to have lunch with my family. Mom usually makes a meal after church."

Brenna propped her body up on one elbow. "That sounds nice."

"It'd be nicer if you came along. You've never tasted Italian food like my mom makes. And she always makes too much." Luke had no idea what he was doing right now. Taking a woman home to meet his parents was serious, and the exact opposite of what he was trying to do with Brenna. He couldn't stand the thought of not being with her on his day off though. "They don't bite—I promise."

Brenna looked completely taken aback. "You want me to meet your parents?"

"It's not a big deal," he clarified.

Disappointment flashed in her honey-colored eyes.

"I mean, I guess it is but don't let it scare you off. All I know is that I want to spend the day with you. What do you say?"

"I say I want to spend the day with you too. And authentic Italian food is too good to pass up."

He kissed her, lingering longer every time their lips met. If he didn't pull away now, he'd never leave this bed. "I'll be back in a couple hours."

"I'll be ready and waiting," she said with an easy smile. Her hair was rumpled from the bed they'd shared. She wore no makeup, and she'd never looked more gorgeous in his eyes.

His mom was going to flip when he showed up with a woman for Sunday lunch. She was also going to fall in love with Brenna immediately; he had no doubt in his mind about that. They both had similar personalities. His mom, like Brenna, was completely self-sacrificing, especially when it came to her children. Also like Brenna, she was one of the most giving women he knew.

Luke had thought dating another neighbor was a bad idea because he'd never get any space and might feel suffocated. But the challenge with living next door to Brenna was that he couldn't seem to stay away. He could see her anytime he wanted, and that seemed to be *all* the time.

* * *

Nerves wound tightly around Brenna's abdomen like a bride's corset, making it hard to take a deep breath as they drew closer to Luke's parents' house.

He looked over and reached for her hand as he drove. "Relax."

"I've never been good at meeting the parents," she said, turning to look out the window. Whispering Pines was a scenic mountain town much like Sweetwater Springs but it was better known for its ski lifts than its scenic and touristy locales.

"Have you gone home with dates to meet the parents a lot?" Luke asked.

"No. Just with my ex-fiancé. I grew close to his parents. Thought of them as my second family." She turned and looked across the seat at Luke. "Give me a fallback subject."

"A what?"

"A topic that, if I have nothing to say, I can bring up and your mom will take the bait and do all the talking."

Luke chuckled. "This is where you two will get along

famously. She loves to cook. Get her talking about food, and she'll never stop."

And that was where everybody was wrong about Brenna. She didn't exactly love to cook; she was just good at it. That was a secret she told no one. What caterer didn't enjoy preparing food?

Luke turned his truck onto a narrow road and drove slowly past a string of houses guarded by greenery. Then he turned into the driveway of a small ranch-style home with wood siding. "This is it."

"This is the home where you grew up?" she asked without thinking.

"For half of my childhood at least."

Her mind filled in the blanks. The half of his childhood after his family's home burned down. She closed her eyes briefly until she felt his hand reach over and cover hers. "Relax," he said again. "It's just food with people who don't know you yet. But give them an hour and they'll love you."

Brenna sucked in a deep breath. "Okay. Food and people. That's what I do all day every day. Piece of cake."

Luke got out of the truck and went around to open the passenger-side door. Then they walked up the steps, and Luke opened the front door without ringing the bell or knocking. "It's Luke!" he called out as a greeting.

"Luca!" a woman's voice exclaimed from the other side of the house.

Luke turned back to Brenna. "By the way, I'm Luca when I'm with my mom. She'll never call me Luke."

Brenna laughed, which eased the tension inside her. Then she heard a shuffle of feet and saw a shorter woman with Italian features that were much more pronounced than Luke's appear with her arms open wide. She stopped when she saw Brenna, and Brenna immediately knew that Luke hadn't told his family he was bringing a guest to Sunday lunch.

"Who is this?" His mom looked from Brenna to Luke. "You brought a lady friend?"

"Emphasis on *friend*," Luke said.

Whereas Brenna was pretty sure his mother's arms were wide to hug him at first, she held them out to Brenna now and wrapped her in a strong hug. "My Luca hasn't brought a woman home in so long," she said once she'd pulled away. "You must be special."

Luke gestured to Brenna. "Mom, this is Brenna. She's my next-door neighbor."

"Oh, how nice is that? And what a beautiful name for a beautiful woman. My name is Maria." His mom opened her arms and hugged Luke as well.

"Smells good," he said of the scent of spices in the air.

"Of course it does." His mom swatted his arm as she pulled back. "I've been poring over the stove since church."

"Is Nick here yet?" Luke asked.

"Oh yes. Nicholas is at the table with your dad. I'm about to start serving."

"Can I help?" Brenna offered.

His mom looked at her. "You're a guest. You sit, I'll serve, and then I'm looking forward to getting to know one another."

Twenty minutes later, Brenna was more relaxed and chatting with Luke's parents and brother like she'd known them forever. It'd been a long time since she'd sat down for a family meal. Her idea of a family meal over the last few years was when Eve decided to grace her with her presence.

"Where is your other son?" Brenna asked as they ate.

All activity at the table froze.

Brenna chewed the bite of pasta in her mouth, realizing she'd said something wrong, but for the life of her, she didn't know what. "Luke said he had two brothers." She looked at Luke. "Marco, right?"

He reached under the table and squeezed her thigh reassuringly. "He's, uh, not here." He offered an apologetic glance at his mother.

Okay. What was Brenna missing?

"Mom," Luke said, "the lasagna has a new ingredient. I can taste it," he said, changing the subject quickly.

Maria looked pleased. "I was wondering if you all would notice. It's a secret ingredient."

Brenna spoke without thinking. "Turmeric."

His mom's eyes widened. "Wow. You really know your stuff."

"Sorry. It's one of my favorite ingredients too."

Then the conversation flowed again, like a river on its course. Brenna didn't dare bring up Luke's younger brother, Marco, again at the table but she intended to just as soon as she got Luke alone.

* * *

The sun was on its descent behind the mountains as Luke drove back home with Brenna, quiet in the passenger seat beside him. He wasn't sure if her silence signaled that something was wrong or if his family had simply worn her out. By the time he pulled into her driveway, he wondered if perhaps she was sleeping.

She stirred as he cut the engine. Then she looked around, blinking heavily.

"You okay?" he finally asked.

"Mm-hmm."

Neither of them moved to get out just yet. "You and my mom got along great," he said.

"I guess it's true that food brings everyone together… Luke?"

He heard a note of hesitation in her voice, and he was pretty sure he knew what was coming. "Yeah?"

"What happened to Marco?"

His brother's name made him shift uncomfortably.

"When I asked where he was at dinner, the tension in the room was palpable," she said in a quiet voice.

Luke swallowed painfully. "I should have told you, I guess."

"Told me what?"

Luke swallowed again and then again. He looked over at Brenna. "I told you about the fire when I was seven. Marco and I were trapped upstairs."

"And a fireman showed up and saved you. Another came for your brother," she said, filling in the parts that he'd already disclosed. He'd intentionally skipped a very important piece of the story when he'd shared it with her, jumping to how he'd gotten the injuries on his back. He'd told her that the fireman had put him in an ambulance, and he had been carted away in a flash of chaos and pain. As far as he was concerned as he left the scene, Marco had been rescued just like him.

Luke's breaths grew shallow as he braced himself to tell the rest of the story. He didn't tell it often. "The other firefighter, the one that went in to help Marco, didn't make it out."

Brenna's eyes widened as she watched him. The inside of the truck was dark, and shadows danced around them as the trees outside swayed against the wind off the creek.

"The authorities think the fireman had a heart attack while he was in the house. Bad timing. Bad luck." Luke sucked in another breath, and pain splintered in his chest. It felt like it might rip him apart but he knew from experience that it wouldn't. "By the time the fire department realized he wasn't coming out, it was too late to send someone else in after their firefighter... and for my brother."

Brenna's eyes welled with tears as she reached for him, taking his hand in hers. "Oh, Luke, I'm so sorry. I had no idea."

"The report said he died from the smoke." Luke had tried to reach Marco himself. That's how he'd gotten burned. The fear and the pain had stopped him in his tracks. For a long time, he'd wondered if he should have tried harder.

Luke steeled himself against the surfacing emotion. He was done blaming himself and getting emotional about what happened so long ago. Instead of crying, he'd put his energy into his passion for firefighting. Marco's death somehow meant something if he could use it as motivation to save lives. That's what Marco would've wanted.

"We lost more than our home that day. Our family changed forever," he said, focusing his gaze on the sky. There were thick clouds blocking the stars tonight. "It was a long time ago," he added. He'd found that things were easier to hear if they were removed with time and distance.

He sucked in a breath and blew it out slowly, thinking of Brenna and wanting to comfort her. It wasn't an easy story to hear. "I'm sorry I didn't tell you before."

"I'm sorry I brought it up to your family," she whispered. "I didn't know."

"It's okay. The Marinis are strong. We're survivors, just

like the McConnells," he said, veering the subject away to a safer place.

She swiped at a tear that had splashed on her cheek. "I guess our families are bound together by more than food, huh?"

A soft sprinkle of rain started to hit the windshield as they sat tucked inside his truck. It gained momentum, pounding harder as they stared into each other's eyes. Thunder rumbled somewhere beyond the mountains.

Luke reached for her, finding comfort in the feel of her skin. He ran his fingers over her arms, traveling up past her shoulders to the curve of her bare neck. Then he leaned across the seat to press his mouth to hers. They kissed as the rain grew into a heavy downpour all around them.

"If we don't stop, the neighbors will see," Brenna whispered once they'd pulled away for just a moment.

He slid his seat back and pulled her toward him, urging her body to rest over his. "The only neighbor I care about is you."

CHAPTER NINETEEN

A few days later, Brenna awoke in Luke's bed. This was becoming the norm for her, and she loved it. She contemplated staying a little longer but the lure of gourmet coffee at her house got her up and crossing his lawn toward hers. She turned on the coffee maker and sat at her kitchen table, breathing in the heavy aroma of roasted beans in the air and thinking about Luke. When the coffee was done brewing, she poured herself a mug, grabbed a stack of mail that needed flipping through, and sat back down.

There was a letter for Luke at the top. Apparently, their mail carrier was still having a hard time keeping their boxes straight. This would give her an excuse to walk over tonight, not that she needed a reason anymore.

Her cell phone buzzed as she sipped her coffee and continued thumbing through the envelopes. Eve's name popped up on the screen with an incoming text.

Are you awake?

Brenna glanced at the time on her phone's screen. It was only eight a.m., still early, but she'd slept in this morning by her standards. Aunt Thelma had offered to open the shop and she'd taken her up on it. She had an event later this afternoon, but there was no reason to rush right now.

Brenna typed in a quick reply. Yes.

Want to have breakfast? Eve texted back.

Brenna clutched the phone with both hands. Maybe she wasn't awake, because the sister she knew would never suggest getting together. It was always Brenna who had to press for such an idea. Sure.

They made plans to meet at a little diner in town, and Brenna hurried around her house getting ready. A social invitation from Eve was rare, and Brenna really did want to work at behaving like sisters again. Just sisters.

After pulling on a pair of blue capris and a soft white T-shirt, she slipped her feet into some sandals and drove across town to the sixties-themed diner where she and Eve had agreed to meet. Eve was already seated in a booth waiting for her when she arrived, which was a relief because Brenna had halfway wondered if she'd be stood up again.

"Hi." Brenna slid into the booth in front of Eve. "Have you been waiting long?"

"No. I already ordered a Sprite for me and a cup of coffee for you."

"You know me well."

Eve tapped a finger to her chin and pretended to think. "Yes, I do. That's why I know you've probably already drunk half a pot of coffee by now."

Brenna had needed it this morning because she and Luke had stayed up late last night. And the night before that. She decided to leave that detail out. "I'm glad you wanted to meet."

Eve looked around the diner. There were only a handful of other patrons right now. "I missed you. And I had a hankering for a stack of pancakes."

"I could've made you some, you know," Brenna pointed out.

"You could have but I wanted to treat you," Eve said. "Asking you to cook wouldn't be treating you."

"You're treating me?" Brenna's lips parted. "What did I do to deserve this?"

"Well, I got my first paycheck at the station, and"—she shrugged—"after all you've done for me, I thought I'd buy you breakfast. It's nothing huge, but . . ." Eve's voice trailed off.

Maybe not to Eve, but this was huge to Brenna. "Thank you." She reached across the table for Eve's hand, a little surprised when Eve didn't yank it away. "And I'm proud of you, going after your dream and not letting anyone stop you."

Eve narrowed her eyes but she was grinning. "You're the only one who wanted to stop me," she pointed out.

"Well, I was wrong. I'm proud of you, and I admire the heck out of you." Her throat tightened. Brenna pulled her hand away as a waitress came to their table, delivering their drinks and taking their orders.

Brenna stirred some sweetener into her coffee as she thought. "So what's going on with the guy you were with at the Tipsy Tavern last week?" Brenna held up a hand. "Don't worry—I'm not going to lecture you on underage drinking."

"Because you know Luke already did." Eve jabbed a straw into her soda. "As you know, Ryan works at the station. He's helping me study for my license to drive the engines. It's not required for my current job but it doesn't hurt to have it." She leaned forward and took a quick sip of her drink before continuing. "As a woman working in a mostly male job, I've decided it's best to build my résumé as much as possible so that I'm considered for promotions."

"So Ryan's your study partner, huh?" Brenna asked with a teasing tone.

Eve blushed softly. "No comment. And enough talking about me. I want to hear about you. Any takers on buying A Taste of Heaven?"

Brenna shrugged. "Janelle said someone is interested and wants to see it. She plans to take the potential buyer for a tour after hours tonight."

"Really? Who is it?" Eve asked.

"Some out-of-towner." Brenna reached for her coffee. "I'd feel better selling to someone local but there haven't been any bites since it listed."

"And time is of the essence since you're off to college soon." Eve grinned. "I'm so excited for you. But I have to say I'll miss having you so close."

"Just say the word and I'll come home for a visit," Brenna said. "You can move back in our house on Blueberry Creek if you want. I won't be there that much."

Eve hesitated as she seemed to weigh her response. "Or you could rent the house out for a year. It's too big for one person. We could split the revenue."

It was too big for one person, but it still felt homey. "I'll need a place to come back to when I'm in town. And I don't like the idea of strangers in our house." She also wanted to be able to come home and see Luke, not that they were going to keep their relationship going. "Do you need money?" Brenna asked, suddenly worried. "Is that why you want to sell the house?"

Eve narrowed her eyes. "Firefighters aren't rich but I'm doing just fine. Stop worrying about me."

"Working on it," Brenna said, relaxing into a smile.

The food arrived and for the rest of breakfast, they talked easily, just like the old days. When it was time to leave, Eve made the first step toward a hug in the parking lot.

"We should do this more often." Eve pulled her keys from her purse.

"Anytime." Once Brenna was in her own car, she sat there for a moment, soaking in the good feelings coursing through her body. She'd awoken beside a man who made her feel things she hadn't felt in a very long time, and she'd rekindled a relationship that had been long suffering. Everything in her life seemed to be perfect for once. Except for the fact that she would be leaving it all behind this summer.

* * *

The fire alarm went off just before noon. Luke jolted out of his chair and darted toward the engine. Tim was already suited up, and Eve was nearly done. It was just them and the volunteers today. Ryan and Wally had been on the night shift.

Luke watched Tim climb into the driver's seat.

"Come on, Max," Luke called to his dog. "We're up."

Max's gaze bounced from Luke to the engine and back. Then, being the brave dog he was, he trotted and jumped onto the engine's platform.

"That's the way," Luke praised. He slid into the seat beside Eve as a radio fed them details.

There was a fire on Blue Spruce Road. Luke had just been in that area the other day when he'd gone to visit Granger. It was a scenic drive with the mountain backdrop in full view. When Luke had walked around the property with him, Granger had mentioned the dry weather this year. Luke wondered if that accounted for the fire they were heading toward.

"I want to work the hose," Eve shouted over the sirens.

"You're not ready." Luke kept his gaze forward. "You stay on the sidelines and watch. That's how you learn."

"I've been a volunteer forever. I went to the fire academy. I've learned, and I'm ready."

"Not yet," Luke said more firmly. Yeah, part of his stance was because of Brenna. She'd asked that he keep Eve safe, and that was affecting how he treated the younger McConnell sister. Otherwise, he probably would loosen the reins a bit. Eve was proving to be helpful and she deserved a chance. "We'll see," he amended, glancing over at Eve.

The radio buzzed with more details. Smoke and flames. Blue Spruce Road...Merry Mountain Farms.

Luke's heart dropped into his stomach. The farm was large, covering several acres of land. He wondered which part was in danger, not that there was any good part to go up in flames. Every aspect was part of the Fields's livelihood, from the Christmas trees to the strawberry fields to the orchards.

But the most important thing to protect was human life. The Fields family lived on the same property as their business, and Granger had two little girls.

Luke gripped the handle beside him, holding on tight as the engine screamed down the road. They were less than three minutes away, but every second counted. They couldn't get there soon enough.

The engine slowed as it took the turn onto Blue Spruce and then gained momentum again, following the curves of the road until it reached the end. Luke looked out the window, seeing the balloon of smoke as thick and dark as the distant mountains.

"Where is it coming from?" he shouted.

"Looks like the tree farm," Tim called back.

Luke was afraid of that. The tree farm brought in the greatest revenue for the Fields family. It would also feed the fire the fastest. It sat up against the woods, putting the forest beyond and Evergreen Park in danger.

Luke jumped off when the engine had barely jolted to a halt. "We need more manpower. See if Ryan and Wally can come in," he told Eve. "The volunteers are on their way. Stand by to call in stations from surrounding towns."

Thankfully, Eve was done arguing. "I'll take care of it," she said.

Tim was already working on clearing a path to get closer to the tree farm. Luke gave a cursory glance to Max, who was on the ground now, his nose pointed in the direction of the fire. Luke didn't worry that Max would run in that direction. His job was to guard the truck or support the family, which he usually did instinctively.

"Luke!" someone called, gaining his attention.

Luke turned to see Granger running toward him. He ran to meet his friend. "Get your family to a secure place. We'll handle the rest."

"My youngest daughter, Willow," Granger said, his face pale and drawn.

Chills ran the course of Luke's body in record speed. He already knew what Granger was about to tell him.

"We can't find her," Granger said in a panic.

Luke swallowed hard, thinking of his brother Marco.

He pushed the worst-case scenario from his mind. "Don't worry. We'll locate her," he promised Granger. "It's unlikely she's out there. She probably saw the fire and got scared. She's probably safe somewhere."

Probably was the best promise he could give, and that wasn't good enough.

Granger didn't look convinced. "Give me a suit because there's no way I'm staying on the sidelines while my daughter's life is at stake."

Luke hesitated. "That would break protocol," he told Granger.

"I don't care about protocol. I care about my daughter," Granger said. "I'll get the suit myself." He headed toward the engine, and Luke didn't blame him one bit. When someone you loved was in trouble, the rules went out the window.

* * *

Brenna had just wrapped up catering an event at the local chamber of commerce when she got into her car to drive back to A Taste of Heaven. Just before she pulled onto the road, two engines from Whispering Pines sped past her on the two-lane road. Tension wound tightly at the center of her chest. Instead of turning in the direction of her business, she followed the engines.

It wasn't that she was nosy. Engines from neighboring towns were only called in when something serious was going on, and Luke and Eve were in the middle of whatever it was.

She saw the bloom of dark smoke in the sky as she followed the sound of the sirens. Pulling onto Blue Spruce Road, she followed the familiar path to the Christmas tree farm where she got her tree every year. The fire was at the farm? She knew the Fields family. They were some of her favorite people in town. Granger's girls were still young, and sometimes they sat with her at the coffee shop on Saturdays.

Brenna parked in the gravel lot across from the farm, jumped out of her car, and hurried toward Granger's parents, who were standing with their oldest granddaughter, Abigail, and watching the scene unfold. Max was on the ground, leaning against Abby's leg. "Are you all okay?" Brenna asked once she reached them.

Mrs. Fields looked at her through red-rimmed eyes. "No."

"Where's Granger? And Willow?" Brenna asked, her heart rising into her throat.

"Willow is still out there. Granger is helping the firefighters look," Mrs. Fields said.

"Oh no." Brenna turned to watch the scene as well, feeling helpless to do anything else. She wasn't like Eve. She didn't run into danger, and even if she wanted to, she didn't have the equipment. "They'll be okay," Brenna said. "They're in good hands." She was telling herself that as much as she was telling the Fields family.

Abigail looked up with terror-stricken eyes, her hand reaching for Max, who was propped up on her leg. "I'm scared for my sister. She needs me."

"I know, sweetie. I know. I'll stay here with you until she's safe, okay?" Brenna knew how it felt to worry about a sister. She knew the plight of being the oldest sibling and feeling responsible for her.

"I just don't know how this could've started," Brenna heard Mr. Fields say on the opposite side of Abigail. "I couldn't care less about my trees as long as my granddaughter is okay." He held one of the firefighter's radios. It buzzed to life in his hand.

"I think I see her," Luke's voice said through the speaker. "I see movement under the deck of the house. I'm headed in that direction."

The radio buzzed again. "Granger, here. I'm on my way."

Brenna held her breath and reached for Abigail's small hand, waiting for the radio to give another report, hoping it was good news. *Please let it be good.*

"I found her!" Luke finally said. "She's okay!"

The Fields doubled over at the news, crying out in relief.

"She's coming to the front with Granger," Luke reported. "I'm going back to my crew."

A minute later, Brenna saw Granger and Willow running toward the fence that surrounded the property.

"Daddy!" Abigail called, letting go of Brenna's hand and running toward them. Max dashed beside her. "Willow!"

Tears filled Brenna's eyes as she watched Mr. and Mrs. Fields run up to wrap their arms around Granger and Willow too. Brenna brushed a tear from her eye, watching the family find comfort in one another. Then she directed her attention back to the fire. Her family, Eve, was still out there.

CHAPTER TWENTY

$\mathscr{T}$wo hours later, the fire was out, and everyone was safe and accounted for. Willow was shaken up but laughing by the time her family escorted her to their vehicles on the gravel lot across from the farm. The smoke in the air was too thick to stay on the premises.

"Brenna?" Luke blinked as if maybe his eyes were playing a trick on him when he saw her standing by the fence. He walked toward her. "What are you doing here?"

"I followed the engines and wanted to make sure you were okay. Are you?" she asked, running her gaze over him. His face was smudged with dirt and ash but he looked unscathed by the fire.

"Fine. Eve is fine too," he said, knowing her all too well.

"And the farm?" she asked, thinking about Granger and his family.

"They lost a pretty big portion of the tree farm, but not all of it."

Brenna blew out a breath. "That's good, I guess."

"It could've been so much worse. I told them I'd rather they stay somewhere else tonight as a precaution. It only takes one spark to get it going again. I called Kaitlyn Russo and got them a couple rooms at the Sweetwater Bed and Breakfast."

Brenna nodded. "That's nice of you. It'll feel almost like a vacation for them, if they can find a way to relax... I've never stayed at the B and B myself but I've always wanted to."

Luke cocked his head to one side. "Are you dropping hints?"

Her lips parted. "No. Just thinking out loud. My nerves are shot if you can't tell."

He leaned on the other side of the fence, drawing closer to her. Then he brushed his lips to hers.

"People will see us," she warned quietly once he'd pulled away.

"I just risked my life." His gaze lifted to hers. "I'm not worried about what people see."

"My sister..." she said, stopping short of saying anything more.

Luke shook his head. "Eve will get over it just like every other thing that ruffles her feathers. I'm tired of hiding. I'm ready to kiss you whenever I want."

Brenna smiled. "Me too." Then she kissed him again, staying longer this time. "I know you have to work. I'll see you at home tonight."

Luke subtly pulled away. "Home, huh?"

Her cheeks heated. "You know what I meant. Our homes are in the same vicinity."

"I know what you meant but I didn't mind what it sounded like either. See you at home," he called over his shoulder as he turned and headed back toward the engines.

* * *

Eve's hands were on her hips as Luke approached. "Were you seriously just kissing my sister?"

He didn't hesitate. "Yep."

"She's my sister. You can't..." Eve made a series of hand gestures. "That's disgusting."

Luke looked between her and Ryan. "I told you two just to make sure you didn't do it at work. I can agree to do the same with Brenna if it bothers you. That's all I'll agree to though."

Eve's mouth hung open. "So you...like her? Like, *like her, like her?*"

Luke massaged his forehead. "Yeah, I like her. But I'm your acting fire chief, and we aren't discussing my personal life right now. All I want to discuss is what a great job you did out there. You too, Tim and Wally," he called to his other two firefighters on the truck. "This fire could've been much worse. The reason it wasn't is because we moved fast, called in help, and had each other's backs. Chief Brewer would be proud...I'm proud. Well done."

He dipped and patted Max's head. "You did a great job sticking by the family's side," he told his dog. "Good boy. There's a treat in your future tonight."

Max grew more excited by the *t* word.

When Luke looked up, Eve was still wearing a sour face.

"My sister?" she asked again in disbelief.

Luke chuckled and ignored the question. "Let's head back."

After a formal debriefing meeting with the crew at the station, Luke called Chief Brewer to fill him in on the day. The chief had already heard about the blaze and was expecting Luke's report.

"Did you figure out what started the fire?" Chief Brewer asked.

Luke clicked the top of his pen repeatedly as he talked. "Granger's youngest girl was playing in the trees. She lit a candle on a mud pie."

"A candle on a mud pie?" Chief Brewer repeated. "I can't say I've ever heard that one before."

"Apparently, it's her mom's birthday." Luke knew the little girls' mom had left after Willow was born and never came home. It couldn't be easy for such a young child.

"Well, I'm glad no one was hurt. That's in large part thanks to you, Luke."

"Thank you, sir."

"Now you can go home and relax. Enjoy a beer and the company of a beautiful neighbor."

"Planning on doing just that after I stop by and check on Granger and his family at the inn. I want to make sure they're settled."

"And *that* is the sign of a good fire chief," Chief Brewer said. "I already knew you were capable, but looking out for the families we help beyond the crisis—that's the sign of a true leader."

Luke chewed on Chief Brewer's praise as he drove to Mistletoe Lane and into the bed and breakfast's driveway. He climbed the steps of the Sweetwater Bed and Breakfast and rang the doorbell.

Kaitlyn Russo answered a moment later, wearing a flower-print apron and a welcoming smile. "Hi, Luke. I hear you had quite the day."

He'd cleaned up at the fire station so he didn't mind following her inside the beautifully designed inn. Kaitlyn and her new husband had renovated together. Even though it was only a couple of miles away from Blueberry Creek, Luke wouldn't mind having a getaway with Brenna here.

Luke stood in the front room. "I just wanted to check on the Fields family. How are they doing? Do they need anything?"

Kaitlyn shook her head. "I think they're fine. They've been up in their rooms since they arrived. Granger asked if he could have some Chinese food delivered but I told him I didn't mind making dinner tonight. I expect they'll be down soon. Would you like to join us?" she asked. "You're welcome too, of course."

Luke shook his head. "Another time. But thanks for the invitation."

"Would you like me to call Granger's room and see if he can come down and talk to you?" Kaitlyn asked.

"That's not necessary. Just give me a call if they need anything at all—anytime, day or night."

Kaitlyn nodded. "Of course. I'll tell Granger you stopped by."

"Thanks. Have a good night." Luke walked back out the front entrance toward his truck.

"Luke!" Granger's voice called just as Luke was about to get in. "Hey, I thought I heard you downstairs. I can't thank you enough for today, man. I just..." He shook his head, lifting one hand to his chest. "I think I aged ten years back there."

Luke stepped closer to the front porch. "Fear around fire is healthy."

"I guess so. I can promise you that Willow will never play with matches again. She's still shaking like a leaf. I don't know what she was thinking."

"She's six, right? She probably wasn't thinking that her little birthday candle would cause such a big commotion."

Granger frowned. "No, probably not."

"Looks like it only affected the tree farm. The house and orchards were salvaged."

"I plan on going there tomorrow and seeing how many of the trees were lost. Then I'll assess the ground and maybe do a little research about regrowing after a fire," Granger said, his tone of voice grim. "Right now I'm just thankful that my family is okay."

"I hear that."

Granger patted a hand on Luke's back, where his skin was scarred. Only Brenna knew about those scars. And now she knew about Marco too. That was more than any woman in his life had ever known. More than he should have disclosed to someone who was just supposed to be temporary.

"Thanks again, buddy. Next time we go out, I'm buying all your drinks."

Luke chuckled. "You don't have to but I'll let you. Just no more drinking games."

"Agreed," Granger said. "I better get back inside. Talk to you tomorrow?"

"Sounds good. I want to know how things are with the farm after you go over there."

"You got it."

Luke watched his friend jog back toward the inn's porch, and then he got into his truck and headed to his home at Blueberry Creek. For the first few months here in Sweetwater Springs, the house was the only place that felt like home but now the entire town felt homey.

There was also Brenna. She felt like home to him these days too. How was he going to let her go this summer?

* * *

Brenna had only been home for an hour but she'd cleaned every square inch of the kitchen, bathrooms, and laundry room in that time. Janelle Cruz was showing the potential buyer A Taste of Heaven right now. They'd either love it or hate it.

She hoped the buyer loved it, even if that thought also saddened her. Her mom had worked so hard to buy that place and turn it into something special.

Brenna's cell phone buzzed from the counter, and Brenna dashed across the room, stopping right in front of it. Janelle's name lit up the screen. Before answering, Brenna patted her hand over her heart, willing it to slow along with her breaths. "Hello?"

"Brenna! I have good news."

Brenna's knees went weak. "Really?"

"The buyer loves it and is planning to put in an offer. He wants to do that with a different Realtor instead of making me dual agent, which I completely understand. That just means he wants to haggle on the price."

Brenna pulled out a chair and sat down at the kitchen table. "Oh. That doesn't sound good."

"It's just the way things are. That's why our asking price is more than what we were hoping to get. No one pays full price anymore," she said.

"Oh." Brenna nodded. "So it's a sure thing?"

"Pretty much. Just looking at his face, I'd say he's completely in love with the place."

"He's a caterer?" Brenna asked.

"Oh, no. He wants to renovate and make it into an antique store."

"An antique store?" Brenna repeated.

Janelle chuckled. "What are the odds that another caterer would come along and want to just take over A Taste of Heaven? If the place sells, who really cares what they do with it?"

Brenna knew Janelle was right. She was just being sentimental. "Yeah. Okay."

"I'll let you know when I have the offer in my hands. But this is a good thing. It's not time to celebrate just yet, but soon."

"Thank you, Janelle," Brenna said. They said their goodbyes and disconnected. Then Brenna sat for a few minutes longer, trying to convince herself to be happy. People loved antique stores. Especially in a small, mountain valley. The tourists would enjoy shopping there. It would be a lovely addition to the downtown shopping area.

A knock on her front door got her attention. Brenna went to open it and her heart sped up at the sight of Luke.

"Ready?" he asked.

"Ready." She stepped onto the porch and closed the door behind her. Then they headed toward the creek to take a walk. He'd texted her about doing so an hour earlier and said he wanted to clear his head after the eventful afternoon. She needed to do the same.

"Something on your mind?" he asked when she remained quiet.

She glanced over. "Janelle says that a potential buyer is working on an offer for A Taste of Heaven."

"Wow," Luke said. "So why don't you look happy?"

She shrugged. "They want to turn the place into an antique store. I guess I was just imagining that it would continue to be A Taste of Heaven, just with different owners."

Luke reached for her hand. "If you're going to let it go, you have to let it go completely," he said.

She nodded. "I know." Her heart pinched softly. The same was true about him. They'd have to say goodbye and let each other go. She'd tried to hang on to her ex when she'd moved down here for Eve, and that had been a slow-motion disaster. She didn't want to go through that again. "I've always loved walking along Blueberry Creek," she said, changing the subject before her emotions got the better of her.

"I bet. It's beautiful out here," Luke said.

"It's a great place to think too." Even though right now she didn't want to think. There was too much weighing on her mind. "Did Eve have anything to say about our kiss at Merry Mountain Farms?"

The look that Luke gave her told her Eve did.

"Uh-oh."

"She said it was disgusting, and I promised not to kiss you in front of her," he said. "I tried not to kiss you in the first place, and that didn't work out so well." He slowed his steps, turned to face her, and lowered his head to give her a quick kiss. "See? I just can't seem to help myself around you."

She laughed as they pulled back and continued walking. When they were standing in front of their houses again, Brenna turned and placed a hand on his chest. "I know you're tired after the day you had so I'll leave you here."

"I'm too tired to even protest," he agreed.

"Good." She gave a definitive nod. "Sleep well, Luke," she said, thinking about the fire and how he'd told her he was restless sometimes afterward. "But if you need me to, I can stay with you tonight."

Something shifted in his eyes. "It's probably best if I'm alone."

She didn't feel the least bit offended. Instead, she felt close to him, knowing the reason he wanted to be alone without him even having to tell her. Somewhere along the way, they'd crossed a line. They knew each other's strengths and weaknesses, hopes and fears. There were a million messy feelings in play, binding them in an impossible web. Maybe she and Luke had been foolish to think they could keep things between them simple.

"Good night, Luke," she said as they leaned in for one last lingering kiss, knowing she would see him again tomorrow. It would be much more difficult when they said the real goodbye.

CHAPTER TWENTY-ONE

*L*uke drove to Main Street the following week and wished he could go inside Brenna's shop to say hello. Instead, he continued driving. She was working right now, and he had other things on his to-do list. First up was meeting Granger and Jack at the Sweetwater Café for a midafternoon snack and drink. It was partly for social reasons and partly for business.

Luke parked and headed inside. He ordered a pastry and a coffee from Emma and headed over to where Granger and Jack were already sitting.

"Fancy meeting you two here," Luke said, taking a seat. "How are the girls?" he asked Granger.

"Good. Willow had a few restless nights, a couple nightmares, but she's okay now."

Luke hoped her nightmares would fade for her sake.

"We're back home now," Granger continued. "Looks like we lost about an acre of our trees. We plan to clear some of the wooded area that got burned and add on to the farm. All the way up to the border of Evergreen State Park."

Jack nodded as he listened. He was the park ranger and therefore responsible for the hiking trails and wildlife in that area, among other things. "You'll need to fence that back section to make sure hikers don't trespass onto your property."

"I was thinking the same," Granger said. "I don't necessarily like the idea of strangers wandering onto the farm without me knowing about it. And I don't want the girls accidentally wandering off the property." He turned to look at Luke. "I was also thinking about the school field trips and presentations that we do at the farm during the school year. Seems like the perfect place for the fire department to do safety talks, especially now that we've had our own little forest fire. What do you think?"

Luke took a sip of his coffee as he considered the idea. "I think that's a pretty great idea but I'm not dressing up as Smokey Bear."

Granger and Jack chuckled.

Luke looked at Jack. "You could join in. A park ranger has just as much at stake in keeping forest fires down. It'd be a great place for the three of us to make a difference together."

Jack leaned back in his chair. "It's a good idea," he agreed. "But I'm not dressing up as Smokey either."

"You kind of look like him without dressing the part," Granger teased.

Jack rubbed his jaw. "I guess it's time to shave if you're comparing me to the wildlife around here."

Granger grinned. "Here I thought we were an unlikely trio meeting up at the Tipsy Tavern a couple months ago. Looks like we would've united anyway." He bit into his croissant.

"You men look like you could use a refill," Emma said, walking over to their table. She stood beside Jack, and Luke couldn't help noticing the way Jack shifted restlessly. She was a pretty woman. She wasn't Brenna though, and Luke had never had any interest. If he had to guess, however, he'd say that Jack did.

Jack pushed his cup in her direction. "I'd love a refill. Thanks. Can never get enough caffeine."

"Not true," she said, looking down at him. "Too much and you'll find yourself staring at the ceiling tonight."

Jack held up a hand. "I solemnly promise I'll quit after this one."

She laughed softly and then filled his cup and looked at Luke and Granger.

Granger shook his head. "No more for me."

"I'm good, thanks," Luke said.

Emma's gaze swept back toward Jack's. "Don't call these guys when you're battling insomnia later."

"What about you? Can I call you?" Jack asked.

Emma's lips parted, and Luke was pretty sure she was looking for a nice way to tell his friend no.

"Hey, man," Luke intervened. "You can't flirt with the pretty café owner when you're out with the guys. Save that for another time," he teased.

Jack turned to frown at him. "She knows I'm just teasing. Emma and I have been friends forever. Our moms were best friends, once upon a time."

"It's true. I'm used to him," Emma said. "Let me know if you guys need more sustenance. And tell your girlfriend hello for me," she told Luke before turning and walking away.

"Girlfriend?" Jack asked. "I thought you and Brenna were just having fun."

"We are," Luke lied. "I mean, she lives next door and we're pretty much seeing each other every day but neither of us are in the market for something serious right now."

Granger shifted as he dug in his pocket and pulled out a five-dollar bill. He slid it across the table to Jack.

"What's that for?" Luke asked.

"We had a bet that you'd be the first of this new trio of friends to go down," Jack told him, swiping the bill from the middle of the table.

"Go down?" Luke asked.

"Another one bites the dust," Granger sang off tune.

"You guys are serious?" Luke folded his arms over his chest. "You bet on my love life?"

Both Granger and Jack shared a look. "Did he just say love?" Granger asked. He curled his fingers in a gimme gesture at Jack, and Jack handed the five-dollar bill right back. Evidently, they'd bet on the intensity of Luke's feelings too.

"All right, all right. Have your fun. But both of you will be lonely tonight, and I'll have someone to keep me warm," Luke said.

Granger held up the cash. "This money will keep me warm."

Luke looked at Jack, who was nursing his coffee. "So, Emma, huh?"

Jack caught his gaze. "Stop looking at me like that. We're just friends."

"That's right. Jack's a loner who spends most of his time in the woods," Granger said. "He's not interested in anything serious either. It's pitiful, really."

Jack pointed a finger. "Do you want me to rehash your story?"

Granger averted his gaze. "Nah. Mine is more pitiful than yours."

Luke ran a hand over his hair. "Enough love-life talk, then. Let's return to talking about something a lot less complicated, like work."

* * *

Like clockwork, the bell on the entrance to A Taste of Heaven jingled as Hannah pushed inside after school on Friday afternoon, a smile spread across her face from ear to ear. She practically ran toward the counter where Brenna was standing.

"Good day, huh?" Brenna asked with a small laugh. She pushed a plate of cookies toward the girl.

"The best day!" Hannah said excitedly. "I got my report card, and you're going to flip."

Brenna's eyes narrowed. "Flip in a good way?"

Hannah's head bobbed up and down. "All A's! I made the principal's list, and it's all because of you."

"Sweetie, that's amazing!"

Hannah ran around the counter and threw her arms around Brenna's waist in the biggest hug Brenna had gotten in a long while.

"But it's not thanks to me. I didn't take those tests and quizzes. You did."

Hannah pulled back and reached for a cookie. She handed it to Brenna. "You get a cookie today too. We're celebrating."

Brenna laughed. "Okay. Then I think we should add milk, don't you?"

Nate walked toward the front. "I just heard all of that, and I'm so proud of you, Hannah Banana. Can I join in on this cookies-and-milk party?"

Hannah giggled. "Of course, Uncle Nate." She gave Brenna a sheepish look. "Can we just celebrate and take the afternoon off from tutoring? Just this once?"

Brenna narrowed her eyes. "Okay, but just this one time."

As Brenna went to get the milk out of the fridge, her smile dropped along with her mood as her thoughts went to the fact that at this time next year, this place could be an antique store. She would be living in a whole separate town. Nate would be working somewhere else, still wearing bad T-shirts and spreading his sarcasm like wildfire.

And Luke would still be on Blueberry Creek, possibly winning over another woman's heart as easily as he'd won hers.

This isn't the time, Brenna. This afternoon was for celebrating, and she fully intended to drink her cares away with a tall glass of milk and a cookie chaser.

She grabbed the milk and three glasses, then carried them over to where Nate and Hannah were sitting.

"You're leaving?" Hannah asked with a huge frown. "Uncle Nate says that you won't be able to tutor me next year."

Brenna sat down at the small table with them. "That's true. But you're finishing out your school year on a good note. You won't need me next year."

Hannah's frown deepened. "I will need you. What if my grades start slipping again? I want to stay on the principal's list."

Nate grimaced and gave Brenna an apologetic look. "I thought she should know. I didn't realize it would kill the celebration."

"It's not," Brenna said, forcing a big smile. "Hannah, you got this. You're smart, and you can always call me.

We can do FaceTime on your uncle Nate's phone if you're stuck with your homework. I'm not abandoning you."

"Really?" Hannah asked.

"Of course. And I'll only be gone a year."

"Then you'll return to Sweetwater Springs?" Hannah asked hopefully.

Brenna shrugged. "I might. I'll have to get a job. I'll be a real teacher then."

"Hey," Nate said, trying to lift the mood, "maybe she'll be your teacher, Hannah."

The girl's smile returned in full. "That would be so awesome!"

Brenna laughed and reached for a cookie. "Yeah, it would." When her first cookie didn't do the trick in keeping her own fears and insecurities from creeping into the forefront of her brain, she grabbed another.

* * *

Later that night, Brenna and Luke prepared all the fixings for the fire station's family-style picnic lunch tomorrow.

"I've never been a fan of potato salad but I have to admit yours looks pretty tasty," Luke said.

Brenna grabbed some plastic wrap from the cabinet and measured out a piece to cover the finished dish. "Confession: I loathe potato salad."

Luke leaned against the counter as he watched her. "So many things to learn about you and so little time."

She swallowed, keeping her focus on the task, but her hands were suddenly shaking. *This isn't the time to get emotional, Brenna.* She started to press the plastic wrap against the sharp metal edge of the box and then cried out when it sliced her thumb instead.

"Let me see," Luke said, immediately reaching for her hand and inspecting the thick, red drop of blood. "Ouch." His gaze lifted. "My fault for distracting you."

"I won't argue." She pinched the tip of her thumb with her opposite hand to keep the blood from contaminating the food and making a mess of the kitchen.

"You sit," Luke said, pointing at the kitchen table. "I'll get a Band-Aid."

"In the bathroom cabinet," she told him, watching him head in that direction.

He returned a minute later with her entire first-aid kit. "Stay calm, Miss McConnell," he said in a deep, professional voice. "I'm a firefighter and trained in emergency situations such as this one."

She grinned as she watched him kneel in front of her chair. "It's nice to have the attention of a handsome firefighter. Maybe I got hurt on purpose."

He looked up from the kit and narrowed his eyes. "Did you?"

"No. But I might in the future."

He continued to look at her, his brown eyes so intense. "Speaking of the future," he said, trailing off while he looked down and fastened a Band-Aid on her thumb.

Brenna didn't breathe for a moment. Luke was kneeling in front of her, wanting to discuss the future, but they didn't have one. Not together at least. "Thank you," she said once the Band-Aid was secure.

"You're welcome." He lowered his lips to her injury and kissed it gently.

The gesture would've taken her breath away if she were still breathing at all. All breath had frozen inside of her at the mention of the future. "Rule breaker," she said quietly. "No kissing in the kitchen, remember?"

"Ah, that's right. Sorry." He looked up at her again. "We're done cooking though, so I thought you'd let it slip."

"Just this once. Or twice." She leaned forward and kissed him for real, unable to help herself. The kiss was slow and lingering. Then she grabbed his hand and tugged him out of the kitchen space and into the living room, pulling him down on the couch with her.

"That was a lot more work than I anticipated for one little picnic." Luke wrapped an arm around her as they sat together. "I'll be better prepared for next year."

"Next year, huh?" she asked. Was that the future he was talking about? Maybe she could come home to help with next spring's picnic. Or like with Hannah, she could Face-Time him while he cooked.

"This is much better," Luke said, brushing his lips over hers. "Now I can kiss you as much as I want to."

When they pulled away, Brenna looked at him. "In the kitchen, you said something about the future." She bit down softly on her lower lip. "But you didn't finish."

"Right." He nodded. "I have something important to ask you."

"Oh?"

"Mm-hmm. The picnic tomorrow is for the firefighters and their families. Or their significant others." He cleared his throat. "I was wondering if you'd be my significant other."

Her lips parted. "I think that's a step up from 'your annoying neighbor.'"

"We're way past that," he said as he looked at her.

"Your secret lover?" she asked, teasing him.

"It's not a secret anymore. My crew knows. Even Granger and Jack know."

"What exactly is it that they know?" she asked. Because she was at a loss on what was going on between them these days.

"That I'm crazy about you. I didn't even have to tell anyone. It's pretty obvious, I think."

Brenna swallowed. "I guess it is."

He reached for her hand, running his thumb over the back of it and causing goose bumps to flesh on her skin. "Please say yes, Brenna," he said, hovering mere centimeters from her lips, tempting her with a kiss. "Go to the picnic with me."

"You'll have to convince me," she said, teasing him. "How good are your persuasive skills, Chief Marini?"

He started trailing kisses from her lips to her neck, spreading them out achingly slow. "Very good," he said in a raspy whisper.

She sighed happily.

"Have I convinced you yet?" he asked, lifting his head to look at her.

"Not even close. It might take all night," she warned, feeling his body shudder as he chuckled.

"Whatever it takes to have you by my side tomorrow."

Tomorrow. That was the future they were talking about. Anything past that wasn't an option.

* * *

The weather was perfect for the SSFD picnic. Luke couldn't have planned it better. And having Brenna help him made it an extra-special occasion. Everyone in town loved her food, and he pretty much loved everything about her.

Brenna finished setting up and went to stand beside him.

He wrapped an arm around her and leaned in for a kiss, stopping short when Eve approached.

"You're not a firefighter," Eve pointed out to Brenna.

Brenna raised a brow. "Is that your way of telling me to get out of here?" she teased.

"No, but..." Eve shrugged.

"I'll have you know I was invited. I'm Luke's significant other."

"His what?" Eve asked on a laugh and looked between them. "Are you serious? I believe the hip term is 'friends with benefits.'"

"That's not what we are," Luke said. "I mean, we are friends, and there are benefits, but..."

"Ew!" Eve held up a hand. "Stop right there. You can stay, Bren, as long as I don't have to listen to any more details about what's going on between you two."

"Well, I'm sure your significant other is here as well," Brenna said.

Eve blushed, which was unusual for her. Instead of responding to that last statement, she changed the subject. "Don't forget that we're getting together next week. I have a day off. I might even help out at A Taste of Heaven. Work it one last time."

If Luke wasn't mistaken, Brenna looked a little sad at the reminder of her business's closing. That was to be expected, he guessed. A Taste of Heaven had been a huge part of her life to this point.

"Nate would appreciate that," Brenna said. "He and Chris have been needing a little time together. It's been so busy lately that we're working nearly every day."

Eve took a few retreating steps. "Actually, I also have tomorrow off and no plans. Want to get together then instead?"

Luke was hoping he'd get Brenna to himself tomorrow but he knew how much working on her relationship with her sister meant.

"Sure. That sounds wonderful," Brenna said.

"Great. I'll meet you at your house in the morning." Eve gestured over her shoulder. "Well, I need to get back to my...significant other."

Luke shook his head when Eve was gone. "Thanks a lot. I'll never live that down if she tells the others."

Brenna turned toward him, hugging her arms around his waist. "Your words, not mine."

"I thought it was romantic at the time," he said, his voice dipping low for just her ears.

"Oh, it was very romantic."

He bent and kissed her. In broad daylight for anyone to see.

"We should probably get in line before all the chicken wings are gone," she suggested once they pulled away.

"Good idea. Although I know the cook, and I'm pretty sure I could get her to agree to make me more if we miss out here."

Brenna cocked her head. "Pretty sure of yourself, huh?"

"When it comes to you."

He and Brenna got in line and filled their plates and then set up a blanket next to Eve and Ryan's. Tim and his wife were on the other side. Wally had set up a blanket on his own but he looked content. The volunteer firefighters were here with their families too, mingling with the crew that they helped on a regular basis.

"I remember these picnics with my dad. I always dreaded them because they sounded so boring but I always ended up having a good time." Brenna tipped her face up to the sky for a moment.

Luke did the same. "Good food, good company. It's a tradition worth carrying on."

"Chief Brewer looks like he's feeling a lot better," Brenna commented, looking in his direction.

Luke followed her gaze. "I think he is. He seemed to enjoy his break from work more than he realized he would."

"Good thing he had you to handle things in his absence. Are you going to miss being the fire chief?"

Luke considered the question. "I never thought of myself as a leader but it felt good." He lifted his sandwich and took a bite. He chewed as he thought and then swallowed. "Not bragging, but I think I did a decent job." He watched Brenna pop a chip into her mouth.

"You did an amazing job," she agreed. "As your significant other, it's my duty to say so."

He grinned. Then he noticed Chief Brewer walking out in front of the picnickers, limping just slightly. Luke imagined that sitting on a blanket on the ground this afternoon wasn't the best for his back.

"What's he doing?" Brenna asked, leaning over to Luke. "I'm not sure."

When Chief Brewer got to the front, he cleared his throat loudly and waited for everyone's conversations to die down. "I'm happy to see this tradition getting picked back up. It's a good sign that the Sweetwater Springs Fire Department is getting stronger. Our bond as a station gives us strength when we need it." His gaze scanned over all the people watching him, sticking on Luke for a long moment.

Luke hadn't thought about Chief Brewer giving a speech here at the picnic but it made sense that he would. He'd been out of work for a month, and he was transitioning back into his role as chief.

"I just want to thank you all for working so hard. Being your fire chief has been one of the most amazing honors of my life, only second to being my wife's husband." He looked over at Mrs. Brewer and held her gaze. "I wouldn't leave if I thought you needed me to stay. This injury showed me that you don't need me anymore. I mean that in a good way, of course. Luke Marini was—is—a very capable leader." He looked at Luke again. "I can retire knowing that my firefighters are in good hands. That is, if Luke is willing to continue on as the SSFD fire chief."

Luke looked around, shocked and overwhelmed.

"I already spoke to Mayor Everson about this," Chief Brewer said. "He agrees that you're a fine choice. If you say no, Luke, Mrs. Brewer will be a very sad wife, and that old saying 'Happy wife, happy life' is fairly accurate. What do you say? Help an old man retire?"

Luke blinked, unable to speak for a moment.

Brenna nudged him. "I think you need to respond."

Luke stood and walked up to Chief Brewer. "I'm caught a little off guard." He swallowed. "But I'd be honored, sir."

"Say that a little louder so everyone can hear you," Chief Brewer said.

Luke looked out at the group of firefighters in front of him. "Of course," Luke said. "I'd be honored."

CHAPTER TWENTY-TWO

"How does it feel?" Brenna asked, lying in Luke's arms later that night.

He glanced over at her, his face close enough to kiss. "What?"

"Success. You got a huge promotion today."

The corners of his mouth lifted. "A promotion I had no idea was coming."

"But you deserve it." She snuggled closer into his arms, unable to get close enough. After the picnic, they'd come here and had a private celebration of sorts. They weren't hungry for food but they'd devoured each other like it was their last night on earth.

"It feels..." Luke hesitated. "Scary if you want the truth."

She lifted her body up, propping herself on one elbow. "But you've been doing this job for the last month."

"There was an expiration date on the job though. I wasn't doing it forever, and Chief Brewer was still making the decisions. Everything wasn't all on me. Now it will be. That's a little terrifying."

She trailed a finger down his arm. "I believe in you, Luke Marini."

His gaze met hers. "I believe in myself when I'm with you. I'm glad you're here."

"Versus next door?"

He gave a small nod. "Otherwise, I'd be lying here wondering if I was dreaming. If I have what it takes. It's kind of hard to believe this promotion is real. But I know you're real. I've been pinching myself every day lately to make sure I'm not dreaming with you."

"Aw." Brenna leaned in and kissed his mouth. "That's maybe the sweetest thing someone has ever said to me."

His arms clasped around her back, holding her there. "I can prove it. I have bruises from pinching myself."

She laughed. "Liar."

"It's true. If it wasn't so dark, I'd show you." He was right. The sun was down now, and just a small slant of light was coming in from the window. "I can prove it tomorrow morning, after we wake up together."

Brenna tilted her head. "Is that your way of asking me to stay the night?"

"I thought that was a given," he whispered. "But yes, please stay."

"It's so hard to say no to you." She lay back against the mattress. She had no intention of leaving. If she weren't lying here beside him, her thoughts would overtake her as well. She was happy for Luke. Thrilled. There was also some small part of her that was silently aching, for a reason she didn't quite understand.

Eve was following her dreams. Luke's greatest dream was now realized. And her best friend, Halona, was getting married. Brenna was living her dream too. She was selling the catering business and going back to college just like she'd wanted for so long. So why wasn't she happier?

* * *

Brenna woke in Luke's bed early the next morning and slipped out to go to her own home and prepare for Eve's visit. When the doorbell rang an hour later, she hurried to open the front door and smiled when she saw her sister. "Hey. Come in."

Eve walked inside and closed the front door behind her. She looked around the house for a moment. A little knot of guilt formed inside Brenna's chest. This was where Brenna had grown up but it was also where Eve was raised.

"Make yourself at home," Brenna said.

Eve gave her a hesitant look. "This isn't my home anymore."

"Of course it is, Eve. This will always be your home no matter where your permanent address is. I already said so but it's worth repeating. You're always welcome to move back if you need to, you know," Brenna said. "I promise— no more interfering in your life."

Eve followed Brenna to the kitchen and sat on one of the stools. "Wow, I never thought I'd hear you say that."

"Well, here's another thing you probably never thought you'd hear me say. I was wrong to ever try to dissuade you from following your dreams to work as a firefighter."

Eve let her jaw hang open in a dramatic fashion. It was so dramatic that Brenna burst into laughter when she looked at her.

"Come on. Was I that bad?" Brenna asked.

Eve smirked. "Have you heard of a bridezilla? Well, you were a momzilla."

"Except I'm not our mom. I could never replace her, and I wouldn't want to, you know," Brenna said. "What I really want is for us to be close again. The way we used to be. The way that sisters should be." Brenna folded her arms and leaned over the counter toward Eve. "Please."

Eve shrugged. "I don't want to be the way we used to be, Bren."

Brenna's heart sank. Was it too late? Had she played the parent role so long and so poorly that she'd lost her sister forever?

"Gotcha!" Eve teased. "I don't want to be the way we used to be," she said again. "I want to be an even better version of us. Sisters and best friends."

Brenna's throat tightened against her rising emotion. "I want that too," she said in a low voice. "More than anything. Okay, well, since we're spending the morning together, I have a few ideas. Feel free to veto them," Brenna said.

"Oh, I will." Eve laughed. Then she got up from her stool and collected her purse. "What were you thinking?"

"First, I was thinking that we should grab a coffee at the Sweetwater Café and talk about this new boyfriend of yours a little more."

"So you can decide if you approve or not?" Eve asked suspiciously.

"No. I told you—I'm your sister, and that's it. You're free to make your own choices. I just want to hear all about him. I want to know what makes him so special."

"Okay, but only if you talk about your boyfriend," Eve countered.

"I thought you didn't want to hear about me and Luke."

"Well, I changed my mind. If he makes you happy, then I want to hear every detail. I'll just pretend like you're talking about someone other than my moody, by-the-book boss."

Brenna laughed. "Deal. And after coffee, I was thinking we'd go to Sophie's Boutique and look at the sales rack. I'll pick out something for you, and you pick out something for me. My treat," Brenna added.

Eve's eyes widened. "Now you're talking. I definitely won't be vetoing those plans. That sounds like the perfect morning to me."

It sounded perfect to Brenna as well. In fact, she couldn't wait to spend the next several hours with her sister. That hadn't happened in a very long time but she hoped it would be happening much more often.

* * *

Luke yawned loudly, drawing a look from Chief Brewer. "Sorry," Luke said. "I didn't sleep much last night."

The chief chuckled. "I don't even want to ask why." Chief Brewer was packing his things today. Then this office and desk would officially belong to Luke.

"I didn't get a chance to say thank you," Luke said from his seat behind the desk.

"You did. A dozen times already." Chief Brewer stopped what he was doing and looked up.

"But not really." Luke folded his arms in front of him. "You didn't have to pick me to be your replacement. You could've hired someone from another station. Another guy, or woman, who has a decade more experience than I do."

"It wasn't necessary. You proved you were the man for the job while I was gone." Chief Brewer grabbed a picture of his family off the desk and loaded it into the cardboard box he was filling. "End of story."

"When I first got hired here, I knew I wanted your job one day. In my mind, I was thinking that day was fifteen to twenty years from now. I never dreamed it would be six months later."

Chief Brewer looked up from the box. "I remember when I first became fire chief. It was the second happiest day of my life. The happiest was when I married my wife. You'll see."

Luke thought of Brenna, which unnerved him. They'd only just started dating. It was too soon to even consider getting that serious but that's how he was. Once he was in, he was all in. He didn't do things halfway. He liked her, and there was nothing casual about it.

Lately, he'd been considering a possibility that he and Brenna had taken off the table at the very beginning of their relationship. What if they didn't end things when she left? What if they tried the long-distance thing? People did it all the time. Why not them?

Chief Brewer packed the last item on the desk and started folding the flaps of the box shut. "This desk is yours now. Do great things but don't follow my example. Make sure you have a life outside this job."

Luke stood and grabbed the box on the desk. "Thank you, sir."

"You're the boss now. You don't work for me anymore, and you don't have to carry my stuff."

"I don't want you to reinjure your back. You have a retirement to enjoy," Luke said, lifting the box and carrying it out. "Ryan!" he called as he headed toward the parking lot. "Can you get the other box on my desk and help me carry it to the chief's truck?"

"You're the new fire chief, Luke. I'm just Frank around here from now on."

Ryan headed toward the office. "Hey, Frank," he said, gaining the former chief's attention. "Don't slip on your way out the door."

Luke froze in place and looked back at his young firefighter. Frank froze as well. Then they all broke into an uproar of laughter.

"You know I'm joking, sir," Ryan said once they'd all caught their breath. "You'll be missed. No one can ever fill your shoes." Ryan looked at Luke. "But he can try."

Frank patted Ryan's back. "Invite me to next year's picnic. Once a firefighter, always a firefighter."

* * *

Smoke filled the kitchen of A Taste of Heaven on Monday morning.

Brenna coughed and grabbed a dishtowel to wave under her fire detector. The last thing she needed was Mrs. Roberts at the seamstress shop calling the fire department again.

"Are you trying to burn this place down?" Nate asked. "Because that might change your buyer's mind."

Brenna let out another forceful cough. "I forgot I had more pastries in the oven. They're burned to a crisp."

The smoke thinned a little, and Brenna stopped waving around the dishtowel.

"That's not like you." He put his hands on his waist. "Correction, that's not like the old you."

She narrowed her eyes. "What's that supposed to mean?"

Nate shrugged. "I don't know. You're just different these days. And I mean that in the best way possible."

"Burning pastries is not a good thing," she said, grabbing her oven mitt and pulling the tray out of the oven.

The phone on the wall rang.

"How much do you want to bet that's Mrs. Roberts worrying that the shop is on fire?" Brenna asked as she headed to answer the call.

Nate laughed. "I'm not a betting man but I bet you're right. I'll get the phone."

Brenna paused. "I love you."

He looked over his shoulder as he reached for the phone. "Save that for your boyfriend."

Brenna shook her head as she inspected what would've been tomorrow's pastries for the Sweetwater Café. They were unsalvageable, and she'd have to start all over again.

A moment later, Nate hung up the phone and turned to Brenna. "I assured Mrs. Roberts that we were all safe."

"And she believed you?"

"Of course. I have excellent persuasive skills. I was on the debate team in high school."

Brenna took the tray and dumped the pastries in the trash can. "I did not know this about you."

"I considered going to college and going into politics because I was so good at arguing a topic." He shrugged. "Didn't happen, as you can see."

Now he had Brenna's full attention. "Do you regret not going?"

"Where?" His expression twisted in confusion.

"To college. You said you wanted to go into politics."

Nate thought about her question for a moment. "Not really. I wouldn't have met Chris if I'd gone away, and I wouldn't have started working here. Despite what it seems, A Taste of Heaven is my happy place. I guess I'll have to find a new one, huh?"

Brenna frowned. "Sorry."

He shrugged. "Don't apologize. You know, Chris and

I discussed buying this place. Chris's job is only part-time right now. It'd be awesome to take over and run the catering gig together."

Brenna pulled some dough from the refrigerator and brought it over to a piece of wax paper that she'd laid out on the counter. She grabbed a rolling pin from where it hung above the sink and started rolling the dough into a thin sheet. "Can Chris cook?" she asked.

"He's better than I am."

Brenna put her weight into the rolling pin, making the pastry paper-thin. "I didn't know that."

"We decided it wasn't the right time for us to be investing in a new venture. It would take all the money we have in savings and then some." He shrugged. "It just wasn't meant to be."

"You might have grown tired of each other if you worked together," Brenna offered.

"You and I work together, and we're rarely in the kitchen at the same time. And when we are, I never tire of you."

This was true.

"Anyway, I might open a place like this on my own one day. I've got my own little dreams brewing."

Brenna wished she could help him with that endeavor. "I like that idea. What would you call your catering business?"

"Not sure. A Date with Nate?"

Brenna tilted her head. "Not bad, not bad."

He shrugged. "Or I'll just call it A Taste of Heaven. If you were okay with that."

Brenna swallowed. It was just a hypothetical right now. Who knew if Nate would even get to the point of opening his own business one day? Even so, the thought of her mom's business continuing on in some way made her feel like crying.

"Oh no," he muttered.

Brenna narrowed her eyes. "What?"

"You're not going to cry, are you? I take it back," he joked. "A Date with Nate it is."

She grabbed a dishtowel and swatted him with it. "I wasn't crying. It was the smoke burning my eyes," she fibbed, making him laugh.

"Liar," he said.

Aunt Thelma walked into the kitchen and looked between them. "If you're going to fight in the kitchen, at least don't throw the food," she finally said. She looked at Brenna. "Summer Rivera stopped me at the store this morning and asked about booking an event. I told her I'd ask you."

Brenna put her dishcloth on the counter beside her. "When is it?"

"This summer sometime," Thelma said.

Brenna hesitated. She didn't have an offer in her hand just yet but Janelle assured her it was coming. Brenna needed to draw a line in the sand. "I'll call Summer back and tell her we can't do the event. This will be A Taste of Heaven's last month in business. We're not booking past the end of May."

* * *

After work, Luke briefly stopped at Brenna's but he was fighting a headache tonight and told her he couldn't stay. It was no wonder his head hurt. He'd been thinking entirely too much these past couple of days.

He retreated to his own home and headed straight to

bed. The house felt quiet and empty without Brenna, and some part of him considered heading across his lawn and spending the night with her despite what ailed him.

Instead, he lay back and stared up at the ceiling until his cell phone rang from the bedside table. Reaching for it, he hoped that it was Brenna. Instead, it was his brother Nick.

"You awake?" Nick asked.

"Yeah, but the chick next to me isn't," Luke said, echoing his brother's words from a couple of weeks ago.

"Brenna?" Nick asked.

"No, I'm alone. Just kidding with you." He heard Nick exhale. "Everything okay?"

"Yeah. Just...I guess it's time for you to return the favor. I'm restless tonight."

Luke rolled on his side. "What's going on? Mom and Dad okay?"

"Oh yeah, they're fine. I was just thinking about Marco. I've been thinking about him since Brenna came to lunch the other day."

"I'm so sorry, man. I should've told her. I wasn't thinking..."

"Not your fault," Nick said quickly. "But she was right. Marco should've been at that table. He wasn't there but he should've been. He'd be twenty-six if he'd have lived. Who knows what he'd be doing right now? Probably fire-fighting like you. Certainly something more important than supervising ski slopes," Nick muttered.

Luke frowned. "You make sure people are able to enjoy themselves while staying safe. Your job is important."

Nick sighed. "I knew you'd say so. That's why I called you."

"You gonna be okay?" Luke asked. "Need me to come down and meet you for drinks?"

"Maybe later in the week. I'll be okay. Just missing Marco—that's all. Sometimes I feel it more than others."

Luke's throat was tight. "Me too. We'll have drinks soon, and have a couple for him too."

Nick chuckled. "He'd like that. I like Brenna, by the way. She seems like a sweet woman. I can tell that she's good for you too. I could see a change in you the other day."

"A change? What kind of change?" Luke asked.

"I don't know. You seemed happier. More relaxed. Does she have a sister?" Nick joked.

Luke knew his brother was fine when he asked that question. "Yeah, but trust me—her sister isn't your type, and she's dating someone anyway."

"Darn," Nick said on a small chuckle.

They talked a few more minutes before disconnecting. Then Luke lay back again. Nick was right. He was changing. He could feel it.

A couple of months ago, he would've preferred to be lying here alone. Tonight, he would prefer some company. A couple of months ago, talking about Marco would've left him staring at the ceiling for the rest of the night. But he'd found a certain peace these days that had evaded him since his brother's death. He wasn't just living his life to fight fires in his brother's memory. He was also leading a crew, mentoring them, and filling his life with other things.

He really had changed, and he never wanted to go back to living the way he had before he'd come to Sweetwater Springs. Before he'd met Brenna. He couldn't.

He had to tell her how he felt about her. He was willing to cope with the distance between them when she left. What he wasn't willing to do was live without her.

CHAPTER TWENTY-THREE

Brenna hurried through the downpour outside and met Halona at Blushing Brides, a bridal store that sold some of the most beautiful dresses in the valley.

"This is great," Halona said sarcastically. "Now I'll look like a drowned rat in every dress I try on today." She used a towel that Lilly Williams, the store owner, had handed her to dry off her hair.

"You'll look gorgeous. Rain is good luck," Brenna reminded her.

"On your wedding day maybe but not the day you try on dresses." Halona laid the towel on the door handle of the dressing room and turned to a rack of dresses that Lilly had already selected for her to start with. "And I don't want it to rain. Mud splashing on your expensive white dress is not good luck, no matter what anyone says."

Brenna considered any bride lucky who made it to the altar. At least if the couple was actually in love. She was lucky that her ex-fiancé had run when he had. At least she knew what he truly valued.

Halona hung a few dresses inside her dressing room and disappeared inside, while Brenna took a seat on one of the cushy chairs. She oohed and aahed every time Halona came out modeling one of the gowns, which were all lovely. Whenever Halona disappeared back inside to peel one off and put on another, Brenna found her heart aching.

What is wrong with me? Her best friend was getting married, and she should be happy for her. At one point in her life, all her friends were graduating from college. Now they were all getting married. She hoped for those things in her own life too. More so lately.

The dressing room door opened again, and Halona walked out. "Well?"

Brenna blinked past sudden tears in her eyes. "You look beautiful."

Halona narrowed her gaze. "Me in this dress brought you to tears?"

Brenna dodged that question because no, that wasn't what had brought her to tears. "I think that's the one," Brenna said, running her gaze over the simple white-satin, formfitting dress.

"Really?" Halona's face brightened.

"It's gorgeous but it doesn't steal the show. You're the one that people will be watching coming down the aisle. Not the dress," Brenna said.

"I couldn't have said it better myself." Lilly stepped up beside Brenna. She brought a hand to her chest as she looked at Halona. "This is why I love my job. I love matching a bride-to-be with her perfect dress. It gives me a thrill every time. I'm sure you feel the same way about your flowers," Lilly told Halona. "You're not making your own bouquet, are you?"

Halona nodded. "Yes, but I don't mind. I've been sketching up exactly what I want since I was a child."

Lilly looked down at Brenna. "And you're catering the wedding reception, I presume?"

Brenna hesitated. "I'm, um... well..." She guessed she might as well start telling people. And in this town, everyone would know by the end of the day. "I put A Taste of Heaven up for sale. I already have a buyer who is interested." And wanted to turn it into an antique store, but she didn't need to disclose that.

"Oh. I didn't realize," Lilly said. "I'm so sorry."

"No, don't be. It's a good thing. I'm going back to college to finish my degree. But of course, I'll cook the food for the reception if Halona wants me to. My current business partner, Nate, will have to cater though since I'm a bridesmaid."

"Oh, perfect," Lilly said, clapping her hands together and looking at Halona. "You'll have the fanciest flowers and food in town... What do you think? Do you love the dress?"

Halona angled back and forth in front of a long mirror. "I do," she said, a large smile engulfing her cheeks.

"Save the *I do*s for the wedding." Lilly winked at Brenna. They all laughed.

"Yes, this is the one." Halona gave them a definitive nod.

"Well, that was easy. If only it were that easy to find the love of your life," Lilly said. The words tumbled off her lips, making Brenna wonder if she said that to every bride once they'd found their perfect dress. "Love is the hardest thing to find. If I could match women with men the way I do with dresses, I'd be rich."

Brenna smiled and nodded. Love was the hard part. Halona knew that as well. This was Halona's second time getting married. Her first husband had died tragically in a skiing accident. Brenna wished the very best for her friend in her second chance.

Brenna had never wanted another chance at love but that's what it felt like with Luke. At least on her end of things. She had no idea how he felt. Maybe he was still thinking they were having a temporary fling until she left. If he felt the same as her though, she might not leave.

* * *

When Luke was young, he used to love a rainy afternoon. Now he understood the dangers, and it was harder for him to look forward to them.

Rain sometimes brought fender benders and chaos. This afternoon was no different. Luke and the crew had worked two minor road accidents and helped the drivers into the ambulance for transport to the local hospital.

Eve walked up beside him.

"Good job on the scene," he told her.

"Even though you barely let me do anything," she halfway whined.

"Not true. Someone had to write up the report."

Eve rolled her eyes. "You're just as bad as my sister, you know that?"

"I, for one, think your sister is pretty awesome."

This won another eye roll from his rookie firefighter.

"Whatever, Chief," she said, dragging out the last word in a teasing fashion. Then she gave him a serious look. "One day, I'll be chief, you know. If you ever loosen up and let me do the job, that is."

He looked at her with interest. "Already plotting to kick me out of my position? I just got the promotion. Let me enjoy it a bit, would you?"

"I meant after you retire. You're way older than me," Eve teased. "You may be Sweetwater's youngest chief but I'll be the first female one."

"I like your ambition." He climbed back onto the fire truck. "But first, you have to make it out of your probationary period."

She plopped onto the seat of the engine.

"You probably would've made a good college student," he said, watching her scowl from the corner of his eye.

"Please tell me Brenna isn't pushing that issue again."

He held up a hand. "Let me finish. You would've done well in college but you shine out here. When you're ready to take my job, just let me know."

The engine pulled into the SSFD driveway a few minutes later, and Luke climbed off. He collected his things and spoke to the next crew members on shift. Then he got into his Ford truck with Max and drove home, looking forward to spending the evening with Brenna. When he walked over to her door and knocked, however, she didn't answer.

Her car was in the driveway. Maybe she'd gone for a walk. There had been brief moments between the rain showers today. What if she'd gone out and had gotten hurt somehow and was unable to return home?

Fear deflated his good mood as he grabbed his waterproof jacket from the back cab of his truck and headed down to the water. Max needed a walk anyway, and his dog didn't mind a little rain. Halfway along the creek, he spotted Brenna sitting on a bench, staring ahead at the water, seemingly unfazed by the springtime downpour.

"Go get her, buddy," Luke said, unclasping Max's leash. Max took off toward Brenna, his ears flying out behind him. Luke picked up his pace and followed until he was standing right in front of Brenna. "Hey," he said, scanning her body for visible signs of injury.

She looked up from Max to him. "Hey."

He sat down beside her while Max leaned against his leg. "You okay?"

"Yeah," she said, but she looked miserable. "This is where I come to think."

He remembered that she'd told him that before. He followed her gaze to the creek and the tiny circles being cast with each drop that hit it. "In the rain?"

"In any type of weather."

He reached for her hand. "What are you thinking about out here?"

Brenna met his gaze, and he knew she'd been crying. That knowledge socked him in his gut, and he immediately wanted to make whatever it was go away.

"I guess I'm just stressed with everything that's going on. Selling the business. Moving. Going back to college...leaving my family and friends." She blinked as raindrops hit her lashes. "Maybe my timing is off. Maybe I shouldn't go back to college right now."

Luke sucked in a breath. "I thought this was what you wanted."

"I thought so too. And it is. I've always wanted my degree." She blew out a breath and returned to looking out at the creek. "But I have a life that I love here. Some parts, at least."

"This life will still be here waiting for you when you get back," he said.

"Will it?" she asked, her eyes searching his.

Luke swallowed, wondering if she was talking about him. Things were getting more intense between them. He thought about her all day, waiting for the moment when he could wrap his arms around her again. "What are you asking?"

"I don't even know. I guess I'm just having a pity party out here in the rain, which is silly." Brenna shook her head.

He squeezed her hand, waiting for her to look at him again. "It's not silly. But we are getting wet out here. Let me get you out of the rain before you catch a cold. Then we'll have some hot tea and talk things through." He'd been wanting to have a conversation with her but hadn't known how to start it or what to say. She was still here for another month, but somehow he knew that wouldn't be enough time with her. He wanted more, and he knew that wasn't fair. It wasn't what they'd agreed on, but if he was reading her right, maybe she wanted the same thing as him.

They headed back along the path toward their homes, and he led the way to his front door. "I'll get some towels," he said, closing the door and barring the growing storm outside.

He grabbed three towels and brought them back into the living room, handing one to Brenna. Then he squatted and dried off Max before toweling off his own body. "Tea or coffee?" he asked, tipping his head and gesturing for Brenna to walk with him to the kitchen.

"Tea would be nice."

As he prepared the tea, she sat on a barstool at his kitchen island, her hair in wet clumps that collected on her shoulders. What was she doing sitting out there in the rain to begin with? She hadn't even had an umbrella with her.

A few minutes later, he carried two mugs of tea to the counter, readying himself for a conversation he'd been mentally rehearsing for the last week. He slid one mug in front of her and sat on the neighboring stool with his own tea.

"Brenna, you have to go. You can't afford to have second thoughts."

She stared into her tea. "Too late."

Luke reached for her hand. "Your family and friends would never stand in your way—you know that."

"I know," she said quietly.

"And you and I...well, we're just..." He chewed on his words carefully, wishing he'd had a little more time to rehearse. What were they? Friends? Neighbors? Lovers? "We're..."

She stared at him intensely.

He needed to get this right. "Well, we went into this thing with no expectations and no strings attached. And that's still true. I don't expect you to change any plans for me. But maybe we could keep seeing each other when you go. Maybe it doesn't have to be the end."

"Long distance never works, Luke," she said with such conviction that he couldn't argue with her. "If I go, I'm going."

Luke remembered what she'd told him about her ex. Long distance hadn't worked out for her that time, and it was obvious she wouldn't consider going that route again.

"No ifs," Luke said quietly, his hope spiraling out of him. "You've waited long enough and sacrificed too much. You have to go, Bren." He squeezed her hand as he held her gaze. The truth stared back at him, unveiled and unmistakable.

He wanted the very best for her. He wanted all her dreams to come true and for her to be happy. The truth was plain for anyone to see but it had taken a while for him to face it. He loved everything about Brenna McConnell, but more than that, he was *in love* with her.

CHAPTER TWENTY-FOUR

$\mathscr{B}$renna got up and darted to the back of the room, holding her sneeze at bay until she was several feet away from the tray of rolls she was preparing for an event. Over the last several days, ever since her whole self-pity fest in the rain with Luke, she'd had a cold. She guessed that old warning not to go out in the rain because you'll catch your death was true. Now she had watery eyes and a runny nose.

She walked back over to the tray, picked it up, and slid it into the preheated oven. Then she grabbed a Kleenex and blew her nose. She was never crying in the rain again. Bad idea.

The back door to the business opened, and Brenna turned to see Janelle Cruz walking in. She wore a short gray business skirt and a silky peach-colored blouse.

"Brenna!" she said, cheerful as ever. She approached the counter and laid down a large stack of paperwork. "I just need you to sign where I've placed the signature Post-its. Then it's official. The buyer knows you're finishing out the last of the scheduled events on your calendar. After that, you can close up this place and move on with your life."

Brenna nodded. "Yes, that is wonderful." She'd been waiting to move on with her life for a while now. "Thank you."

"Of course." Janelle pulled a ballpoint pen out of her designer purse and handed it to Brenna.

"Now?" Brenna asked, panic sweeping through her chest.

"No time like the present," Janelle said in a singsong voice. "And I'm in no hurry."

Brenna submitted to another sneeze into the crook of her elbow. "Right," she said with a nod.

"Take your time. I'll just sit over here in one of these comfy chairs while you do that," Janelle told her. "Then I'll take the papers with me."

Brenna lifted the pen and stack of papers, along with a box of Kleenex. "I'll be right back." She carried the stack to her office and sat down heavily, giving herself a mental pep talk. Her mom would be okay with this. There was no reason to stay. Luke certainly wasn't asking. He'd made it clear there were still no strings attached on his end. Selling and moving on with her life, as Janelle had put it, was what needed to be done.

Brenna pinched the pen tightly between her fingers and started signing until she made it through the pile of papers. Then she walked back into the front area and handed the stack to Janelle, who was staring at her phone's screen with a look of consternation.

Her smile returned easily, and she stood. "Great! Congratulations, Brenna! Now you can officially celebrate the sale of your business!"

Brenna forced a smile that she didn't feel. "Thank you, Janelle. For everything."

"Of course. I'll be in touch," Janelle said before breezing past Nate as she left and he walked in. Today Nate's T-shirt read ASK ME WHY I'M SMILING.

Brenna was tempted to ask but she also wasn't in the mood right now. "What are you doing here?" she asked instead.

"Working, of course. I told Thelma not to worry about coming in today. I'm taking her shift," he said.

"That's nice of you."

Nate shrugged. "I don't want to be home anyway. Chris accused me of being needy."

"Ouch." Brenna grimaced.

"It's true. I am needy." He gestured at the door where Janelle had just left. "So what was that about?"

Brenna forced that fake smile again. "This place has officially sold."

Nate's usual smile vanished, making the text on his T-shirt false. "Wow. That's great news," he said, even though it was obvious he was disappointed.

"Yeah. It is," Brenna agreed. She stopped bothering with the fake smile. She didn't need it for Nate, and most days he seemed to see right through her.

"I guess I was kind of holding out hope that this thing you have with Luke would change your mind. Selfish on my part, I know."

"If I thought he felt the same way, it might have changed my mind," Brenna confessed.

Nate's eyes widened. "You have real feelings for him?"

Brenna considered his question. She had so many feelings that she couldn't even begin to sort them out. "It's too soon to talk about love and the like."

Nate's eyes widened even farther. "Did I just hear you say love?"

She shrugged her shoulders.

"Well, what does Luke have to say about it?"

Brenna had hoped he'd say a lot more than he did. "He says that I have to go. I'll always regret it if I don't. And there are no expectations or strings attached in our relationship."

Nate scrunched his face. "Please tell me he didn't say that. Because I've seen the way he looks at you, and there's more to that story. He has feelings for you too. I know it."

Brenna sighed. "He said we could do the long-distance thing maybe but I shot that down. I know it would be just a way to drift apart without a harsh breakup. No one likes breakups."

"Maybe it wasn't that at all. Are you sure you read him right?"

Brenna dropped her face into her hands. She wasn't sure of anything these days. All she knew was that if he felt the same as her, he'd have fallen to his knees, begged her to stay, and confessed his undying love for her. "I don't want to think about this anymore."

"Okay. What do you want to think about?" Nate asked.

Brenna looked up. "Well, Janelle said I should go out and celebrate."

"Great idea! We should," Nate agreed.

"We?"

"Yes, we. You and I are going out to the Tipsy Tavern tonight after we close. We're going to drink, laugh, relax, and talk about anything and everything except for college and Luke. Those two topics are off-limits." He held up a finger. "And Eve."

"What's left to talk about?" Brenna asked before succumbing to another sneeze. She reached for a Kleenex in her quickly emptying box.

He shrugged. "Who cares? You need to give your mind a break. And we need to have fun. Just you and me."

"Okay, but I should warn you I'm on cold meds, which probably shouldn't be mixed with alcohol."

"I'll make sure you get home safely. Your home or Luke's?" he asked.

"Luke is working late tonight, so mine." She needed to stop spending every night with him anyway and wean her heart off slowly.

"After work, I need to run a few errands. I'll meet you at the Tipsy Tavern around seven. Sound good?"

"Sounds great," she said, relieved by the idea. A night out sounded exactly like what she needed.

* * *

One of the crew had called in sick this evening so Luke was pulling a double shift. It came with the territory of being the new fire chief. He didn't exactly mind but it would mean he probably wouldn't see Brenna until much later, if at all. He minded that. If they only had one more month together, he couldn't spare a single second.

His cell phone buzzed on his desk, and he reached for it, seeing a text from Brenna flash on the screen. He opened it and read:

I'm going for drinks with Nate tonight.

Everything okay? he asked.

Yeah. We're celebrating. A Taste of Heaven has officially sold!

Luke frowned as he texted his reply. That's terrific! Congratulations!

Thanks! Don't wait up. We might close down the bar.

He'd never known Brenna to be much of a drinker but he also hadn't known her very long. Do I need to pick you up? I don't mind, he offered.

No, it's okay. We'll call an Uber. TTYL!

He stared at the TTYL. Talk to you later. Four friendly, little words whereas he wanted to use three important words. Doing so would only hold Brenna back though, he reminded himself.

"What's got you looking so grumpy?" Eve asked, stepping into his office. "Never mind. It's probably something about my sister, and I don't want to know. Especially if it pertains to your sex life."

Luke blew out an exaggerated breath. "You can't talk to your fire chief that way, Eve. If you ever work under someone else, you need to know how to speak to your chief. And the rest of the crew takes cues from one another. If you talk to me like that, everyone will."

Eve stuck one hand on her hip. "Right. I hear you loud and clear. From now on, I'll talk to you with the utmost respect while we're at the job. I can't promise to do that when I'm home…um, at Brenna's house." Eve looked away.

"I'm sure Brenna would agree that it's still your home too. You grew up there."

Eve put her other hand on her hip. "We're not doing family therapy on the job, Chief."

Luke held up his hands. He'd never wanted to get in the middle of Brenna and Eve's home life anyway. But it came with the territory.

The radio buzzed to life with a fire call from Mrs. Roberts at the seamstress shop.

Eve groaned. "Seriously? Another false alarm?"

Luke stood. "We still have to check it out regardless."

"I know," she sighed.

The radio buzzed back to life. "Flames spotted," the 911 operator said.

Luke shared a momentary look with Eve. "Gear up!"

"Are you going to let me work it this time?"

"No," he said without thinking.

"Chief," Eve said, "with the utmost respect, I ask you to reconsider. I've worked hard and trained on everything you've asked me to. I'm ready. And this is my turf. I need to do this one."

He turned and looked at her. There was no time to argue, and she was right. If she were any other firefighter, she'd be working the scene. She'd more than proved her competence. "Okay. You're on the front lines with this one. Don't make me regret it, Eve."

* * *

Ten minutes seemed like a lifetime to get to the seamstress shop and A Taste of Heaven Catering. When they got there, Luke jumped off the engine with Max at his heels.

Luke scanned the scene. It was all hands on deck, and volunteer firefighters were already pulling up across the street. He spotted Mrs. Roberts wringing her hands on the sidewalk and ran over to where she stood.

"Anyone inside?" He touched her arm to get her attention, noticing that she seemed to be in shock. "Is there anyone else inside?" he asked again.

"I don't...I don't know. I knocked on A Taste of

Heaven's door when I first smelled the smoke, and no one answered. I don't think anyone was inside. But I saw Brenna earlier. She must've left right before it happened." Mrs. Roberts shook her head, her bottom lip trembling. "I tried to call her cell phone but she didn't answer either."

"Thanks." Luke gestured for a paramedic to attend to Mrs. Roberts and went to help his firefighters with the hose efforts. Fortunately, the flames were staying contained to the right-hand side of the catering shop.

Wally had the hose, and Eve ran up to meet Luke. "I need to go inside and search for Brenna."

"I'll be her partner," Ryan offered.

Luke looked onto the scene. "I don't think she's in there. Mrs. Roberts said she knocked and no one answered."

"Sir..." Eve pressed. "I'll be quick. I need to make sure. She's my sister."

Luke was tempted to go in as well. He needed to help Tim fight the flames from the outside though. The fire wasn't out of control but it could get that way if they didn't act fast. "Be quick," he told Eve and Ryan. "Go in, check for human life, and get out. Use your radio if you get into trouble."

"Yes, sir."

They turned and ran toward the building, where smoke bloomed overhead. Luke didn't believe Brenna was inside but he wasn't sure about Nate or Aunt Thelma.

Max whined from the ground.

"It's okay, buddy," he said as he pulled his cell phone out and dialed Brenna. She didn't answer. He texted her.

Where are you?

Seconds passed with no response.

Call me as soon as you get this message. It's urgent, Brenna!

He called Nate next, impatient as the ringing played in his ear.

"Hey, Luke," Nate said as he finally answered.

"Nate. Where are you?" Luke practically snapped.

"Waiting at the Tipsy Tavern for your girlfriend," Nate said. "She better not be standing me up."

"Do you know where Brenna is?" Luke asked, his heart rate picking up speed. If she wasn't with Nate, could she be inside? If so, every second counted.

"I spoke to her after my last delivery. She said she needed to run back to A Taste of Heaven. She forgot her purse."

Fear continued to gather inside of Luke. "What about Thelma?"

"She didn't work today," Nate told him. "Everything okay?"

"No." Luke pinned his gaze to the building, where flames and smoke escaped from the roofline. "There's a fire at A Taste of Heaven. I have to go. Call me if you hear from Brenna," he said before disconnecting the call. He spoke into the radio at his shoulder. "Eve? Ryan? Any sign of Brenna?" If she was inside, he was going to charge into that building to pull her out himself. He'd just found her. There was no way he was going to lose her now. "Eve? Respond!"

"Luke?" a voice said behind him.

Luke whirled to see Brenna walking toward him. Her eyes were wide; her face was pale. Her mouth hung open as she looked at her shop. "Thank God you're okay. I wasn't sure if you were inside," Luke said, stepping toward her. This was no time to wrap her in his arms but he wanted to. And when he did, he never wanted to let go.

"I came back for my purse," she told him numbly, her eyes still focused on the flames. "What happened?"

"We're not sure yet. We're getting it contained." Luke's radio buzzed to life, and Eve's voice came through.

I'm here, sir. No signs of life.

"Eve? Is that my sister? You let her go inside?" Brenna said in a shrill voice, fear and anger warring on her expression.

Luke didn't have time to respond to Brenna. Not when his crew were still in danger. "Brenna's here with me," he said into his radio. "Nate and Aunt Thelma are accounted for too. You and Ryan come out now."

The radio buzzed again. Luke waited to hear Eve's voice. After several long seconds of silence, he spoke again. "Eve? Ryan? Report!"

A loud crash was heard from inside the building.

"Eve? Ryan?" he called more forcefully. "Report!"

The radio buzzed to life with Ryan's voice this time.

"Eve is hurt, sir!" Ryan called. "I need assistance!"

* * *

Brenna's heart nearly exploded. "My sister is hurt?" Before she could even think, she was charging toward A Taste of Heaven. Toward the flames and the smoke. She didn't care. She'd lost so much in her life but no way was she losing her sister. Not today.

Two arms wrapped around her and pulled her back as she lunged forward. "You can't go in there, Bren," Luke said. "You don't have a suit. It's dangerous...Let me do my job!"

"Your job?" She yanked herself free and spun to point her finger at him. "If you were doing your job, Eve wouldn't be in danger right now."

"I can't help Eve if I'm here fighting with you. Stay!" Luke ordered before softening his voice. "Please."

Brenna lowered her voice as well. "You promised me she wouldn't get hurt. You promised to take care of her." Tears suddenly streamed down her cheeks. "If she's not okay, I'll never forgive you, Luke. Never. Now go save Eve," she said. "Go!"

At the order, Max darted toward the building, a blur of brown and white fur. Luke looked stunned for a moment. Then she watched him talk into his radio before charging inside the front entrance. Brenna's chest heaved, and her throat burned from the smoke. She stepped farther away and turned to assess what was going on around her. There were two firefighters with a hose. Volunteers were rushing around doing various jobs that they'd spent their free time training for. Mrs. Roberts was standing on the curb.

Brenna turned back to A Taste of Heaven. It wasn't a big fire. She didn't even see any flames anymore. Just smoke, but she knew smoke inhalation was dangerous too.

She coughed as she tried to take in a full breath. Then she felt someone grab her from behind. She whirled to find Nate standing there, still wearing that stupid T-shirt, his expression a mixture of awe and grief. She stepped into his embrace. "Eve is inside. She's hurt."

"It'll be okay, Brenna." Nate led her to the curb, keeping a hold of her and talking to her quietly.

"I can't lose her too. She has to be okay," Brenna said. He probably couldn't hear her over the ambulance sirens.

Moments felt like hours as she watched and waited for her sister to emerge with Luke and Ryan.

Then Luke appeared with Eve sandwiched between him and Ryan. They had their arms around her as she limped. Max trotted alongside them, barking loudly as if alerting everyone of their presence and calling out for help.

Brenna broke free and started running toward them. "Eve!"

Luke and Ryan handed her off to the paramedics, who loaded Eve onto a stretcher.

"I'm okay," Eve choked out with a cough. "I think I broke my leg but I'm okay."

"Your leg?" Brenna ran her gaze over Eve's lower body, worry and panic flooding her veins. She felt Luke lay a hand on her shoulder, and she yanked herself free. "Don't touch me," she snapped. "This is all your fault...Just go away, Luke. And stay away."

She saw the hurt flash in his eyes. All she could care about in this moment was Eve though. She'd been juggling a million and one emotions lately, and they were all raw and on the surface. She couldn't begin to control them, not even if she tried.

Turning, she followed the stretcher and climbed inside the back of the ambulance with her sister, leaving everything else behind her.

CHAPTER TWENTY-FIVE

$\mathcal{T}$his is all my fault," Brenna whispered to herself later that evening as she curled into a chair beside Eve's hospital bed and watched her sleep. "And Luke's." She couldn't make up her mind who she was madder at—herself or him because he was the one who'd let Eve run into danger.

Brenna knew it was irrational of her. Her sister was a firefighter. Of course she would run into burning buildings. But the anger was also somehow keeping Brenna afloat right now. Without it, she'd just be sad. The business was gone. Eve was injured. And soon Brenna would be alone in a new town without Luke. At least if she was angry, she could pretend like that last part was okay.

Brenna reached for Eve's hand, running her thumb over the back of it. "Why did you run into that building?"

Eve stirred, shifting in her bed and turning her face toward Brenna's. Then her lips parted but her eyes remained shut. "For you."

Brenna straightened, uncurling her legs and placing her feet on the floor as she leaned forward. "Eve?"

"You asked why I ran inside." Eve grimaced as if speaking was a painful feat.

Brenna grabbed her large thermos of water and stuck the straw against Eve's lips.

Eve sipped, swallowed, and then her eyes cracked open, revealing the vibrant green color of their father's eyes.

"Have you been awake this whole time? I thought you were asleep."

Eve scoffed playfully. "Who can sleep when you're talking to yourself like that?"

Brenna laughed, despite the tears suddenly flooding her eyes again. She couldn't seem to stop crying tonight. "Sorry."

"To answer all your questions, no, this wasn't your fault. No, it wasn't Luke's fault. And I ran inside for you. I'd do it again if I thought you needed my help."

"You would?" Brenna asked.

Eve gave her a small eye roll, and Brenna realized that she'd missed those lately. "Because you've always been there for me. You've never let me down."

Brenna squeezed Eve's hand. "That's not true. I've let you down too much, especially lately, it seems. And I'll probably let you down some more. I'm not perfect, you know. But I do love you."

Eve smiled. "I love you too. And I'm sorry for everything. Including scaring you half to death in this fire."

Brenna lifted the thermos of water to Eve's lips again and watched her take a sip. "All that matters is that you're safe." And that was thanks to Luke.

Brenna dropped her face into her hands. So much for staying angry with him. With that emotion peeled away, all she could do was miss him. And love him.

* * *

The next afternoon, Brenna wheeled Eve down the hall of the hospital.

"I can totally walk on my crutches," Eve huffed as Brenna pushed her.

"Hospital policy. You ride until you're out of the building. Then I'll drive you home."

Eve glanced over her shoulder. "I can return to my own apartment too."

Brenna stopped pushing and punched the elevator button on the wall. The elevator promptly dinged, its doors opened, and Brenna pushed Eve's wheelchair inside. "You can but the doctor said to take it easy on that leg. You can do that better at the house where I can make you meals and fluff your pillows."

Eve laughed. "The only reason I'm agreeing to this is because I don't have Wi-Fi at my apartment just yet. And if I'm going to be resting, I should at least get to surf the web."

The elevator stopped and the doors opened on the bottom floor. Once they reached the main entrance, Eve grabbed her crutches and propped herself up. Then they slowly made their way through the parking lot. "Ryan is allowed to come over, right?"

Brenna clicked the unlock function on her key fob as they approached her car. "Eve, the house is just as much yours as it is mine. You don't have to ask permission to have your friends over."

After Eve was safely resting in the passenger seat of the car, Brenna walked around to get into the driver's spot and cranked the engine.

"What about Luke?" Eve asked.

Brenna felt her heart stall at just the sound of his name. He'd texted last night to check on her and Eve, and she'd updated him briefly on Eve's status. Nothing else. He had every reason to be upset with her. She'd questioned him. Insulted him. And if she wasn't mistaken, she'd kind of broke up with him when she told him to stay away.

Brenna swallowed and pulled out of the parking spot. "What about Luke?" she asked Eve.

"Well, I'm on crutches. I can't work. Do you think he'll fire me?"

"The crutches are temporary and only because you were doing your job. He'd be crazy to let you go," Brenna said, crossing the parking lot out to the main road.

Eve turned to look out the window, falling quiet for a minute. "When I fell in there, for a moment, I thought I might die. It was kind of weird, you know, just like they show in the movies. Except my life didn't pass before my eyes. It was more about all the things I'd miss out on if I didn't make it out. There's a lot left that I want to experience in this life."

Brenna glanced over from the road just for a second. "Like what?"

Eve's voice became wistful. "For one, I still want my CDL. I want to get married and go on an amazing honeymoon. Maybe to Jamaica. Maybe I'll have kids one day." She looked over. "It's the stuff that most people want, I guess," Eve said.

Brenna raised her hand. "I personally have no desire to drive a fire engine."

Eve giggled. "You know what I mean. If you were stuck in a burning building, possibly dying, what would you regret not having done?"

Brenna offered a humorless laugh. "Dramatic much, sis?"

"Humor me. Just name something."

Brenna thought as she navigated the roads home "Okay, well, I want to see you have those things you just listed."

"Nope. You can't live through me. What do you want for yourself?"

Brenna swallowed past the ache that threatened to consume her. She wanted to get married, go on a honeymoon, and have kids too. She wanted to go to college, get her degree, and be a teacher. She wanted it all. Everything. "I'll figure out what I want once you're all better. How about that?" Brenna continued driving and then pulled into the driveway in front of her house. She stepped out and hurried around the car to help Eve.

"We're not done with this discussion," Eve said, "so keep thinking."

"Role reversal. Now you sound like Mom," Brenna pointed out as she reached into the car and grabbed her purse.

Eve laughed as she swung her body forward on the crutches. It was going to be a long, immobile summer for her. Her cast would come off just before Brenna left town.

Brenna stood and watched her sister for a moment. Then she felt compelled to look across the yard at Luke's place, and a little gasp caught in her throat. Luke was watching her from his porch.

She lifted a hand and waved. He waved back. Then he turned and disappeared inside his house. She considered calling after him. Resisted taking back everything she'd said last night. She didn't mean those words. Any of them. She was proud of Eve and of him. And ashamed of herself.

Instead, she reminded herself that losing him was inevitable anyway. Best to do it now.

Brenna headed inside and closed the door. In answer to

Eve's question, perhaps in Brenna's dying moments, she'd regret every second that led to this one without Luke.

* * *

Luke walked inside his house and slammed the door as Brenna's words from last night pounded his brain along with the headache he hadn't been able to temper since then. She had been upset in the moment. He knew that but her words still bothered him.

Max came darting toward him, barking furiously as if something were wrong. "Everything's okay, buddy. Just me having a temper tantrum." To prove his point, he bent and petted Max's head, talking to him in a gentle voice. "See? Everything is just fine. And you are a great fire dog. No more running into the fires though, okay, buddy? You stay on the outside."

Luke had been shocked when Max darted into A Taste of Heaven last night. Some part of Luke thought maybe Max knew one of the crew was in danger, and he was going in to help. Max had faced his fear for the good of the crew, and Luke was proud of him.

Luke wasn't so sure he'd done his own job well though. Maybe Brenna was right. Had he been wrong to let Eve work the fire? Was she ready? Perhaps he wasn't ready to be chief.

Luke's thoughts swirled around in his head as he took a quick shower and changed clothes. Then he headed to his truck while glancing across the yard in Brenna's direction. There was no sign of her, which was just as well. He wasn't ready to face her just yet. He didn't think she'd meant what she'd said but what if she had? What if things were over between them?

He drove over to Chief Brewer's house and knocked on the front door. They hadn't talked since Frank had packed up his office and officially handed it off to Luke. It was an honor but, after last night, one that maybe Luke didn't deserve.

Instead of Mrs. Brewer coming to the door, Frank answered this time.

"Hey, Chief," Luke said.

Chief Brewer shook his head. "Just Frank, remember? I'm no longer the chief."

Luke felt a frown pull on his face. "Yeah. That's what I came to talk to you about."

Frank patted his shoulder. "Let's sit on the patio. The weather's nice today."

Luke followed Frank to the back porch, and they sat.

"Don't tell me you've changed your mind about accepting the job," Frank said, crossing his arms over his chest.

Luke looked up. "Not exactly. But I'm not going to lie. I am having second thoughts after last night."

Frank narrowed his eyes. "I'm sure last night was hard. One of your crew got hurt. But no one said the job would be easy."

Luke looked at his hands clasped in his lap. "Trial by fire."

"Have they figured out what caused the fire yet?"

Luke shook his head. "Not yet. The fire marshal is supposed to be investigating. I'll try to catch him over there."

Chief Brewer nodded. "Eve is okay, right? I called the hospital and checked on her myself."

Luke gave a nod. "She'll be fine."

"From what I hear, you and Ryan are the ones who saved her. That's a good day. I've had days where that wasn't the case."

Luke swallowed thickly. He had too. He'd lost his brother Marco on one such day. If he'd have lost Eve last night…He didn't even want to think about it. "Brenna blames me. And I don't blame her for that. I treated Eve like any of the other crew when she isn't any of the other crew. She is a new firefighter, and I should've had her right beside me." He ran a hand over his hair, resisting the impulse to pull at it.

"You're a good leader, Luke. If you made the decision to loosen the reins last night, it was the right call. You couldn't have known that Eve would get hurt."

"The scene was personal to her," Luke said. "That in itself was reason to keep her on the sidelines. It was a family business." Luke leaned forward over his knees, feeling sick to his stomach. "I should have considered that but I didn't."

"Okay," Frank said. "There's a learning curve to running a station. That's one thing no one tells you."

"The learning curve is steep if someone gets hurt. Or worse." Luke stood and started pacing, needing to walk off his energy.

Frank stood and walked over to him, laying a calming hand on his shoulder.

Luke froze.

"A chief who was unfit for the role wouldn't be here right now," Frank said. "He wouldn't care. You care, and that makes all the difference. That's one of the reasons I picked you. You're the right man for the job. I have no doubt."

"But I do. How can I be any good if I second-guess myself and doubt my abilities?"

Frank smiled, which confused Luke. "There should be a guidebook for new chiefs with all the secrets you should know. Everyone second-guesses themselves. Everyone doubts. Everyone is afraid at times. But not everyone keeps going. Some turn back. You're not quitting today, Luke," Frank said with finality. "I won't allow it."

Luke didn't budge. He didn't even breathe for a moment. "What am I doing, then?"

"Getting your head on straight, for one. Don't do anything rash. Remember what made you want to be a firefighter. Remember what made you work to get where you are. Can you do that?"

Luke looked away and blew out a breath. Frank had no idea what he was asking of Luke right now. Remembering his family's fire and the brother he'd lost had the potential to make matters worse, not better. "Since there's no guidebook, maybe I'll just keep coming to visit you every now and then. It helps to have someone to talk to when life feels like too much."

Frank patted his back. "My door is always open for you, son. Forgive me if it's none of my business but I think it's Brenna's door you need to go knock on right now though."

* * *

Brenna's alarm clock still went off at four a.m. the next morning. On autopilot, she got up, used the bathroom, made the coffee, and set about showering, dressing, and fixing her hair and makeup. It wasn't until she got into her car and started it that she remembered the fire at A Taste of Heaven. She didn't have a job to go to.

She cut the engine, got out, and walked back inside her home. She would've gone back to bed but her morning dose of caffeine would make that attempt futile. Instead, she checked on Eve and made her breakfast. When it was almost seven, she got back into her car and drove to the Sweetwater Café.

Halona's eyes widened when she walked in for her morning coffee. "I didn't think you'd be here today," she said, beelining to where Brenna was sitting.

"Where else do I have to go?"

Halona frowned and then opened her arms wide for a hug. "I'm so sorry. What do you need me to do?"

Brenna pulled away. "I don't know. Maybe give Nate a job because now he's out of work."

"Already done," Emma said, walking over with a cup of coffee in hand for Brenna. "I emailed him this morning and offered him employment. He hasn't responded yet but the offer is there. I need extra hands making the beverages. I have a kitchen in back where he can make the pastries too, if you're okay with that. Then, once you've rebuilt, you can have him back."

Brenna suddenly felt overwhelmed. "Thank you for that. But I was closing the catering business anyway. I sold it, actually, although the buyer will likely back out now."

Emma laid a hand on Brenna's shoulder. "Whatever you need from me, just ask."

"Same," Halona said.

Brenna swallowed past a sudden rush of emotion. "Thank you. You two are amazing."

"You'd do the same for us." Emma gestured behind her. "I hate to leave but I have to run the counter."

"It's okay. I'm fine," Brenna said.

Emma nodded. "Talk to you later, ladies."

Halona slid into the chair across from Brenna and pulled her coffee to her. "Is Eve okay?"

"She's fine. Her leg will heal, and she'll be charging back toward danger in no time. She's just tired and weak from the whole ordeal right now."

"I'm sure." Halona reached for Brenna's hand and gave it a squeeze. "We'll get through this, okay? I know you have Luke but you have me too. Don't hesitate to tell me what you need."

Brenna looked away. "I'm not sure I have Luke anymore." In fact, she was pretty sure she didn't. "I was a huge jerk to him at the fire. I was scared, and I lashed out. It's like I couldn't control what was coming out of my mouth. And I'm pretty sure I broke up with him."

"What?"

Tears threatened behind Brenna's eyes. "I told him everything was his fault and I never wanted to see him again. Or something like that. It's all a blur of smoke and sirens." Brenna closed her eyes, embarrassed by her lack of self-control.

"I'm sure Luke understands," Halona said softly. "Have you spoken to him since then?"

Brenna shook her head. "Not really. He called the hospital and checked on Eve."

"That's nice," Halona said, taking a drink of her coffee.

"It is." Brenna nibbled at her lower lip. She wrapped her fingers around her cup of coffee. She'd barely sipped from it since Emma had handed it to her. "I don't think I'm going to talk to him. It was time for us to break up anyway. And what would I even say? 'Hey, I'm sorry I freaked out the other night. Thanks for saving my sister. Can we go back to being in love?'"

Halona's mouth dropped open.

Brenna's did too. She clapped a hand over her mouth. She hadn't meant to say those last words out loud.

Halona nodded. "That sounds pretty good to me. Yeah, say that."

Brenna swallowed. "Except I'm the only one in love."

"Are you sure about that?" Halona asked.

Brenna shrugged. She wasn't sure about anything right now. "It doesn't matter. I messed up. He's avoiding me, and it's over. End of story."

"Bren, Luke is not your ex," Halona said. "He's not going to walk because of some heat-of-the-moment fight. Or because you're leaving for a year."

Halona's words hit home. Brenna was so used to losing—her parents, her ex, her chance at a college degree—that she was bracing herself to lose Luke too. She'd been bracing herself the entire time she'd been with him. "How do I know that for sure?"

Halona tilted her head. "The only way to know is to talk to him." Halona leaned over the table, drawing closer to Brenna and lowering her voice to a whisper. "The plus side is after you apologize, you get to make up." She waggled her dark eyebrows playfully.

Brenna shook her head, a small laugh bubbling out of her unexpectedly.

"I'm speaking from experience," Halona said, leaning back in her chair with a satisfied grin on her face.

"I'll keep that in mind."

"And you'll go talk to him?" Halona asked, looking serious again. "Sooner rather than later."

"I'll think about it."

"No," Halona said with conviction. "No more thinking. Not when it comes to matters of the heart. With those, you throw caution to the wind."

"It seems to me you kept your heart pretty guarded with Alex last year," Brenna reminded her friend. "And that's smart, in my opinion."

Halona nodded. "Yes, but eventually you have to let your guard down. I wouldn't be picking out a wedding dress and dreaming of my happily ever after right now if I hadn't. And I have no regrets."

Brenna envied her friend that. "There's no guarantee that Luke and I would even work out."

Halona frowned. "Love is always a risk—you're right. I mean, who knows? Luke might transform into a jerk. He might leave you when you need him most, just like your ex did. He might pretend to love you, and then his actions might prove him to be a liar."

Brenna scrunched her brow. "That's not Luke. He wouldn't do that."

"No, he wouldn't," Halona said with another satisfied smile as if she'd just proven her point.

$\mathcal{C}$HAPTER TWENTY-SIX

$\mathcal{L}$uke dipped under yellow police tape and stepped inside the cavernous remains of A Taste of Heaven, breathing in the familiar smell of charred wood and plastic. Tom Shiver, the fire marshal for the area, was doing the investigation today, and Luke had wanted to come over and check in.

He spotted Tom in the back of the store and headed that way, stepping over wood beams that had fallen as the building came down. "Hey, Tom," he called.

Tom looked up. He was maybe forty years old and typically had a clean-cut look. This afternoon, however, his face was unshaven and smudged with char. He wore a nice pair of black pants and a short-sleeved shirt that also had black smudge on it.

"I spoke to Eve about what happened. Brenna told her the fire must have started in the oven," Luke told him, stepping up to where he was. "She baked some cinnamon rolls on the evening of the fire."

Tom glanced over. "That's the story I got from the report too. It just doesn't check out."

Luke narrowed his gaze. "What do you mean?"

Tom shrugged. "It looks like the oven was turned off. That's not what started the spark and the eventual flames." Tom gestured for Luke to follow him toward the wall that stood between A Taste of Heaven and the seamstress shop. "There's some wiring here in the walls that's burned to a crisp. The burn appears to start in the seamstress shop at the plug for one of her sewing machines. We've written up Mrs. Roberts before and thought the issue was fixed."

Luke shook his head. "She always insisted that Brenna's business smelled like smoke. Are you saying the fire started over there?"

"Seems that way," Tom said. "In the wall. She had a lot of damage too. Fortunately, Mrs. Roberts recently put in a new sprinkler system that saved her business. She was always paranoid about a fire happening here. Maybe some part of her knew it was just a matter of time."

"Brenna had a sprinkler system too," Luke said, even though Tom already knew that. If she hadn't, the fire might have been even more destructive.

They continued to walk through, discussing the details of the blaze, while Tom jotted down notes. On their way out, Luke spotted a baker's rolling pin toward the back exit where he'd found Eve lying on the night of the fire. Wood beams were down, and it was amazing one hadn't pinned her under its weight. Maybe if it had, things wouldn't have ended so happily. If you could call this a happy ending.

Luke bent to pick up the rolling pin. It was smudged with char as well but otherwise okay. "Mind if I take this from the scene?" Luke asked Tom.

Tom shook his head. "I'm done here. Take it. I'm

heading next door to talk to Mrs. Roberts. She'll need some electrical work done to ensure her business is safe."

"I don't envy you with that conversation. I'm going back to the station."

"Congrats on the promotion, by the way," Tom said. "That's great news, buddy. The town is lucky to have you."

"Thanks. This was my first fire as the permanent chief, and it was kind of a rough one."

"There'll be good days and bad days," Tom said, "and days you wonder why you ever wanted the job."

Luke looked over. "I've already experienced all of the above."

"And you're still here. That's a good sign."

Chief Brewer had told Luke the same thing.

They walked out of the building, said goodbye, and then Luke headed to his truck with the rolling pin in hand. As he drove, he called to check on the crew. He had planned on going back but he wanted to return the rolling pin to its owner. There was also the part of him that wanted to see Brenna and make sure she was okay. But that's all he would do.

He'd had a lot of time to think, and he wasn't upset with her about the other night. But before the blaze, he'd been wrestling with his knowledge that she'd always regret not going to college if she stayed on his account. And on the night he'd found her in the rain, he'd started to see the hesitation in her eyes. She was considering staying in Sweetwater Springs, and he loved her too much to let that happen.

That's why he wasn't going to wrap his arms around her when he saw her. Or pull her in for a kiss the way he wanted. That's why he couldn't tell her how he felt about her. Instead, he was going to hand her this rolling pin and walk away.

* * *

Brenna had spent the afternoon on the phone. First, getting news that the buyer for A Taste of Heaven was backing out as she'd predicted. Then she'd spent several hours handling the insurance paperwork and discussing plans for rebuilding the business with a construction crew on the phone; she couldn't sell the business as it stood now or leave the charred rubble as an eyesore for the community.

It was all too overwhelming to think about. She could rebuild on the same land or find a new location, away from other businesses and the complaint of smoke from the seamstress shop next door, which might be best. She wasn't ready to make a definite decision just yet. Nothing felt right at the moment.

The doorbell rang, and Brenna blinked away her thoughts. She got up and walked down the hall, hesitating behind the front door.

What if it was Luke? If so, what would she say? How would she greet him? He lived next door so it was just a matter of time before they ran into one another. At some point, she needed to apologize. And maybe take Halona's advice and let him back in. Lower the guard on her heart and throw caution to the wind. Isn't that what Halona had advised? What would that even look like?

The doorbell rang again.

On an inhale, she opened the door, and there he stood. Her heart danced around in her chest. *Down, heart.*

"Hi," he said through the screen door.

"Hi." She swallowed, still unsure of what to say. "About the other night..."

He held up his hand. "You don't have to. It's okay." He

looked down at his feet. "Maybe you're right. Maybe Eve wasn't ready to go in on a situation like that. I don't know what I was thinking."

Brenna stepped onto the porch toward him. "You're her chief. You were thinking that it's her job to fight fires. Luke, you saved Eve's life. If I made you feel like you were at fault..."

He looked up, his expression shifting. "If?"

Brenna looked down at her feet for a moment, guilt swirling in her stomach.

"Anyway..." He shrugged as if it were no big deal and held up a rolling pin. "I didn't come over here to discuss the past."

The past. Right. If they couldn't discuss that, surely it wasn't the time for discussing the future.

"I came to bring you this."

Brenna looked up and sucked in a breath as he handed it to her. "It survived the fire? It was my mother's. We used to bake together every Sunday afternoon, and she'd always tell me the food was 'made with love.' We'd each eat just one of the treats, and then we'd deliver the rest to our neighbors."

Luke's eyes narrowed just a little. "Your neighbors must have loved you."

"This rolling pin..." Brenna's words caught in her throat, and she couldn't finish her sentence. She looked at him. "Thank you for bringing this back. And for rescuing Eve. And for being so amazing."

"You're giving me too much credit, but you're welcome."

For a moment, she saw something spark in his gaze. He looked at her again the way he used to. Like she was the most interesting, beautiful, smart, and funny person in his world. "Would you like to come inside? I can make coffee," she offered.

He took a step backward, and that flicker of affection in his eyes dulled. "No. I better get home. I have a few things to do."

Brenna swallowed painfully. "Maybe later, then?" she asked, realizing she sounded a little desperate. Was that what Halona meant by throwing caution to the wind?

Luke met her gaze. "We had our fun, Brenna. I think we both know it's time we went back to just being neighbors. We crossed a line that we never should have."

"Fun?" she repeated.

He turned his head, looking in the direction of his house. "We always knew this day was coming. I'm your sister's boss, and I'm your neighbor. That's it."

He was more than that to her. So much more. "I see." Brenna steeled herself against her emotions. "You never thought dating between neighbors was a good idea anyway. Looks like you were right." Brenna looked down at the rolling pin in her hand. "Thank you for dropping this off."

"You're welcome. See you around."

The coldness of his goodbye left her feeling empty inside as she watched him turn and walk away, leaving her standing on the porch and struggling to breathe. Then she stepped back inside, closed the door behind her and leaned against it, allowing her tears to stream down her cheeks.

* * *

Later that night, Brenna stared at the rolling pin that lay on the bed in front of her. She was amazed that it had survived the fire intact. It didn't even have any evidence of smoke or ash. She rolled it forward and back over her bedspread, her thoughts oscillating in a similar rhythm between her business and Luke.

"Is everything okay?" Eve asked, propped on her crutches in the bedroom's doorway. "Usually you're in the kitchen cooking something around this time."

"I'm fine. Are you hungry?" Brenna's voice lifted on a hopeful note. Cooking was a good distraction, and she really did enjoy cooking for the people she loved. "What would you like? I can make anything you want." She'd even be willing to go to the store to get the supplies if she didn't have them in the fridge. Anything to distract herself from sulking over Luke.

Eve's gaze dropped to the rolling pin on the bed. "Is that what I think it is?"

Brenna followed her gaze. "Luke dropped it by earlier."

Eve's eyes lit up. "I can't believe it! It survived the fire?" She hobbled to the bed and picked it up. "It's a miracle it didn't burn up. Everything else in that blaze turned to ashes." She looked up with bright eyes. "You know what this means, don't you?"

Brenna shook her head. "No. What?"

Eve's wide-eyed wonder reminded Brenna of the way she'd looked when she'd gotten excited as a child. "Mom was there."

Brenna narrowed her eyes. "How hard exactly did you hit your head in that fall?"

"This is her rolling pin, and it survived, Bren. She was there, and you can't convince me otherwise." Eve ran her hand along the smooth wood. "It isn't even discolored. It's like new."

"I admire your passion and belief. When I grow up, I want to be just like you, little sis." Brenna swallowed. Then she got up and carefully wrapped her arms around Eve.

"Just don't ever run into a burning building on my account again. Please. If Mom was really there, I'm sure you nearly killed her all over again."

Brenna pulled away and looked at Eve, suddenly needing to tell her something. "I don't want you to think that you ever held me back. You know you didn't, right? I just put what's most important first. And slid the rest to the back burner."

"A cooking pun. How appropriate." Eve's expression turned serious. "And I know that. I'm grateful for everything, Brenna. Even if I haven't always acted like it."

Brenna nodded.

"So what's important to you now, Bren?" Eve asked.

Brenna swallowed as she thought, surprised to find the answer to that question so simple. She was older now. She didn't want to run off to her dream college anymore. She wanted to stay here on Blueberry Creek. Wanted to be among her family and friends.

She still wanted to finish her degree and be a teacher but there were other ways to have that. "I can finish my degree online, and maybe do my student teaching at Sweetwater Elementary... I'm not going to Western University," Brenna said quietly, talking to herself just as much as to Eve. "I don't want to leave. I'm staying," she said, as relief flooded through her.

And it wasn't because anyone was holding her back. It was because this was what she wanted now. Truly wanted. She still wanted Luke too, but she wanted a new arrangement with him. Temporary wasn't going to work for her anymore. She wanted expectations and strings. She wanted forever.

CHAPTER TWENTY-SEVEN

$\mathscr{L}$uke felt restless but not because of this week's fire. This time it had more to do with his neighbor. Seeing Brenna and not being able to hold her, kiss her, or tell her how he felt—that would be torture, and it was the exact reason why he'd resisted getting romantically involved in the first place.

At least they wouldn't be neighbors for too much longer. She'd go off to Western University just like she should. Maybe they could reunite after that but he wasn't holding his breath.

Everything inside him felt hollow. He pulled out his cell phone and tapped his brother's contact. Nick answered after a couple of rings.

"What's going on, man? It's not the middle of the night."

Luke plopped into a chair at the kitchen table. "You busy?"

"Not really. You sound out of sorts. Is this about a fire?" Nick asked.

"No. I mean, yeah, there was a fire, but…it's about Brenna. We broke up," Luke said, feeling achy all over. He'd forgotten that heartbreak felt pretty similar to the flu.

"Aw, man. Whatever you did, just apologize."

"Your advice is off base this time. She's the one who apologized."

"Then what's the problem?" Nick asked.

Luke stared out the window toward the creek. "It's complicated. I'm the last thing she needs right now. Being with me will hold her back." Luke leaned back in his chair.

"So don't hold her back. Wherever she's going, pack up and go with her."

Luke stilled. "She's going to college, three hours away. I'd have to quit my job." And give up this new life that he loved on Blueberry Creek when he'd just gotten settled in. He'd also just gotten a promotion that meant the world to him…but Brenna meant more. "Go with her?" he asked, struck by the fact that he hadn't even considered that option.

Nick made a noise into the phone. "Mom will kill me if she finds out that I suggested you move even farther away. But why not? Life is short. A job and a nice house don't mean a whole lot without someone to enjoy them with."

Luke's heart was racing in his chest. He'd considered the long-distance thing but he was pretty certain that Brenna wouldn't go if they didn't cut ties completely.

He'd never considered that he could pick up and leave. He loved his new home but he loved her a thousand times more. "Send me a bill," Luke said, a sense of urgency overwhelming him. He needed to find Brenna.

"Only if you promise not to tell Mom it was my idea if you move."

Luke laughed. "Deal." They disconnected, and Luke

stood. Who would lead the Sweetwater Springs Fire Department if he left? Was there even a job he could take near Western University? He supposed he could easily rent out this house and come back to it later. So many new possibilities were suddenly circling his mind.

The doorbell rang, and Max hopped to all fours, barking with just as much urgency. Luke headed to open the door and stared back at Brenna. Her dark hair was down and blowing in the breeze off the creek. Just the sight of her righted his world. That old saying that when you loved someone, you had to let them go was garbage. When you loved someone, you did whatever it took to be with them. Even if it meant letting go of everything else.

"Hey," he said, stepping out onto the porch. Max followed and propped his paws on Brenna's knees, apparently having missed her just as much as Luke.

"Hey." She gave him a sheepish look, and it was all he could do not to pull her into his arms this very moment and kiss her. "Can we talk?"

* * *

Brenna's heart was beating so hard that she thought she might drop the box of doughnuts in her hands. She couldn't tell what Luke was thinking but she wished she could. All she knew was that she had to get out all the thoughts racing through her mind.

"I'm sorry, Luke. You wouldn't let me apologize earlier, and I need to." She took in a breath and blew it out to the side. "I'm sorry that I yelled at you. That I didn't trust you. That I flipped out and accused you of things that weren't true. You're a good leader, and you're good for my sister." She held out the box of doughnuts.

His gaze lowered to the box and back up to her. "I thought those were just to welcome new neighbors to Blueberry Creek," he said, finally cracking a smile.

A nervous laugh tumbled off her lips. "And apparently to ask for forgiveness."

He took the box and stared at it for a moment before looking back up at her. "Thank you," he said, holding her gaze hostage.

Brenna swallowed. That wasn't all she'd come to say. "I also wanted to tell you something else."

"I have something to tell you too. And I can't wait a second longer," he said, cutting her off. "I know you're leaving, and I want you to go."

Brenna's heart sank. She'd come over here determined to make things right, to begin again and start fresh. Strings and all. "What?"

"But I'm not ready to say goodbye either," Luke said. "I never want to say goodbye to you, Brenna. That's why I've decided that I'm going with you."

Her mouth fell open. "What?" she asked again.

"I mean, only if you want me to, of course. But I love you, Brenna. I thought that meant letting you walk away and chase your dreams but I've decided that's wrong. If loving you means leaving this house, this town, and my job to follow you and support you in going to some big college out there, then I'll do it. I'll drop everything. For you."

Brenna pressed a hand against her racing heart. She considered pinching herself to make sure this wasn't a dream. "You just said you love me."

He grinned and stepped closer, reaching for her hand. "Yeah, I did. I do."

Her eyes welled. "Quitting your job and leaving this house is a huge sacrifice." For as long as she could remember, she'd been the one making all the sacrifices. "You would do that for me?"

His gaze didn't waver. Neither did the look in his eyes as he ran his thumb along the back of her hand, the touch sending shivers through her body. "Letting you go would be a bigger sacrifice, Brenna. Now that I've found you, I don't want to lose you."

"I know the feeling," she said, breathless as her chest quickly rose and fell. "But you didn't let me finish what I had to tell you. I'm going to college, Luke. I need to finish the degree I started. I need to follow my own path and do what I love. I want to teach."

"You'll be a great teacher," he said.

"But I can do all of that here. I've decided to finish my degree online."

"What?" Luke asked, sounding the way she had a few moments earlier.

"A big university was the young Brenna's dream. I don't need that anymore. I can finish my degree while staying here, where I have friends and family...and you."

He gave his head a subtle shake. "Are you sure?"

"One hundred percent. And I didn't make this decision for anyone but me. I don't want to go. I have another dream these days."

Luke raised a brow. "Oh? What's that?"

"You. Sharing afternoons on Blueberry Creek together, taking long walks, going to bed and waking up together. That's what I want more than anything."

He smiled that smile that always made her heart skip. "I like that dream a lot. And it's my personal mission to make all your dreams come true, from this point on. I guess that's what a man does when he's in love with a woman. I love you, Brenna."

Brenna's heart swelled to the point that it might burst. "I love you too."

He gazed down at her, the look in his eyes so full of warmth. "So what do you say we live out that dream of yours, starting right now?"

She laughed even as her eyes teared up. "I say yes."

"There's only one thing left to decide, then." He dipped his head until his lips hovered in front of hers.

Brenna swallowed. She was done with thinking and weighing big decisions. "Oh? What's that?"

He brushed his lips to hers, kissing her softly. "My house or yours?"

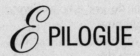

EPILOGUE

$\mathscr{I}$t was seven years after she was supposed to graduate, but the long wait only made this day more special.

Brenna put on her cap and gown and looked in the long mirror in front of her. "I'm tempted to say I feel silly," she told Luke, who was lying on the bed watching her. "But I don't. I feel..." She took stock of her many emotions and then turned from the mirror to face him. "Amazing. I did it. I finished college, and I'm graduating today." It wouldn't be a big ceremony like at the large-scale universities she'd once dreamed of. This one would be small, cozy, but no less perfect.

"I'm so proud of you." Luke stood and stepped toward her, wrapping his arms around her waist. "You wanted something, and you didn't give up, even though a million and one things got in your way. Including me."

She laughed as she folded into his arms and tipped her head back to look at him. "You were a minor obstacle. But I'm glad I get to have my cake and eat it too."

"Are you comparing me to cake?"

She laughed. "Kind of. I am still technically a caterer, even if I'll be just a silent partner and leaving the business in the hands of Nate and Chris after today." Aunt Thelma had officially retired in the last year, and Nate had accepted Brenna's offer to take partial ownership of A Taste of Heaven. He was good at the job, and they'd all trained Chris over the last several months. He was proving to be a master caterer. Everything was falling into its perfect place.

"It's almost time. Guess we better go," Luke said. "Don't want you to miss walking across the stage."

"I wouldn't miss it for the world," she said.

"Neither would I."

They headed out to Luke's truck, and an hour later, they arrived at the small college Brenna had taken online classes from. She'd had to come here for a few projects and presentations, so she was familiar enough with the campus.

She hurried to the auditorium, holding Luke's hand, excitement swelling in her chest. Eve and Ryan were coming today. Aunt Thelma too. Halona, Alex, and Theo were also invited. Brenna just wished her mom and dad could be here to share in this moment. Maybe somehow, in some way, they were.

She stopped walking and turned toward Luke before going to join the other graduates seated up front. "Thank you for supporting me in this. I couldn't have done this without you. And thank you for being here."

"Where else would I be?" Luke asked.

She shrugged. "I don't know."

"Well, let me make that clear for you. I'll always be by your side, Brenna, cheering you on. Forever. That's a promise."

Goose bumps rose on her body even though she was already hot under the gown. "Sounds serious," she teased.

"It is." He pulled a box out of his pocket and looked at her. "The last thing I want to do is distract from your big day and all that it means." His gaze was steady on her. "So if you want me to put this away for another time..."

She swallowed as tears burned her eyes. Her heart thumped under her gown as she looked at him. "It would only add to this day and make it mean even more," she said. "If it is what I think it is." Now she felt silly because what if it wasn't?

Luke dropped to one knee and looked up at her, something vulnerable flashing in his brown eyes. "I'm not all that great with words but I only need three. I love you."

A tear slipped down her cheek. "I love you too."

He grinned and opened the box, flashing a diamond that caught the overhead lighting and seemed to shine like a light of its own. Her heart immediately soared into her throat.

"Brenna McConnell, you make my life better. You make me better. Will you marry me?"

Her hands flew to her mouth. "I don't know what to say."

"Say yes," he said. "To us. To forever."

She didn't even need to think about it. Her heart had been saying yes to him before there was even a question. It was her mind that had needed convincing, but not anymore. "Yes," she said softly.

He slid the ring on her finger, and then he stood and kissed her. "It's time for you to go walk that stage," he said, pulling away. "I'll be the one cheering the loudest for you in the audience. Always."

She looked at her ring and then back at the man she loved. All of her dreams were coming true today but new ones were already taking root. And she couldn't wait to chase each and every one with Luke at her side.

The Only Pancake Recipe You'll Ever Need
from *Skillet Love* by Anne Byrn

When Brenna makes pancakes for Luke, she aims to impress so she doesn't just get out the biscuit mix. She uses a basic recipe that can have added ingredients— blueberries, walnuts, etc.—to make the pancakes her own. A good cook knows that separating the eggs and using cake flour is what makes these special. And the buttermilk, of course! And now you know too. I hope you serve these as part of breakfast in bed for a loved one soon. Love, Annie

Makes 18 to 24 (3-inch) pancakes (6 servings)
Prep: 20 minutes / Cook: 4 to 5 minutes per batch

- ½ cup (1 stick) unsalted butter
- 2 large eggs, separated
- 2½ cups buttermilk
- 2 tablespoons sugar
- 1 teaspoon vanilla extract
- 2½ cups cake flour or all-purpose flour
- 1 teaspoon baking powder
- 1 teaspoon baking soda
- ½ teaspoon salt
- 2 teaspoons vegetable oil
- Sliced fresh fruit, melted butter, maple syrup, and/or honey, for serving

1. Preheat the oven to 275 degrees F.
2. Melt the butter in a small saucepan over low heat, then let it cool to room temperature.

3. In a large bowl, whisk together the egg yolks, buttermilk, sugar, and vanilla until well combined.

4. In another large bowl, whisk together the flour, baking powder, soda, and salt. Pour the buttermilk mixture into the flour mixture and stir just to combine. Pour in the cooled melted butter and stir until smooth.

5. In a medium bowl, beat the egg whites with an electric mixer on high speed until soft peaks form, 1 to 2 minutes. Fold the egg whites into the batter until just incorporated.

6. Heat a 12-inch skillet over medium heat. When it is hot, add the oil and tilt the pan to spread it out over the bottom. When a few drops of water dance on the skillet, you are ready to cook. Measure out ¼ cup batter per pancake and cook three pancakes at a time. Cook until bubbles form on top, 2 to 2½ minutes. Turn the pancakes and let them cook on the other side until bubbles form and the underside is lightly browned, 2 to 2½ minutes. Transfer to an oven-safe platter or baking sheet and place in the warm oven while you make the remaining pancakes.

Serve warm with your favorite toppings.

About the Author

Annie Rains is a *USA Today* bestselling contemporary romance author who writes small-town love stories set in fictional places in her home state of North Carolina. When Annie isn't writing, she's living out her own happily ever after with her husband and three children.

Learn more at:
  AnnieRains.com
  Twitter: @AnnieRainsBooks
  Facebook.com/AnnieRainsBooks
  Instagram: @AnnieRainsBooks

Sealed with a Kiss

MELINDA CURTIS

or Kimmy Easley, potentially showing up at her ex's
vedding without a date is unacceptable. She's got to find
omeone—and fast—or the gossip will spread through
unshine Valley quicker than wildfire. Convincing her
hildhood friend Booker Belmonte to go with her is fairly
asy. But when the matchmaking Sunshine Valley Widows
Club sets their sights on this couple, nobody's heart is
afe...

A bonus novella from *USA Today* bestselling author
Melinda Curtis follows.

FOREVER

$\mathscr{P}$ROLOGUE

$\mathscr{I}$'ll see your two cents. And raise you two cents." Clarice Rogers tossed pennies into the pot in the middle of the card table. "Was I the only one who didn't get an invitation to Haywood and Ariana's wedding?"

It seemed like everyone in the town of Sunshine, Colorado, was going except Clarice. Rumor had it the reception had a Bohemian theme, and Clarice dearly loved anything Bohemian.

Clarice and her two closest friends were playing a high-stakes poker game at the cozy home of Mims Turner.

Bitsy Whitlock checked her cards and then tossed in additional pennies. "I'm not sure why I received an invitation." She adjusted the black bow in her bobbed blond hair. Her hair bows had a tendency to slip. Nothing else about Bitsy ever slipped. "I only met Haywood last Christmas."

"You helped Haywood pick out an engagement ring when you were having your jewelry cleaned." Mims Turner tossed in two cents. "Besides, everyone knows you give good gifts. I got an invite because Ariana's grandmother is my cousin. Call. Two pair." She snapped down her cards and tugged at the ends of her beige fishing vest. "Winner!"

Not waiting for Clarice, Bitsy fanned her cards gracefully on the table. "Two pair, kings high. Looks like I win again."

"Wrong! Full house!" Clarice tossed her cards down with such verve that her gray braids bounced. "The pot and game are mine." And as the winner, she was allowed to choose whom they applied their matchmaking expertise to next.

"Who should I choose?" she wondered aloud but it wasn't a rhetorical question. Clarice had been thinking about whom she'd select if she won ever since Haywood and Ariana first announced their engagement. Happiness swirled inside her chest like courting pigeons on a spring day. Weddings generated lots of events, many of which created pressure to bring a date. And the need for dates opened the door to matchmaking opportunities.

Clarice tapped her chin as if she was perplexed. She said again, "Who should I choose?"

Mims and Bitsy rolled their eyes.

The trio made up the board of the Sunshine Valley Widows Club, a group devoted to providing emotional support to those who had lost their spouses. Privately, they called themselves the Sunshine Valley Matchmakers Club, a group devoted to helping Cupid's arrow find its mark. They were more successful than those swiping dating apps.

"Just say it, Clarice," Mims grumped, gathering the cards. She was on a losing streak.

Clarice drew herself up, tossed a braid over her shoulder, and said, "I choose Booker Belmonte."

Mims stopped sweeping up cards. "Booker's not a widower."

"He's not even divorced." Bitsy gave Clarice a gentle

frown. "You should know that's against the rules." The people they matched were on their second time around.

Rules. How Clarice loved them. As club secretary, she had the pleasure of reminding members what the rules were. But in this situation... "I present a special case. Booker is nearly thirty-two and on the brink of success. And you know what can happen to a man when he's trying to catch the success train."

"That's right." Mims nodded, grumpiness fading. "He loses life balance."

"And he waits too long to find love." Bitsy's tone implied that she found merit in Clarice's selection.

"It's like a public service." Since her friends were warming to the idea, Clarice spoke with more confidence. "And the timing couldn't be better. His best friend Haywood is getting married." The wedding Clarice wasn't invited to. "Booker will have marriage on his mind."

"He'd be a good fit with Wendy Adams," Mims suggested with a fluff of her round white curls. "She's so easygoing."

"Or Avery Blackstone." Bitsy nodded, black velvet bow slipping again. "She has a certain flare."

"All good options. But..." Clarice raised a hand and her voice, which made her realize she might have forgotten to put in her hearing aids again. "I was thinking more like Kimmy Easley. She and Booker hung out in the same crowd in high school. And I always thought there was a spark between them."

Mims and Bitsy both sat back, their mouths making small Os. The three widows had been together so long their brains often shared the same track.

"Kimmy worked at the Burger Shack for years," Bitsy said quietly. The restaurant was owned by Booker's family.

"Along with the groom and Booker." Mims raised her gaze to Clarice's. "Didn't she date Haywood once when he and Ariana took a break? That could be awkward."

"Indeedy. It could be." Clarice rubbed her hands together, so filled with glee that she would've gotten up to dance if she'd had a good pair of knees. "Oh, she'll be looking for a wedding date, all right. The perfect wedding date."

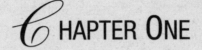

CHAPTER ONE

There was a line at the deli in Emory's Grocery.

Kimmy Easley took pride in the deli's popularity and hurried to move the lunch line along.

"What's the special today, Kimmy?" Clarice Rogers leaned on her hickory walking stick. The free-spirited former hippie had been slowing down lately and claimed to be holding out as long as possible before having her knees replaced.

"Garlic-butter Italian-sausage sandwich." Kimmy finished assembling a ham-and-cheese panini for Everett Bollinger and put it on the grill. "It's served on a crusty baguette with melted cheese on top. Can I make you one?"

"Yes. It sounds delicious, like something my Fritz would've liked." Clarice eyed the selection of salads, her long gray braids swinging against the orange paisley of her blouse. "And a side of the wedding salad." She chuckled. "I have weddings on my mind. Specifically, Haywood's." Her expression turned wistful. "Are you going?"

"Yes." Kimmy tried not to let talk of Haywood's marriage diminish her shine. She was happy for Hay but she had a little over a week to find a wedding date. She sliced open a baguette for Clarice and stuffed it with garlic-butter-soaked sausage.

Welcome to my thirties. The reality decade. Unmarried. No prospects. And light-years behind her peers in getting a career in place.

"I'm sure you have a date already." Kimmy could tell Clarice was trying not to seem like she was prying. But this was Sunshine. People pried. When Kimmy didn't immediately respond—what with being busy prepping the sandwich—the old woman added, "Not that an independent woman like you needs a date."

Oh, Kimmy needed a date, all right. She needed one like Batman needed his mask.

"I haven't thought that far ahead," Kimmy lied. She slid Clarice's sandwich into the toaster oven, checked Everett's panini, decided it needed more time, and dished out Clarice's wedding salad.

"Did you know the Widows Club is hosting a bachelorette auction Saturday night?" The reason for Clarice's visit became clear. "It's a great way to meet someone new and perhaps find a wedding date."

Kimmy hadn't signed up. She never signed up. She expected being on the auction block at Shaw's Bar & Grill on a Saturday night to be like showing up at her high school reunion in a sundress and forgetting to shave her legs. Mortifying.

But mortification was exactly what she was going to experience if she showed up at Haywood's wedding dateless.

If only it were the fall, which was when the Widows Club hosted its *bachelor* auction. Kimmy would rather be empowered to choose her own date, not wait for someone to bid on her.

Kimmy rang up Clarice's order and then sighed. "Do I have to give you an answer now?"

"No, dear." Clarice paid in cash, dollar bills plus exact change, which she counted out in pennies. Thirty-seven of them. "You can sign up until the bidding begins." She smiled kindly. "Hope to see you there."

A few customers later and her boss, Emory, came behind the counter. He was old school and wore a white button-down with short sleeves and a red bow tie. "I'm worried."

"I can handle the line," she reassured him, working on a sandwich for Paul Gregory, one of her regulars and the owner of the local exterminator business. "It moves quickly."

"I'm not concerned about you." Emory shook his grizzled head. "I'm worried about the Burger Shack. I hear Booker is back for the wedding."

She'd heard that too. The news had given her a warm, fuzzy feeling. She, Haywood, and Booker had been close in high school.

"You should be anxious, Kim." If the worried emoji had been based on a real face, it would've taken inspiration from Emory's. "Booker bought his parents out and plans to change the menu."

Kimmy couldn't worry about that. "It's about time." The Burger Shack menu hadn't been updated in forever.

"You don't understand." Emory shook his head once more, this time causing a lock of stringy gray hair to fall onto his forehead. "They're adding gourmet burgers."

A tremor of unease worked its way through Kimmy. "Gourmet?" Gourmet sandwiches were her thing. Emory's was the only place in town you could get gourmet anything.

Used to be the only place in town.

"Yes." Emory rubbed a hand behind his neck. "Fancy burgers."

The unease turned into apprehension.

A tall man with thick black hair got into the end of the line. He stood next to Clarice's friend Mims Turner, chatting amicably.

Booker Belmonte. He'd been her rock throughout middle and high school. Maybe he still was. Just looking at him settled her nerves and turned the inclination to frown into a smile.

"Speak of the devil." Kimmy nodded in Booker's direction.

"He's here to check you out." Emory, being in his seventies and a bit naive, didn't catch the double meaning of his words.

"My sandwiches, you mean," Kimmy said under her breath, because Booker was like family to her. She handed Paul his order. "Did you get new uniforms?" His shirt was lime green and printed with brown cockroaches, vaguely reminiscent of a Hawaiian shirt.

"Yes." Paul turned to show her the back, which was more of the same. "Do you like it? I got tired of boring blue."

"It's a bold choice." Kimmy gave him a thumbs-up.

"The American species is a bold creature." Paul tapped a cockroach on his shirt. "He takes what he wants. I've decided I should be more like him. And since I've been wearing these shirts, business is up."

"Please don't say the *c*-word." Scowling, Emory scrubbed the top of the deli case near Paul.

"Congratulations, Paul. See you next time." Kimmy

gave Paul her patented customer-service smile and turned to the next customer before he could go in depth on the bugs he loved to terminate. They'd taken some classes together at the community college in Greeley so she knew Paul loved to talk about his work.

"Will there be a next time?" Emory muttered, wiping down the counter because he was a stress-cleaner. "Everyone's going to want to check out the sandwiches at the Burger Shack."

"Maybe a time or two." Kimmy gestured to Lola Williams that she was ready to take her order.

Kimmy looked upon the Burger Shack with nostalgia, having worked there for three years during high school. At the Shack, she'd been one of the guys, along with Booker Belmonte and Haywood Lawson, boys higher on the popularity ladder than Kimmy. They'd taught her how to grill, and she'd taught them the importance of loyalty and keeping their word. Her father always said a kept promise was a true sign of character.

When it came to making promises, Booker and Haywood had balked at girlish pinkie swears. Instead, they'd given their word while holding a hand over a hot basket of French fries. Silly kids' stuff. But it had meant something to her, even if Booker's promises had often come with conditions.

"If our customers head to the Burger Shack for lunch more than a time or two," Emory said mournfully, "I'll have to cut staff hours, maybe even resort to layoffs." The old man spoke as if gourmet burgers at the Burger Shack were already trendier than gourmet sandwiches at Emory's Grocery.

Truthfully, at the words *cut* and *layoffs*, the bottom dropped out of Kimmy's little world. Six more paychecks and she could afford a new transmission for the food truck she and her dad were restoring. If she lost this job before the truck was ready...

She glanced at Booker. At broad shoulders and the face of reliability.

It wouldn't come to that. It couldn't come to that.

Still, it took her a moment to work up enough saliva to reply to her boss in an upbeat voice. "It'll be okay, Emory. Can you work the register for me?" Kimmy tried to take Lola's order, not to mention smile and not look like Emory had put her off her game. But she reached for jalapeños instead of green peppers for Lola's wrap, something her customer pointed out.

Somehow, Kimmy made it through four more specials, two wraps, and a chef's salad before Emory was called to the front of the store and Booker appeared before her.

With his jet-black hair, deep-brown eyes, and infectious smile, Booker had always been handsome. But the years had given him an air of hard-won confidence.

Confident enough to put the competition out of business?

No. Never.

But the seed of doubt had been planted. Gourmet sandwiches weren't just her thing; they were her future. She needed some confidence right now.

And a wedding date.

Not necessarily in that order.

Staring at Kimmy working behind the deli counter, Booker Belmonte was at a loss for words.

Which was unfortunate since he had a lot to say to her.

Doubly unfortunate since Mims Turner was filling the void during their wait in line with good-natured babble that kept him from collecting his thoughts. He slid his damp hands into the back pockets of his jeans.

Mims finally came to her point as they reached the front of the line. "Booker, it would be a pleasure to have you as a guest emcee for our bachelorette auction this Saturday."

The old woman had gray curls and a full-cheeked smile like Mrs. Claus. Unlike Mrs. C., however, Mims wasn't helping Santa make a list and check it twice. Nothing Mims and her Widows Club cronies did was ever that straightforward. Mims wasn't fishing for an emcee. She was out to make a love match.

Booker glanced at Kimmy, who was wiping down the counter.

"Say you'll accept the honor, Booker." Mims stared up at him as if she didn't expect to be rejected.

"I'm just the new owner of the Burger Shack." Booker tried to put Mims off, even as he smiled at Kimmy, ignoring the tension between his shoulder blades. "I'll take the special."

He hadn't seen Kimmy Easley in what seemed like forever. They kept up with the occasional tag on social media. He was happy to see she looked the same. Same vivid brown eyes. Same dark-brown hair contained in a neat braid. Same tug at his heart when he set eyes on her.

In high school, Kimmy hadn't liked making plain burgers, the Burger Shack's bread and butter. It wasn't unusual for her to take an order and suggest to a customer that they add garlic hummus, mushrooms, or aioli. After hours, she'd practiced her sandwich-grilling skills by feeding Booker and Haywood. So it was no surprise that she'd put her own stamp on things when Emory had hired her to work the deli counter.

What was surprising was her response to his order. "Sorry, Book. We're all out of specials." Her lively brown eyes were guarded.

Does she know?

"Darn it." Mims pouted, just a little. "I should have come earlier. But I got to talking to Booker, and...I suppose I'll have a grilled cheese."

"Shoot." Kimmy's gaze softened but only when she looked at Mims. "I'll make you a surprise special."

"And me? Your old friend?" He hoped they'd still be friends when he confessed what he'd done.

"I can scrounge a grilled cheese for a childhood friend, I suppose." Kimmy cut him no slack. "Plain and simple, like those burgers you serve."

He sensed it was time for damage control. "Let me apologize."

"For what?" Kimmy was still looking at him warily but her hands were moving—buttering bread, sprinkling seasoning.

Watching her work in the kitchen had always been mesmerizing. "I'm assuming you're going to tell me what to apologize for. You always do."

Kimmy scoffed, cheeks turning a soft pink, not an angry red.

Booker drew a deep, relieved breath.

"Are you going to participate in the bachelorette auction this Saturday?" Mims asked Kimmy.

"I'm thinking about it." Unhappily, if her expression was any indication. "And don't"—she shook her knife in Booker's direction—"give me any grief about it."

"*Moi?*" Booker tried to look offended. "Make fun of you? I'd never." As teens, they'd joked that the Widows Club events were for the dateless and desperate.

"I'm not either of the things you're thinking of." But Kimmy looked grim. Datelessly grim.

What was wrong with the male population of Sunshine that they couldn't see the appeal of Kimmy Easley?

Booker leaned over the counter for a closer look at what Kimmy was using on Mims's sandwich. It looked like spicy guacamole, heavy on the garlic. Garlic being her obsession.

If he was honest, it was his too.

"So, I can count on you on Saturday, Kimmy?" Mims was nothing if not persistent. "All proceeds go to the Sunshine Valley Boys & Girls Club."

"I suppose." Kimmy relented. "Unless something comes up."

Booker frowned. What was going on here? Kimmy was pretty and clever and creative. She should have had guys dangling from a string, waiting for a chance to date her. When they'd been in school, she'd had Booker on a string, and she hadn't even known it.

"Thanks, Kimmy." Mims paid for her sandwich, hefted her yellow pleather purse onto her shoulder, and fixed Booker with a stern stare perfected from years of working in the school cafeteria. "You'll be our emcee, won't you, Booker? It'll give you a chance to talk about the Burger Shack's new menu."

Kimmy sighed but didn't glance up from her work.

Booker reluctantly nodded. "I suppose I'll have to agree if one of my best friends is helping raise money for a good cause." Although, judging by the look on Kimmy's face, he suddenly feared their friendship had fallen by the wayside. His shoulders knotted. Booker needed Kimmy to be his friend. Friends forgave each other's bad decisions and betrayals.

"Oh, I'm so happy you'll be our emcee, Booker." Mims hugged him. Her purse banged against his side with the weight of a brick—or a very large handgun, which Mims was rumored to carry.

With her mission accomplished, Mims took her sandwich and walked toward the exit.

No one was behind Booker in line. Earlier diners were busy eating what looked to be a darn good sandwich. Emory had disappeared somewhere. And Kimmy had her back turned to Booker, smashing his sandwich with a grill press.

"I have a break in five minutes," Kimmy said in a distant voice. "Meet me out back?"

"Sure." Relief skimmed through Booker, untying his knots.

Their history was flooded with work breaks taken together behind the Burger Shack, where they'd sit on a sturdy plastic picnic table and dream of leaving Sunshine and making their mark on the world. Kimmy by opening a specialty sandwich shop. Haywood by selling million-dollar homes. Booker by owning and managing a chain of high-end restaurants.

Only two of their trio had achieved anything close to their dreams—Haywood and Booker. Only one of them had left town.

Kimmy had unwittingly played a role in Booker's success.

And now Booker had to make up for it.

CHAPTER TWO

I haven't seen you in years and you show up with Mims?" Kimmy pushed the back door of Emory's open and didn't stop walking until she'd reached the employee picnic table on the back patio near the receiving bay. She sat down across from Booker with her sandwich and a bottle of water. "What's happening here?"

Her gaze caught on him. On handsome him. And something deep inside her stirred with interest.

I need to date more.

Who was she kidding? She needed to date. Period. Starting this week.

"You made me lunch. That's what's happening." Booker held up his grilled cheese sandwich. "Cheddar, Muenster, and Swiss. But you spiced it up with..."

"Grainy Dijon mustard, walnuts, and super-thin apple slices." Pride had her smiling back, despite a small voice in her head whispering that Booker was the competition now. Her attractive competition.

Stop. This is Booker.

The guy she'd studied geometry with and thrown French fries at. The guy who'd taken her to prom because neither of them had had dates, although that had turned out to be a disaster. He was her friend. He could still be her friend.

As long as he doesn't kill Emory's lunch business in the next six weeks.

She sighed. "It makes the cheese more interesting, doesn't it?"

"I've never done more than salt and pepper on a grilled cheese sandwich. Well done." Booker took another bite. "You know what would make this better? Two thick slabs of French toast."

"Heavens, no." Kimmy unwrapped a shredded-chicken sandwich she'd made for herself. "The imbalance of bread to cheese wouldn't work."

Booker's smile fell a little.

"Maybe it would work between waffles," she said kindly, intrigued by the flavor combinations.

Behind him in the loading dock, several teenage boys were doing tricks on skateboards.

"Isn't that your brother?" Kimmy pointed to a teen who was shorter and skinnier than the others. "Dante?"

Booker turned, scowling when his eyes lit on his kid brother. "Dante! Aren't you supposed to be in school?"

Dante skidded to a stop, flipping his board vertical so he could grab the front axle. "We had an assembly today. Short day at school."

"Then shouldn't you be at the Burger Shack?" There was no mistaking the command in Booker's voice.

Dante shrugged. Translated from teen speak that meant *Yes, but I'm not going.*

The other two teens—the Bodine twins—took off in the other direction.

"Gotta go." Dante waved and followed them.

"But..." Booker twisted back around in his seat to face Kimmy, his expression dark. "Aren't you glad you have an older brother? Because..." He gestured toward the escaping Dante.

"At this moment, yes." Looking into Booker's dark eyes, she nearly forgot why she'd come outside to join him. *Mental head thunk.* Her future. "I hear you're changing the menu at the Burger Shack." Might as well address the elephant in the room.

"My parents' business has been struggling, and they wanted to retire. And I've been playing with the menu in the store I opened in Denver." His voice dropped into that low, soothing range usually reserved for lawyers and ministers dealing with sensitive topics. "The restaurant in Denver is all mine, and it's exceeded my expectations."

"You're a success." And she was just the deli clerk at Emory's.

Only for the next six weeks.

Kimmy bit into her sandwich, pausing to relish the blend of basil pesto, melted mozzarella, baked chicken, and olives. They could take away her job but they'd never take away her ability to make magic in a sandwich.

"It's not exactly the dream I talked about when we worked at the Burger Shack." He pulled what remained of his sandwich in half, stretching the cheese as he did so and then wrapping it around the bread before taking a bite. "But it's just what my family needs. I hope to have the staff trained before the wedding. I've got to get back to Denver soon afterward." He paused to smile but it was a tentative thing. "I want to show you the menu."

He wants my input?

Kimmy made a noncommittal noise and took another bite of sandwich, considering the cowlick at Booker's temple. The rest of his hair fell straight and in line. And that was Booker's life in a nutshell. He knew what he wanted and marched straight toward it, overcoming obstacles like a tank on a battlefield.

Her path to her dreams was slower paced and more circuitous. Not that she wanted to discuss her plans with Booker, owner of the Burger Shack. Or help with his menu.

She switched gears. "I need to find a wedding date." She set down her sandwich, thinking it could use a bit more garlic. "Maybe I am desperate. Can you imagine? Me up on the stage at Shaw's?" Gawked at and bid on. She shivered.

What did I get myself into?

"You'll earn the highest bid of the evening." That was Booker, ever the optimist.

Booker back in town. Kimmy needing a date. The Widows Club at her lunch counter. Suspicion worked its way into her thoughts.

"I'm just going to be frank here." She wiped her fingers clean with a napkin, wishing she could just as easily wipe away her promise to be auctioned off. "You walked up to my counter with the president of the Widows Club. Mims cornered you to emcee the event and maybe something more."

"It's not what you think." Booker held up his hands. "My mom brought her into the kitchen at the Burger Shack, and then she said she had something to talk about but wanted to get her steps in, and suddenly I was in your lunch line."

Kimmy picked up her sandwich and was about to take

another bite when she hesitated. "You don't think they're targeting the two of us as..."

Booker looked stricken and released a strangled "*No.*"

He either believed that or was friend-zoning her.

The friend-zoning stung given how smitten she was by his good looks today.

It's a by-product of my need for a date.

"Yeah, you're right." She stuffed some chicken back between the bread. "If they were trying to match the two of us, Mims wouldn't have asked you to emcee. You can't bid as the host."

"Bullet dodged," Booker muttered, not meeting her gaze.

Was the richness of the sandwich getting to him? Or was this conversation turning him off?

A cool mountain breeze swirled around them.

"I can still get out of the auction if I find a wedding date." Kimmy took another bite of her sandwich and savored the flavors.

"But...you promised."

Kimmy lifted her chin. "I caveated my acquiescence."

"High school vocabulary words aren't going to get you out of this." He wasn't teasing. He was serious. "You always said—"

"That a promise isn't to be broken." She hung her head. "Yeah, yeah, yeah. I can show and get bought, and the schmo can buy me dinner. But forget about that guy being my wedding date." She'd heard stories about drunken cowboys bidding. "Who can I ask from our high school class?"

Booker smirked. "First off, you want someone to talk to about the food they serve."

It was calming the way he knew her so well. "Yes, there's that."

"And someone who's willing to put up with your extraordinary dance moves." Booker grinned.

What Kimmy didn't have in smooth moves she made up for in enthusiasm.

Booker was eyeing her sandwich the way her father's dog eyed a hot Shack burger. "How about Jason Petrie?"

"He's still Darcy's guy." When Jason came home from the rodeo circuit, which was almost never.

"Iggy King?" Booker watched her take another bite. "I hear he's running a legitimate business now."

Kimmy swallowed and frowned. Iggy would be a fun wedding date if she wanted to drink too much and wake up in the wrong bed the next morning. *Pass.* "I'd put him in my last-resort category."

Booker seemed relieved. "I'd offer Dante but that seems a little extreme."

His kid brother? "I'm no cradle robber." Dante was thirteen years younger than she was. She pushed the remains of her sandwich away.

Booker scooped it up and took a bite. "Oh, man," he said after he swallowed, "this is good." He took another bite before asking, "Why don't you go stag?"

"Oh, I don't know." Kimmy propped her chin on her fists and adopted a sarcastic tone. "Maybe because ten years ago I went on a date with Hay."

It had been wonderful. Dinner in Greeley, followed by a movie and then a drink at Shaw's. He'd brought her home and kissed her good night. She'd been melting in his arms—her childhood crush, a tender kiss, visions of wedding veils dancing in her head.

And then Hay had broken it off, rested his forehead on hers, and said, "That was weird, wasn't it? I'm sorry."

He'd turned and walked away so fast that Kimmy hadn't

worked up the nerve to say, *That wasn't weird. It was wonderful, you idiot.*

And he'd driven off, apparently straight to Ariana's house. *And that, my friends, was the end of that.*

"You aren't still freaking out over that kiss, are you?" Booker rolled his eyes. "Hay told me it was like kissing his sister."

And Booker had made sure he'd told Kimmy that, more than once. "We don't have to rehash it."

"But you've been rehashing if you're thinking you need a date because of that one mistake a decade ago."

"Ariana still looks at me funny." Like she wasn't sure Kimmy could be trusted around her man. "I'll ask Avery if she's got a castoff I can use." Avery was an avid dater.

Booker pulled a face. "Man up and go alone."

"No. Jeez. Don't you get it? This is Ariana's big day. I don't want her to look at me and think, *That woman is in love with my husband.*"

"Do you love him?" Booker's dark brows lowered.

"No." Crushes weren't love. When Booker narrowed his eyes, she tried to clarify. "It's like...when you're young and you look at a famous actor—in your case, an actress— and you imagine what it would be like to be with them. But you know it's not going to happen." Although in her case it had, but not with the desired result.

"So you do still love him." There was an odd note to Booker's words that she couldn't place.

"No." Kimmy made a frustrated noise deep in her throat. "I love both of you but I'm not *in love* with either of you."

"Well then..." Booker was building a grin, along with his point. "Ariana's not going to be jealous of you."

Like I'm not someone to be jealous of?

"Way to make me feel good about myself, Book."

"Kim"—he shortened her name too—"you have mad kitchen skills. You should feel good about yourself and let the past stay in the past." Booker crumpled their sandwich wrappers together. "Now, about my menu..."

He didn't understand. "I don't have time to fawn over your menu." Kimmy stood, awash in disappointment. "My break's over."

"Right. Time constraints." He threw the balled wrappers into the trash, a gleam in his eye. "Speaking of, you should get yourself a wedding date quick, before the good ones are gone. Don't forget what happened at prom." When they'd both hesitated and ended up going together. "But first, tell me what you put in your sandwich besides garlic." He blessed her with a grin that tugged something in her chest.

"Spill my secrets?" Kimmy wasn't falling for Booker's charm that easily. "Help me get a wedding date, and maybe I will."

"Hello, parents. What are you doing here?" Booker stood in the back entrance to the Burger Shack, where he had half the staff practicing making gourmet sandwiches. He wanted to check on their progress and then find Mims. "Go home. You're supposed to be retired." The business was his now, and he planned to manage it from Denver.

His dad looked down his nose at a pimento-chicken sandwich with waffles in place of bread while his mom was poking a finger at a jalapeño- and meatball-stuffed ciabatta. Both his parents had dark hair threaded with gray and wore the Burger Shack black button-down and black slacks, along with grease-stained running shoes. They'd come prepared to work.

"I don't know, Booker." His dad pulled a face. The one he'd used when Booker came home after curfew. "The Burger Shack isn't known for sandwiches."

The tension that had sat between his shoulder blades while he'd stood in line for one of Kimmy's sandwiches and when she'd refused to look at his menu returned. "I've proved both concepts work together." With the restaurant he'd opened in Denver. "People want options."

"But these sandwiches..." His mom looked just as grave. "They're like what Emory's Grocery offers."

The sandwiches were exactly what Emory's offered, since they were the same sammies Kimmy had made while they were in high school.

Those were the sandwiches Booker knew how to make. He hadn't thought anything of his use of Kimmy's creations until his lawyer suggested he create fanciful names for items on his menu and trademark them. The process of legal protection had made him realize the sandwiches had never been his to begin with. He had to buy the rights from her.

The double knots threaded their way up his spine, tightening at the base of his neck.

Booker needed to come clean. But he'd been putting it off, putting out smaller fires instead, like saving the original Burger Shack from bankruptcy. And now he had no firebreak. The fire was upon him.

"Booker?" His mom rubbed his shoulder. "Are you reconsidering?"

"No," he blurted. He needed the higher income the sandwich line brought if he was going to put Dante through college and pay his parents retirement dividends. But...His stomach did a slow churn. It wasn't as if Kimmy didn't need the money too.

"Booker," his father said in that firm voice he used as a start to a lecture.

His trainees were looking like they didn't want to witness their current and former bosses arguing.

"Guys, these sandwiches sell well." Booker took each of his parents by the arm and walked them to the door. "They'll help fund your golden years. Now, why don't you go look at those travel brochures I gave you?"

His mom slipped a glance at his dad, a hopeful smile on her face. "I did like the river cruises."

"Maybe next year when I don't feel so useless." His dad took the sunglasses from the top of his head and slid them on. "We ran this business for more than forty years. It'll take me more than a month to stop worrying about it."

"I appreciate you allowing me to take your vision and make it succeed another forty years." Booker glanced back inside the restaurant. "Where's Dante?"

"He's at school." His mom beamed, naive as to her youngest's whereabouts. "He's at track practice, and afterward he's going to Theresa's to study for their chemistry test."

His dad had on his poker face, staring to the west and Saddle Horn Mountain, which was still blanketed in snow despite the spring sunshine. He likely knew what Dante was up to.

"Uh-huh." Booker decided not to mention that skateboarding wasn't a track event. "I wanted Dante to come to the Shack today." He had a sneaking suspicion that Dante had a severe case of high school senioritis, not conducive to part-time employment. "He should be shadowing me, like I did with Dad. He's going to help me manage the business one day." A string of Burger Shacks.

"Don't be hard on him," his mom said in the nurturing

voice she reserved for her youngest. "You know, we demanded too much of you, Booker. Let Dante be a kid awhile longer."

Dante was almost eighteen, almost an adult. At eighteen, Booker had been writing payroll checks and prepping the Burger Shack ledger for their accountant.

"Our little Dante is special." His mother laid a hand on Booker's cheek. Her eyes filled with tears. "You never know what the future might hold."

True that.

When Dante had been three, their mom had found a lump on his leg, just below the knee. It'd been cancerous. Booker was sixteen at the time and had to step up and run the Burger Shack while his parents shuttled Dante to and from treatments in Denver.

But Dante was tough. He'd beaten cancer and been clean ever since. And ever since, he'd been doted on by everyone in the family.

"Dante is special, Mom." Booker squeezed her hand, squeezing back the wish that someday his parents might see him as special too. "That's why I want to make sure he gets the best college education."

CHAPTER THREE

*H*ow's my baby?" Kimmy walked up her parents' drive-way and knelt in front of a jacked-up food truck, still thinking about Booker's successes.

In ten years, he'd hustled, started his own business, and bought out his parents. Envy banged around her head, making her temples pound. By comparison, Kimmy was a slacker. And so was her business plan, at least if you looked only on the outside.

Her food truck was rusted, dented, and dinged, but it was all hers. And someday soon—hopefully in six weeks—she was going to quit Emory's Grocery and make her living catering and selling grilled sandwiches out of it.

Her dad rolled out from beneath the engine. He still wore his blue-stained coverall uniform from the tire shop but he didn't look weary. He was as excited about Kimmy's venture as she was. "The new muffler came in this afternoon. I was just making sure everything's ready to put it in."

"And the stove?" Kimmy opened the van's door and stepped inside, conducting a slow inventory, wondering what Booker would say when he saw this.

He'd tell her Sunshine didn't have a large enough population to support three sandwich options—Emory's, the Shack, and hers. He'd point out she'd need to move from Sunshine to make a decent living. He'd remind her how close she was to her family, how important they were to her, the same way his family was priority one to him. He'd ask her whether she was willing to leave Sunshine to make it big.

Kimmy rubbed her temples. This time it wasn't envy banging around her head. It was impending sadness.

Leave Sunshine?

She drew a deep breath. An industrial kitchen on wheels and all her own. Kimmy thought it was beautiful. She didn't care if it never made her rich.

She'd bought the truck from someone in Denver who'd set the kitchen on fire and was getting out of the business. New paneling covered newly installed fire-resistant insulation. On the passenger side, the external features hadn't been damaged. The metal awning over the customer-service window swung up, and there was a customer counter that folded down.

She set her purse on the floor and ran a hand over the stainless countertop. She'd installed red-checked linoleum on the floor. Elbow grease had scoured the sink, the fixtures, and the cabinets until they gleamed. All she needed now were appliances—a fridge, stove, chargrill, fryer, panini press, steam table, warmer, and microwave.

And a special-order transmission.

She'd committed to everything. She'd ordered everything. All she needed was a couple more paychecks, and she'd be debt-free.

"Hank said the stove *might* come in today." Her dad joined her inside, wiping his hands on a rag. His dark-brown hair was gray at the temples but nothing about his knowledge of vehicles was aging. "Too bad it didn't."

Five months of work. Kimmy couldn't have restored the food truck on her own. Her dad, her uncles, her cousins—everyone had chipped in.

"It's okay, Dad. It's so close to being finished." She was so close to fulfilling her childhood dream of opening a specialty sandwich shop. "I can already imagine cooking in here."

Her dad slung his arm over her shoulder and gave her an affectionate squeeze. "The Garlic Grill is almost ready for launch."

"Hey." Her mom joined them inside. She had a streak of dirt on her cheek, and her hands were red from using cleaning products all day. She ran a small maid service in town. "Are you free on Sunday, Kimmy? Haywood hired me to clean his bachelor pad. He's having family and friends over Monday night."

"Um…" Kimmy didn't mind cleaning her friend's home but Booker's achievements proved Kimmy needed to take a step toward her dream every day to make it come true. "I was hoping to work on this but…"

"But we won't have all her appliances in," Kimmy's dad finished for her. "Of course she can help you. That's what family is for."

"Of course," Kimmy echoed, swallowing back guilt and excuses. She didn't want to appear ungrateful, and there were lines of fatigue on her mother's face.

"Thanks, honey." Her mom's expression eased. "Dinner in thirty minutes." She left, heading toward the house.

Kimmy and her father took in the fruits of their labor in silence.

"If my stove had come in, I could have cooked in here," Kimmy said wistfully.

"When this is done, my baby will be flying on her own wings." Her dad squeezed her once more. "I couldn't be prouder."

"Oh, Daddy." Kimmy tried not to cry.

"Hey." Uncle Mateo bounded into the truck, taking the stairs as if he were a much younger man. He lived just a few houses down. "I have logo designs for you from Ian." He smoothed wrinkles out of long sheets of paper with colorful renderings of the Garlic Grill food truck on them. "My boss at the shop says I can paint this beauty just as soon as you get her running."

They spent nearly thirty minutes admiring her cousin's graphics. She couldn't stop herself from wondering which design Booker would advise her to choose. Certainly not the one with pink. She wasn't selling cupcakes.

But Kimmy gravitated toward it anyway. The design featured a bright, happy sun in the top left corner, radiating across the side. "The name is really easy to read." In big pink letters.

"I'll tell Ian." Uncle Mateo placed that design on top. "He promised me he'd come by for dinner tonight and bring my grandkids." He grinned. "I haven't seen them in three days. And they live right around the corner. Crazy, huh?"

That was what Kimmy loved about her large, generous, close-knit family. They all pulled together. Helping to fix each other's vehicles and homes. Celebrating life's milestones. Supporting each other's dreams. It helped that her

family lived in a four-block radius on the south side of Sun
shine.

Kimmy hugged Mateo. "Tell Ian I remembered my
promise to make his family lunch every Saturday for the
next month." She was lucky her family let her barter for
services.

"Lunch every Saturday for a month," her dad said, chest
puffed out in pride as he looked at Kimmy. "A kept promise
is a true sign of character."

"And love," Kimmy murmured.

"I won't have to remind Ian." Uncle Mateo rubbed his
stomach. "He knows how good your food is. We all do."

The front screen door screeched open. "Dinner!" her
mom shouted, letting the door bang closed behind her.

Kimmy grabbed her purse. "I haven't even cleaned up."
She ran out of the truck and up the stairs outside the garage.

Skippy, her three-legged cat, met her at the door. The
small apartment felt larger now that her sister, Rosalie, had
moved out.

"We're running late, Skippy." She scooped up the gray
tabby and gave her a cuddle as she crossed the small living
room to the bedroom.

The only thing going slow in her life was the food truck
renovation. Everything else was coming at her fast—Hay's
wedding, Booker's return.

What could possibly happen next?

"Mims." After sending his parents home, it had taken
Booker three hours to find the Widows Club president.
"Can we talk?"

Hair wrapped in big pink curlers, Mims sat under a
hair dryer in the Sunshine Valley Retirement Home salon,
sound asleep, arms crossed over her fishing vest.

"Shhh." Lola Williams was fixing Harriet Bloom's hair. "Her hair will be dry in five minutes. Then you can wake her." Lola sprayed Harriet's hair, teased it with a long comb, and then sprayed it once more for good measure until it looked like a gray helmet.

The salon was small and looked even smaller with one wall painted a dingy rose color. The liveliest thing in the room was a large black feathered headdress hanging from the wall. It looked like something a Vegas showgirl would wear.

"Lola, I wish you'd master the art of a comb-out, instead of wasting your time on shopping for frivolous clothes." Harriet pointed to Lola's legs. "Have you ever seen such unusual legs, Booker?"

"Uh . . ." Booker hedged.

"Hush. You're embarrassing the man," Lola said but it was the hairdresser who was blushing. She wore an elegant black dress and lug-soled black boots. But what had caught Harriet's attention was her white stockings with edgy black tattoo patterns on them. "There's a viewing for Brillo Bryson later." Lola also worked as a hairstylist and makeup artist for the mortuary. "He was a biker. He'd appreciate my choice. And even if he wouldn't, sometimes a girl has to make a statement."

Kimmy had made a statement. She wasn't interested in seeing Booker's menu. He had to get her buy-in before he began officially selling sandwiches in Sunshine, because his sandwiches were her sandwiches. He wanted to make Kimmy an outright offer for her recipes. Cash money. But it wasn't the kind of business transaction you just tossed at a person without discussion and the appearance of negotiation.

The appearance.

Inwardly, Booker cringed. Never in his wildest dreams had he imagined his financial position would hinge on the work of someone else. He had to set things right without losing his friendship with Kimmy.

Mims snored. The loud kind that should've woken her up. It didn't.

Booker checked the time on his phone. Three minutes to go before her hair would be dry.

"I hear you're the best man at Haywood's wedding." Harriet caught Booker's gaze in the mirror. "That's a big responsibility. You've gotta make sure the groom doesn't have second thoughts."

"He won't." Hay had loved Ariana since they were in the sixth grade, probably since the time Kimmy had been crushing on Hay and Booker had been crushing on Kimmy.

"But he could," Harriet continued, holding her sharp chin high while Lola swept hair from her neck with what looked like a large paintbrush. "Who's your backup?"

"The other groomsmen?" Not that he needed them.

"No." Harriet made a derisive noise that deteriorated into thick coughs. It took her a moment to catch her breath. "I mean your wedding date. You need a date to keep you sane when Haywood's toes catch a chill."

"I…" He glanced at Mims, hoping she'd wake up and save him from this conversation. "I thought I was there to carry the rings."

"Nonsense." Harriet scoffed, turning her head to and fro to check out Lola's work. "You're there to have an escape plan in place for Haywood, if needed."

Lola laughed, heading toward a waiting walker. "Don't let her throw you off your game, Booker."

She already had.

"Have pity on me." Harriet inched her chair around with the toes of her white orthopedic shoes. "I don't get out much. Who's your wedding date?"

"I don't have one yet." He'd been hoping to ask Kimmy. But even though they'd discussed her options, she hadn't seen Booker as anything more than a man who appreciated her sandwiches.

She'll never know how much I appreciate those sandwiches.

That wasn't true. Booker planned to tell her. Of course, if he told her, it was a certainty that she wouldn't be his wedding date. Which was why he had to talk to Mims. He had a feeling the secrets he had to tell would send Kimmy running. He needed her to sit still and listen.

Lola rolled the walker to Harriet and helped her out of the chair.

"You could take Lola," Harriet said without any tact. "Her husband's dead."

"Only just." Grief flickered over Lola's features. "You'd try the patience of a saint, Harriet."

"Foolish girl." Harriet worked her way slowly toward the door. "Look at Booker. He's prime real estate. You need to strike while the iron is hot."

"Crotchety old woman," Lola countered, albeit good-naturedly, as if their arguments were common. "You owe me a nickel for whining about my work." She glanced at Booker and then gestured toward a shelf, where her whining jar was halfway full of nickels and pennies.

"I'll bring a dime next week." Harriet cackled. "Same day. Same time."

Lola turned off the standing hair dryer, startling Mims awake.

"Booker. What are you doing here?" Mims opened her

eyes wide. "No one is supposed to know I'm here. Barb over at Prestige Salon cuts my hair but she's booked, and my grandchildren are coming to town. Not to mention there's the bachelorette auction this weekend. I don't want to look like an unkempt mountain woman."

"Nobody's going to tell Barbara." But Lola made time to close the salon door behind Harriet.

"Mims, we need to talk," Booker said firmly, prepared for an argument. "I can't emcee the bachelorette auction."

The old woman blinked at him. "Why not?"

"Does it matter?" He didn't want to tell her the truth. "I promise to show up and bid." If he won Kimmy, she'd be his for an hour. The bachelorette auction included an informal dinner at the bar immediately afterward.

"Ah, I see." Mims gave him a forgiving smile. "Bring lots of cash. We don't accept credit or checks. And I expect Kimmy to go for a high price."

"Kimmy?" This was why Booker avoided Widows Club events. They could read minds and weren't shy about butting in where they weren't wanted. "Who said anything about Kimmy?"

"Who indeed?" Mims chuckled as Lola began unrolling the big pink curlers.

"Please don't get any ideas." His words had as much chance of being respected as a snowball in the Sahara. "Kimmy's made it very clear on several occasions over the years that she just wants to be friends." Which made his attraction to her inconvenient. He valued Kimmy's friendship too much to attempt to date her. "But if I do buy her—for reasons that have nothing to do with romance—can you make sure she gets a wedding date?"

"My boy, I have the perfect man in mind for her."

Mims's smile wasn't reassuring. There were plans springing in that head of hers.

"Great." Booker said his goodbyes and headed for the door. "As long as you're not talking about me."

Her laughter followed him out into the hallway.

$\mathcal{C}$HAPTER FOUR

"$\mathcal{H}$ow do I look?" Kimmy smoothed her green lace sheath over her hips. "I was going for sexy and sophisticated but now that I'm here, I think I might look grandmotherly and dated."

"You look fabulous." Her friend Priscilla Taylor was quick to reassure her. "If my divorce was final, I'd put myself out there too."

Kimmy was glad Priscilla wasn't joining in the auction festivities. She'd always been the center of male attention, while Kimmy had always been the girl on the outskirts of the crowd, male or female.

And speaking of crowds, Shaw's Bar & Grill was packed. The local hangout had a big stage and a dance floor on one end, and on the other were padded booths and large wooden tables surrounding a well-used pool table. The center of Shaw's featured a long, narrow bar ringed with stools. There were license plates on the walls and saddles mounted on the rafters. And on Saturday nights, customers tossed shells from free peanuts onto the floor.

It being Saturday, Kimmy had to watch her step in heels.

"Look at all these women." Priscilla grabbed on to Kimmy's arm. "They're lined up like it's Black Friday and there's a great deal on Michael Kors handbags."

Kimmy stopped walking and took count. Fifteen women. That was a lot for Sunshine. "This is a mistake." But she couldn't back out. She'd promised.

"It's no mistake." Priscilla pointed toward the dance floor. "Look. Have you ever seen so many cowboys?"

Kimmy hadn't been looking at the men. But now she could see there were cleaned-up cowhands milling about the dance floor, as well as local men in all shapes, colors, and sizes. Paul Gregory was wearing a suit and elbowing his way to the front of the stage, holding what looked like a strawberry daiquiri.

"The good news is I don't see my brother." Priscilla dragged Kimmy toward the line of bachelorettes up for auction. Her older brother was the sheriff, and when it came to fun, Drew was something of a wet blanket.

"The bad news is he would've made a good wedding date." Kimmy wouldn't have had to worry about Drew drinking too much and making advances. Although he probably wouldn't have been able to talk intelligently about food. Or more accurately, he might have dozed off while she did so.

"You're here!" shouted Clarice. She checked something off the list on her clipboard and took Kimmy's other arm. "Right this way." She gave Priscilla a frosty stare. "It's against the rules for married women to participate."

"I guess I'll be at the bar." Priscilla grinned and headed toward the center of the room.

"I wrote an introduction for you." Clarice continued to use her outdoor voice. Who could blame her? The crowd noise was nearly deafening. "Do you want to read it?"

Kimmy shook her head.

Clarice made another check mark on her clipboard and hobbled off without her walking stick, her purple tie-dyed muumuu swaying with each step.

Kimmy took her place behind Darcy Jones at the end of the line. If Darcy was up for auction, Jason Petrie was most likely in the audience. Since they were an item, Darcy's purchase was a sure thing. Kimmy, being last, wasn't such a sure thing. She wasn't showing as much leg, as much cleavage, or as much makeup as most of the young women in line. By the time it was her turn, most of the rowdy cowboys would have lost their enthusiasm for the sport or already purchased their date.

Confidence. She needed confidence.

Lacking some, Kimmy started to sweat.

Mims moved to center stage and turned on the microphone. For all Kimmy had made jokes about the Widows Club and events like this, Mims's poise was calming. She wore a blue dress and white sandals and looked as comfortable as if she were wearing her fishing vest and blue jeans. "Thanks for showing up to the Date Night Auction to benefit the Sunshine Valley Boys & Girls Club. The bachelorettes for auction tonight—"

The crowd erupted with applause, whistles, and hollers.

Mims made a settle-down gesture with her hands. "Our ladies will be available for prescreening for the next few minutes on and around the stage." Mims stared down at the crowd. "Gentlemen, as a reminder, bidding starts at one hundred dollars. This is a cash-only event. Any man who sets foot on the stage makes an immediate purchase. Winning bidders also pay for dinner and drinks afterward."

Paul Gregory sauntered along the line. He'd lost the straw for his daiquiri, the drinking of which had stained his upper lip, making him look as if he had a red mustache. He stopped by Kimmy and said, "You look pretty tonight without your apron."

"Thanks?" Kimmy murmured, not wanting to encourage him, but he was a good customer and a good exterminator. And she did so hate bugs.

The cowboys who ambled by next checked out the women up for auction the way she imagined they checked out cattle for sale. Kimmy smiled, in case good teeth were important in their judgment.

More residents came by. Dr. Janney, who did her annual exam. Jay Parker, a plumber who still wore his work coveralls. Darnell Tucker, a mechanic at the local garage. All customers at the deli.

During a lull, Kimmy touched Darcy's shoulder. "I feel awkward." Like she was lined up in gym class to be put on a soccer team.

"You'll be fine," Darcy reassured her. "Just remember it's for a good cause, and these people are your friends. Except for some of the cowboys. In which case, just remember dinner only lasts an hour." She turned to speak to the woman in front of her.

"Right," Kimmy said under her breath. "Good cause. Good friends. One hour."

Iggy King walked by. He paused when he saw her. "Hey, Kimmy. I've never seen you on sale before."

On sale? Panic set in. She grabbed his arm. "Iggy, I'll give you free sandwiches for a week if you buy me."

Booker appeared at Iggy's shoulder, looking handsome in a suit and tie. "You look great, Kim."

Ditto. But she couldn't say it. He'd think she wanted him to buy her.

"Thanks?" she said instead.

Who was she kidding? She'd be thrilled if he did. Not that he would. He was more likely to bid on someone from his side of town. And even if he did, it wouldn't solve her wedding-date dilemma.

Kimmy tried to catch Iggy's wandering eye.

"I'll think about it, Kimmy." Iggy headed toward Priscilla and the bar. "Good luck."

Shoot. That sounded like Iggy had thought about it and made a negative decision.

"Hey." Booker leaned in close enough to be heard over the crowd. "Are you okay?"

"I'm at the end of the line." Kimmy's heels were beginning to pinch her toes. "I think Iggy is my last resort." Heaven help her.

Booker frowned. "If it's stressing you out, don't do this."

Easy enough for him to say. "I have to. Wedding date, remember?" She straightened her spine. "Plus I promised." An Easley always kept a promise.

"It's time to get this party started." Mims's voice raised the roof once more.

A few minutes later, the bidding began.

Mims was a skilled auctioneer. Paul bid often but lost every time. He ordered another daiquiri and continued to suck his drink down without a straw. His bright-red mustache deepened in color. Winning bidders escorted their dates to reserved tables. Iggy and Priscilla were yukking it up at the bar, which in hindsight was where Kimmy should have been.

And every few minutes, Kimmy took a few steps closer to the stage. When Darcy's name was about to be called, she turned to Kimmy and wished her luck. And then Darcy was walking out on stage. Sure enough, Jason was in the audience and bid on her. He outbid Paul, who must have been on his fourth daiquiri.

"And now..." Mims smiled at Kimmy and gestured for her to join her on the stage. "Our last bachelorette of the evening, Kimmy Easley."

There were weak whoops and a round of applause, nothing like the enthusiasm for Mims's opening remarks.

Mims read Clarice's introduction. "Kimmy is a Sunshine girl. She creates gourmet sandwiches at Emory's Grocery. She likes long walks in the park, and in her spare time, she likes to garden."

Gah! She sounded boring.

"A hundred bucks." Paul swayed near Kimmy's feet.

Kimmy swallowed, seeking out Iggy in the crowd. He wasn't even looking at her!

"One twenty-five." That came from a cowboy with a friendly smile.

She hoped he loved long walks in the park and food, especially garlic.

"One fifty." That bid came from the back of the crowd. Kimmy couldn't see where.

"Two hundred," Paul said wearily.

Kimmy would've felt sorry for him if she weren't his last chance for a date. The whole purpose of this exercise was to find a man who might be a good wedding date, someone who'd talk about food, not bugs.

"Two and a quarter." The cowboy was still smiling. He was wearing a straw hat and a blue chambray shirt that looked soft to the touch. He probably loved grilled steak.

She made a mean T-bone.

"Two seventy-five." Whoever was bidding in the back must have been short or hidden behind several Stetsons beyond the stage lights. Kimmy still couldn't see him.

"Three fifty." Paul set his drink on the stage, placed his palms on either side of it, and hung his head as if he might be sick.

Mims and Kimmy exchanged a glance and backed up a step.

"Four hundred dollars!" came the bid from the back.

The crowd gasped. It was the highest bid of the night.

The cowboy made a cutting gesture across his throat.

Paul lifted his heavy head and tried to spot his rival. He wasn't the only one looking. Everyone up front was turning around.

"We have four hundred," Mims said into the microphone. "Going once. Going twice. Sold!"

The crowd was parting, cowboys moving out of the way as the lights came up.

And then a man approached. A well-dressed man. A solid man.

Booker.

Buying Kimmy hadn't netted Booker the response he wanted—Kimmy's gratitude.

Yes, there was relief in her eyes, but only temporarily.

Added to that, Paul and the cowboy who'd bid against him were lingering nearby.

"My hero," Kimmy said to Booker when they were seated in a booth in the back with two glasses of champagne and a dinner order placed. Her gaze darted around Shaw's, around his competition. "But let's be clear. Although I appreciate the save, you need to circulate through the crowd and find me a wedding date. You promised."

Fat chance, honey.

Bidding on Kimmy against other men had stepped on a nerve, one connected to a proprietary feeling for her. She might never see him romantically but for the next hour, she was going to be his.

"Look, we're here." Booker raised his champagne glass. "Let's toast. Here's to old friends and new beginnings."

With a sigh, Kimmy clinked her glass against his. "Hear, hear."

"We should take this time to catch up." Booker had a lot of explaining to do, and his hour alone with Kimmy had begun. "We didn't get a chance to do that the other day. What's new?"

"What's new?" Kimmy smirked. "I put myself out there in the Widows Club bachelorette auction." She'd looked miserable up there, smiling on command. "And that's about it for me. You?"

"I want to increase Burger Shack profits and put Dante through school." Booker was proud that he'd be able to do it. That is, if he could increase earnings at the original Burger Shack. And to do so, he needed Kimmy to sign a contract.

Instead of regarding Booker with warmth and respect, Kimmy frowned. "Why do you want to give Dante a free ride when you never had one? From what I hear, Dante doesn't even work at the Burger Shack anymore."

"He can't work because he's on the track team." And before that he'd been on the basketball team. And in the fall, the football team. Although there was the matter of the skateboard that shed doubt on Dante's school activities. Regardless, Booker had to stay on point. "Have I told you how hard it was to work and go to college?"

They'd talked more in the four years he was in college than in the last four years.

"Are you complaining? Seriously?" Kimmy sipped her champagne and stared at him over the rim of her glass. Her mouth tipped up at the corners. "From the way you talked, you loved every minute of it."

He had but Booker denied it anyway. "I ran an underground grill from my dorm room. I could have been kicked out at any time."

Kimmy crossed her arms over her chest. "Again, you loved every minute of it."

"I was exhausted and stressed 24/7." It had been a continuous adrenaline rush. "It probably took ten years off my life. I don't want it to take ten years from Dante's. Or worse, make him sick again."

She rolled her eyes. "Is your mother here? I think I just heard her talking about Dante's life expectancy." Although Kimmy was fond of Dante, she'd never been fond of the way Booker always came last in the family. "Oh, no. It was you who was babying him."

"Here it comes." Booker cupped a hand behind one ear. "The work lecture."

Paul passed by. He'd had too much to drink and was strutting like a peacock, all despondency over being dateless gone.

Kimmy's gaze chilled. "Hard work builds character, Booker. You know this."

"Is your father here?" Booker refilled their glasses. "Doesn't he always say that?"

"Touché." Kimmy and her siblings had been told, not encouraged, to find jobs as soon as they were old enough to drive. "Would you take it back? All those years spent working with your family at the Shack? I wouldn't." She leaned forward as if what she had to say needed to be private, despite the fact that they had to talk loud enough to be heard over the bar's music. "Don't you love cooking? Wouldn't you rather be in the kitchen than anywhere else? I know I would."

Before Booker could answer, Clarice showed up at their table. "Sorry to interrupt," she shouted.

Mims was right behind her, pointing to her ear and a bright-red clip-on earring. "She forgot her hearing aids."

"I didn't forget." Clarice bristled. "I don't need them in here. Everybody is shouting."

Mims patted her friend's shoulder. "We just wanted to ask Kimmy if she'd participate in our bake sale next week. It benefits the Little League."

Kimmy sat back, her expression turning wary. "Isn't that competitive?"

"No, no, no," Mims reassured her. "I mean, Wendy Adams always sells out her Bundt cake first but it's all for a good cause."

Booker was trying hard not to smile. Kimmy had given the Widows Club an inch, and they were trying to take their mile. She'd be a prime target for every fund-raiser they had from now on.

"Oh, Booker." Mims smiled down at him. At first glance, it was a benevolent smile. But upon closer inspection, it was a smile that meant business. "Did you ever find a wedding date?"

"No." It was Booker's turn to fall back against the seat.

"There's Wendy now," Clarice shouted. "She was late and just missed being up for auction."

Sure enough, Bitsy, another Widows Club board member, escorted Wendy toward their table as if Kimmy or Booker were in need of her.

As if I want Wendy to be my wedding date.

Booker's shoulders cramped, sending a sharp twinge up his neck.

"I have an idea," Mims said, still smiling. "Why don't you two team up for the bake sale?"

"Booker and me..." Kimmy's eyes narrowed. "We don't bake. We grill."

Clarice frowned at Mims and shouted, "I think there's a rule—"

"There is no rule, Clarice," Mims said at the same volume. The Widows Club president wasn't good at hiding the high sign. She made wild eyes at Clarice and drew a make-believe zipper across her mouth. And then she turned to Kimmy with a big smile. "You could grill dessert." She cleared her throat and turned to Booker. "Together."

"I was just talking to Iggy," Clarice shouted at Kimmy. "He loves fried food."

Kimmy paled.

Booker wanted to laugh. The Widows Club was trying to match Kimmy with Iggy. But it wasn't a laughing matter. They were trying to play Cupid with him and Wendy and eating into his time alone with Kimmy. The auction had promised an intimate date but Booker wasn't getting his money's worth.

Bitsy and Wendy paused at their table.

Wendy, the shiest, most withdrawn girl from their high school class.

Paul danced past, scooting through the crowd. He'd fastened his tie around his head like a sweatband, and he had his dress shirt open, revealing a stark white T-shirt.

"Hi," Wendy said to Booker in that meek voice of hers, one he had to strain to hear.

He and Kimmy were better at secret high signs than

Mims and her widows. Booker pressed his lips together and stared at Kimmy, willing her to read his mind: *Red alert. We're being cornered.*

Paul danced back doing the "Look Alive" dance, drawing Kimmy's attention away from Booker. "I'll buy Wendy." The town exterminator didn't stop dancing. "Two hundred. *In cash.*"

Everyone blinked.

Paul planted his feet but his hips kept moving, as did his shoulders. And there was a side-to-side head bob. The cobra dance move. Despite being drunk, the man had moves. People around them were applauding his skill.

Paul extended a hand toward Wendy. "Come on, girl. Are you ready for this?"

The Wendy he remembered from high school would have shrunk back. That wasn't this Wendy. She put her hand in Paul's.

"Sweet." Paul skipped off, dragging her after him.

The Widows Club huddled together. This was Booker's chance. Not just to communicate without words to Kimmy but to confess what he'd done. Beg forgiveness. Offer money. And perhaps salvage their friendship.

"Kimmy," Booker said sharply, staring at her with mind-meld intensity.

She stared back. And then understanding dawned in her eyes as she seemed to receive his message.

"I've got this." Kimmy tapped Mims on the shoulder. "Can you excuse us, ladies? Booker paid a lot for a date with me, and I'd like to give him his money's worth."

CHAPTER FIVE

"It's official. We're being targeted for wedding dates," Booker told Kimmy as soon as the Widows Club set off to rescue Wendy or collect their two hundred dollars. It wasn't clear which.

"Why are you panicking?" Kimmy sipped her champagne. "You never used to freak around the Widows Club."

"They brought me Wendy Adams." He'd have preferred they brought him Kimmy. Instead, he'd had to buy her outright. Nothing was going right tonight. "They've never flaunted a date in front of me before."

"You're older now. And still single." Kimmy glanced toward the dance floor, where Wendy was doing the mom dance and Paul was bouncing around her like a pogo stick. "Besides, Wendy's got a smidge more personality now."

Was that a smile twitching at the corner of her mouth?

Kimmy faced him squarely, not a hint of a smile on her face. "Besides, I should be the one who's nervous. Clarice mentioned Iggy. My last resort."

They stared at each other for a moment and then burst out laughing.

Kimmy drank more champagne, mischief in her eyes. "You know what this means?"

Booker shook his head.

"You'll have to be my wedding date." She said it with a straight face.

Booker sucked in a breath, afraid if he blew it out, he might just break his cheeks by giving her the biggest smile on record. "You're asking me..."

She nodded.

Booker's heart swelled. He'd hidden his feelings for Kimmy for two decades. But he had to hide them a while longer. She was asking him out at the worst possible moment—right as he was about to confess to basing his sandwiches off her concoctions.

He blew out a breath. "No." It pained him to refuse her.

"Hang on." She laid her palms on the table and narrowed her eyes. "*No?* Is this about prom?"

Prom. She'd debuted her dance style there. And he, as her let's-go-as-friends date, had been unwilling to step out on the floor and join her.

Stupid, fragile teenage ego.

Paul tossed bills at the widows and then ran to the bar. He scrambled onto a stool and then onto the bar itself. A swing of his arms and his button-down sailed into the crowd, which was clapping and egging him on. A twist and a shimmy and his T-shirt followed. And then he boot-scooted toward the far end of the bar.

"Booker. Book." Kimmy waved a hand in front of his face and glanced Paul's way. "This is about how I dance, isn't it? Wedding dates are obligated to dance."

"This has nothing to do with your dance moves." And everything to do with his obligations to his family.

"I'm not asking you to promise to have and to hold until death do us part." Her shoulders were bunched around her ears. "It's one date between friends. Don't make such a big deal out of it."

Booker ran a hand over his face. It was hard to present logical arguments with Paul dancing a few feet away. The town exterminator reached the end of the bar and boogied along the short end, not caring that the bartender was on the phone, most likely with the sheriff.

And then something Kimmy said sank in. "Hold the phone. Did you just say *promise*?" Booker stilled, trapping Kimmy's gaze with his own. "You know how I feel about promises." And he knew how she felt about hers.

"Promises to you always come with conditions." She studied him carefully, shoulders lowering. "Name yours."

This is your chance, his inner voice whispered.

Yes, his chance to clear the air about sandwiches and the past. But maybe a chance to win her heart as well.

"If you don't agree," she said impatiently, "the widows will try and set me up with all kinds of men for the wedding. And you... Wendy Adams was just the start for you."

Booker shook his head. "You know how they get." The widows. They were like a bouncy Labrador who kept bringing his owner a different toy to play with until... "I need more than a wedding date this week. I need a girl-friend to avoid more permanent matchmaking."

The words dropped between them, drowning out the music and the crowd noise and the approaching siren.

"So..." Kimmy was looking at him as if he were a box of spices that was unlabeled, one she couldn't believe she was considering purchasing. "You're saying we date for real?" Her head was shaking before she'd finished her sentence.

"I'm saying we *pretend* to have fallen for each other." Easy enough on his part. "We show up at the wedding events. There's a family-and-friends barbecue Monday, the wedding party celebration on Wednesday, a rehearsal dinner on Friday, and then the actual wedding on Saturday."

"You do remember prom," Kimmy said, staring at her hands and grimacing. "I want to dance."

"It'll get you out of the bake sale." One less Widows Club event to worry about. "And I'll get out on the dance floor. I promise."

Her barriers were coming down. Kimmy was no longer looking like she'd swallowed vinegar. "Still…"

"You've got nothing to lose." Whereas he…This could definitely boomerang. In fact, it would as soon as he told her about the contract.

Kimmy reached across the table for his hand, rubbing her thumb over his knuckles. "We're putting years of friendship on the line."

Sometimes you had to fish or cut bait. "We'll be fine." Booker came around to Kimmy's side of the booth, sliding in next to her. "We'll hold hands, like this." He took one of her hands in his, noting the way her eyes widened. "And occasionally, we'll brush the hair from each other's eyes." He smoothed her hair back from her forehead, noting the way her breath hitched. "And every so often—just to sell it, of course—we'll kiss." She held herself very still as he leaned in and pressed a kiss to her cheek. "You can do that, can't you?"

He wasn't sure anymore that he could. He wanted to

sweep her into his arms and kiss her somewhere besides her cheek.

"Promise me you'll be my pretend girlfriend all week long." This was important, perhaps more important than him proving that she wouldn't reject his touch. "Kim. Promise me."

"I promise," she said begrudgingly.

"Say the rest." Luckily, a waitress delivered their food— two blue cheese burgers with two sides of sweet potato fries—just in time.

Kimmy's eyes flashed to her fries and then back to Booker's face. "Did you plan this?"

"Nope." He shook his head. "Do you want me to go first?"

Eye roll. Huff. Kimmy put her hand a few inches over her fries. "I promise on an order of hot fries to be your wedding date for a week so you won't be harassed by the matchmaking Widows Club." She took a fry. "And you?"

He put his hand over his fries. "I promise on an order of hot fries to make sure Ariana knows you're no threat." The bride knew that anyway. He picked up a fry.

They both took a bite and then grinned at each other.

That's when the guilt set in, heavy on his shoulders. He knew Kimmy wouldn't renege on their deal no matter how mad she was at him.

"This is such a bad idea." Kimmy lifted the top of her burger and sliced it open to check the inside. "Medium rare. Love."

"Jeffrey's cooking in the back. My dad taught him everything he knows." Booker checked his burger. Also medium rare. "I've always admired how you keep a promise." He wrapped his fingers around his burger.

Kimmy was ahead of him. She took a bite and then made a sound of approval.

"You know my college grill?" he asked.

She nodded, snagging another fry. "Needs more garlic."

"I never told you what I put on the menu." Booker was coming up on her slowly, carefully. "And you never asked."

She'd teased him instead. *What's on your menu, Booker? Plain burgers? Doubles? Extra-large patties on an extra-large bun?*

And when she'd finished her teasing, he'd always nod and say, *"Something like that."*

"It was your business," Kimmy said now, nodding her head slightly.

Guilt pressed down on him harder. Not just on his shoulders. It closed around his throat, trying to halt his words. He pushed them out anyway. "The reason I was so successful...The reason I had loyal customers...It was because I used your sandwich recipes." Not at first. But that didn't matter.

For just a moment, Kimmy's head continued to nod. She continued to chew a fry.

And then her brow furrowed. Her head stilled, and she swallowed. The corners of her mouth turned down. "You what?"

"I—"

"You jerk." She shoved him out of the booth and ran.

"You're on his side?" Kimmy stopped digging through a box of kitchen utensils her aunt Mitzy had purchased at a garage sale for her, and straightened in the food truck. She clutched a metal spatula. "Booker's?"

She'd been dumping the events of last night in her father's lap while he installed her stove.

"Do you know how lucky you are?" Her dad slid the stove into place and rubbed his palms on his coveralls.

"You have a large extended family supporting you. And he—"

"He stole from me." Kimmy shook the spatula in the air. She hadn't been able to sleep last night, not with betrayal burning her heart worse than too much four-alarm chili.

"Haven't you always told me the Belmontes give everything to Dante and nothing to Booker?" Her father laid a hand on her shoulder.

"So that makes it right?" Every time he'd asked her what was in a sandwich, she'd been filled with pride that he'd enjoyed her creation enough to ask. And all along, he'd been pilfering her work.

"I know this hurts." Her dad's gaze was soft. "Do you remember when you took my set of screwdrivers to Emory's to fix the loose storage lockers?"

"Don't try to say that's the same." Kimmy couldn't believe they were having this conversation.

I should have told Mom. She'd understand.

"I didn't begrudge you the use of my tools." He was in dad mode, words slow and deliberate, as if he knew her mind was circling around the possibility that she'd been betrayed. "I did ask you after a month to bring them back when I knew I was going to need them."

"Tools are not sandwiches."

"But you borrowed my tools without asking," her dad continued.

Kimmy swallowed a groan of frustration.

"You don't have to admit I'm right." His hand fell away. "But you know I am. Ninety-nine percent of the time."

Kimmy stared at the freshly painted ceiling.

Her mother climbed onto the lower step of the truck. "Are you almost ready to go? I promised Haywood I'd be there soon. He left us a key under the mat."

"Yes, Mom, but can you weigh in on this?" Because Kimmy would like to have someone on her side.

"Sure." The pleasant smile on her mother's face hinted at expectations of a food truck opinion. She had no idea there were much heavier issues at hand.

Kimmy explained what Booker had done.

Her mother didn't hop up and down in anger. "You're saying Booker used your sandwiches to finance his way through college?"

"Yes." Maybe her mother was doing a slow burn on this.

"Don't you create new sandwiches every week?" She was in mom mode, calmly presenting her arguments. "Do you even remember what sandwiches you were making ten years ago?"

No. "That's not the point."

A truck pulled up outside. It was a new truck, and Booker was driving.

Kimmy's pulse kicked up a notch.

"Family goes the extra mile, honey." Her mom hopped down and waved to Booker on her way back inside the house.

"Family." Kimmy watched Booker approach. She had on her grubbies: jeans and a T-shirt she didn't mind getting dirty. He wore pressed khakis and a black Burger Shack polo. "He's not family."

"Isn't he?" Her dad waved Booker inside. "For years, you would've argued he is."

She hated that her parents' arguments made sense. Scowling, Kimmy set her hands on her hips.

"Hey." Booker bounded up the steps and looked around. "What's all this?"

"Kimmy's future." Her dad excused himself and left them alone.

"Family's got your back," Kimmy muttered. "Not."

"What's that?" Booker ran a hand over the countertop the same way Kimmy did when she came in, a greeting of sorts to the kitchen. He glanced around and then faced her. His gaze was soft, forgivable.

Do not forgive.

"This is my big move forward," Kimmy said instead, planting her feet. "When we were kids, we always talked about having businesses of our own. This is mine." She plastered a smile on her face and shored up her defenses for his criticism. "I know it's not brick-and-mortar or white tablecloth but it's a start."

"What a great idea." Booker began opening cupboards, checking out her space.

My baby.

"Low overhead. Freedom to change locations if the grass is greener elsewhere." He poked around the box of utensils from Aunt Mitzy, muscles flexing as he moved things around. Every hair in place except that cowlick. His voice familiar, comforting, approving. "You can make your own hours. Work the catering circuit."

"You stole from me." There was no escaping that fact.

"Yes." He leaned against the counter, not running from anything.

"You operated an illegal grill from your dorm room. No health inspections. No business license." At the time, she'd thought he was daring for doing so.

"Yes."

"And because you cheated the system, you thought you could cheat me." Her words were roughened by hurt. "You didn't ask. I would've been okay if you would've asked." Because what her parents had said was true. He was like family to her.

Booker's gaze didn't drop from hers. "My dad gave me an indoor grill as a graduation present. I used it to cook meals. And then my college friends wanted me to grill for them. They were willing to pay." He scratched at his cowlick. "My roommate was a business major. Somehow, it went from this little thing to a big thing overnight. Except...people got bored with burgers."

"So you turned to sandwiches." Hers.

"It was weird," Booker said slowly, nodding. "When I prepared your sauces and put them on the grill, it was as if you were next to me, helping me, working with me." His gaze was so dark and sorrowful she knew she'd forgive him. "I miss us working side by side, bumping elbows and scooting around each other." His gaze took in the food truck's kitchen. It was just the right size for bumping elbows and scooting.

But he's not going to be cooking in here with me.

"I'm sorry I didn't ask permission." Booker's eyes were filled with regret. "I'm sorry I waited so long to tell you the truth."

The air between them seemed thick with significance.

Kimmy could forgive him, and their friendship would carry on. Or she could hold on to the hurt, letting it sit like the taint of rotten eggs. She wasn't the grudge-holding type. But she wasn't the brush-it-off-and-everything-is-hunky-dory type either.

Kimmy sighed. She'd forgive him and hope time would heal the wound he'd made. "You should have asked or at least told me sooner. But you always were a procrastinator." That wasn't true but a truce sometimes required levity. And there was the promise she'd made about the week ahead.

Booker gave her a rueful smile. He knew he was still on shaky ground. "There's something else. I—"

"Kimmy!" Her mom banged out the front door. "Time to go."

"I have to help my mom with a client." Kimmy moved toward the door. "Can we talk tomorrow?"

"Sure." Booker had a bewildered expression on his face. "What time?"

"What time?" Kimmy paused on the top step. "What time are you picking me up for Hay's party?"

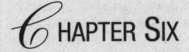

CHAPTER SIX

$\mathscr{K}$immy took Monday off to drive into Greeley.

She needed dresses, a pedicure, and a stylish haircut if she was going to spend the week pretending to be Booker's girlfriend on the wealthy side of town.

What I need is my head examined.

This was the one time she should've broken a promise. Her hesitation wasn't just because she was still in the process of forgiving Booker. Growing up, she'd never felt as if she fit with the kids who wore expensive tennis shoes and name-brand blue jeans. For heaven's sake, she'd cleaned Haywood's house yesterday for the party she was attending tonight. If that wasn't proof she was out of her element, she didn't know what was.

At the mall in Greeley, Kimmy ventured deep into foreign territory—a department store dress department.

"May I help you?" The woman who stepped between the racks had a style Kimmy envied. She wore a figure-flattering dress and a pair of attractive heels that didn't look tortuous.

"I'll have one of those." Kimmy's gesture encompassed the woman. "I need three dresses to wear to wedding events and one to a wedding. Plus shoes. And..." She sighed. Might as well just admit all her failings. "This is what I normally wear to work." She gestured to her blue jeans and red T-shirt. "Your mission, should you choose to accept it, is to make me look like I know what I'm doing in the dress department."

The sales clerk—Lydia, her name tag said—took Kimmy by the arm. "I've been dreaming of you my entire life. Come on."

An hour later, Kimmy was armed with four dresses she'd never wear after this week, a pair of heels she could stand to wear for a few hours, and a referral to the spa in the mall.

At the spa, the hairstylist wasn't as excited to see Kimmy as Lydia had been. "What kind of product do you use on your hair?"

"Shampoo." By the woman's frown, she could tell that was the wrong answer. "I have to wear my hair back for work every day. I don't need product."

The hairstylist tried to run her fingers through Kimmy's frizzy hair but her hands moved slowly through the thick mass. "You need product. Good product."

Kimmy took that to mean *expensive*. She couldn't afford expensive. That was why she didn't go to Prestige Salon in Sunshine. With all her credit card spending today, she was setting her food truck timeline back a week.

The hairstylist ran a comb carefully through Kimmy's hair. "And you need bangs."

"I don't want bangs."

"You need bangs."

"No bangs."

"I'll change your mind."

"No, you won't," Kimmy said as politely as she could.

"You're tense." The woman continued combing Kimmy's hair.

"I'm tense because you keep talking about bangs."

"You need a complete spa treatment. Massage. Facial. Wax. Mani-pedi. Hair. Afterward, you'll feel like a new woman." Her recommendations sounded convincing. Her hair, skin, and nails were flawless. Not to mention she styled hair while wearing high heels. She looked like she belonged at Hay's party more than Kimmy ever would.

"Okay, fine." Her credit card balance was going to be huge. "As long as you promise me no bangs."

The woman didn't promise.

Hours later, Kimmy left the mall with her purchases, muscles aching from a deep tissue massage, upper lip red from waxing, and bangs falling in a straight line across her forehead.

If it hadn't been for her promise to Booker, friend and sandwich thief, she might not have opened the door when he came to pick her up for the barbecue.

"Whoa." Booker took a step back. "Somebody's been out shopping and..."

"You hate them." Kimmy tried to pull her bangs down, hoping to help them grow out quicker. Like in the next ten minutes. "I don't blame you. I hate them."

"I wasn't looking at your bangs." He swooped in and ruffled them up. "That's better."

Kimmy doubted it.

Skippy sauntered out to rub against Booker's legs.

"I recognize you from your pictures." He leaned down to scratch her behind the ears. "Tell Kim she looks awesome, Skippy."

On cue, Kimmy's cat blinked up at her and meowed.

Kimmy took a moment to stare in disbelief. "Okay, let's get this show on the road." She grabbed a sweater and then locked her apartment door behind them, hurried down the stairs, and headed toward Booker's truck. When she noticed Booker wasn't with her, she stopped and turned "What is it now? Did I leave a tag on?" She turned this way and that, tugging at her skirt.

"You have curves," Booker said, almost in awe. "And legs."

Kimmy sent her gaze skyward. "How many years have you known me?"

"Twenty-seven." He approached, circled, and smiled The really good smile. The one that practically lifted her spirits along with her lips. "I can't remember ever seeing your knees after the sixth grade."

"That can't be. We went to prom..." She hadn't wanted to bring that up again.

"Everyone has an unfortunate event in their past." Booker caught her hand and led her to his truck. "So you ordered a prom dress online."

"It wasn't anything like the picture." Or anything that flattered her teenage shape in any way. "No big deal. I just wore my coat all night." And sweat like she'd taken hot yoga until one of the chaperones forced her to remove her coat in case she was harboring everyone's alcohol. And then Booker and Hay had dared her to dance. And she'd gotten out there—horrid dress, horrid dance moves, and all.

Booker opened her door and helped her into the seat. "If you want to feel better, I could tell you about my preteen acne, which required a prescription and a nightly treatment from my grandmother—who made a sickly smelling poultice."

"Enough said."

When Booker was behind the wheel, he slipped her another smile. "I know I'm going to say this wrong but you look beautiful."

Kimmy's cheeks heated. "Which is another way of saying that normally I don't."

"That's enough whining." He brought the truck to a stop at an intersection and then brushed his knuckles gently over her cheek.

The air went out of her lungs.

"I've only recently learned about penalties for whining. Per the retirement home rules, you owe me a nickel." He drew his hand back and then made a right turn. "However, I'm willing to waive that fee since I owe you for the use of your sandwiches. I'll pay for that dress you're wearing. I'm sure you wouldn't have bought it if not for our pact."

Kimmy indignantly sucked in air. "You're not paying for my clothes."

"Then I'll get you something for your food truck."

"No thank you." She sat stiffly in the seat, fully cognizant that she could use the money. "You don't need to offer me money to make yourself feel better."

"Kimmy, I want to pay you. I want to make this right. —"

"If you offer me money again, I'm going to have to break my promise." Her words tumbled out too quickly and at too high a pitch. Her cheeks began to heat again.

Booker glanced at her as he neared the town square. Her sister, Rosalie, was walking with her fiancé and their dogs. She waved.

Kimmy raised a limp hand. "If we both think this dating ruse is a bad idea, we can stop this now." She'd return the other dresses and ask Paul to be her wedding date. She was sure he'd dance with her.

"This isn't a bad idea," Booker said firmly. "And I should know. I'm the king of bad ideas."

"That you are." At least he was fessing up to it.

Booker took Kimmy's hand, and when she gave him an incredulous look, he said, "We need the practice."

And then her cheeks were heating for an entirely different reason.

They reached Haywood's place and went around to the backyard.

Kimmy stopped just inside the gate. She'd cleaned the inside yesterday but that had been before the decorators and caterers had come. "So pretty."

"Yes," Booker murmured next to her.

"Just look at all this." She dragged him forward. "It's wonderful."

"It is." His voice was gruff. His gaze intent. But he wasn't staring at the backyard. He was staring at her.

Attraction fluttered in her chest. She swallowed. "You're not even looking." She turned and pointed, focusing on her surroundings rather than Booker.

There were Chinese lanterns in orange and blue. Twinkle lights were strung from the trees, their warm glow just beginning to challenge the dusky sky. Places were set on white tablecloths with bouquets of spring flowers. Cushy blue chairs and couches sat around a stone fireplace with a roaring fire. Perfect for a chilly outdoor mountain evening.

It was everything the magazines depicted for garden parties, everything Kimmy longed to have someday if she could earn enough money. It made her sad that she'd be turning into a pumpkin at the end of the evening and going back to her two-room apartment with its outdated, cat-clawed furniture and plain white walls.

"Booker!" Haywood set down his beer and strode across the lawn to greet them. "You brought my favorite coworker in the whole wide world, Miss Kimmy Easley." He hugged them each in turn.

Once released, Booker took Kimmy's hand and gave her a look that seemed to say, *Here we go*.

"Book, you haven't seen the house since I bought it." Hay gestured around. "What do you think? Kim, Ariana, or I can give you a tour tonight." Hay winked at Kimmy.

Booker raised his brows.

"I'll explain later," Kimmy said quickly, because Ariana was drifting across the lawn in an exquisite green dress and a delicate pair of taupe sandals with a mane of blond hair that had never been tortured with bangs.

"Booker. Kimmy." Ariana noted their joined hands, and her smile broadened. "I was wondering when this would happen."

"What?" Kimmy's mouth dropped open. She wouldn't have noticed if Booker hadn't lifted her chin to close it.

"The chemistry between you two has been off the charts for years." Ariana clapped her hands. "Come on. Hay's been grilling but everybody knows he can't hold a candle to you two in that department." She hooked her arm through Kimmy's and led her to a bar setup. "How about a glass of wine?"

"Sure."

"Cabernet? Sauv blanc? Pinot noir?" Ariana tilted the bottles as she read the varieties.

The last time Kimmy had wine, it had been strawberry moscato and sweeter than soda pop. "I'll have whatever you're drinking." Because she had no idea what kind of taste to expect from the wines before her. But she was determined to fit in and finish whatever was in her glass.

"Sauv blanc. This one's from South Africa." Ariana poured white wine into a glass and handed it to Kimmy. She paused, staring at Kimmy's forehead. "Those bangs..."

"I know, right? Huge mistake." Kimmy tugged at them.

Ariana gently moved Kimmy's hand aside. "They should have blended them, whoever it was. Bangs are the right idea with the shape of your face, but not blunt cut. What was your hairstylist thinking?"

"I don't know."

"Come into the salon tomorrow at eight."

"Oh, I couldn't impose." No matter how awesome it felt to be asked.

"It'll take five minutes. Ten tops." Ariana fluffed Kimmy's bangs again. "And you'll feel ten times better."

"Okay." Who could argue with ten times better?

"What are we talking about?" A long, heavy arm came to rest over Kimmy's shoulders.

Kimmy would never admit Booker's touch sent her heart fluttering or that she edged closer to him.

"I was just about to say that you two are needed at the grill." Ariana smiled at Booker. "But you're so cute together."

Kimmy stopped a reflexive disbelieving eye roll. Booker being gorgeous and Kimmy being bang challenged—a cute couple they didn't make.

"We are, aren't we?" Booker drew Kimmy closer, next to his firm chest and his body heat.

Instinctually, Kimmy wanted to turn into him, to snuggle closer, to lift her face for a kiss.

But this is Booker.

"Whew." Kimmy skirted out from under his arm on unsteady feet, balancing her wineglass with one hand. "It's getting hot out here. Come on, grillmaster. Let's see what's for dinner."

For a moment, there was a look in Booker's eyes that Kimmy didn't recognize, a gleam that left her feeling breathless.

This isn't my Booker.

But then Booker fluffed her bangs and glanced away.

Kimmy stared at him, trying to reconcile this Booker with the Booker she'd known most of her life and failing.

"Go mingle," Booker told Kimmy in a gruff voice. "I've got this covered."

"Are you sure?" Kimmy cradled the bowl of her wineglass between them.

"Yep." He went over to join Hay at the grill.

Leaving Kimmy feeling oddly bereft.

"Well, aren't you a surprise?" Haywood poked a steak with a fork, releasing some of its juice.

"Did you learn nothing while working at the Burger Shack?" Booker took possession of the fork, leaving Hay to pick up his beer.

"How long have you and Kimmy been dating?"

"Long enough."

"Best-kept secret in Sunshine," Hay teased. "That is, if it's been longer than a day."

Booker jabbed the meat harder than Haywood had. "You don't have to go telling everybody." In case things crashed and burned sooner than the wedding.

"Are you kidding?" Hay moved closer, lowering his voice. "Let's tell everybody. This is what you've wanted for years."

"You always did gossip like a girl." But Booker smiled. "Don't jinx it."

Hay sipped his beer and stared toward the outdoor fire-place, where his guests were congregating. "Don't break her heart."

"I won't." Booker knew he couldn't have Kimmy's heart *and* her sandwiches. "This is just a friend helping out a friend."

"Who's helping who?" Hay turned serious. "Hurt her and I'll have to give you a pounding."

"I told you, I won't." But Booker's shoulders were as stiff as steel.

Kimmy laughed at something Ariana said. The sound of her laughter was magnetic. Who was he kidding? Kimmy was magnetic. Smart, attractive. And she was gutsy. That food truck...He'd looked into the business once. It took hustle to make those profitable. If anyone could succeed at it, she could.

Hay raised his beer bottle toward her in salute, cheery on the outside, threatening with his words. "Have you told her?"

"I told her about college." He'd been interrupted trying to tell her about the menu at the Burger Shack.

"She must have taken the college part of your story well." Hay studied Booker's expression. "Or not."

"You never should've taught her how to give a charley horse." He rolled his arm where she'd shoved him at Shaw's and then turned the steaks.

"Good for her." Hay grinned. "You know, I had a late lunch at the Burger Shack today, hoping to see you. Got a glimpse of Dante. He looked like working there was punishment."

He'd whined like it too. Booker needed to get a whining jar for the Shack. "He'll get over it. I did."

Hay shook his head. "Your dad started you there when

you were ten. Dante is seventeen. He's not going to get over it."

"Hard work has a way of changing people."

"It changed us," Hay agreed. "But that's because we had to work—you so Dante could get well and me because my family needed food on the table." And now Hay was a successful real estate agent. Maybe not selling million-dollar homes the way he'd dreamed as a kid, but he did okay.

"Whatever's being said here is way too serious." Kimmy came to stand between the two men. She had no idea how beautiful and sexy she looked. Kimmy stared at the steaks and breathed deeply. "There is nothing like the smell of grilled meat."

Booker put his hand on Kimmy's waist and tucked her to his side. He was nearly overcome with a sense of rightness, a need to pull her close and keep her there.

She gently pinched his waist. "I said, there's nothing like the smell of grilled meat."

"Ah, the sensory game," Hay said, draining his beer. "I haven't missed playing that at the Shack."

Booker knew from his friend's wry grin that wasn't true. Hay liked mental challenges, and the sensory game was full of them—sights, sounds, tastes, touches, smells. "We're doing good aromas? I'm partial to the *smell* of buttered popcorn."

"Coffee, first thing in the morning." Hay set his empty bottle down on the grill's side table. "Too easy."

"It's only too easy if you win the game," Kimmy insisted. "Mention a smell we both dislike and you lose. I like the smell of chocolate chip cookies."

"Oh, man. We haven't played this game in forever. I'm rusty." Booker curled his fingers around her hip, trying to think of an answer. "There's nothing like the smell of..." He drew in a deep breath.

There's nothing like the smell of Kimmy's hair.

Hay and Kimmy were staring at him, waiting.

His gaze caught on the flowers on the table. "There's nothing like the smell of roses on a hot summer day."

That earned him dual groans.

Barbara Hadley approached. She was the town queen bee, the owner of Prestige Salon, where Ariana worked, and the mayor's wife. She was too thin, too put together, too brittle. Although she was smiling, she looked as if she knew something they didn't. "Well, well, well. Booker and Kimmy. What a surprise." She tossed her blond hair artfully.

Next to him, Kimmy stiffened.

Barb sidled closer, a spider looking for a fly. "How long have you guys been seeing each other?"

"Not long." Booker pressed a kiss to Kimmy's bangs.

"But long enough." Kimmy slipped her arms around Booker's waist and stared up at him. She was smiling broadly, and if he fuzzed his vision, he couldn't see the hint of worry in her eyes.

The queen bee could be cruel. And if Barb sensed their relationship was a sham, not only would she expose them but she'd never let them forget they couldn't fool her.

"Long enough?" Booker murmured, dipping his head. "Long past due, you mean."

And then he kissed her.

$\mathcal{C}$HAPTER SEVEN

Holy moly. The man could kiss.

Kimmy nestled closer, drawn to the warmth, drawn to the intensity, drawn to the combination of strength and softness. Drawn to...Booker.

Hot. Dog.

"Nothing to see here." Hay's words drifted to her through the fog of desire.

Booker pulled away enough to stare into her eyes. It was the same face she'd grown up with. Handsome, strong. Dark eyes that gave away only the secrets he wanted you to know. This time she recognized the look in them. Booker wanted her. He wanted to kiss her again.

She stiffened because...

Holy moly. I want him to kiss me again too.

This was wrong. All wrong. They were friends. They'd always been friends.

And yet it felt right. So right.

She half expected Booker to pull back farther and laugh,

that deep chuckle he released when he'd pulled one over on somebody, as if that kiss had been a joke. And if he did that, she'd have to laugh, force air through her lungs and make a lighthearted sound that said she knew what he'd done was all in fun, and she approved of the kissing charade.

Booker and Kimmy and Hay. The trio used to be a team. Working together like a well-oiled machine at the Burger Shack for years. Ribbing each other and the world at large good-naturedly.

Booker and Kimmy and Hay. They were friends. Regardless of her childhood crush, they had had fun together.

But that kiss...That kiss had been Booker and Kimmy. Friend zone breached. No fun intended.

Her knees were weak, and it wasn't just because of the way Booker's kiss had affected her. It was because it was a surprise.

Booker and Kimmy, no Haywood. The dynamic wasn't exactly wrong but it was different. New.

She'd felt attraction for Booker before he'd returned but she'd never picked up on his want, his need. She didn't know how to react or what to say.

Without moving away, Kimmy slid her gaze toward Hay, seeking out the familiar connection of the three musketeers.

Immediately, Booker released her. "Meat's about to burn."

"I'll get it." Kimmy reached for the fork.

Booker held it away. "I've got it." The chill in those words. She got the message. He thought she cared about Hay's reaction to their kiss.

She didn't. She stepped back, taking in Hay's beautiful backyard. The guests' upbeat chatter. Barb's melodious laughter. Ariana's delicate beauty. The twinkle lights. The Chinese lanterns. The breeze swaying the branches.

Kimmy stared at Booker's broad back and remembered...

Summers when she helped her mother clean Ariana's house or Barb's. Watching Barb and Ariana sun themselves in the backyard while she dusted their pretty, expensive things. Every visit making her realize the differences between them.

She remembered winters when they couldn't keep the heat on higher than fifty in the house at night because they couldn't afford their electricity bill. Sleeping in two layers of clothes and beneath two blankets and a sleeping bag to stay warm.

She remembered high school bells ringing. Kids running to after-school activities—sports, clubs, causes. And Kimmy running to work at the Burger Shack. She was a member of the family at the Shack. Never cold. Checked on by Mrs. Belmonte if she called in sick.

And then there were Booker and Hay.

For three years, the teens had done the heavy lifting at the Shack while little Dante battled for his life. They'd signed up for the most shifts and worked the most hours.

Oh, they hadn't been complete angels. There'd been food fights and grill-offs. And competitions. Man, the competitions. Who could eat the most burger patties in five minutes (Hay). Who could clean the dining room the fastest (Kimmy). Who could prep and slice the most potatoes for French fries before Mrs. Belmonte came back from the dentist (Booker).

Three teens who enjoyed each other's company and shared the value of hard work.

And now?

It was as if they shared nothing.

The only time Kimmy saw Haywood was when he

stopped in for a sandwich. She hadn't seen Booker in years. What kind of friendship was that?

Kimmy knew the answer. It wasn't a friendship. She didn't belong here.

She took another step back.

She could leave. No one would miss her.

She could walk home a mile or so in heels. She'd suffered through worse. She was suffering now.

Another step and...

"I'm glad you came." Hay took her hand and gave it a squeeze.

"Don't go." Booker took her other hand and gave it a squeeze.

She felt their gazes upon her but couldn't look at them. If she had, she might have done something stupid, like shed a tear, grateful as she was for their past friendship.

But here in the present, Booker had kissed her.

And she was afraid nothing was ever going to be the same again.

"Did I hear right?" Booker's mom came through the back door into the Burger Shack, dressed for work in black slacks and the Shack's black polo shirt. The thick streaks of gray in her hair glimmered under the fluorescents. "Are you dating Kimmy Easley? Can I say I heartily approve? It's about time you took a moment to think about your future."

"Mom." Booker jumped into the void when his mother took a breath. He'd been prepping potatoes, and he dried his hands on a towel. "Don't start planning my wedding. Kimmy and I have always been good friends."

"And she always had that crush on Haywood." His mother tsk-tsked. "Patience really paid off for you, didn't it?"

Patience? He'd kissed Kimmy at the first opportunity. And when it was done, she'd looked at him in just the way he'd imagined. Slightly breathless, slightly dazed, completely blissful.

And then she'd looked at Hay. *Shades of summers past.*

Booker gritted his teeth.

And then Hay had taken her hand, sensing—much as Booker had—that Kimmy wanted to bolt.

Booker's jaw clenched so hard that it popped. He'd driven her home but the ride had been quiet.

"Can you imagine the two of you together?" His mom opened the supply cabinet and grabbed a bag of napkins. She was like a savant, sensing the staff who'd closed last night hadn't refilled the dining room's napkin holders. "Dark-haired babies with your smile and her smarts."

"Mom." Seriously, the woman needed a hobby. "Shouldn't you be home? Gardening or knitting or something?"

"Knitting?" His mom rushed to his side, dark eyes wide and hopeful. "Baby booties?"

"No. No babies." Booker put his hands on her shoulders. "I meant you shouldn't come in the Shack every day. I bought it from you so you'd be able to enjoy life. You've given so much to Dante and me. It's time you focused on you. Book a massage at Prestige Salon." If she didn't, he'd make the appointment for her. "Join the gym."

"But..." She crushed the napkins to her chest. "This is my life. And when Dante leaves for college..."

"You'll have Dad," Booker was quick to say. He drew her back toward the office. "You can travel, like you always talked about."

His mother sat down in a chair by the door, still embracing the napkins. "Your father doesn't want to travel. All he's interested in is the television remote. He discovered he can record shows last night. And this morning, he's watching all the shows he recorded."

Booker frowned.

"So you see, Booker"—his mother turned puppy-dog eyes his way—"unless you're going to give me a grandchild, the Shack is all I have."

"Your bangs bothered me all last night." Ariana shook out a black polka-dot cape and fastened it around Kimmy's neck. "I even dreamed about them."

"I'm sorry?" Kimmy was still unsure of her footing where Ariana was concerned. Add to that the fact that she'd helped her mother clean the salon a time or ten and it felt odd to sit in a client chair. "I didn't know hairstylists were bothered by the botched work of other hairstylists."

"All the time." Ariana picked up Kimmy's bangs and let them fall. Repeatedly. "So." Her gaze met Kimmy's. "What was it that finally got you and Booker together? Hay and I have talked about the chemistry between you guys for years."

"Years?" That couldn't be.

Ariana chuckled. "Were you the last to know?"

"Apparently." It was hard to believe that others had noticed an attraction and she hadn't. Booker was just… Booker.

Caring. Considerate. Smart. Handsome. Sandwich thief. Booker.

Ariana lightly sprayed Kimmy's bangs with water and took thinning scissors to her hair. "To think we were all in high school together. It's funny, isn't it? I was such a dork back then. Trying so hard to fit in."

"You did fit in." Ariana had hung out with Barb and the in-crowd.

She shook her head. "I felt like I was one wrong shoe decision away from expulsion. If it hadn't been for Haywood…" Ariana fluffed Kimmy's bangs. "He's so grounded. And funny about money. I wanted to get engaged way back. You know, when we had that little break."

Oh, I know.

Kimmy pretended the silence wasn't awkward as she waited for Ariana to continue.

Haywood's bride-to-be worked some mousse into Kimmy's hair. "There was a reason Hay didn't want to get married when we were younger. He wanted to make sure we were financially stable. His parents never have been."

Kimmy kept silent.

Hay's parents, like Kimmy's, were blue-collar workers. But Hay's sports ability had earned him a place on the popularity ladder, which Kimmy had been unable to climb. But she wasn't about to admit any weakness while in Prestige Salon—the hub of town gossip.

"So I waited because he's so totally worth it."

Booker might be worth it too.

A dangerous thought. So Kimmy chose silence again.

"And then at the town's tree-lighting ceremony, he proposed with the choir singing Christmas carols and the lights sparkling in the trees. It was perfect." Ariana grabbed a hair dryer and blew Kimmy's bangs dry, raising her voice to be heard. "I hope Booker is as romantic as Hay is."

Kimmy wanted to say, *That man is not going to propose to me.*

Kimmy should say, *I hope so too.* If only to keep up the ruse that she and Booker were indeed infatuated with each other, which would give the impression that Kimmy was no threat to Ariana's special day.

But Kimmy managed only a meek "Yep."

Who was she kidding? Booker was going to be gone in a week, managing his growing restaurant empire from Denver. He'd probably forget about that kiss before he returned home. If he was thinking about settling down, he certainly wasn't thinking about settling down with Kimmy, chemistry or not.

Ariana returned her hair dryer to its place near the rest of her tools and picked up a flat iron. After a few passes over Kimmy's bangs, it was time for hair spray and a final fluff. "There." She whipped off the drape as dramatically as a stage magician. "Booker is going to love this. Parted to the side, it gives interest to your face and makes your eyes look huge."

The face that stared into the mirror looked the same to Kimmy. She was the woman behind Emory's lunch counter. The woman who'd stood in the crowd in the town square when Hay had proposed to Ariana.

Kimmy stared at her reflection and nodded. Bangs made no difference whether blunt cut or fluffed to one side. Same woman.

She'd best remember that.

$\mathcal{C}$HAPTER EIGHT

$\mathcal{S}$ee you tomorrow, Emory." Kimmy shut off the lights behind the deli counter. She had to hurry home and get ready for another wedding-related event.

She hadn't seen Booker since the dinner at Haywood's house two nights ago. She wouldn't be surprised if he texted and gave her an out for the evening, regardless of whether he'd noticed chemistry between them for years or not.

Emory walked into her path, blocking her exit. His bow tie today was a solid blue. "I hear they're testing their new menu at the Burger Shack this Friday at lunch." His tone had the quality of Eeyore's doom and gloom. "I don't expect much business that day. And you shouldn't either."

Kimmy resisted the urge to check the time on her cell phone. "We'll be fine." Of course, she experienced a niggle of doubt as she said it. She was just the lunch-counter clerk, not the store manager. "People are loyal to us."

Emory considered her words, pursing his lips until he came to a judgment. "You and Booker..."

Oh, not Emory too. Customers in her line today had asked Kimmy about her relationship with Booker.

"Booker is loyal to you," Emory was saying. "He'd show you their new menu if you asked. And if you saw it, you could design something better for us."

"That seems kind of low, doesn't it?" Besides, she'd declined to review it twice. How would it look if she asked now?

"It's called survival." Emory shook his head. "You know, Kimmy, there's a push to turn that abandoned mill down by the interstate into a distribution center. If that happens, everything's going to change. New homes will go up out there. New businesses too. And we'll be left here to wither away."

"No." Regardless of her short-term-employee mentality, Kimmy refused to believe Emory's prediction.

"Mark my words." Her boss eyed her. "Unless you come up with something new and slam-bang, something that keeps customers here, the Burger Shack will ruin things for this store."

Then Emory was paged to the front of the store, leaving Kimmy to ponder his opinion and whether they applied to food trucks too.

"I was just about to call you." Kimmy stood in the open doorway of her apartment, trapped between the hot late-afternoon air and Booker climbing her stairs and the cool air-conditioning and the safety of her normal life inside.

Should she kiss his cheek hello? Drag him inside for a lip-lock? Or ask about his menu?

Booker hurried toward the door in a dark suit and tie,

checking his cell phone and looking like a businessman from Denver, not her childhood friend.

"I thought you might cancel." She'd give him an out. After all, Booker still hadn't looked at her. That kiss. Every second that passed made it more awkward to bring up.

He drew his brows together, released them, and then pocketed his phone. "I'm late, that's all. Dante was out at the old mill with some friends and somehow got left behind." He stopped on her welcome mat and looked at her. A slow smile built on his face. "Now that"—he gestured toward her from head to toe—"all works together, bangs included."

Booker's attention was building her confidence. Her dress this evening was a sapphire-blue sheath. Kimmy was getting used to the new haircut and dressing like an adult. She could get used to Booker's compliments too. And yet she felt deflated. The fact that they hadn't talked about that kiss had to mean something.

"What's wrong?" His smile fell, and he hustled her inside, closing the door behind them.

"This." Why beat around the bush? She gestured from him to her. "Us pretending. Me holding your hand. Being in your space. Kissing you."

Booker tilted his head and studied her face, saying nothing as the heat built in her cheeks.

"Say something," she whispered.

"I'm just putting everything in context." He came forward slowly until he was close enough to brush the bangs from her eyes, although he didn't touch her. "You're taking responsibility for a deal we both agreed to. It isn't you deciding to hold my hand. As far as I recall, I've always reached for your hand first."

So true. Her cheeks burned with embarrassment. "We don't have to do this."

"Oh, but we do." His hands came to rest on her shoulders, sliding slowly down her arms until his fingers closed around hers. "You haven't been moving into my space. I've been dragging you into it. And that kiss the other night? *I* kissed *you*, not the other way around."

"I didn't just stand there," Kimmy mumbled.

"No." He broke out that infectious smile. "You didn't."

"But..." How to say this? "Everyone's been telling me this..." She held on tight to his hands and shook them. "That this was bound to happen. That all the signs were there."

Booker stared at her tenderly. "And you didn't see these signs?"

"No."

"Does that mean you want to call things off?" There was a wary note to his voice that hadn't been there before. "Like you suggested the other night?"

"And go back on my word?" *Yes. No.* She didn't know which would be worse.

"I know you'd never break a promise." He leaned closer and pressed a kiss to her forehead.

"I can tough it out," Kimmy said, unsteady in her heels. She risked looking at Booker, so close she could have leaned forward and kissed him again. "If you can."

His trademark smile returned as his arms came around her. "Like it's a hardship." Before she could ask him what he meant, he'd released her, grabbed her purse and her keys, and ushered her out the door.

The dinner for the wedding party was being hosted by Ariana's parents. Another home Kimmy used to help her mother clean.

"We need a set of tongs." Ariana's mother glanced around.

"I'll get them." Kimmy hurried from the patio into the kitchen.

Booker followed her, although not as quickly. "I thought you might need help rifling through Camilla's drawers." He slowed to a stop at the large kitchen island, where Kimmy stood holding the tongs she'd dug out of a drawer. "How did you..."

"Mom and I used to clean this house." She'd never told him that. Back in the day, it'd been too embarrassing. "Come on." Kimmy retraced her steps. "Don't look at me like that. This is my Cinderella moment. As soon as the wedding reception is over, I'm turning into a pumpkin."

He fell into line behind her. "Besides the fact that Cindy doesn't turn into a pumpkin at midnight, you were never Cindy. You were Sleeping Beauty, and I'm sorry it took me so long to show up and give you a kiss."

Kimmy's breath caught. That was without a doubt the most romantic thing a man had ever said to her. And he'd spoken the words when she was wearing a beautiful dress, standing in a beautiful home, and having a good hair day. Could life get any better?

Booker caught Kimmy's arm, bringing her around to face him. "In fact, I'd like to give you another."

Kimmy stared at him through her lashes. If he was going to kiss her, she wasn't going to object. "Camilla needs her tongs."

"Camilla can wait." Booker's arms came around Kimmy. He tilted her chin up and gathered her close, hesitating, lips practically touching hers. "You want another kiss, don't you, Sleeping Beauty?"

Kimmy's heart pounded out an answer he couldn't hear so she had to say, "Sometimes the magic takes more than once to work."

His eyes sparkled, and he was smiling when his mouth came down on hers.

Their last kiss had been soft and surprising. A first-date kiss stolen on a whim.

There was nothing soft or whimsical about this kiss. There were heat and hunger, demand and declaration.

This. Him.

Her heart pounded harder, emboldening her to kiss deeper, to hold on tighter.

The floodgates opened in her head, and she put together pieces of memories she hadn't allowed herself to previously. The flutter in her chest when Booker's shoulder brushed hers in the school library as they worked through a complex equation. The weakness in her knees when his smile connected with hers in the school hallway. The tremble in her fingers when he asked her to scratch his nose while he was elbow-deep in dirty dishwater.

Yes, she'd been attracted to Booker as a girl. But he was going places, and everyone knew it. Kimmy was the daughter of an auto worker and a maid. She might have talked big dreams about going to college with Booker but she'd known the truth. She wasn't going anywhere. Haywood came from her side of town. He was the more logical choice.

But now...

But this...

She was falling in love.

"Wow," Booker whispered.

"Ditto." Dizzy, Kimmy had to lean against the wall.

"Hey," Camilla called, "do you need help finding those tongs?"

"Found them." Kimmy drew a deep breath and pushed Booker back, gaining much-needed space.

Booker followed her out to the patio. "I think we found more than tongs."

"Kimmy looks happy." Haywood nudged Booker and gestured with his beer to the cluster of women sitting on the enclosed patio.

"She makes me happy." But for how long? Once Kimmy knew the whole truth... The grilled oyster appetizers he'd eaten squirmed in his stomach. Booker should have told her the rest of the truth at Shaw's or in her food truck or tonight before he kissed her.

The two men stood at the outdoor bar. Haywood was opening beer bottles. Booker was mixing another pitcher of margaritas.

"You told her though, right?" Hay asked, counting beers and then comparing his number to a head count. "About the menu?"

"Not yet." Booker doled out ice cubes in tall bar glasses. "But she'll understand." He held on to a sliver of hope.

Hay stopped double-checking his beer order and began giving Booker the stink eye. "She won't. I wouldn't. It's one thing to use her sammies to work your way through college." He lowered his voice. "It's another thing entirely to use her to make your fortune."

Booker kept his voice just as low. "You know how Kimmy is. She'd give you the shoes off her feet if she thought you needed it." Those oysters banked and rolled in his gut.

"And what would you give her if she needed it? A share of the profits? Part ownership in the Burger Shack?" Hay waited for an answer. When he got none, he gathered beer necks between his fingers. "You know, I showed her a lot of empty buildings to buy or rent when she was considering opening her own sandwich shop here in town. She couldn't afford any of them. And yet you..."

"I'm going to give her a fair offer, Hay." Booker sucked down some water, hoping to drown the oysters who'd taken on the role of his conscience. "She'll get paid. I promise."

"I understand you wanting to protect the family business but..." Haywood nudged Booker's chest with a handful of beer bottles. "But Dante..." He bit back whatever he'd been about to say.

"Dante what?" Booker pushed the beer aside.

"Dante doesn't deserve a free ride." Hay's voice was hard and unforgiving. "Yeah, I know he had cancer back in the day. But what has he done with his life since then besides being a mama's boy?"

"Don't you remember what he went through?" Outrage shook Booker's voice. "Pale. Sunken eyes. Tubes coming out of him." Half-dead before he was even four.

"I remember what he looked like *when he was a toddler*." Hay blew out a breath. "Has it ever occurred to you that we turned out so well because it was either sink or swim? Adversity builds character. Let it build Dante's."

"So you'd have me stop everything? Change the menu back to burgers only?"

"Yes. And do you know why?" Haywood leaned closer. "Because you love Kimmy."

The oysters hardened. Booker rubbed his chest, trying to relieve the heartburn, unable to deny Hay's statement.

He loved Kimmy. He'd always loved Kimmy.

But he didn't deserve her.

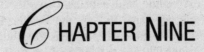

CHAPTER NINE

After that hot kiss in the kitchen, Kimmy had expected a hot good-night kiss.

She'd received a very chaste peck on the cheek at her door.

But she was nothing if not optimistic and fully expected Booker to call or text or swing by Thursday after work.

That was a big nada.

She made excuses for Booker: he was busy preparing for a relaunch; he was busy with ownership responsibilities for two businesses. But it wasn't until she remembered that Haywood's bachelor party was tonight that she stopped making excuses and relaxed.

He'd call. He'd call tomorrow.

Friday dawned clear and bright, belying the forecast of overcast skies and afternoon thunderstorms.

Kimmy went to work and prepped the lunch counter for the day's special sandwich—bacon, zucchini, and spicy mozzarella paninis. Her sauce was divine. The grill was hot. And she had a date with Booker tonight. Who cared if a storm was on the horizon?

At eleven thirty, Emory came up to the counter, wearing a dark expression and a black bow tie. "I haven't seen any of our regulars. Today's the Burger Shack test run with their new menu. All proceeds go to charity. If I wasn't so nervous, I'd appreciate how brilliant Booker's strategy is."

"The bell hasn't tolled on us yet." But Kimmy smoothed her clean, already smooth apron. "You'll see."

By noon, she'd served five customers instead of ten and was getting nervous.

Emory walked past slowly, raising his brows at her one customer.

By one thirty, Kimmy was ready for an early lunch break. With Janet behind the counter and no line, Kimmy removed her apron and walked the two blocks to the Burger Shack under gathering clouds.

Thunder rumbled over Saddle Horn Mountain. Trepidation rumbled inside her.

Kimmy went around to the back.

"Kimmy!" Mrs. Belmonte sat at the outdoor employee table, the same one where Booker, Haywood, and Kimmy had taken breaks on summer days. She closed a travel magazine and scurried over to give her a hug. "Seems like I haven't seen you in ages." She held Kimmy a little too long. And her smile was a little too big. "I'm so glad you and Booker are finally dating."

Kimmy made a noncommittal noise and entered the Burger Shack, looking for Booker.

She'd worked at the Shack on some popular burger holidays—Memorial Day weekend, Fourth of July, Labor Day. It had never been this chaotic before. What kind of menu change had Booker made that had created such a feeding frenzy?

The chill hand of suspicion grazed the back of her neck.

Seven people were working in the kitchen. They had the fryer crackling and the grill sizzling. There was a crew working the assembly row, nervously checking the posted ingredient lists as they put together sandwiches and then placed them on a panini press.

Sandwiches.

She moved deeper into the kitchen, peering over Agnes Hempstead's shoulder to see what she was making.

Monte Cristo Waffle Sammy.

The bottom dropped out of Kimmy's world. It was one of the first few sandwiches she'd created in this very kitchen. For Booker and Hay.

She stepped to the left, looking over Joyce Jamison's shoulder.

Mac and Cheese and Pepper Panini.

Again, it was a sandwich she'd created for Booker and Hay. Her heart flattened as if someone had put it in a hot panini maker.

She circled around the assembly stations, finding more familiar recipes. Somewhere along the way, she found her anger. It flamed hot, burning romantic hopes to ash.

"Hey." Booker, standing tall but maybe not so proud. A man who knew he had some explaining to do.

Thunder rolled across the valley—*boom boom boom boom.*

A voice in her head echoed its cadence—*fool fool fool fool.*

"Outside," Kimmy told Booker. "Now." She didn't look

to see whether he'd follow. She was too busy trying to make sure her legs didn't give out.

She pushed through the back door and stomped out from under the cover of the portico.

"Is something wrong, honey?" Mrs. Belmonte asked from her place at the table.

"You need to go inside, Mrs. B." Kimmy worked hard to keep from shouting. "There's a storm coming."

On cue, thunder cracked overhead. Lightning sparked through her.

Mrs. Belmonte went through the door, passing Booker on his way out.

They stared at each other. Kimmy, feeling empty and betrayed, standing unprotected from the elements. Booker, looking handsome and unreadable, standing beneath the portico.

"You said you used my recipes while you were in college." Her words were as jagged as the lightning flashing overhead.

"Yes." His answer was disappointing.

She'd expected him to apologize, maybe grovel a little. It might have been a fantasy but hearing him beg would've been good for her heartbroken soul. But no. He'd gone for taciturn. He was going to make her dig out every transgression.

Kimmy wasn't going to play that game. "I need to hire a lawyer."

His eyes widened. He probably hadn't counted on her cutting right to the chase.

Thunder shook the buildings around them. It shook the legs beneath her.

"I..." He faltered then, gaze sliding toward the Burger Shack.

She knew the family business had always been his top priority, overriding everything. Apparently even what little honor she'd ascribed to his character.

Booker swallowed. "I drew up a contract to pay for your recipes. I was waiting for the right time to show it to you."

"Now. Now would be the right time. Or last weekend before the auction. Or before that first time we kissed." *Before I fell in love with you.*

She felt so empty. There was nothing inside left for him to hurt.

Big, fat drops began to fall, striking the pavement angrily. They were like her tears, those drops. The tears she didn't want to fall.

Booker held out a hand. "Come inside. We'll talk in my office."

The pace of the drops increased, along with the pounding of her heart.

"You had your chance to talk." She was being pelted by drops but it was a good thing because tears were rolling down her face nonstop, and she didn't want Booker to realize she was crying. "You had days of chances to talk."

Her chest was folding in on itself, brought down by heartache and betrayal. And the rain was dumping on her, harder and faster, the way life was dumping on her. The way life always dumped on hardworking people reaching for the elusive American dream.

"Your lunch business is going to shut down Emory's lunch counter." She knew that for certain now. "I'll be out of a job."

Just six more weeks.

She didn't think Emory would keep her on the payroll that long.

"I'll hire you." Oh, how he was quick to speak now.

She hated him for that speed. And the hate rose up inside her like too much fiery kimchi. "I'm not going to work for you on the assembly line. Those are my sandwiches. *Mine!* And you stole them the same way you've stolen...'

My heart.

Her breath hitched, and she could no longer speak. He'd betrayed her trust. He'd sabotaged her dreams.

She had to go. She had to run.

Into the heart of the storm.

And away from him.

Booker sank into his chair in the office and put his head in his hands.

"Everything okay, honey?" His mother closed the door behind her. "Was it safe for Kimmy to leave in this storm?"

"No, Mom. No." But he'd been unable to stop her, because every word she'd thrown at him had been true.

"If it wasn't safe, why did you let her go?" His mother came around behind the desk and put her arm around his shoulders.

"Because I've always put you and Dad and Dante first.' Only this time, he'd gone too far. He hadn't listened to Hay's warnings, even though he'd known in his heart he should have.

"I love her." The words sounded raw and lost.

"I know, honey." His mother rubbed his arm consolingly. "You've always loved her. Such a good, sensible choice."

"Love isn't sensible." If it were, he'd have done everything differently. He'd have asked Kimmy's permission. He wouldn't have stayed away while building the business, burdened with guilt. He'd have stopped trying to prove to his family that he could solve all their problems and ease all their worries. "Love isn't sensible," he said again. "Especially not in this case."

"You're selling her sandwiches, honey. Without her permission, I imagine."

He nodded.

She slapped him upside the head, not hard but with enough verve to get his attention. "What were you thinking?"

"You hit me." He stared up at his mother in amazement. She wasn't one to discipline with more than stern words. He'd never even been spanked.

"Well, someone's got to knock some sense into you." She crossed her arms over her chest. "We've never given you the credit you deserve for holding this family together. But you can't just make a mistake this humongous and then wallow in self-pity. You've got to own up to those boo-boos and set things to rights."

Booker rubbed his head. Not because it was sore but because he knew it would annoy his mother. "So my humongous mistake is just a boo-boo, eh?"

"Has Dante's experience taught you nothing about life being too short?" She began to pace. "I've been thinking about life a lot lately. About your father. About you. About Dante."

"If this is your midlife crisis, all I can do is beg you not to leave Dad." His old man would never recover.

"If it is my midlife hurrah, then I'll do as I please." She tossed up her hands. "And if I needed to divorce your father, I would. But he's having a little crisis all his own." Judging by her tone, her patience with his dad was at an end. "Why do you think I come here every day? Your father has been trying to come to terms with this new life stage. It's...It's pitiful." She shook her finger at Booker. "And if you tell him I said that, I'll deny it."

The fire in her eyes went out, and she dropped into a chair. "We can't sell Kimmy's sandwiches."

"Not without her permission, I know." He would have talked to her about it if he hadn't kissed her Monday night. Or Wednesday night. "I was afraid that I'd lose her when she found out." And now he had.

"You were blinded by the dollar signs, I suppose." His mother sighed. "Before you were born, your father tried selling pizza. Burgers and pizza. The way he talked about it, you would've thought it was the second coming." She huffed.

"What happened?"

"Our good friend Jerry over at Sunshine Pizza paid him a visit." His mom wore her I-told-you-so smirk. "He told your father he'd blanket the town with coupons and deals so great that no one would ever order pizza here again, much less burgers. And your father—valuing Jerry's friendship, of course—returned the pizza oven he'd purchased and stuck to burgers."

"You're saying I should honor the original menu of the Burger Shack." Booker stared at his hands. Burgers wouldn't finance Dante's college education.

"I'm saying it's your business." His mother stood, back straight, chin high. "Do what you will. But make it right with Kimmy. You love her. And you'd make such beautiful children together."

CHAPTER TEN

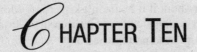

"I hear you need a wedding date." Clarice stood on Kimmy's doorstep, leaning on the doorframe and shouting. "May I come in? I brought my hearing aids." She dug a small container from her raincoat pocket and rattled it gently. "Didn't want them to get wet."

If it hadn't been raining, if Kimmy hadn't been crying, she'd have politely declined. But it was raining and she had been crying. In a moment of weakness, she opened the door wider.

She ushered Clarice inside, took her coat, and found her a seat that wasn't covered in cat hair.

Skippy lumbered out, sniffing at her visitor.

"You have a three-legged cat." Clarice was putting her hearing aids in. Already, her volume was below shouting range.

"I got her from that rescue Eileen Taylor runs." Kimmy brought Clarice a glass of water and a small bowl of almonds. "I don't have much else in the house to offer you."

Today was payday, and under normal circumstances, she
would have done her grocery shopping after her shift ended,
but she'd been too drained emotionally to push a cart
through the store.

"Now, let's get down to business." Clarice fiddled
with her ear before patting the couch next to her, waiting
for Kimmy to sit before continuing. "I'm breaking
the rules here but it had to be done. I wanted you to have
the perfect wedding date for Hay's wedding, someone
who'd make it a most glorious evening, one you'd never
forget."

"Never fear. I'm not going to go to the wedding."
Kimmy couldn't bring herself to attend, not when Booker
was the best man.

Skippy wound her way around Clarice's rain boots.

"That seems rather cowardly." Clarice bent to pet the
cat. "And you don't strike me as a coward."

"It's more complicated than me breaking a date with
Booker." And she'd given him her word, sworn over
French fries. But he'd honored nothing, not even their
childhood friendship. "He stole from me. And he wasn't
going to tell me." That much was clear. "I went to see
Rupert Harper today. He's going to represent me in this
case."

According to Rupert, it was going to be drawn out and
messy and cost her a small fortune. There went the money
she needed to pay for her transmission.

Damn you, Booker.

"Well"—Clarice slapped her palms on her pink poly-
ester pants—"you've picked up the pieces of your life
rather quickly. More quickly than Booker, who—from
what I hear—hasn't come out of his office since you
stormed away from the Burger Shack."

"You mean the Burger & Sammie Shack." Apparently, a broken heart made Kimmy snarky.

"It will always be the Burger Shack to me." Clarice waved a thin hand. "Just like your memories of Booker will always be tied to your grill."

Kimmy tried to speak but she didn't know what to say, so only a strangled noise came out of her mouth.

"Anyway…" Clarice petted the cat in long strokes, head to tail. "I don't think you should hide from the wedding tomorrow with Spanky."

"Skippy."

"That's why I came here with a solution to your problems." Clarice drew herself up. "I want you to go to the wedding, and I'd like to be your plus-one."

Booker was waiting for Dante in the kitchen when he got home on Friday night.

His little brother carried his skateboard and a teenage smirk.

Where Booker took after their father, with his broad face and shoulders, Dante took after their mother, with her lean frame and delicate features. But the family value for hard work…That seemed to have shot past the mark in Dante's case.

"Come on over here, little brother." Booker pulled out a chair for him. "I made empanadas at the Shack."

"Cool. Those are my favorite." Dante sat down, dumping his stuff on the floor next to him. He grabbed the largest empanada on the plate and took a big bite, wiping at his face with his fingers and then licking his fingers clean.

Booker handed his brother a napkin. "I've been thinking about your summer," he said, being careful to sound upbeat. "I talked to Mom and Dad."

"Cool." There was less enthusiasm to Dante's response this time. He practically inhaled the next empanada.

"I got you an early graduation gift." Booker gestured toward an electric grill in an unopened box in the corner. An indoor model that was large and smokeless. "It's the same gift Dad gave me when I graduated high school. Do you remember?"

Dante shook his head, giving the grill a sideways glance. He picked up his third empanada.

"I know I told you I'd pay your college tuition and living expenses, but something's come up, and I don't have the cash flow I'd expected to have."

Kim's drenched, tear-streaked face came to mind as powerfully as a punch to the gut.

"Wait." Dante nearly dropped his empanada. "What?"

Booker nodded, continuing to keep his tone light. "I can't keep my promise to you. You're going to have to pay part of your way through college." He gestured toward his graduation gift. "By working."

"Mom." Scowling, Dante pushed his chair back. "*Mom!*"

Booker tsk-tsked. "I wouldn't wake her. She and I already discussed this. She's one hundred percent on board, same as Dad."

"Nuh-uh." Dante may have been in honors English but he wasn't showing any of that vocabulary.

"Yuh-huh, little brother." Booker gestured toward the grill once more. "I suggest you pick up some shifts at the Burger Shack this summer. You'll need to know how to grill if you want to supplement what I give you."

"But...but..." Dante swallowed hard and said almost rebelliously, "I have cancer."

"No, you don't. You've been clear for almost twelve years." Booker clapped a hand on Dante's shoulder. "Let's look at the positives. You're healthy. You're smart. You're good at sports. And you've got a great scar to impress the girls. That and a good grill will get you far."

He left Dante sputtering.

Phase one of his plan was complete.

He wouldn't sleep a wink tonight, wondering whether everything would go well with phase two tomorrow.

CHAPTER ELEVEN

The church was decorated with white ribbons and pink roses.

Organ music, brightly dressed guests, and murmured voices filled the sanctuary proper.

Kimmy sat in the back of the church, surrounded by the board of the Widows Club—Clarice next to her near the aisle, Mims and Bitsy on her other side. She fanned herself with the wedding program.

"It's lovely," Clarice said in a loud whisper. She had her hearing aids in but Kimmy suspected she didn't have an indoor voice in her vocal arsenal. "And look, Mary Margaret is wearing a fascinator."

The redhead passed by with her fancy hat on.

"I hear the reception has a fairy-garden theme." Clarice hugged herself.

Kimmy raised her eyebrows and told her date, "I'm beginning to think you offered to be my plus-one because you needed an invitation to Sunshine's biggest event of the year."

Clarice's leathery cheeks turned rosy as Mims and Bitsy laughed.

A tuxedoed man walked behind Kimmy and around her pew and sat down in front of her.

"Hay, what are you doing out here?" Kimmy touched his arm. "Is everything okay?"

"Do you have cold feet?" Clarice asked breathlessly.

Bitsy and Mims shushed her.

"Not even a cold toe." Hay winked at Clarice. "I'm showing my face and drawing all kinds of attention..." He pointed to the assembled, who were turned to get a good look at him. He waved. "Because I thought it was important to tell you about Booker."

Kimmy crossed her arms over her chest. "This isn't middle school. I don't accept apologies by proxy."

"Good one." Clarice elbowed Kimmy.

Hay's expression sobered. "He's been in love with you longer than I've been in love with Ariana. But you've been strong-arming him into the friend zone for decades."

"True, but that doesn't excuse what he did." Kimmy waved Haywood off. "This isn't a conversation we should be having on your wedding day. This is between Booker and me."

"You're right." Booker came around from behind them and stood at the end of the pew, looking like he should wear a tuxedo every day of the year.

The entire church seemed to have turned and was watching them. No one was talking. Even the organist had stopped playing.

"Which part is she right about?" Clarice demanded.

It was a good thing she asked. Kimmy couldn't speak. Booker was supposed to be in the bowels of the church, telling Haywood what a great day this was turning out to be.

"Kimberly Anne Easley has been right about everything she's ever told me." Booker paused, stared at Clarice, and raised his brows. "*Everything.*"

"That's my cue." Clarice stood and edged toward Booker and the aisle.

Her cue? What did that mean?

"Where are you going?" Kimmy latched on to Clarice's arm, nearly dragging the old woman into her lap. "You're my plus-one."

"I...I...I have to go to the bathroom." Clarice lifted her chin and extricated herself from Kimmy's hold, leaving no buffer between Kimmy and Booker.

"Your cue?" Kimmy said, understanding dawning. A quick glance around those sitting close to her confirmed Kimmy's suspicions.

Mims and Bitsy gave her encouraging smiles. Hay winked at her. Clarice hesitated at her back.

Kimmy glared at Booker. "This was all part of your evil plan." And he'd recruited Haywood and the Widows Club board.

"Yes," Booker said unapologetically.

Kimmy's head hurt, right behind her eyes. And her heart felt as if it were withering in her chest. All the pain, all the sadness, all over her body. But she wasn't backing down. She wasn't running away. Not today.

"Hay's right too." Booker's dark gaze captured hers. "I should have told you I liked you when we were thirteen and lab partners. But it didn't strike me as romantic when you were making moon eyes at Hay while we dissected our frog."

"For the record..." Hay turned to his wedding guests. "While this was going on, I was making moon eyes at Ariana."

Booker ignored Hay and stared at Kimmy. "I should have told you I liked you when we had ice cream during freshman orientation. But you were making moon eyes at Hay."

"I sense a theme," Clarice said loudly in Kimmy's ear.

Kimmy batted at her as if Clarice were a pesky fly.

Booker ignored Clarice. His gaze never left Kimmy's face. "I should have told you when I picked you up for prom that I loved you."

The wedding guests were quiet but at that statement, a hush fell over the room as if everyone was holding their breath. He'd gone public and declared he loved her. Kimmy wasn't holding her breath with the rest of them. She was huffing like Emory during the Thanksgiving shopping rush when they ran out of turkeys.

Booker wasn't quiet. He wasn't huffing. Hay's best man was unflappable. He kept right on talking. "I should have told you the day I drove off to college that I loved you. Or when I was away at college and missing you. I should have told you when I called. I love you, Kimmy Anne Easley."

"I sense a theme," Clarice piped up.

"I do too." Kimmy turned in her seat, facing Booker squarely. "You love me. Great."

He loves me.

Kimmy wanted to curl up into a ball and die.

"Yes. I love you." His calm was finally broken. His voice rose. "I love how you check your ego at the door. I love how you help your mom in her job and your dad in his. I love that you're restoring a food truck so you'll have a business of your own. I love how you talk. I love how you walk. I love how you dance. It's unconventional and the sweetest thing ever."

Kimmy rolled her eyes.

But Booker wasn't done. He ran a hand through his black hair, upsetting that cowlick. "I love how you don't take any guff from me. You call me out, even if it means I'll call you out in return. But mostly, I love how you love me. There were days this week when we knew we were meant for each other. It scares me how much I love you."

She waved off his fears and declarations of love. "That doesn't excuse what you did to me."

"Just so we're clear"—Booker's eyes narrowed—"and so everyone knows...We're talking about my using your sandwich recipes."

Oh, that was low. He was admitting all his sins to the town.

"Stealing." Kimmy nodded.

There were gasps from the crowd.

Kimmy played to their audience. It was obvious she was going to need them. "I forgave him for using them in college. Although it was still a betrayal of trust, but—"

"I was wrong," Booker said loud and clear. "All my life I've tried to do the right thing. I tried to be part of the team that made it possible for Dante to beat cancer. I tried to plan for the future so that I could fund my parents' retirement and my brother's college years. And in the process, I cut corners, and I leaned on you because deep down I hoped—*no, I believed*—that'd you'd forgive me. Which is why, four weeks ago, I had my lawyer draw up a contract, giving you ten thousand dollars for the right to use your recipes."

Hay's wedding guests had opinions about that. Their voices rose up and gave Booker and Kimmy a small measure of privacy.

"That's not enough, Booker." Kimmy didn't know where she got the guts to say it. She didn't believe it was true. Ten thousand dollars was a lot of money. She could pay for the food truck's transmission. She could stock the cupboards with food and fill the gas tank. She could hit the road with confidence about what was ahead.

Even as she left everything she loved behind.

"You're right about the money." Booker pulled a folded sheaf of paper from his inner pocket and ripped it up. "It's not enough."

The room went still. The pages didn't flutter to the ground. They flopped. Along with Kimmy's dreams.

"I don't understand." Reeling, Kimmy leaned back against Mims, who sat next to her in the pew.

"I'm here to offer you a better deal." Booker raised his voice so that everyone could hear his proposition. "Half ownership in the Burger & Sammie Shack."

Kimmy couldn't breathe. Not one breath. She clutched the neck of her dress and stared up at Booker in disbelief.

"Say something." Clarice whacked Kimmy on the back. "She's in shock."

Kimmy slurped in air and wheezed. "Thanks, Clarice." She shook her head at Booker. "You need a better business manager." One who'd caution him against making such bad business deals. "I'm just a sandwich maker."

"Kim." Booker dropped to one knee and took her cold hands in his. "You're more than a sandwich maker. You're the love of my life. You make me smile." His gaze shifted to Hay and then back to her. "Oh, how you make me smile."

Kimmy was horrified to discover her eyes were filling with tears.

"What good is having a business if I'm not having fun with it?" Booker ran his thumbs over the backs of her hands. "You and I...we were meant to be together. To bump elbows as we cook and to laugh when you can't convince someone to add garlic to their burger. We're meant to prep food at the same station and sneak sandwiches together on our breaks."

Was this... Was he... proposing?

Kimmy couldn't breathe. She couldn't swallow. She couldn't move.

His parents stood in the corner behind him, beaming at him. Her parents stood next to them, beaming at her. And there was Hay, of course, beaming like he'd helped plan it all. Which he probably had.

They'd known. They'd all known.

They should have known she couldn't say yes.

"Say something." Clarice whacked Kimmy on the back again. "Shock," she said again by way of explanation when people turned frowny faces her way.

Kimmy looked at them all—the wedding guests, her family, and her friends—and still she couldn't speak.

She stared at Booker, taking in his warm gaze, his tender smile, his gentle touch. He loved her. The sincerity of his words was sinking in, having snuffed out some of the hurt and anger at what he'd done.

"I don't want to be your business partner," Kimmy said softly.

"What did she say?" someone at the front of the church asked.

"She said she doesn't want to go into business with him," Clarice shouted.

Mims and Bitsy shushed her.

"I just want to be your wife," Kimmy said in a small voice. "I knew back in the science lab that you were special. I knew at freshman orientation that I loved you. And... And... And all those times afterward. I know the difference between a crush and love." She freed one hand and cupped his cheek. "But I valued your friendship too much to step up and risk telling you how I felt." Her throat threatened to close. "In case you didn't feel the same way. Because we come from different places and we've always been going different directions."

"I can't hear," someone at the front of the church complained.

"She said..." Clarice tossed up her hands. "Ah, someone will tell you later."

"Do you know what I think?" Booker placed a kiss on her palm. "I think we've always been headed in the same direction, just on different paths. Let's meet somewhere in the middle. I think we have a lot of time to make up, you and I. And I promise you—"

"On an order of fries." Hay lifted a small paper basket of fries he'd had on the pew next to him. "Sorry, no longer hot."

Kimmy's chest constricted around her heart. These two men, her friends, she loved them both but she was in love with only one.

"And I promise you," Booker said again, holding their hands over the fry basket, "to tell you I love you every morning, noon, and night. No more holding it in. No more holding it back."

The wedding guests heaved a collective sigh. Both sets of parents beamed. And Kimmy struggled not to cry. It was the most beautiful moment in the history of beautiful moments. And it involved food, which made it even better.

Booker drew her closer. "Kimberly Anne Easley, will you make me the happiest man alive by agreeing to be my wife?"

"Yes," Kimmy said thickly, blinking back tears. "Yes."

"I take offense to the happiest-man-alive comment," Hay said, munching on a cold French fry. "Seeing as how it's my wedding day."

"Kiss her," Clarice said, a sentiment echoed by the assembled.

And Booker did.

He made Kimmy's heart full.

He made it fuller at the wedding reception, after the bride and groom had their special dance.

Booker showed up at Kimmy's table while Clarice was admiring the reception's Bohemian decorations. He drew her to her feet. "Honey, I think I owe you a dance."

"You certainly do." Kimmy couldn't wait. She practically led Booker to the dance floor.

The DJ spun "It's Raining Men."

The dance floor filled, and after a bit of sidestepping, Kimmy let the music move her. She had her own version of the Dougie, while Booker was more of a Carlton man. It didn't matter that his dance moves were from the generation before hers. He had better rhythm than she did.

Paul danced over to Kimmy, and they did the floss and the cobra. And then he bounded over to the bride and groom.

After a few fun songs, the DJ put on a slow dance.

Booker drew her into his arms, which was exactly where she wanted to be. "Your dance moves have improved."

"Paul and I took lessons." At the junior college. "Only Paul got so good they asked him to teach." Whereas Kimmy had learned just enough steps to dance better than she had in high school.

Booker laughed. "How was your dinner?"

"My steak was grilled to perfection." She swayed closer

because a man who'd ask her about food deserved an extra cuddle. "It even had enough garlic."

"I'll tell you a secret." Booker's smile morphed into a mischievous grin. "I had the chef prepare a steak specifically for you."

"I knew there was a reason I loved you." That deserved a kiss. And then another.

They might have kissed all night if the DJ hadn't spun "Can't Stop the Feeling!" That brought out more wedding guests and more dance moves than anyone could put a name to.

Everyone was outdanced by Paul but no one seemed to care. It was a wedding. And for two couples, it was one of the happiest days on earth.

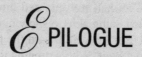

EPILOGUE

"How's the stock of paninis?" Kimmy ran a finger down the supply list.

Booker opened a cupboard with a Vanna White flourish. "I bought enough to feed a small army."

Kimmy scoffed. She'd go through that in one day. "What about chicken? You know I don't like the frozen stuff."

"It's all fresh." Booker opened the refrigerator. More flourishes occurred.

"What about fresh garlic?" Kimmy scanned the counter. "Did you buy enough garlic?"

"Yes." Booker produced a mesh bag large enough to hold a basketball. It was full of garlic cloves. "Can we go now?"

"No." Kimmy set down her list of supplies, wrapped her arms around Booker's neck, and kissed him thoroughly. "I don't think you've met your promised quotas of *I love you*s for the day."

"I love you, honey." Booker framed her face with his hands. "But if we don't get this food truck down to Greeley, we won't get a good spot for the festival."

"You're right." But Kimmy kissed him one more time anyway. She loved being able to show him her love whenever she wanted. She headed toward the front of the truck and then stopped. "Wait. Who's running the Shack today?"

"Dante." Booker's younger brother was becoming skilled at the grill. "My parents went to Denver to check on our location there."

His parents had decided they wanted to be semiretired. They were part of the Burger & Sammie Shack management team.

"You think of everything." Kimmy wound her arms around his neck again.

"Not everything," Booker admitted, drawing her closer. "Just you."

About the Author

Melinda Curtis is the *USA Today* bestselling author of lighthearted contemporary romance. In addition to her Sunshine Valley series from Forever, she's published books independently and with Harlequin Heartwarming, including her novel *Dandelion Wishes*, which is currently being made into a TV movie. She lives in California's hot Central Valley with her hot husband—her basketball-playing college sweetheart. While raising three kids, the couple did the soccer thing, the karate thing, the dance thing, the Little League thing, and, of course, the basketball thing. Between books, Melinda spends time remodeling her home by swinging a hammer, grouting tile, and wielding a paintbrush with her husband and other family members.

Learn more at:
   melindacurtis.net
   Twitter @MelCurtisAuthor
   Facebook.com/MelindaCurtisAuthor

*Fall in love with these charming
contemporary romances!*

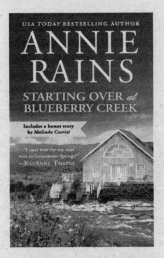

STARTING OVER AT BLUEBERRY CREEK
by Annie Rains

Firefighter Luke Marini moved to the small town of Sweetwater
Springs with the highest of hopes—new town, new job, and new
neighbors who know nothing of his past. And that's just how he wants
to keep it. But it's nearly impossible when the gorgeous brunette next
door decides to be the neighborhood's welcome wagon. She's sugar,
spice, and everything nice—but getting close to someone again is
playing with fire. Includes a bonus short story by Melinda Curtis!

Discover bonus content and more on read-forever.com.

*Find more great reads on Instagram with
@ReadForeverPub.*

RETURN TO MAGNOLIA HARBOR by Hope Ramsay

When a knee injury put an end to his dreams of playing professional football and a car accident forever altered his life, Christopher Martin knew it was karma. He's not proud of the man he used to be, and now the only thing he wants is to hide away from the world. When he meets his new architect and realizes she's the woman he hurt all those years ago, he starts to wonder if it's possible to make up for a lifetime of wrongs. But can he convince Jessica to forgive him?

MERMAID INN by Jenny Holiday

Inheriting her aunt's beloved Mermaid Inn is the only reason Eve Abbott is coming back to the tiny town of Matchmaker Bay. She's definitely not ready to handle nosy neighbors, extensive renovations, or the discovery that a certain heartbreaker—now the town's sheriff—still lives down the street. Includes a bonus novella by Alison Bliss!

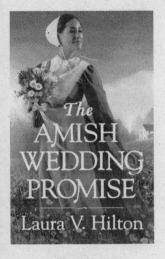

THE AMISH WEDDING PROMISE by Laura V. Hilton

Zeke came to Hidden Springs to assist a community in need after a tornado swept through the town. He didn't expect to meet his soul mate. Determined to ignore his feelings, Zeke promises to help reunite kind, beautiful Grace with her missing groom. But after spending time together, Grace confesses that she might not want to marry her fiancé after all. Can Zeke convince her that her true love is standing right in front of her? And can she find the courage to follow her heart?

CAN'T HURRY LOVE by Melinda Curtis

Head over heels in love, Lola Williams gave up everything to marry Randy, including a promising career in New York City. Now, after one year of marriage and one year of widowhood, Lola finds herself stranded in Sunshine, Colorado, reeling from the revelation that Randy had secrets she never could have imagined. She swears she's done with love forever, but the matchmaking ladies of the Sunshine Valley Widows Club have different plans...Includes a bonus short story by Annie Rains!

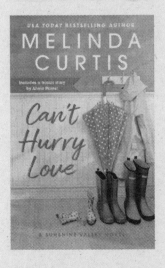

STARLIGHT BRIDGE
by Debbie Mason

Hidden in Graystone Manor is a book containing all the dark secrets of Harmony Harbor, and Ava DiRossi is determined to find it. No one—especially not her ex-husband, Griffin Gallagher—can ever discover what really tore her life apart all those years ago. With Griffin back in town, it's more important than ever that she find the book before someone else does. Because her ex is still angry with her for leaving him. And he still has no idea Ava never stopped loving him…

PRIMROSE LANE
by Debbie Mason

Olivia Davenport has finally gotten her life back together and is now Harmony Harbor's most sought-after event planner. But her past catches up with her when Olivia learns that she's now guardian of her ex's young daughter. With her world spinning, Olivia must reconcile her old life with her new one. And she doesn't have time for her next-door neighbor, no matter how handsome he is.